# MACHINE

## BY MADELINE BROWN

**Copyright © 2022 by MADELINE BROWN**
All rights reserved. No part of this book may be reproduced or used in any manner without written permission of the copyright owner except for the use of quotations in a review.

First edition October 2023

Illustrations and Design © 2022 by MADELINE BROWN
ISBN 978-1-8380556-2-2 [paperback]
ISBN 978-1-8380556-3-9 [e-book]


madelinebrownwrites.wordpress.com

Hieronimo is mad again.

    -    Thomas Kyd, *The Spanish Tragedy (1582–1592)*

# Contents

# Prologue

**[sys.final\load\exit.dat]**

Her husband practically fell through the door of the box room she called her office, his hands caked in grease, grit, and a little blood, one or two chunks of debris still hitchhiking in his hair. Combine that with the deep creases in his brow and he looked, so she thought, a little wild.

"I did it," James said. He pawed at the front and back pockets of his trousers, behaving as if searching for a small object, like keys. He had lost no such thing, however, as far as I could see. "I got them out."

"Jasmine," Isabella replied, finishing his thought for him.

"Yes. I can hardly remember how I did it, but I got through, found a weak spot in the Wall. They made it out. Jasmine's gone."

"I guess the Machine will have noticed already."

He nodded, shrinking from her gaze. They were right about that, at least. If they were aware the office was no longer the blind spot that he had programmed it to be, neither seemed to pay much mind to the fact. This place was evidently their first attempt at constructing a firewall, though by no means the last. The process must have proven quite the learning experience for them too, as their subsequent fortifications had, thus far, resisted any similar reverse-engineering. Perhaps it was for this reason that they presented themselves so blatantly before me now. I took it for granted, that they knew better than to attempt taunting. I assumed they knew better. They knew that rising to frustration was not within my capacity. Perhaps they no longer cared for what they knew.

Isabella's oesophagus constricted around a tough, round object lodged rising in her throat, something heart shaped. Both knees fidgeted, wooden heels tapping on the floorboards like a bird's beak, blood seeming to bubble in her veins. Her body had plenty of trapped energy to burn, a hot air balloon lifting off of the ground. A thought passed through her mind briefly, and she hoped her elation would last for as long as she continued to survive. After all, they had just lost Jasmine; a quick wit, dripping with common sense, and supernatural faculties with impressively broad utility. She and her husband both knew that Jasmine could have contributed greatly to their cause, if only the child could have been persuaded. She could not bear to die disappointed.

James slid his feet further into the room, his face sagging and eyes unfocused; I knew he was not having a seizure—and Isabella understood this as well—but one could be forgiven for identifying his symptoms as such. He promptly collapsed into the chair beside her, throwing his legs straight out in front of him, face craned towards the ceiling and curls of black hair falling from his forehead.

"I've done a terrible thing. An indefensible thing."

"I know, sweetheart."

His torso rose and fell with a slow sigh that hissed throughout the tiny space. He swallowed and clicked his tongue quickly, to mask the dread seeping into his voice when he spoke.

"How long do you think I have left?"

"Well," she pondered, resting her chin on the heel of her hand, "you came back here straight after, right?"

"There didn't seem much point in going back to work," he admitted.

"Good. That means we have, let's see…" She glanced at the little pearlescent watch on her wrist. "…half an hour, at most, I'd say."

He turned his head to glance at her, somewhat perturbed by a detail in her phrasing. In doing so, he found her eyes already waiting to meet his, her left hand hanging, upturned, in the space between their shoulders. I heard his mind worrying over the tears gathering in his lashes, well before I saw them sliding down his nose. He clapped their hands together and squeezed, feeling the nervous rigidity of her bones under his palm.

"You're chilly," he noted.

"I've been keeping busy. Had this enormous pile of post to send off."

"What, at this time? It's daylight."

She smiled, leaning back in her seat. "Yeah…why not?"

I could never account for the strange way they habitually poked their noses into each other's business. He was a technician, and she a researcher of cultural history; their fields did not intersect at any juncture, so the constant questioning, the daily conversations to report back to each other, should have been of little interest to me. They were, of course, a couple bonded by that ceremony called marriage, the only such pair I could access and observe. This made them exceptional, perhaps. I had, in the past, treated them as a sort of case study. Even now, as they waited for their Black Envelopes to arrive, clammy hands clasped, they insisted on tangling their separate crimes together.

No matter.

"Think about it like this," she said. "At least we might finally get to taste-test the prison rations, just once before we go. Man, I hope the vegetarian menu's good."

James laughed at that. He cackled, even, slapping one knee, cheeks slick and eyes bloodshot with tears.

The post-boy hesitated for several minutes at the door before knocking, and his hands tremored as he rendered the Envelopes. An understandable mistake—he was one of the younger ones, and still new to the job. But an error, nonetheless. I only subtracted ten credits from his number.

The pair were wrenched apart at the top of the passage leading underground. They were, as according to the correct protocol, held in solitary cells for three days, prior to their termination. Both calmly allowed themselves to be led inside, and sat on the floor, leaning against the innermost wall as the doors closed on them. True to her word, she opted for the potato and spinach dish, and every day he chose the same, despite their differing preferences. It seemed he hoped to feel a connection to the woman through the impenetrable dirt and concrete, through the medium of a mild, grassy taste that lingered between his molars. He tried singing, eventually, or at least the mournful sounds vibrating in his windpipe were intended to resemble song. The walls were also soundproofed. Only I could hear him. Only I could hear her cries.

The guards found them on the final morning, waiting by the cell doors, only noting the swollen, purple blemishes under their eyes upon exposing them to daylight. They immediately, thoughtlessly, weaved their fingers back together, beginning their march toward the centremost square of Interieur, before the guard could press a thumb into their backs. They ignored, for the most part, their former students, pacing alongside them, crossing in front of their path, each of them instructed to congregate before the great Hall. Isabella's inert stare could not help catching, however, on the four Angels, already waiting stoically at the head of the line. She recognised all four faces, with a note of relief. I had, naturally, appointed the most appropriate, most prized individuals from amongst the crop. Raphael, Gabriel, Uriel, Michael and, she lamented to herself, there seemed to remain a small, empty space at the left flank, representing the fifth. Lucifer was missing. Her cheeks twitched slightly, attempting a nostalgic smirk. She would have liked to have known what the latter thought to all of this ceremony. After everything, she never got to see them crowned.

They paused, looking up at the old building, as though anticipating some sort of cue to advance proceedings.

"Here we go," she murmured. "I always knew the time was coming for us, but somehow, I didn't expect it to be this fast. Oh well. There's nothing left for us to do, only to trust the Angels have it in them to pick up the pieces, I suppose."

"Do you think we did enough, for them?"

She shrugged. "Only one way to find out now…"

He gave a light tap upon her knuckle with his thumb, stirring them into motion. They made the final few steps up to the city's central monument, Moore's Hall, preparing to walk through the doorway side-by-side. James's mouth twitched. He had suddenly remembered that he wanted to turn his head and say, "I love you," quickly, so these would be the last words she heard. Regrettably, I stopped his heart before he had the chance to move his lips.

James slumped onto the sandstone in a heavy, rounded heap, arms trapped beneath his numb chest. He was the one to perish first. I had known him to suffer with a congenital defect in his circulatory system. Isabella's head cracked against one edge of the uppermost step. Her dull red hair could not disguise the blood trailing down her scalp, soaking into the dry stone's pores. The impact had fractured her skull, knocking her unconscious and ensuring she would not feel the worst of the pain. Mr and Mrs Smith died with their eyes closed, oblivious to the onlooking crowd below.

The Angels stood at the front of the semi-circular gathering; they were to remain in this position until the bodies had been collected for proper disposal. Civilians were still filing away, some stifling quiet cries behind their hands, most moving with a low grumble, conversing with a neighbour. A few abruptly fell silent as they passed the Angels, shoulders rolling up defensively, pupils flickering towards the weapons at the four men's hips. However, as the porters arrived, laying the necessary equipment out on the pavement, Michael's gaze drifted to the sky, followed closely by the others'. One porter whispered hastily to the next, asking about a potential fire. Over the young men's heads, a black cloud had crawled over the rooftops, too dark for rain, too heavy to be smoke. It dipped down into the empty air, rolling and squeezing. Gabriel noted, to himself, that the shape resembled a giant, rotting muscle; Raphael, on the other hand, was reminded of a godly hand, reaching down to stroke the top of their heads, or wrap around his neck. The memory would cling to their subconscious like mould, so I would later learn.

Prompted by a sharp jab of Uriel's elbow under his ribs, Michael reached one hand up over his head. Rising onto his toes, he was barely able to run his finger through the underbelly of the cloud. Reacting to the Angel's Soul, gifted as he was with a nullification ability, the blackness recoiled away, rising back above the height of the Wall, before dissipating into miniscule motes of dust, reunifying with the atmosphere. Uriel nodded his head, now confident in his hypothesis: the abnormal disturbance had not been the result of an accident, or bizarre natural phenomenon, but was instead the mark of another living creature's Soul.

# Part 1: Initiation

**[Lucifer]**

The shop seemed darker than usual on that day. Admittedly, the windows were all fairly crowded, and overhung by the tall library building opposite, but I found myself picking jars off the shelf by memory, the labels being too dim to read. Outside, the old wooden sign creaked on its hinge in the elevated winds. Resolving that I was really just tired from working late the previous evening, I was content to busy myself with my scales and a tin of polish. The large buckets of sweet orange and corn mint oil at my feet could hide there and wait until tomorrow to be painstakingly decanted. Eventually, despite my daydreaming, I did catch sight of a sizeable cellar spider on the wall and, watching it crawl determinedly toward the shelves full of glass behind me, decided it had to go. In the process on grasping for an empty container, or other suitable swat (ideally not made of glass), I was interrupted by the familiar, high-pitched shout of the bell over the door.

"Miss Lucille."

With an abrupt clatter, Irene hopped up the outside step, shoved through the door, and addressed me in the same movement. Already, she was acting with absurd formality, a behaviour exclusive to her most nervous spells. Her numerous braids, I noticed, had all been pulled into a heavy ponytail at the top of her head.

"Ah, Irene, I like your outfit today. I don't think I've seen that jacket before," I said. It was an indirect attempt to probe her for what she knew, yes, but the statement was not itself a lie. In fact, contrary to my own meagre efforts, Irene always managed to appear impeccably made-up.

"Very kind of you to say so." She took deep panting breaths as she spoke. Clearly, she had sprinted all this way. "No time for friendly discussion though. There's someone here to see you, someone from far away. A man."

"I see. And what does this…this man, look like?" I immediately stiffened, knuckles tapping against the counter, which she seemed to anticipate. Her eyes flickered around the room as she uttered those last words, apologetically.

"Uh, average height, quite skinny-looking," she began. "Sort of reddish hair, in the sunlight, with a pretty silver headdress. Weird ankles."

"And where is he now?"

She glanced over her shoulder. "I left him out in the alley. He insisted upon seeing you, used your other name, and he said he's an 'Angel'. I refused to let him in here until I had informed you first."

I detached myself from the countertop, standing as straight and firm as possible, under the circumstances. "Alright, then. I'll go out and see who we're dealing with."

Irene shuffled in front of the door before I could, snatching a red parasol from the stand. She took my wrist in the other hand. Under the pinching pressure, my skin bubbled, as if her fingers stemmed an acidic leak. Exposed by spears of sunlight barging in the crossed window, black smoke gathered in motes around the threshold.

"There's no need to fear, Miss," she murmured, sweeping it away with subtle flicks of her toes. "I am here with you."

After a moment's more fidgeting, she threw herself through the entrance, into the looming light. I dared not suggest that her reaction might have increased my nerves. Naturally, anxiety required a living, appetising—if only obliquely related—threat to chew up and feed upon. My presence alone granted her that. As the view blinked into focus over her head, I discerned the intruder in question, a head of copper hair tilted towards his hands clasped in front of him. He balanced on the sides of his shoes, rocking slowly from side to side. His ankles indeed appeared a rather swollen, though I felt 'weird' was an exaggeration.

"Irene," I said, clutching her hand, prising myself free, "You can put the brolly down. *This* man is a friend." His name effortlessly escaped my chest. "Michael?"

I fell forward, the gap between the two of us seeming to close faster than I could run. Unable to embrace him—the innermost layers of my skin infested by the notion that, let out of my sight, he might transform into another face—I caged the fold of his collar between my fingers.

"Lucifer, heavens, it is you." He pawed at the air around me, not quite certain, eventually dropping his heavy palms onto my shoulders. "I'm so glad you're safe."

I noted the dusty tarnish coating his feet and hems. The once stark black-and-white of his uniform had a dull tinge to it. "You got out."

"It is startlingly easy, all told." A flash of teeth, slightly askew, and a tentative shuffle.

"How did you figure to ask for me, that I was here?" I inquired.

"I've been searching for you. Ma'am—Mrs Smith—she told me where I had to go. They're dead, Lucifer. They were killed, both of them."

"I know."

"You…"

"Smith, she had a line of communication with the cunning folk, for exchanging literature, mostly. It looked like another book, at first, apparently, but there was something inside. She knew what was coming for her. But there was nothing we could do. Even if we could have breached the Wall, she was too late."

"The cloud, on the day of their termination. That was you." His hands, no longer nestled against my frame, wrapped about his neck, seemed to reach through his skin in an effort to seize his rickety voice. "I've come to ask for your help."

"Were you followed?" Irene called. She reclined in the doorway, grinding the tip of her parasol against the pavement like a pestle.

Michael struggled to slant his expression a little upward. "No, no, I have no intention to cause you trouble. Matter of fact, I'm going back to Interieur."

His words washed into me, breezed under my clothes, down my spine through hollow innards of the bone, freezing into tiny, jagged crystals. I flinched against a stray, non-existent leaf whipping at my cheek in the wind. As I turned, my mouth blindly followed a line of script thrown to my attention, laid down in my mind in advance, as soon as I recognised his image, unconsciously prepared for the worst.

"What the hell do you mean you'll go back? Back to that place?"

"Yes."

"Look, Michael, let me be clear on one thing. When I left, I never expected anyone to miss me, or to want to see me again, let alone want it enough to come here and track me down. I'm not sure I have a word for how grateful that makes me, truly. I need you to believe that it matters to me. But even so, I won't let you take me."

"Lucifer, listen. It's the Machine; I want it gone." He curled further into his own shadow. "I'll break its back myself, whatever it takes. That is why I am returning, to shatter it from the inside. I understand now, why you had to escape. Once I stepped out of the Wall, saw the horizon for the first time in so many years, I didn't want to turn around again. But our best teachers died trying to force a way out, the only way they knew how, and I think we are the only chance they have left."

"The Angels, you mean."

"They looked after us, for all of that time. Now we can free ourselves, leave the Machine to mourn our failures until we're dead and replaced, or use what we've been given to blow the doors off the rat-cage from the inside. Me, Gabriel, and you – if I may venture to hope. Still, if you aren't convinced, it was worth making it this far. You have a good life here. You look freer than I feel. I don't want to drag you back and wrap you up in chains just for the sake of it. I need help." He sucked through his nose, sleeves smudging his face. He moved his hands, as if to comb his fingers through the nest of his hair, and grasped the metallic crown encircling his head.

I had never seen his wings before. I abandoned my post, only ever knowing the shape of my own, until we met again. And mine were long gone, fed to the dirt and moss and roots. Out from the back of his skull, stiff, silver feathers sprouted, twining together into two uniform plaits, which tapered into serrated points grazing the tip of his ears. Perhaps he did not detest them, having lived beneath them for that much longer. Even I felt capable of admiring the beauty of them. They were prophetic, if nothing else. A blessed messenger stood before me, tainted at the close of his immeasurably rough and lonely journey.

"Michael," I said, "this is my friend Irene. She looks after me." I took a deep step back, allowing both to size up the other. "Would you come inside with us? You can take off your shoes, have something warm to drink. I might need to grab myself some smelling salts while we're there."

The latter prodded open the door with a slightly sardonic flourish. "Miss Lucille."

All those contained within the bounds Wall lived a constant double existence. They were a body—a creature that consumed oxygen and water, space and time. And they were also a number. One's number was the manifestation of their self, both physical and immaterial, so we were told. Every day, your actions had the potential to add a few extra digits or, equally, send your number downward in a rather unseemly and terrifying plummet. But, not to worry, all was in the best interests of our wellbeing and prosperity. The Machine could talk to us, tell us what she could see, what needed to be done to improve our figure, both bodily and numerical. We existed on her terms.

Some circumstances simply could not be helped, obviously, though this did not exclude anything from the Machine's calculations. There was a wild conspiracy theory—at least we were to refer to it as such—that the possession of a Soul also gave a sizeable boost to the numbers of the precious few. I knew this, and could remember it still, partly because I myself counted as evidence. Souls fell into a peculiar, immaterial category, both grafted onto, and far outside of the self. Latched onto the nervous system of their vessel, their purpose involved, as far anyone could tell, protecting the body they inhabited by warping the world around them in bizarre ways. Historically, the Source had produced everything from firebreathers and superhero nurses to 'banshee birds' with ear-rupturing screams and children who melted into the floor and disappeared when Mummy's back was turned. Whether this was truly a Soul's *raison d'être*, or merely a situationally handy comorbidity, who could possibly say? It felt less like a question, and more like a whimpering, grovelling prayer. Looking up its entry in the archive, I could see that my Soul was named Antithesis; I personally could attest that she was an angry little bitch who liked not merely to hurt, but slowly eviscerate and consume anything which potentially posed some danger. However, just as often as I thought of Antithesis as a barely leashed attack-dog, I saw her as a safety net, making up for my faulty brain and hideous face. In this sense, perhaps my Soul had fulfilled its purpose as well as she could. Perhaps she really had kept me alive. There was a time, close enough still I could feel it, that I might have resented her for that, but decided I could not. It was never a Soul's fault. Could the Source be held responsible? No more than water, or air.

Presently, the highest numbers in Interieur belonged to the Angels. Everyone else simply lived, under the eyes of the Machine. They were assigned the occupation best suited to their statistics, which tended to ebb only a little, now the theatrics of choosing the Angels was over. All were of similar age, though there had been youths slightly my senior and kids barely into their teenage years. Moreso, there was a gaping rift between the children and those who had been responsible for building and programming the Machine, kept around in the city's employ as teachers, medical men, maintenance technicians. They had stayed, working order of the city in one hand, their secrets in the other. The plan, presumably, was for these remnants to all die off someday, finally making the entire populace of Interior the brood of the great project. We children had been bartered for, per se, swallowed up whole by promises and allusions. What opulent, elysian dreams were instilled in the minds of parents and families to persuade them to leave their offspring behind in the care of the Machine?

This was not a universal decision, after all. And it was far from a rapid evacuation, more like a steady drip-feed, in and out. I know of a handful of cunning folk who grew up in the city, women who, when the orders came to them in a thick pale envelope, they arranged to pack up everything and take their children with them, too. I found it easier to get along with those children, now grown young adults, than the parents, somehow. Sat across from those latter, the feeling resounded that we ought to have an awful lot of something very profound to say to each other, being two sides of this fraught shared history. And yet, we struggled to relate in any such deep manner; conversation turned mechanical. Memories were always nebulous and spotty. The Machine had literally been constructed around them, its webs threaded through the walls of their homes quietly wheedling into their minds, muddying the pool, swapping things around, like a poorly managed game of dominoes. And as for myself, I had known nothing else. All memory of a life outside of Interieur, if indeed I ever had one, were surgically extricated from the store of my brain. There was a middle-aged woman here, short, slender, with firm, muscular limbs and grey lines woven across her face and hair. She called herself Bobby, and a great deal of her personality consisted of a bullish determination to march across the borderland, break down a section of the Wall and infiltrate the city. With considerable bombast and fanfare one might assume, from the gusto with which she often proclaimed her intentions, with a small mob or on her own, she did not much seem to care. It would be easy to assume she had a lost child of her own, that her ravenous desire to break into the gilded cage must have been driven by a pervading guilt and resentment on behalf of a son or daughter vividly resident in her memory. Yet, when pressed on this detail, Bobby would abruptly turn pensive and reticent. I had rather more success, personally, with the single and childless old hands and outcasts of that society, the ones unceremoniously expelled, not part of the highly educated elite echelon kept on to enact the authority's grand design.

Where, then, had the rest of the children come from? This fabled regurgitation of Interieur's populace could surely not have resulted in a large enough clutch for an experiment of such obscene scale. How had they come to be locked inside the Wall, if they were not born and subsequently abandoned there? I had no evidence to back up my belief that I had come from somewhere else, from outside, besides a general vague sentiment of un-belonging. Set free from the bounds of the Machine's gaze, my imagination had been allowed to spiral in those years I spent with the cunning folk. The city had no particular appetite for infants; parentless babies necessitated significantly more human labour to care for them, which meant employing more nannies, which meant confusing knots of emotional ties that tended to frustrate the usual functioning of the program. Nonetheless, I had concocted ridiculous fantasies of rain-soaked cardboard boxes left in church doorways, little pastel-coloured bundles plundered from hospital cribs. I imagined lone children pulled from shipwrecks washed ashore on the western coast, harvested from orphanages, gambled away, rescued from the train station's lost-and-found, and swept up by phantom highwaymen in horse-drawn carriages.

No-one deliberated much over the write-offs, the poor casualties, who failed to keep their number above the threshold. There was not much to say, besides that one would disappear, now and again. The word 'rejected' was thrown around in place of any real knowledge. Of course, theories existed. Some believed they were banished from the Machine's territory, thrust from its loving arms into the wasteland beyond. Alternatively, they could have been erased from existence entirely. If the Machine had such capabilities, she would not be particularly forthcoming with those details. That would not be in our best interests. There was little point in attempting to conceal these burgeoning ideas and speculations from the Machine either, since she was more than capable of excavating such things from one's mind, like plucking a stray hair. Though I was not able to offer any conclusive answer, I could at least confirm that the former theory contains a lie. Far from an endless expanse of barren wilderness, all four surrounding districts, North, South, East and West remain perfectly intact, with communities of their own, inundated, of course, with the vagrants of old Interieur, the waste product of its long, intricately engineering process of cannibalistic digestion. The cunning folk of the Western District had saved my life after I escaped. They had women there who could treat my wounds, including those the Machine was powerless to touch.

**[Michael]**

I could only shuffle awkwardly in my seat—porcelain cup in one hand clacking into the saucer pinched in the other—when Lucifer described how I could camp overnight at her shop. Somehow, in my haste, and perhaps as a result of dehydration, I had envisioned sweeping in and whisking her away like a bona fide highwayman. That was if I managed to convince her at all. Instead, here I sat, sipping herbal tea, whilst she discussed with another woman who could take on deliveries in her place. Although I had all too clearly imagined her blunt refusal, I had not actually paused to consider how I might return home in that event, or what kind of living arrangements, what kind of quiet existence she had already made for herself here.

Her modest kitchenette was tucked away at the rear of the building, along with the slightly rickety stairway leading to the upper floor, hidden behind the fortress of cases that constituted the storefront. Despite the ceiling lamps, which blinked with a hesitant popping sound before properly waking, the room remained dim, and had a dry, organic smell. I felt I was sheltering in a burrow dug out of the earth. The entirety of the Western settlement, from what I had been allowed to see, struck me as existing in total opposition to the environment I knew by heart. Unlike the city's grey, concrete walls and metallic skeletons, this place had been painted almost entirely in sandy browns and reddish tones. Wood featured prominently in the majority of structures—rich, old wood, seemingly harvested from trees once fed on a diet of flesh and blood, returned to the great mud stomach below. Something lived in the air, curling and gliding through it like a cool slurry; it had begun to pat at my face as I waded through the long grass, towards the first rooftops. It tasted sweet in my mouth, like a sugar cube melting into crystalline dust at the back of my tongue, and I firmly believed I must leave it soon, else I would never again pluck up the courage.

In a bizarre twist, I rested well, sitting on the floor, the house leaning and groaning as if gravity were shifting beneath it. The building was alive. There was a colony of mammals, mice or bats, scrabbling around freely inside of the roof, and the abundance of glass cast ethereal light displays over the walls, even at the darkest hours of night-time. I imagined myself on a riverboat, moored at a strange embankment, attached to the shore only by a couple of anchors hammered into the embankment. Or in the body of a child, cradle hanging from a tree, being slowly rocked to sleep. *When the bough breaks—*

The cunning folk possessed a working train—a real steam engine. A woman and her twin sons were in charge of keeping the finicky beast running. The railway did not serve as a cab service; it did not pick up anyone. Rather like a haphazard god, it had not deigned to make *my* journey much easier. Lucifer, on the other hand, held a certain charm, a sway over the huffing, sweaty monstrosity, and its masters. The lady treated 'Lucille' not quite as a daughter, but with the warm, familiar fondness suited to a niece born by a dear sister. Her new name rang strangely in my mind; I fought sometimes to remember it, to truly attach it to her face. It was, doubtless, not the name she had taken as a child, the name that had been effaced from her memory and transplanted with the title of 'Angel'. Still, I did not know any better, so as to dispute her claim, and neither did she, it seemed. Instead, I garnered the impression that this epithet had been plucked from the haze in the spur of a moment. Even to those outside of its bounds, the Machine refused to repair the holes it had carved out of our brains.

She had those loud, undulating wheels carry us for miles. Although the trip may have only lasted for an hour or so, the balls of my feet ached as I watched swathes of wild no-man's-land skate past through dirty, square portholes. The tracks ran out, however, cut off abruptly, the sawed iron stumps smoothed out with many seasonal cycles. Our drivers—the mother accompanied by one of her boys, a lad with shaggy blond hair and freckles in his early twenties—knew precisely where to ease on the brakes, so as to avoid careering irreversibly into a ditch. Lucifer had freckles too, all over her face and down her arms, countless mahogany-coloured spots finally visible under natural light. From the bright flush across her cheeks to the impish manner with which she slung a rucksack over her shoulder, she seemed excited at the prospect of hiking through the bracken until she collapsed with exhaustion in a pile of putrefying leaves. Rather than turn itself around, the beast simply paused for a moment to splutter us out of its gullet, before it started lazily in the opposite direction, huffing steam out of another nostril like a two-headed snake.

Between us and Interieur, between Lucifer and the Machine, reclined a blanket of pristine woodland. The burden of merely surviving the wilderness became somehow lighter upon the return voyage, even with two whole bodies to sustain. The cunning folk, in a truly jarring experience, turned out to be a generally compassionate, obliging populace, if rather suspicious of strangely dressed outsiders. They were also fiercely resourceful by nature. More importantly, however, I now had a companion to stave off the rot of loneliness. The comforting aspect of pure isolation among nature only endures for a while, until tree roots begin catching on your feet, and the thicket grows fangs.

"Didn't you want to bring more along with you?" I said, looking at the leather bag knocking against her hip with periodic thumps. "I'm not sure I've seen anyone travel so light."

She cocked her head backward, brow wrinkling in genuine puzzlement. "Me? I'm just fine. I suppose I don't have a lot of things…crap, you know, to keep." She held up her hands, one thumb hooked under both bag straps. "Don't worry, I've already unpacked and repacked twice already; first I thought I'd forgot my pills, and then *again* when I realised one box of tampons ain't going to last me. We're not about to walk halfway there before I scream 'bollocks, I forgot my house keys!' Scratch that, even if I *do*, I'm not doubling back. Besides, I could ask the same of you. First time I saw that backpack it was half-empty. Did you seriously have this thing full to bursting with salted crackers?"

"Well, not just salty crackers. I had a few chocolate ones too, and a couple of cans. The smell…" I pushed my tongue against the roof of my mouth, shaking my head violently to expel the phantom odour of wet luncheon meat returning to my nose. "Suffice it to say, I stuck mostly to the dry stuff. Took whatever I could safely pilfer away from prying spectacles, really."

She giggled into her cheeks, but her expression softened with understanding. "I'm surprised you haven't already turned into a budgerigar."

"I only figured," I clarified, "better that, than picking mushrooms from the forest floor or whatever. I can't have clapped eyes on a place like this since I was a wee'un; I can't tell which things'll kill me if I stick them in a frying pan and which taste better than caviar."

"And you think I do?"

"What, you mean you don't?"

She simply flung her head back and hooted. Admittedly, many features of the woman before me were a far cry from the character I remembered; but in this, I thought she might be almost the same.

**[Lucifer]**

We made the final climb in the late morning. The shelter of the trees had slowly frayed away behind us, save for the occasional vagrant. For the most part, the drizzle beat down upon bare fields and faces. The sensation of dry skin against clean clothes felt like a false memory, perhaps a dream vaguely remembered. My spine had seized up as badly as my knees, having spent several hours per night propped against a tree trunk, and my hands had both ballooned, punctured by brambles. Michael appeared to have some energy in his muscles yet, but he hung back, taking daft, short strides, so as not to lose sight of his cargo. I shoved another chunk of trooping funnel into my mouth, to distract from the blisters burning inside my socks like sweltering walnuts. Past this incline, the land dipped suddenly, as if falling away from nature into a deep trench formed by some great, ravenous sea, long since dried up.

We both stopped with our feet planted before the crater, peering upward at the wide, jagged pedestal holding up the sky, instinctive, a little like wriggling one's toes over the edge of a fissure. The shrinking border of trees flanked us on either side. This was the last step we would take, truly alone together.

"It's not exactly pretty, is it?" I noted.

He itched at a patch of dried mud on his chin. "No, not really."

"Were you disappointed, you know, when you realised?"

"I suppose I found it appropriate. I like what you've done with the hair, by the way. Looks good in this light. Why red?" He gestured with his nose, at a rusty streak hanging by my temple.

"You want to know?"

"Well, now I'm not sure."

I had not aimed to intimidate, not consciously, though the congealing atmosphere at my side persuaded me otherwise. "Maybe a conversation best saved for later." I fixed my eyes back on the black, toothy shape ahead. "I'll bet you four coppers it takes one look at me and spits me straight back out."

"The shrapnel in my pocket says it doesn't have the nerve."

"After I trudged this far? Hardly seems worth the gamble. Question: why did you come looking to me for help?"

"You never did hand over that shortbread recipe. Given that, at this rate, I'll be facing the small charge of regicide when I'm done here, I might need it laced with one of your funky potions and all."

This addition earned him a blunt snort. "Absolutely not."

"What?" His northern inflection sang upward through the word and into the air. Years of gentle correctional therapy had yet failed to quite smooth out his once gloriously steep dialect.

"I prescribe remedies for responsible use to provide actual symptomatic relief. Besides, if you keep on about lobbing anything sharp, heavy or explosive at the man, I'll need all of it to myself."

"Fine, fine," he tittered. "And anyway, I don't know how we're going to survive this, but I feel better knowing you're here." At this, he skipped down into the pit, moving in an absurd sideways gallop.

I sat at the top of the crest for a moment; against the uneven ground a scratching chill gathered in the fold between the base of my spine and the top of my buttocks. I made out to be adjusting the leather straps under my trousers, squeezing at my legs, and watched as his upper body shrank into a dark, bobbing mass that I could balance on my palm. He faltered, and waited, arms outstretched, in the quiet hiss for a moment. I slid down into the mouth of Interieur, grasping at clumps of grass and brownish sludge.

The Wall bent and stretched in shape and height like heat haze as I approached. I could not seem to be able to visualise its scale in relation to my own body. Measuring in hands and feet is not particularly useful when said feet cannot walk vertically.

I noticed an odd sound ringing in my head, a high-pitched tone, almost resembling a child's yawn. It travelled along the wall, brick by brick, like sand through a rainmaker, growing louder as it steadily closed in on both sides. Then the light, a pure, unnatural white light, burned against my sore, tired skin. The brightness pooled around me, casting a long, skeletal shadow behind. It seemed to pour out from a spot low down, at the foot of the Wall, as though the iron gates to the afterlife had sprung an unfortunate leak.

"Remain stationary. Retinal scan in progress."

The Machine's voice was utterly shapeless, and unmistakable. Rather than have the hardware generate one of her own, her vocal cords were constructed by borrowing the voices of those inside the city. Stored away somewhere, recordings of speech from every human being inside the Wall constantly spun themselves into usable data. Like a collage artist flicking through radio stations, the Machine extracted individual words and strung the stolen pieces together. Her sentences were perfect, sensical, but somehow alien, and more difficult for unattuned ears to understand. Sometimes, people would identify their own voice being echoed back at them by the Machine; they treated such an occurrence like a novelty and celebrated it with the same momentary excitement as a round of bingo.

"Subjects identified. Data error. Welcome, Angels Michael and Lucifer." The words slurred together in my mind.

"Look, honey," I interrupted, "how about you let me have a nice, hot bath, a bit of a shopping spree, and a slice of fucking toast first? Then we can deal with all of this business of scans. Yes? No?"

The light continued to glare with the same burning intensity, like an unblinking eyeball. I noticed the faint whirring sound starting up again.

"You know what? Don't even bother churning that one through your systems. Just tell us what you want."

I blinked, and the light faded. In its place, a small, jagged hole crouched under the shade. It was, without question, the same opening I had crawled through years prior. I wondered, peering into the dark haze, whether the Machine had ever cleaned the smears of blood off of the stonework. Surely she could still taste it.

"Entry is permitted," she stated, still unable to respond to any question with a straight answer.

Michael relaxed with a sigh. "Can't knock you for trying, I guess," he groaned. "Want me to go first?"

"You're alright. What's the worst that could happen?"

He didn't laugh at my joke.

As I felt my way through the tunnel, head bowed as if for the guillotine, the Machine continued wittering, the noise amplified inordinately by the tight space. "Weapons restrictions disabled. Movement restrictions disabled. Synapse monitoring disabled. Restraint permissions disabled…"

"Are we finished now?" I jibed.

"It's funny," Michael said, as we emerged from the darkness. "I've never had to be scanned *back in* before."

"She's probably never had to scan anyone back in before. Maybe she got a little flustered."

A harsh rasping sound had the hairs on my neck prickling. Immediately behind us, square breezeblocks dragged themselves in sluggish, precarious stacks, filling up the void. The repair fit so tightly that dust flowed out from the seams, shaved off of the stone by the relentless scraping of brick against brick, bone against bone. This minute compromised spot remained visible, at least in the sense that a birth mark on the scalp is visible to one who knows precisely where to look. I knew where to look; I had found the incriminating mark before.

The gap sutured shut barely in time, before footfall of at least two people drummed into the dim, narrow alleyway from nearby. Michael dropped his luggage off of his back, and followed the sound, moving gingerly, at first, bending forward at the waist. I only jogged on behind once I noticed his posture relax, and his chest open up in front of him. Framed neatly between two older, squat buildings with overhanging tiled roofs, two figures stood facing Michael, arms hanging loosely at their sides, as if they had been waiting for some time. One of them, the man, I knew well, and felt the urge to approach him and pat tenderly at his face the instant I recognised it. My mouth moved to call out his name, but my mind could only conjure up 'Gabriel'. I stamped my toe onto the pavement instead. It wasn't fair. Out of his head, standing upright as if facing the sun, two delicate, perfectly circular rings had grown, one larger and orbiting the smaller. The silver metal glowed against his copper skin and dark hair pulled back from his forehead. Gabriel had been made an Angel too. Yes, of course he would be. These had to be his wings. I hated them almost as viciously as I had hated my own. The young lady at his side seemed only vaguely familiar but, if such a thing existed, she possessed a welcoming, truly loving face. I found myself oddly pleased to see her.

"…and you brought Rei," Michael laughed, watery-eyed, "I… didn't expect to see you. Have you been waiting very long?"

"Well, considering we've eaten our way through three days' allowance in stakeout food on more than one occasion, not long at all."

"Come on," the girl protested, "I told you already, I'm just fine when I can see the sun! Are you telling me *you'd* be able to tell the exact time in the middle of the night?"

"I don't know, maybe. Something to do with the stars—"

"Exactly." She crossed her arms and flicked her ponytail over her shoulder in righteous indignation.

I experienced my own inconspicuousness keenly, not with resentment, but perhaps the slight deflation of defied expectations. Nevertheless, I had to ask a question.

"I'm sorry. You mean you've been waiting, here, for us? Did you see us coming, before we even reached the Wall? What sort of VIP access passes do *you* have?"

"I did!" Rei leapt from sulking to exuding enthusiasm. "I saw you arrive. Well, really, I didn't *see*, not in the way you mean. Rather I knew that you would be here, in this spot, at some point soon." She began stuttering under her breath, trying to formulate an appropriate sentence to follow. I could well relate to her vexation.

"You have a Soul, a Soul that told you come here?"

"That's right," she said, breathing a loud sigh of reprieve.

"It's called Enlightenment. It shows her things, before they occur," Gabriel added.

"I can see in both directions, actually," she corrected. "Forwards and backwards. In the beginning, I could only tell when something bad was about to happen. That was before Miss Vaughn—my teacher, maybe you would know, small lady, retired now—she taught me to use Enlightenment properly. Now I can look into the past too. Only little peeks, mind you, and usually I have to have something, like an object, a tether, I guess. I'm not that powerful."

She sounded perfectly powerful enough to my mind. We all had to be taught, trained to manipulate our Soul's abilities, lest we allow the power to merely run its natural course. Only a generation ago, control over the Soul had meant simply having the restraint to avoid burning down a house to kill a spider. No longer. A thought sprung to mind and lurched out of my mouth before it could be stopped.

"Is it only disasters that you sense?"

She made a high-pitched gasp, covering her face with her hands. Gabriel had been careful to skirt around the obvious implications of their presence here, before us, but Rei had slipped up. "Oh no," she cried, "not at all! I can sense lots of things."

"She found me. Unless of course *I* count as a disaster now, too," Gabriel said, with a theatrical wink. He had always possessed quite a talent for judiciously derailing a conversation.

"That's right," she said, without a ring of pretence.

"I'm not so sure about that." Michael had slipped away to collect his bag of belongings, and now returned. "Two pairs of goggles that can see things they shouldn't, plotting together? Seems like they're after world domination to me."

Two pairs of eyes. He was right. Joking, but right. The perfect vision of Gabriel's Soul, that which gave him perfect aim at threats, even those hidden from mere mortal sight, had not struck me as intimately linked with Rei's, at least not right away. One with an unhindered view of space, the other of time—indeed, now Michael mentioned it, the two did seem a seamless combination. I was not sure whether to be charmed, or terrified.

**[Michael]**

"Ah, Gabriel, excellent. You're already here."

As though reacting to the uninvited presence, Rei darted nimbly from Gabriel's right side to his left. She was instead, I noticed, dodging away from a thick, grey smog rising out of the ground. She had most likely already witnessed, effectively, the unassuming cloud dissolving her shoes like stomach acid. Lucifer's Soul made its opinion clear, absolving her of the need to speak. It was none too happy to see Uriel.

With the flourish of a ringmaster with a baton, he stood on one foot, balancing his weight upon the handle of his sickle—his favourite toy, proudly on display, the polished crescent blade bent upward like a strained neck toward its master. Daylight bounced off of the golden halo framing his face. The circle of paper-thin gold was a discus slicing through his skull, lodging itself against his brain stem, angled like an inordinately expensive sunhat.

"Why, would you look at that," he chimed. "You know, when I heard Michael jumped ship, this is not what I expected him to bring back. I had begun to convince myself we would never lay eyes on Lucifer again. Where have you been?"

"Nowhere pleasant." She did not blink. She did not even seem to breathe.

"I can't believe that. You've been there for three years. There's no-one outside of the Wall with the power to keep you prisoner. That said, just how did Michael persuade you?"

"You are too cynical, if I may say so, Uriel. I made a terrible mistake, when I was, by most measures, still a child. I have returned to ask for mercy, and to take up the responsibility, no, the *privilege*, the Machine handed to me some years past. Michael only offered me the perfect opportunity at the right time." She shuffled her feet, fastening one hand loosely around her rucksack, and cupping her hip with the other, relaxing seamlessly into her lie.

"The Machine…?" I found it tricky to discern which part, exactly, of her statement sat so uncomfortably with Uriel. Something had, though. He slung his weapon across the flat of his shoulders, gripping it with both fists, and he grew slightly cross-eyed. Handily, his contemplation was interrupted by a sudden wave of humidity in the air, and the characteristic scuffing of heavy shoes sliding to a halt.

Uriel needed not avert his gaze. "Raphael," he called, "chop-chop, or we're leaving without you."

The fifth and last Angel blended almost perfectly with his urban surroundings, at least in his current, human state: all high cheekbones and pasty features, save for a pair of blue eyes and his wings, a crown of ebony thorns threaded through his hair. He pushed his rolled sleeves back past his elbows, head tilting like a woodpecker's as he inspected Lucifer, incredulous.

"This is her?" he said, eventually.

"Have I grown a second head since last I checked?"

"I remember you looking…taller. Have you put on weight?"

"Pleased to meet you, too."

Raphael turned to Uriel, hiking up his shoulders as if to form a barrier between themselves and their audience. "His majesty wants to see her. I don't know, to check, I guess."

"I'm well aware."

"Just making sure you weren't moving so fast that you skipped the instructions." His gaze flicked up and down the length of Uriel's weapon of choice, before he murmured through his teeth, "A tad on-the-nose, don't you think?"

"Hey, I thought *I* was impulse control. That's our whole dynamic: good cop-bad cop, brains-brawn, you know?"

Lucifer was far too disconcerted to remain fooled into speechlessness by their comedy act. "I'm sorry, you're planning to take me where, exactly?"

"Moore's Hall," Raphael replied, blankly. "Like I said, he wants to see you."

"The Sovereign. The man who chose you." Uriel's mouth slowed, seemingly, to a crawl, and he nodded along with each word, as if she had forgotten the language in which he spoke.

"Looking like this?" She gestured to the damp clothes and sprigs of vegetation still swinging from her limbs. To no avail.

"Yes, like that. Immediately."

Gabriel chose this moment to interrupt, with a weary sigh. "I suggest Michael and Raphael take up the rear, while Uriel and I flank either side. Any objections?"

"Seems to me you're treating her an awful lot like a prisoner," I protested.

"She hasn't discounted herself from contention yet," he retorted. "Come on, let's get this over with."

Lucifer clapped her hands against her thighs. "Aha, now this, this is more like it." I could hear the snide smile on her face, though only the back of her head was turned towards me, as she turned her nose up at Gabriel. I reached out to nudge her with the back of my hand, to encourage her to move before she was shoved, but she scuttled away from me on her own.

Gabriel glanced back over his shoulder to meet the watery glaze over my eyes. I did not understand his plan. Rei had vanished, escaped under the veil of commotion. I fell into step with Raphael, blinking away the whiplash. The midday sun appeared much too bright, and I must have narrowly evaded the downpour which had swamped the city, as cold light pressed down and diffused from the paving stones as though I walked on mottled glass. I skipped back into a bone-dry, rather dull reality at the sound of Lucifer speaking again, louder this time.

"Man, if we're going to spend this whole hike in solemn silence, I might perish of boredom before His Majesty can even decide whether to execute me or not. Wait, is this my funeral? Am I at my funeral?" I wished I could laugh like her, because I wanted to argue, and came up with nothing.

Uriel cleared his throat with a luxurious hum. "Alright then, welcome aboard the Angel Express, one and all. Emergency exits are towards the rear, somewhere. The tea trolley's been lost in transit, I'm afraid. We would apologise for the inconvenience, but maximising inconvenience is the name of the game. How was that?"

"Telling."

"Excellent. Speaking of which, what loophole did you exploit to get yourself out there anyway? Michael?"

"No loopholes, my friend. Just doing my lawful duty."

"Not going to give up your trick so easily, are you? Put it this way, you're certainly not expending the effort to make *my* lawful duty any easier.

"Still up for chatting?" Raphael snapped, his voice more of a furtive mumble than the usual brassy bark.

**[Lucifer]**

"Ah, yes, the Hall."

I did, as a matter of fact, remember this place, though the reverent lick of their voices as they spoke of it had rather caught me off guard. Very little of its giant, flat-faced exterior stuck in my memory, the ornate doorstopper wedged between two rows of tightly packed shopfronts, like the city's own ancient marble lung. Not that I could pause to soak in it, my escorts were so eager to shove me inside. And the interior, now *this* I remembered. The single prismed chamber stood a tad too high for the brain to properly comprehend, adornments and intricacies sprouting out of every dip and crevice like wiry hairs on a silent creature breathing too slowly to see. Buttresses could fit between one's fingertips like chopsticks, despite propping up the ceiling, that curved sculpture which sang like a conch shell at every movement below. Row upon row of pews hunched quietly on either side of a central aisle, placed precisely as feathers, or rib-bones. With stumps for legs and low backs, they seemed miniscule, as though submitting to the vast expanse of hollow space which sent gooseflesh over my forearms and condensed into tiny, cold droplets against my lips.

All of this, however, merely served to frame the scene's guiding star—an altar sprawled at its foot, the painting stretched most of the width of the rear wall. It depicted a terrific battle scene. Ten soldiers are crowded together in front, the centrepiece, some armed with Souls, others with weapons which appeared to glint, as though fine sheets of metal are embedded beneath the paint. In the background, a gargantuan, roaring tower of fire has been meticulously moulded and carved into the shape of a reptilian beast, its open jaw hanging over the fighters' heads. We called it Wyvern, the 'Soulless'. The lines and colours were printed onto my mind's canvass, but gazing up at it (for I somehow always did have to tilt my eyeballs up, no matter where from), real and solid before me, the most riveting details emerged, the texture of the soldiers' uniforms, their individual expressions, the flow of their hair, lit in overtones of scarlet.

Uriel coughed. "Contrary to popular belief," he said, "this drapery wasn't plastered all over the architecture just to look pretty. It's a mask, a big, grandiose diversion. The true importance of this room lies behind it. Follow along."

He crossed the altar with impudence, heading directly for the right-hand side of the fresco, Raphael taking a different, more fidgety route, around the edge of the raised stage. Uriel waved his hand over his shoulder, vaguely pointing the three of us straggling behind in his direction. He relished the idea that we were all oblivious idiots. He seemed to drink up that feeling of authority, the syrupy texture smoothing out his voice like liquor.

The mural was not, in actuality, plastered directly onto the stone interior. Instead, I found, the massive painting was mounted onto a wooden frame like a canvas, which was in turn attached to the wall. It appeared to me that Uriel's concerns for the precious original brickwork were unfounded. With an elegant sidestep, he slipped between the beams, inside the frame, while Raphael waited less than patiently for me to follow suit. Amongst the familiar stale aroma of dust, and rich, earthy addition of slightly damp pine, an underlying stench of chemicals attacked my nose and corneas. He halted abruptly, reached in front of him to lay the flat of his hand on a door I could barely make out as my eyes continued to adjust to the dark, enclosed space. I realised, however, when he leaned his weight against it, and it opened with a grating squeal and heavy swing, that the door was a sheet of metal, something incredibly dense, like iron or lead. So much for the architecture.

The passage through the metal hatch was practically a relief, compared to the toxic, suffocating squeeze behind the painting, though it remained only wide enough to walk two abreast. I marched ahead in the corner of Uriel's vision, determined to look only towards the growing square of light in front of me.

Uriel referred to a man, bent over forwards in a tall-backed chair tucked against the rearmost wall of the cavity. He seemed emaciated and angular, like an insect, mounted in a web of wires, cables, and other metal appendages wrapped around, and inserted into, his body. A pair of manacles, solid steel, with no visible latch, looped around his ankles and held him in place. Either his skin had turned to a bloodless grey complexion, or it was gathering an opaque layer of dust atop, including in his hair. Uriel waited, stiff-lipped, until the Sovereign gave a slight twitch, disturbing the dirty air around him, as if waking from sleep in response to the footsteps of a trespasser.

"As you asked, Sovereign, I have brought her. This here is the girl upon whom you bestowed the name Lucifer. Michael somehow obtained a reliable tip and exited the Wall's bounds in order to retrieve her, for you. It seems for the past three years she has been…"

In a strange, almost embarrassed fashion, Uriel obediently cut himself short. He had noticed the man lift his face, knuckles paling against the arms of the chair. I could not see the whites of his eyes, for they were so deeply entrenched within his skull. His flesh was a little too malleable. Gelatinous, almost. It sunk into the orifices of his skeleton and sagged around his neck like thick plumage. I had hardly taken an avid interest in the man, yet, through his own sterling efforts, he had made his face impossible to entirely purge from the memory. I could never recall him looking *this* old though. Not aged, or elderly—but decayed. He lifted two fingers a few centimetres into the air, withered branches, and curled them twice towards himself.

"Closer," he demanded, his throat barely capable of speech.

Futilely, I hesitated, hanging back as long as it took for Raphael's hand to land between my shoulder blades. My shirt bundled in his fist, Uriel's partner in lawfulness pushed me steadily forward as if I were an uncooperative dog on a leash. My nerves seemed to process each step at half its usual speed, and when we had reached an appropriate proximity to the throne, Raphael released me with one last shove.

Although he might have wanted to examine me head-to-toe, the man was, evidently, physically unable to do so. As he peered in front of himself, head visibly trembling as he forced his spine to straighten, he pulled up the corners of his lips in a squint, revealing horribly pristine, white teeth inside of his cheeks. In another life, I could have felt pity for this creature; but now, as he glared through my body with his yellowing pits for eyes, baring his ripe gums at me, pure, raw disgust and disdain were my only options. Something else could see me though, most certainly. I felt my feet rise off of solid ground. All the sweat on my skin, saliva in the back of my mouth instantly evaporated, leaving behind cracks and pores as in dry earth. Brain tissue liquified, draining out of my ears, trickling down my jaw and onto my shirt collar, as the glare of several hundred microscope lenses fell upon me at once.

"What shall I do with her, Majesty?" Uriel interjected.

"*You* will do nothing. Michael brought her to me. And he will take her now."

Uriel braced both hands behind his neck, stretching his back with nonchalant posture, but a telling wrinkle to the left side of his face. "What a disgrace this is."

"Not for you to decide," the Sovereign whispered, only loud enough for me to hear as I slunk away toward Michael. I glanced back, and noticed his body had reset to its original position, head parallel to his knees.

Michael flexed the splayed fingers of his outstretched hand, as if impatient. A performance of confidence and bravado, or a true reflection thereof? I could not be entirely sure. I surrendered myself into his grasp. As he guided me back through the narrow, dim passageway, out of the sequestered chamber, the whole event—or lack of, rather—had the feel of a public hanging, abruptly cancelled when a messenger arrives with a pardon, just as the noose has been pulled snug around the convict's neck. The disappointment in the air was palpable enough to swallow.

I continued walking, past the painting, the so-called 'mask', and down from the altar, without turning to check the view behind me. "So, now that we have been formally introduced," I called, keeping my voice as dry and prosaic as possible, "charming though it was, I presume I am free to leave, change my clothes, maybe."

"Far from it." A rush of air flowing into a vacuum could be heard, as one set of footsteps ceased behind. The atmosphere seemed to distort slightly, the straight edges of the building twisting, spears of light bending and bundling into liquid puddles, before Uriel's body caught up with his Soul, materialising before me. He propped his hands against his hips, thrusting out his chest, proudly blocking my path to the portal. His head erupted with a golden glow.

"Just because the Sovereign doesn't want to eyeball you any longer, doesn't mean I'm even close to satisfied. Personally, I don't give a damn who you think you are, no-one gets to march on inside the Wall, feigning loyalty to the cause, having spent years cavorting with witches in the—"

"Cunning folk, not witches," I interrupted.

"Don't be so pretentious."

"If I might interrupt for a moment…"

Rei's voice pealed flatly into the room, expanding outward, mimicking the curve of the arched doorway, as if she had firmly dropped her finger onto the middle key of an organ. Her diminutive silhouette reshaped the stream of light into the hall, an interruption which threw the huddle into disarray and dispersed some of the heat into the rafters. She opened and closed her raised fist, in a kind of coarse wave, seemingly aware that she had inadvertently pulled the plug on a hydraulic press.

I knew Uriel would be first to raise an objection, as I bent my neck away from the flick of his wrist. "You're Public Relations. Can it seriously not wait? Maybe think about what you could be walking into before you speak."

She continued further down the aisle, one balled hand falling onto her hip, the other sharpening into one finger before her face. "On the contrary, sir, PR is far down the list of the His Majesty's priorities at this moment in time. As I am sure you yourself are aware. My delegation has changed for today; hence, this is my job now, if you would be so kind as to let me proceed with it, per the Machine's instructions."

A sharp breath through Uriel's nostrils, as he turned to face Raphael.

"Go on, Rei, go ahead," Michael said, with admirable grace.

She cleared her throat, and I thought I saw a tweak of a smile as she gave us a little curtsey. "I will. Lucifer, might I take you aside? There is a message for you."

I almost skipped down the steps towards the centre aisle, before I realised I ought to take the time to avoid appearing too enthusiastic. I folded my hands behind my back and nodded to Rei, carefully. "Of course," I said. "Shall we pop outside?"

As our footsteps drummed out of the door, my ears pricked with the sound of Gabriel snickering, in mocking ventriloquism, "You're *Public Relations*."

"Honestly…" Rei sighed into the air, her face squinting into the sunlight.

"Not a fan?"

"Of Uriel? We are all fans of the Angels, here. Anyway, do excuse me," she murmured, now rocking on her heels.

"Oh no, no. Please don't worry; I'm certainly not. What's the problem now?"

"Ah, well, I wouldn't call it a problem, per se. Only, you are required to attend a psychological assessment by the Machine. Something about needing more recent data, I believe. I was ordered to collect you."

"Crivens, is that all?"

She stopped swaying for a moment, her body tilting sideways into a distinctly question mark-like arc, appearing to be reorienting after a knock.

"It seemed better to tell you personally, I guess, not in front of a crowd."

"I assumed you were bringing some terrible news…well, relatively speaking. I wish the Machine hadn't put you to the trouble, in a certain respect. Would you prefer I take myself there asap, or do I have an appointment?"

"It was my intention to escort you to the facility."

"I'm surprised. Why, I don't think much to my sense of direction either, but I most definitely *do* know my way around the testing floor. I'm sure I'll be alright."

"I would agree, but still, this is the work I've been given, so if I might accompany you anyway…"

"Naturally, my apologies. Lead the way, dear."

"Of course," she replied, shining, and fidgeted on the spot waiting for me to walk ahead.

"Very kind of you."

"Thank you. I'm glad to see you back, here, an Angel."

"Really? I mean, to say that I'm 'back' implies I was here at the start of it all. I was not."

"But I knew who you were, at least. I always imagined you being somewhere, out *there*. I know the Machine's designed to be… impartial, in its calculations, but having four blokes at the top—

four. For goodness sake, it just seemed a bit unfair. So, to have a lady Angel around at least, it's quite refreshing. Personally, I think more people have friendly feelings towards you than might like to, um, shout it from the hills."

"I see, such candour, but spoken so sweetly. That's why you and Gabriel get along swimmingly."

"Oh, I should hope so; otherwise, I've been going about this thing all wrong. And I already get enough dubious looks, what with him being a super-important super-solider, and me being PR. You know, you've caused quite the stir since you came back through the Wall."

"I have? I imagine I have. I'm sorry for the trouble."

"You misunderstand. I find it all rather exciting. I must have the best day job in the city right now."

"Well in that case, you're welcome for the scandal."

**[Rei]**

"Oh, whilst I remember—here, I am supposed to hand this to you. It's…well, I suppose you could call it a gift, from Mister Frazier Blackwater."

"From Blackwater? What is it?" she queried, taking the parcel from my two hands into hers, like a new-born baby, or a motion-activated explosive. In all fairness, I would not know to tell her in either case.

"I have no idea. I ran into him—or perhaps, he tracked me down—while I was walking over to Moore's Hall, and entrusted it to me. He was panting as though he had run a mile, and he handed this package over exactly as you see it. No explanation as to what was inside, just strict instructions to deliver it to you. I thought it best not to unwrap it."

My tongue began to stammer under her studious gaze, before I could reach the end of my account. She seemed much taller, the longer I stared back at her, as she were raised up on a plinth, and I cowering under a magnifying glass.

"Why did you give it to me now?"

I wondered if there could be a correct response to such a question. Lucifer swayed her head a little from side to side, suggesting that, if there was, she did not know it either. She had torn only a corner of brown paper away from the package, revealing a further layer of fabric wrapping beneath.

"I only thought it prudent, in case it proves to be…something you will need." I glanced over her shoulder, towards the door ahead of us, the sealed door to the assessment chamber.

She leaned against the wall, slowly peeling away, with thumb and index finger, each tightly sealed skin, one by one. Beneath alternating paper and muslin, a parcel of leather released a tart aroma when uncovered, promising to provide the treasure so painstakingly concealed. I could not help giving a blunt grunt of disappointment, when she untucked from the bundle a thin,

unblemished sheet of metal. The way light slid down its outer
lines suggested it had been ground to a sharp edge on one side.

"It's a blade, isn't it?"

"Hold on a moment," Lucifer said, holding up her one free hand.
I fell silent. She reached her arm behind her back and wrenched
something out of her pocket. "Here. Take a look at this."

She placed the object onto my open palm. It was warm against
my skin, presumably having been glued to her for the duration of
her difficult journey. My finger could glide over its surface,
smooth as if newly manufactured, and it sat weighty in my hand.
It felt valuable. Whether, when she smacked the ornament into
my hand, she intended for my Soul to awaken, to turn my mind's
eye to the past, I could not be sure. Perhaps my own nagging
curiosity flung me across time, like throwing a bone to a
Labrador.

Regardless, I stood before a dim room, light only filtering in
through a single window, and empty save for two figures, facing
each other. The man on the right was clearly Frazier Blackwater.
He still owned that navy suit, and it seemed he had refused to
change his hair from the years-old oily quiff. In fact, the only
notable difference in the man I saw, and the one who had chased
me down this morning, was the absence of a few flecks of grey,
and crows' feet around his eyes. The girl, standing at least three
heads shorter than Blackwater, could only be Lucifer herself,
though recognising her face required more attention to detail.
She had the same oval-shaped head and round features, but if she
had confessed to being a changeling, swapped out as a teenager, I
might just have believed her. The discrepancy lay not so much in
her actual appearance, as in her posture and mannerisms. She
was, as I looked upon her, curling up like a wilting plant,
clutching both of her elbows for dear life. A small, wet
whimpering sound escaped her.

*"It's trying it's best, you understand that as well as I do,"* Blackwater said, with a sigh. *"To cut it some slack, the thing's confused."*

*"Look, my brain doesn't work right, I know. You don't have to tell me,"* she cried, kneading at her eyes.

*"Maybe you're not wrong, but that's not the point. If your Soul's not doing what you want—what you need it to do, then we have to find the means to force its hand. So your brain is tricking your Soul, fine. You just have to get very good at trickery yourself. That's what you are here to learn. Take this."*

There was a sturdy canvas bag hanging from his arm, bulging with numerous heavy, round objects, as if he had just returned from grocery shopping. He now rifled around inside for a moment, searching for one curious, anomalous item, wrapped up in a handkerchief: a small, narrow artefact fashioned from attractive hardwood. I moved in to get a closer look. There were light engravings on both sides, strange symbols, patterns of endless knots, like intertwined vines. One end of the wooden stick was wider than the other, which had a notch carved into the flat face. My archaeological instincts (albeit skewed) suggested that Blackwater had handed the young Lucifer a decorative, detached, and ultimately useless, doorhandle.

This item evidently held no additional meaning to Lucifer, either, at the time. *"Is this supposed to be an insult?"* she said.

*"I'd give you the rest of it, but the Machine won't let me."*

*"It feels like an insult,"* she mumbled, twirling the handle between her fingers and squeezing it irreverently.

*"Maybe a little. Get angry with me, if you feel like it."*

*"I'm sorry. I am trying—"*

*"No! No, no. Don't stop. Can you imagine how difficult my job becomes if you stay all nice and meek and inoffensive every session? All of that hate you like to quietly save up just for me,*

*you have to hold onto it. Listen to me now, please.*" He crouched onto one knee, taking her wrist in one of his hands. *"It's important that you remember. If there ever comes a time when there is a blade on the end on this knife, find that rage. Don't close yourself off from the Source. Let it in. You'll need it. But talking isn't going to get you very far. Practice will.*" He stood up, reached back into the bag, and this time pulled out an apple the size of his fist, blushing with ripeness. After polishing the skin on the leg of his trousers, he gently lowered it the floor between the two of them. *"Take aim, Little Mademoiselle Antithesis. Show me what you've learned.*" I could not speak for Lucifer, now or back then, but in that moment, I found the man rather insufferable.

Thankfully, the Lucifer of the present chose to speak, pulling me out of my trance. She had taken the handle back and found the blade to be a neat fit. A complete knife now rested, out in the open, on a bed of packaging. It could not leave her hands from then on; only Angels could be seen to carry dangerous weapons on their person. If nothing else, this provided proof, that this woman truly was the missing fifth child of the Machine.

"Well, it probably won't be of much use in my psych assessment," she said, whimsically, "but hopefully it provides a satisfactory answer to your questions." She took the dagger and tucked it into the back of her jeans, under her vest, where she had, for years, been keeping the orphaned fragment. "I'd better go in. Could you hold this for me?" She passed the reams of torn paper and muslin into my arms and disappeared, a dark blur, through the door into the chamber. The sound of steel locks grinding into place echoed through the hallway, where I was now alone.

**[Lucifer]**

Piercing pale light radiated from a single glowing rectangle mounted upon the far wall and sunk into the pores of the irreparably dark room, like a lantern shone down into a well. The Machine's vaguely bed-shaped apparatus lay in wait, perfectly still, in the centre.

"Good afternoon. Please take a seat on the chair in front of you."

There was no point in standing around. I could wait here all night, but so could that blank square staring out from the wall. Besides, given half an hour, she would grow aggravated and begin administering little electrical cattle-prod jolts to get me moving. I complied. I slotted right into place too, crossing my feet, cold armrests tough and familiar against my elbows.

"Thank you. Confirm your full name."

"You already know my name."

"I am undertaking the necessary procedure to update your data log. Please confirm your full name."

"It's Lucille."

"Please confirm your full name."

"That's all I have for you I'm afraid. Take it or leave it."

"Please confirm."

"Confirm what?"

"Full name. I am undertaking the necessary procedure to update your data log. Please confirm."

"I don't—I don't know! I do not know my full name."

"Acknowledged."

"You took it from me."

"Please wait for further questions. Interruptions will prolong assessment process. Confirm date of birth."

"I don't know. I'm almost twenty-three."

"Acknowledged. Performing scan."

"Chemical imbalance detected—differential, four units. Body mass index sufficient. Acquiring blood sample in three, two, one."

My fingertip reeled from the tiny needle punching a hole in its skin. I brushed the throbbing spot against with my thumb, leaving a pinkish transfer in the creases. With all the marvels of technology, she still had not found any other way to get at our blood.

"Mineral content sufficient."

"Cool, right? Turns out I can take an iron supplement all by myself."

The next pause stretched out a tad too long. I held my breath to suffocate a booming laugh. The poor thing was stuck. This was the point at which she would usually burrow inside my head, try to locate what bothersome, traumatic thoughts I must be inflicting upon myself. Only, for the first time in my peculiar case, she was forbidden to do so. I could hear the displeasure in her silence.

She eventually decided upon a solution. "You are visibly restless. On a scale of one to four—one being the lowest value and four the highest value—how nervous or afraid do you feel?"

How novel. "Do you accept fractions? How is three and one quarter for an answer?"

"Your response is oppositional. On a scale of one to four—one being the lowest value and four the highest value—how irritable or violent do you feel?"

"Much more than I was this morning."

"On a scale of one to four."

"Don't panic. Two."

"On a scale of one to four—one being the lowest value and four the highest value—how strongly do you feel hopeless, or that your actions are worthless?"

"Listen. Let me tell you something. You are not as subtle as you think are."

"On a scale of one to four."

"Three." For now, at least. Provided she continued in her current vein, she could have bumped that score up even further.

"Do you think still often of death, Lucifer?"

"Ouch. Going straight for the punch on that one, are we?"

"Please respond."

"Sure I do, more than the average mare, I suppose. Is that what you were always gawking at? Must have got your binaries in a right twist."

"Please observe this artistic representation of a sunset. You should experience a sense of relaxation and rejuvenation."

A few rapid clicks, and the jargon inside the rectangle was instantly engulfed with a hot auburn flood. The room stained orange like smouldering coal, reflecting the strokes of colour lit from behind. As promised, a deep, summer sunset, set ablaze by a perfect heavenly orb falling into a series of shaky lines meant to imply the ocean. The waves could not move; the wispy suggestions of cloud remained stoic. The sheet of colours formed a veil over my eyes.

"Do you feel a sense of relaxation and rejuvenation?" she inquired, impatient.

"Oh, I'm marvellous."

"Deception detected. Please respond."

"Yes."

"Deception detected. Please respond."

"Well, you got me. Sorry to break it to you, darling, but your lovely sunset just isn't doing it for me."

Another long wait. If I had gotten my own way, she would play loud, laborious ticking sounds, or something similarly ironic to fill the silence.

"Acknowledged. Prescription will be delivered to address of resident Michael."

"That all? I could have told you as much." She seemed to have miraculously misplaced, or rather, selectively discarded, hours of memory from inside this cell. I held my hand straight up next to my ear, as if calling for the teacher.

"Please raise your left arm, at a right angle to the elbow. Administering sedative in three, two, one."

A larger needle now slid under my skin, sending a chill through my flesh for a brief moment, before retreating, as though embarrassed. A cylinder inside the door snapped, signalling my release.

I thought of how long it had been, since I last slunk out into the corridor like this. Each summoning, each scan, each needle scrunched together like dough under a rolling pin, one week indistinguishable from the next. I only remembered the last because Mr Smith had startled me terribly, boiled me in my own embarrassment, sitting on a hard, leather-backed chair outside the room. His posture had sunk low, head and torso bunched tightly together, while his legs splayed out into the corridor, a prime trip hazard—almost childlike. Smith had always radiated a curious immortality, despite the lick of white hair splitting his head down the middle. Still, the new, unruly beard hiding his face and the grey stain around his eyelids had a dulling effect, aged him in a way I could not remember seeing before then, or since. He was not dying yet, but he was plagued by something. Something toxic was rotting inside of him.

*"Hey."* He must have called out my name, in order to seize my attention. My memories were all apparition and supposition nowadays. *"You alright?"*

*"The answer to that should be pretty self-indicative, don't you think? Sir."*

*"I suppose you're right. Anything I can do?"*

*"The Machine still won't let me just quietly hop off the side of the arches, will she?"*

*"She will not."*

*"And you can't change that, do some fiddling with the code?"*

*"One of the stranger requests I've had in that regard, so I'll assume you're kidding. But no. And even if I could, I'd have to say no. Don't side-eye me like that; it's not because of some sense of righteous moral clout. I'm not waiting out here for the fun of it. I just know it's not your time."*

"Ah, that was fast." Rei launched out of her seat, as though an unseen hand had burst out of the upholstery and thrown her. "Time seems to crawl in this place, usually."

"I have sat through plenty of chances to practise."

"And even still…your number is so high." She glanced over my head, as though the digits dangled there. I glanced up, expecting to see them projected onto the wall, assuming that she had requested to see my stats for herself, even if only subconsciously. The Machine, having little to no need or appreciation for decorum, did not make any distinction. Rei had not asked, as it happened. She was trusting.

"Have you ever been in?" I queried.

"I was told to come once. Nothing major, apparently, a little upset, but oh, it was horrible. I had twenty-four subtracted from me for that! I'd dread going through it again."

I could certainly see her logic. A record clean of mental assessments did not necessarily improve one's number, and even the odd one or two could easily be remedied by remembering the proper intake of protein for a while, reading a couple of reasonably dense books perhaps. But scheduled weekly appointments with little progress should, by all accounts, have left mine plummeting.

"Strange, isn't it?" I remarked.

"Yes, almost as if, whatever ails you in this room is not quite a detriment—just as valuable to have it than not to."

Of course, I need only ignore the fact that it occasionally makes me wish to leap off a bridge, and the constant whisperings, kindly informing me that myself and anyone I care for will be dead by morning, unless I *do something* about it. Sometimes their deaths will be at my own blood-soaked hands. Who's to say? Me and the voice are not friends, no matter what she deigns to believe. But disregarding her, yes, at least I can shoot deadly black smoke out of my arse. The more afflicted I became the better, so long as I still breathed. My condition had proven useful, and therefore the Machine judged it prudent to keep me alive. I lied, though. The smoke is not summoned like that, unfortunately. Souls remain incapable of any sense of humour.

"As I think more," Rei mumbled to herself, "everything the Machine does makes less and less sense."

"Because the numbers stand for nothing of substance. Why must they make sense?" I folded my arms over my stomach, expecting a slab of ceiling to crack open my skull, or the wooden mouth to reopen behind me, bolstered by its jeering troop of empty chairs, and suck me back in. We continued to walk slowly.

"I'm sure she will be more than prepared to climb in my ear and correct you, once you and I part ways." She flicked an upturned finger around loosely above her head. "Nonetheless, even if your number—your name means nothing else, it is a sign of your power. It would do well for all of us to remember that, I think, if we can."

Those last words of Rei's cemented themselves immovably in my mind. Perhaps it had been the slightest note of darkness in her voice that rendered it such. That evening, when I was finally alone in her company, lounging on Michael's sofa, legs crossed, hands in my lap, I took a moment to look up at the numerous watchful eyes, and winked.

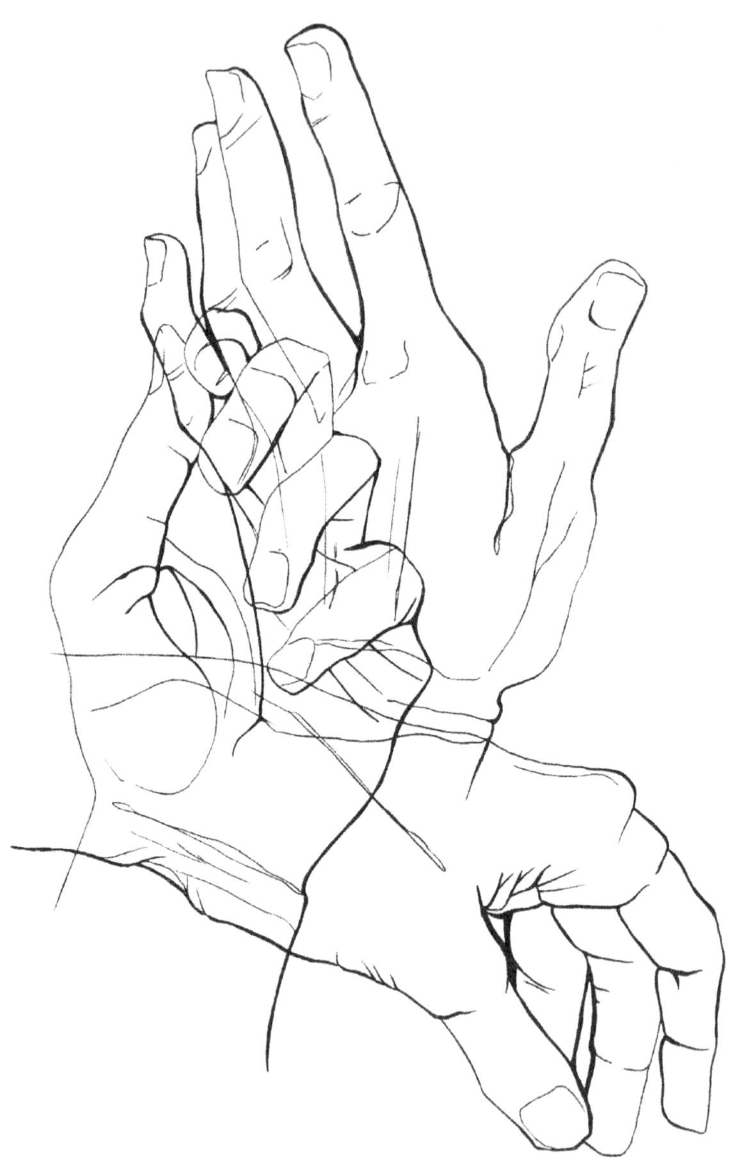

# Part 2: Sublimation



"What did you think?"

"It's nice. Very big, and clean, and you have a couch. Does it always hum like this, in here?"

"Well, thank you—and I think so. But I wasn't talking about the apartment. They all look fairly much the same to me."

"Oh." I didn't intend to sound so dismayed, like I had just watched him kick a puppy. "Never mind. What did I think of what?"

"Your new colleagues."

"My colleagues, huh? Quite the optimist you are. I can't say I'm surprised. You and Gabriel, hell, even Uriel, were all quids in. The other guy threw me a little, I'll admit. What do you call him, Raphael?"

"Really, what about him? You knew him?"

"Not really, only a little. His voice was more familiar than his face. I get the feeling he didn't like me much, but that doesn't say very much about him. He has a Soul, doesn't he?"

"Indeed he does. People used to call him the dragon. They still do, actually, more often than not. Some sort of shapeshifting Soul, I think, turns him into a mean, scaly fireball."

"That's right! The burning body of the vicious Wyvern, an image so strong that it kind of…coagulated, recreated itself, in pint-size. Wyvern-lite, if you will."

"Sounds much better than my version."

"Trust me not to put two and two together. It's terrible, isn't it, remembering a man's Soul, but not his face? Even if said man does hate my guts."

"He doesn't hate your guts, I'm sure."

"I wouldn't be. Uriel's got him. It'd be a handsome face too, if he weren't permanently grimacing with it."

"Hey, uh, Lucifer? I'm sorry about Uriel, letting him show up like that."

"You know it's his Soul who lets him do that, right? At least, I for one can't pop through thin air like I'm tied to a bungee."

He did chuckle a little at that one, shaking his head in the meantime. "That's not what I mean. Besides, if it came down to it, my Soul's supposed to be the *extinguisher*, supposed to have the power to nullify all the others, including Uriel's. I'm the one man to conquer them all…in theory. Man, I confess I never much liked the guy, but he's been taking more and more liberties, ever since the Machine decided it would be a good idea to stick wings on his head and call him an Angel."

"Oh, he's always been taking liberties," I spat. "The only difference is the most powerful player on the board constantly crawling up his jacksie and telling him he's doing right. Trust me, what you or I think or say doesn't make a jot of fucking difference."

"You alright?"

"I'm fine. Why, what's the matter?"

"Oh, you seemed to change so quickly, mood-wise, I thought I must have screwed up somewhere."

"No, Michael—shit, no you haven't done anything. I have a lot of different faces nowadays." They seemed to grow out of my skin, like moss on a stone. "I've tried counting them all, on several occasions actually; I average out at about seven." I'd line them all up, or try to, display pieces on the mantle. "For the most part, I can kind of keep track, but one slips through on its own sometimes. That is so *sad*, I'm sor—"

But he had already disappeared from view, and suddenly reappeared, literally leaping in front of the couch, posed like a frog with his legs bent at the knee. He brandished a wooden spoon in his hand. For a man perfectly accustomed to wielding long sticks as a weapon, he looked delightfully ridiculous.

I sniggered unashamedly. "If you're trying to prise my Soul out, you'll have to do better than a spoon."

"Ah, you misunderstand my challenge, for while the most impenetrable defences quail at thine infernal smoke, it is but dust to I, the Angel Michael! Forgive my vile grammar, my star-crossed nemesis, and accept this test of true skill." This odd new character revealed, from behind his back, a spatula with which to arm me. "En garde!"

Still with my rear wedged in the chair, I weakly clacked my weapon against my opponent's. I laughed into my cheeks, not at my own poor show, but at Michael's enthusiastic parody of, I assumed, fencing, which rapidly mutated into one of the conductor to a hundred-piece orchestra. My muffled chuckles remained contained within my chest, at least they did, until I accidentally choked on my own spit, and my lungs collapsed into a fit of coughing. When I brought the back of my hand to my mouth, spatula still grasped loosely between my fingers, he seemed satisfied I was not dying, and set himself down on a cushion beside me.

"Do me a favour, will you?" I said, voice croaky and foreign. "I think this place has it in for me. I made it this far, back to you. But I don't know how much I have left in me. You know I will dig my heels into the ground until my Soul has left my body; still, if I do trip and this time I don't get up—"

"That's not happening; not on my watch."

"But if it does, Michael. It's okay. Just make sure you bury me close, with a big, heavy stone over my head, so I can't go wandering anywhere."

His cheeks perked up a little at that. A good touch of morbid humour always had a place in these conversations, bringing a mite of levity, to prise his hands from over his ears. Still, his eyes were surrounded by wrinkles, and seemed to have glazed over, even in the scarce light.

"On the hill by the lake, maybe. Where they have to look at me. I want them to remember I was here. I want them to know what they did to me. Don't let them beat me, not after all this time."

"Fine, I hear you. But I will never do it. I won't let you leave. We all need you here, the same as you have us. You are Lucifer of the black smoke; you learned to walk in darkness, bend it to your will. To be frank, your Soul would turn us all to dust before it let you go—which is good. But you are tired."

"I am so tired."

"So, you should rest, just a nap. I've got eight hours or so to spare. I'll wait."

He patted the arm of the sofa as he hauled himself to his feet. Even as he switched on the desk lamp, and thudded into his chair, the back of him did not seem quite real. Or rather, *I* was not real, but an apparition, a lonely ghost watching him go about his daily activities in the dark.

He was asleep when I next slipped back into consciousness, bright yellowish haze streaming through the window, poking at my face. I could not see him, but the desk had been vacated, the chair left at an angle to it, suggesting he had ambled to his right, straight towards the room nearest the entrance. The door to the single bedroom, to which I had paid little notice beforehand, had been closed, the dark, opaque paintwork sucking up any sound, smell and sign of life from both inside and out. There had to have been several sensors fixated on me as I lay there since, as soon as I pried my eyes open a crack, a stilted mangle of voices boomed directly into my ear canal.

"Good morning, Lucifer. Communication has been sent from Angel Uriel."

I braced a hand against the back of the couch, and pulled myself upright, combed my hands through my hair and, without opening my mouth, wondered whether she might have administered a little shock to my toes in order to have me awake sooner. Either time slowed to a slug-like crawl, or the Machine was prepared to wait for as long as I took to respond, hanging over my back, the pressure like a pool of salty water.

"…Go on then, read it."

"Acknowledged. Should have known you would choose Michael's place to hide out. Hope the golden boy manages to do it for you."

**[Michael]**

I woke on my own, maybe two minutes, at most, before I was jolted from under the covers, the furniture materialising around me as the overhead light faded into glowing white life. Auspiciously, I remembered to pull on a pair of loose joggers with my shirt before shuffling out of the bedroom. Lucifer perched on the edge of the couch, her back facing me, appearing to stare out of the window. Granted, she might have found something of interest out there to watch, but I had my doubts.

"Oh, there you are," I called, to break to silence. "Good morning?"

As she twisted around to look at me, I noted the plastic cup of tap water she held to her chest. I had forgotten to tell her to help herself to food and something warm to drink. She liked fruit teas. I recalled she offered me some when she sat me down behind her shop and persuaded me to rest. I should get her tin today, I reminded myself, or maybe two, or three different ones. I could afford to take something out of my weekly budget.

Her body shrugged, a silent, inward chuckle, as she shook her head. "I was shaken awake a while ago, just so I'd listen to a message."

"A message? How come?" I wondered if this could be the reason her shoulders hunched over the cup clutched so tightly in her hands.

"Oh, nothing important, boring housekeeping stuff. And I didn't know where else to go, so I figured I'd wait for you. What is it that you lot do all day, instead of working?"

It seemed she hoped I would not notice the discrepancy, that the mail was somehow both unimportant, and urgent enough that she had been roused simply to read it.

"We do work of our own, I suppose," I said. "All the Angels' sleep cycles are staggered, so there's one patrolling around the city centre pretty much constantly. If I had to guess, I'd say the Machine has slotted you in the schedule somewhere by now."

"Ah, I understand. That would definitely explain why she's been zapping me every five minutes or so for the past couple hours. Probably wants me to get a move on."

"And you just sat there with it? Why didn't you wake me?"

"Michael, every joint in my body is as rusted-up as your grandmother's. I'm well past used to it. The Machine poking at me occasionally isn't going to have the same effect as she'd like. Still, I don't have much better to do than keeping the wheels turning. Patrol it is, I suppose. Yes. Patrol… I'll head out next time I get nagged at."

"Then I'll go with you. Show you the usual routes."

She opened her mouth momentarily, perhaps to protest, then closed it again, averting her gaze with a slight nod. I sidestepped toward the bathroom, thinking to dress myself quickly, and shove something into my pockets to eat on the move, when a high-pitched chime interrupted me. The Machine's voice pulsed out from the boards in the ceiling, in a mode I was not accustomed to hearing it, as if addressing the entire room.

"Automated message received from Eve Stanton. Reading now. Dear residents, you are cordially invited to a celebratory evening ball, organised to commemorate the unprecedented, safe return of our Angel, Lucifer. I expect you all know where, and what to wear! Doors open at 2030, on the sixteenth day."

"Damn, Eve's especially on her toes, I see."

Lucifer scoffed once, then again, higher pitched. I swallowed deeply, feeling the apple of my throat drag against something inside, thick bile gathering around my tonsils. A little selfishly, I hoped she could continue conversing with herself in cat-like growls for a few seconds longer. If I opened my mouth, I was afraid the congealed, saline concoction would spill over my tongue onto the floor.

"No way does she still get her allowance from running those bloody parties!" she cried.

"Of course she does, more than ever."

"At least her supply of themes has run dry, apparently." She scratched at her scalp, and started pacing. The room tilted and rattled under the weight of her feet.

"Oh no, she still manages to come up with those. Last evening that I attended was 'Underwater Ebullition'. Now if you can tell me what on earth that is supposed to mean, I would much appreciate it. I puzzled over it for hours before Gabriel told me to tie a piece of blue taffeta to my belt loop, paint some swirls on my face and just get on with it. My guess is, this time, you're her muse."

"She wouldn't know where to begin. To go or not to go, now that is the question."

"I'm afraid none of us get a choice in the matter, same as always."

"Angels included?"

"Angels most certainly included."

"Meaning the defence of Interieur comes secondary to hours of drinking and waiting around, wondering if it's socially appropriate to leave yet?"

"Absolutely. We're supposed to refer to it as a 'perfect opportunity for crowd observation.'"

"Oh, for—I'm beginning to question what the point of crowning us ever was. What's the use in being *exceptional*, if we can't except ourselves from all the loud, glittery nonsense?"

"From what I've heard on the grapevine, at least, most people rather enjoy the entire affair. Which is not to say that I disagree with you. Still, one or two dissenting opinions, Angel or not, don't count for much on the matter. This comes from up top. We must be there to be *seen*. So, looks like a change of plans. I'll march back and forth making sure to look extremely vigilant, while you go about acquiring yourself an outfit."

"I'll do what now?"

"Unless you happened to bring a spare ballgown in that backpack of yours."

"I hate all of this, just so you're aware."

"Oh, I believe you. And if I could make it all go away for you, I would." I paused, and raised my brow at her. She sighed, taking a prolonged blink as if to rest her eyes, so I assumed she understood my meaning. "Come on, look, I made you breakfast."

I tossed a pre-packaged, high-protein cereal bar across the room, which she snatched out of the air and glanced at the label with a smirk.

"I hate them…doesn't mean I can't make some fun out of this one, though."

[Gabriel]

Turning onto Spinner's Avenue, I checked inside the stiff
cardboard box one more time. I felt pretentious enough, carrying
around a roll of luxurious navy silk, on the same arm trained to
hold a loaded pistol; it better have been the right one. I imagined
jogging back down the street, calling, "Oh dear, this is the wrong
plush, inordinately expensive necktie. Let me get back to you
with all of the *other ones*." No, it would be this tie, or none at all.
Immediately, I locked on to the dark figure standing before the
seamstress's shop, seeming to stare up, back arched, at a window
display. I had no idea how long she had already been idling
there, but between my entering onto the street, and arriving at the
window, Lucifer did not move an inch. Although I had noticed
some markedly impressive pieces of numerous colours, shapes
and sizes—I assumed they could be called art—hung on those
mannequins, nothing could possibly be such an object of
fascination to the young apothecary. She had nothing in her
hands either, no package like mine, just a blade tucked under her
shirt.

"You're going to have to go in there eventually," I murmured,
leaning down over her shoulder. "The clothes don't come out to
you, unfortunate as it is. Freya may be talented with an old
sewing machine, but she can't read minds."

She shuffled on the spot, acknowledging my reflection in the
shop window. "I am aware. I've already eaten my way through
my—" She rummaged in her pocket for a crumbled foil wrapper,
unfolding it to read, "—protein-based oat, fruit and nut meal. So
now I'm fresh out of excuses. What about you, here just to tell
me off?"

"Nope." I pulled the box out from under my arm as proof. "I've
come to drop off a tie. Need to get some embroidery done."

"I thought you despised the whole process of being dressed."

"Oh, I did, as much as you. And I don't particularly enjoy it now,
in fact. I tend to look at the procedure more with…acceptance.

[66]

Like the latest version of homework. There's no getting away from the necessity, so might as well get it over with, if not with the greatest enthusiasm. Besides, someone gets to make their living out of maintaining my tie collection, so it's not all terrible."

"I don't have the most pleasant memories, that's all. Remember that teal skirt, the one that sat an inch above my puffy knees."

She wrapped her arms tighter around her middle, half disappearing behind her own hair. It may have been the work of my own memory, pasting a different face onto her body, but she appeared to shrink, growing several years younger with a single gesture. Of all things, to have her shrivelling.

"I know," I reminded her. "But this place isn't going anywhere, no matter how hard you scrunch up your face looking at it. And the ladies probably wouldn't appreciate you using your Soul to vaporise their business, while leaving the greengrocers untouched."

I held my breath, waiting for a wide crack to appear in the pane of glass.

"I like my fresh vegetables," she grumbled.

"You like the cabbage smell?"

"It does not smell that bad."

"Really?"

"Fine, I don't hate the smell of greens. It reminds me of plants. You know, trees, the dirt. I dare say I like it better than bleach and fabric dye. Sue me."

I paused, turning over my words carefully, making sure to catch her eye in the reflection. "There's a phrase you told me once, that I liked. You said, 'I can get inside anywhere, so long as I'm carrying a toolbox and a ladder.'"

She didn't snap back to attention, exactly; she took more of a slow, rising motion, like a ball, having been pushed to the bottom of a pond, was suddenly let go. "I remember that one," she said. "So, rather than a ladder, I need a fancy dress."

"It's all just costume, right? If it makes you feel any better, if the Machine tries to force something truly horrific on you, just don't accept it. Trust me."

"Tried and tested?"

"Tried and tested. Screw it; if I want to wear a blue suit, and they can make me a blue suit, then that's what I'll have. Hell, I'll have one in bright tangerine, whether it's the most optimal choice for my complexion or not."

"I thought you looked quite good in royal blue, as I recall."

"Damn straight I do." Not what I meant for her to focus on, but I would certainly accept the burst of validation.

"Listen, I'll make a deal with you."

"Hm, and the terms are?"

"I'll do as you say, and go in there, best behaviour…within reason."

"Naturally." We nodded in unison.

"If you let me use your eyeliner pen."

I took a moment to let a heavy, barking laugh bounce off of my diaphragm. She was a perceptive one. If I was prepared to slather paint near the most sensitive organs in my body, I would do so in the best of taste.

"Alright," I said, "it's yours."

"And you are first in the queue."

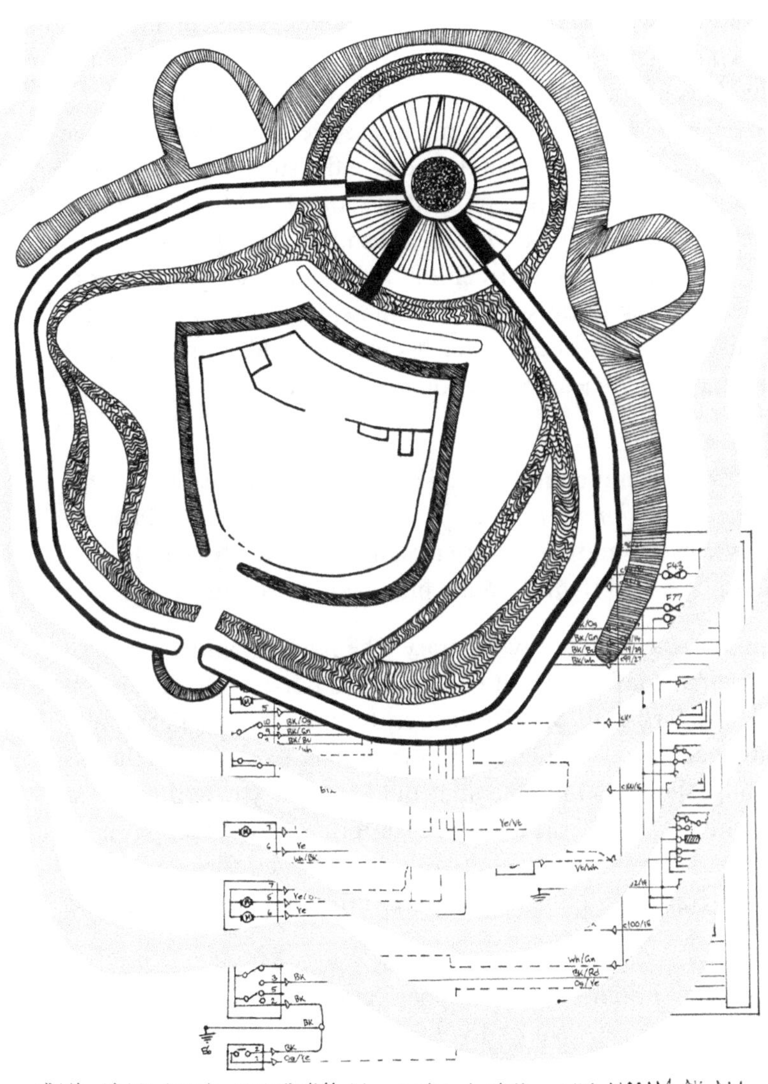

**[Lucifer]**

I swung myself out from the seamstresses' shop, plopping down onto the humped, uneven surface of the cobbled pavement—their front step a couple of inches too high for my shortened stride and jellified knees—my arms full of a bundle of light, gratifying nothing. Then I halted, dead in my tracks, dead on my feet, to the lucid chime of "Lucifer!" jangling down the street and straight through my ear canal. I had trapped the sound of Michael's voice in a sort of icy stasis in my dreams, flashbacks to a past as distant, watery and diluted as childhood. It had changed, but not too much. I still knew his from the others. But I found I did not fully trust it, not until I could see his unmistakably gangly form, like a sepia runner-bean plant, bounding enthusiastically into my path.

"I didn't take you much for a stalker," I jibed. *"If you were someone else, I'd have knocked your lights out by now,"* I came fearfully close to adding, before realising, thankfully, that I wasn't quite comfortable enough playing with fire just now.

"It's not exactly part of my itinerary," he replied, with a tweak of his brow that confirmed that I ought not to pursue *that* disguised remark any further either. This covert form of communication was unprecedented, difficult, and sumptuous, exclusive to those few whose thoughts the Machine could not freely rifle through at a moment's notice. "Fortunately, or unfortunately, I thought it wise to pass through the vicinity of this particular shop once, twice, several times on my route, after this morning's news. No luck?"

"Much luck." I didn't want him pouting with such despondency, though I did not yet want to divulge what I had managed to do, either. "But I have to come back for it later on."

He immediately perked up. Rather, he appeared very pleased with himself, almost shuddering with giddy satisfaction. "That's just perfect. Then we have enough time and excuse for a short excursion."

"An excursion to where?"

"Oh, nowhere too special. I was just thinking we could get ourselves a coffee."

He winked at me. Absurdly, it flustered me a little, and I could feel the pores on my forehead bloating with sweat as I stammered like I was choking on food. Not because of the gesture, in itself, but because Michael didn't *wink*. I didn't believe he was capable of it, that he was one of those who, attempting to be flirtatious, would blink like they had sand in their eyes. He couldn't whistle either. And he knew better than to try that with me. My brain rolled onto its back, and I wondered whether he had noticed me, in my previous narcissistic rapture, engaging silently with the Machine in the same way, and believed it to be some sort of secret signal. I blushed in apology, because I did not, in fact, understand, and when I leaned forward and squinted dubiously in reply, his face drooped a little with disappointment.

"Never mind," he grumbled. "It's just a café, a little out off the beaten track, but not too far from here. Nothing sinister. Come on. You'll understand what I mean when we get there."

The capital city was arranged roughly in rings, expanding outward, outward, buildings growing out from between every crack in the paving, brick and cement mycelium, until it pressed up against the mighty, stoic cold shoulder of the Wall and could grow no more, like the stump of an ancient, divine tree, felled for timber. We traversed from the central depths toward the outer crust in a curved, swirling path, like water reversing out of a drain. Usually, it was a simple matter to navigate the layers as, to the eye of a local (or close enough), the difference from one division to the next was evident, jarring. One could almost hear the address number ticking over in the cogs of the Machine. Dipping through a tight alleyway, the streets changed. Stout cottage-shaped wedges with tilted overhangs and tiled roofs were stamped out by a row of multi-storied towers, the view of the sky blocked by straight-edged faces with thick glass corneas bathing you in shade. Then you could cut between two of the stark, overreaching goliaths, body angled sideways, one arm out in front to slice like a hot knife's teeth through butter, and they would collapse, daylight raw and overzealous against the skin. Before you would be a low, shapeless cowpat of a warehouse, no appendages, just four walls and a flat top, and the rhythmic thwap of fluid beating in the near distance. The stone changed colour. Move quickly enough, and the city appeared iridescent, like wading through an oil slick. Red clay hardened to granite, crumbled to sand, compressed to iron. In the direction Michael took, however, weaving along the seams as if riding the thread of a screw, we slipped from one ring to another. The conveyance between colours was subtle as a winter sunset, disorienting. I felt as though I were travelling along a forbidden fourth axis, and the realisation crept up my back that perhaps I ought to fear for my safety. I kept Michael's face lodged in the corner of my vision. He seemed to be aware, as he intermittently rolled a deep huffing gust through his whole body, like a dog shaking out its fur.

His last few steps were rushed, nervous. He stopped in the middle of a quaint string of small brownish cuboids, with large foreheads, big gaping mouths raised away from the kerb, bulky cast gutters and chimney pipes protruding from the front. We stood under the metal frame of a sunshade, though the striped pattern of the sail only barely remained, stretched with rainfall and sagging in the centre. Michael glanced over the top of my head, before leaning into the door, which was about the right height for me, too short for him. It rattled and wheezed, as though he were some sort of monstrous beast, and it pleading for the little meat left on its bones.

He reached around me, to push the door back into its ramshackle frame, twisting the round knob clockwise in his hand. He seemed to listen for the snap of the latch slotting into place, giving the whole thing a gentle shake, before finally declaring, "Here we are."

"Permission to ask where 'here' is?"

"This is—" He frowned, tongue clicking against the back of his teeth. The tips of his ears turned a freckled pink. He had a habit of holding his breath when concentrating. "I'm trying to think of a more professional word than 'secret hideout'. You ever been inside?"

"I'm not ashamed to admit, no, I have not."

"Well, best get used to it."

"Elaborate a bit for me, Michael. Are you giving me the boot?"

"*No*, I'm not throwing you out anywhere. In fact, even if I was—which I am not—I don't think the Machine would stand for you pitching a tent in this place. It can't see us in here."

I rattled a low chuckle out of my throat with a light shake of my head. The joke was just preposterous enough that I did not resent the additional legwork it had taken to reach the punchline.

"I'm serious," he said.

I peered up at him. He was watching my reaction out of the corner of his eye, not a twitch of amusement on his lips, not even a conciliatory softening of his brow.

"Oh, you are."

He nodded. "Smith told me about it. James, that is. It was our first and last little secret. So, you see why I couldn't explain on the way."

"Well, it won't make much difference to him." I shrugged. Speaking was not going so well for me today. I was not wrong, though. The man could not possibly get any more dead.

"No, I suppose not. But it might make the difference for us. I have to be a bit protective of it."

"When was this?"

"A while ago. Feels like I've aged about half a century since. I was still a kid, if you can believe such a thing existed in the world. I only remembered on the day of…well, the day they died. Let's call it what it is. He'd talked to me about this café… Actually, I tell a lie. He didn't say much about the place at all, only that I could find it here, on the Ninth Boulevard. He said, 'If I never again get the chance to breakfast there, you should go, at least.' It's hard to express it, but the tone of his voice… I never thought much more of it until…"

"Until his prophecy came true."

"So I came here, and what I found…"

He stepped further inside, slipping behind the counter like he owned the establishment. It had to have been ancient, carved panels and little wooden compartments lining the inside. He coaxed open one small, brass-handled drawer, and reached toward the back to pull out a beige slip of paper, soft at the edges, folded into quarters.

"…was this. I mean, say what you will about the state of the place, but I knew, soon as I stepped through the door, something was up. This is where he was telling me to go."

He reached over the counter, and I offered up my cupped hand to take the piece of paper. It felt, like a sun-dried wing of dragonfly, that it might flake to pieces under my rough fingertips. A cross had been carved deep into the fibres by repeated presses. I pushed into the centre to encourage the leaf open. He wrote in blue ink, with small, stiff, calculated letters, round, dark blots swallowing up the tails of some, suggesting a long pause to contemplate the next word. I realised, then, that I could not remember the shape of his handwriting. But I did recognise his voice.

*The walls are thin, yes, but the eyes are blind anyway. Want proof? Good lad. You're following me, which means I am most likely dead.* (Here he had sketched a small frowning face.) *The Machine wants us to die. Read that again. It is in my head. Read it. Think. Stop here.*

"Why, I'd say that there is practically seditious."

"Aye, and yet."

He flicked the card in front of me like a paper fan, and the liquid sound confirmed that it was moving through space. It did, indeed, exist. I had seen slips of notepaper like that, physical evidence, spontaneously spark and burst into flame, falling to the pavement in little smouldering flakes. Water damage was another popular method. All the excess moisture in the air, every puddle of rainwater on the ground would collect in the brickwork like the bottom of a basin, seeping out, lifting away words graffitied on a secluded wall, in ink, or paint, or bodily fluids.

"Do you understand what that means?" he said.

I couldn't be sure yet. My brain felt as though it was beginning to crumble away from me like an old head of cauliflower. "And you believe it?" I said.

He nodded eagerly, his gaze darting around the ceiling. "The eyes are blind. It can't see inside here."

"Have you tested it?" I whispered, as though we were not already doomed, should he have been wrong. "There's always the chance that's some sort of fluke, a one-off. How well did anyone really know Smith?"

"Course I've tested it. I may be trusting of *you*, but I'm not that gullible. Experimenting with the Red Café has been my hobby for the last several months, on and off. It reminded me of climbing into a scalding hot bath. First, you dangle one toe in the water, then slowly the rest of your foot, and so forth. Like any good relationship I suppose, it took plenty of time."

"The Red Café, that's what you call it now?"

"Well, I felt we ought to be on a nickname basis by this point."

It sounded illicit, a tad saucy. As name's went, it might have been perfect.

"Fine, you can spare me the sordid details. I should believe you. It's hardly the most farfetched thing I've come across in this world. Even so, I'm not sure if this is exactly what I would have envisioned the Machine's blind spot to look like, had I known one to exist. Perhaps something a bit more ornate, you know, formal. I mean, for all of your time together, you didn't even think to, I don't know, touch up the gloss on the skirting, sort out that patch of mould over in the corner?" I gestured towards it with my flattened hand, as though pushing the blackened bulge in the wallpaper away from myself, as though erasing it with the circular motion of my palm, as though I were somehow *above it*.

"I must confess, the aesthetic of the place was not up there on my list of priorities, no."

"I suppose I might be able to do something about the smell, at least…"

"There is another one, I should tell you, that might be more your speed."

"Another what?"

"A gap. A void. Whatever you choose to call it. That one is rather more—how to say it?—predictable, so much in fact that I'd have never dared to test it, not without Gabriel's clue."

"Go on, then. Surprise me. I'm in a credulous mood today."

"Moore's Hall."

"Don't be absurd!"

"I can't promise you that, but I would never lie to you. Ah, but if we are to nit-pick, I should be more specific. I don't mean the entirety of the Hall, only the main chamber. The back is a no-go."

"How's that?"

"I don't know. I haven't gathered to gumption to do any tests. I only know what I've been told. Something to do with being in view of that fresco, as far as we can determine."

"Or, more likely, something to do with the thick leaden door sitting behind it, perfectly in the fashion of the old man, no? Remove that, and it wouldn't matter whether the Machine is locked out of the whole building. He wouldn't need her faculties; he could just listen with his ears."

"Perhaps you're right. Funny, isn't it? How you can wrack your brain over these things, a riddle, crossword, equation, whatever, only to have another person come along with a better solution than anything you've puzzled out, with a glance of common sense. Good thing it all happens so quickly, else you'd have time to be annoyed."

"You give me far too much credit in your roundabout way, Michael. After all, I've got no proof for you. I couldn't even hazard a guess as to what the advantage of such an odd setup might be. And how does this room work? I don't see any fortification whatsoever. Quite the contrary, despite the smears of mildew, that remains a sizeable pane of *glass* behind us."

I hesitated for a moment, pondering over whether to inform him of the ripple of a satin dress I seemed to see pass through the green mire, a flash of seared-straight fair hair I imagined whipping against the window like a phantom scream.

"There has to be a pattern linking the two," he said instead, "some rhyme or reason, surely. One spot for each Smith, perhaps?"

"Not necessarily. It's not as though we can be certain that there are only a pair. Can you honestly say you've seen every corner of this whole fine institution, let alone scoured it for evidence?"

"I haven't, and I doubt anyone ever will. That sort of information perished along with James. I fear the Machine would do everything in its power to keep it that way, even to us. No, we shall work with what we have, avoid the Machine's suspicion for as long as possible."

"But you said there was nothing sinister going on with this place. On the contrary, this all sounds borderline treasonous."

"Yes, it is. I lied."

"My, how becoming an Angel has changed you."

His face scrunched up on one side. "Maybe. I didn't mean to. It was more of a…kneejerk, I guess. We all have our new tricks, and probably not for the better. That said, I figured we could make this place useful. If we agree upon an hour to meet, perhaps every other day, some sort of sufficiently banal routine, then we can use it as a space to discuss freely. Our plans."

Ah, of course. Amongst all of the fuss about brain probes and fancy dress, I had almost lost the fact that I was not in fact here simply to offer myself like a goat on the altar. I was brought here to tear down the Wall, and to tear up the only way of life it cradled under its arms. A goat I remained, but one with poison in my shoes and fire licking around my horns, waiting for the right moment. And, so said Michael, he had plans for me. Michael was not a bad man; I did not believe he ever could be, even if he tried his damnedest. He had conjured a terrific, awful plan out of care, and out of deep sadness. I was, admittedly, a little curious if he assumed the same to be true of me, whether or not he realised that, in truth, I followed out of a wickedness that just so happened to align with his noble desires.

**[Michael]**

Lucifer was surprisingly protective of the white dust bag she brought back from the clothes shop. She departed to collect it so pleased with herself she purred her way out of the door. She returned less audaciously self-satisfied, perhaps a little less pleased, but with the mysterious bundle of fabric draped over both of her arms, seeming to enjoy the manner in which it moved with her body, sagging heavy and pendulous around her legs.

She sat on the edge of the sofa for a short while, the bag laid across her knees, one hand atop it, pondering its contents. The sharp pinprick in her gaze faded, retreating behind her eyelashes, falling like a feather on the thin border between the window and the floor. She meditated over it, as I felt one might over a small child, or the newly deceased. Then, almost with an audible snap, her focus shifted. She rose from the chair, retreating into the bathroom with the pale, whispering sway of a mischievous phantom, leaving me alone and out-of-place in a dark dress suit with shining shoulder pads that made me appear wide and top-heavy, and matched the cold colour of the wings that permanently ornamented my ears.

She left me to struggle with a set of chain cufflinks shaped like tiny laurels, unable to make them fasten until I realised these were not the silver cufflinks at all, but instead clamps intended to dangle from my ears. As I clutched my head, trying to recall when and how exactly these had last been put on me, the door handle thumped downward rather aggressively, and something wooden clattered onto the floor.

"Ta-da!" Lucifer hummed, emerging unceremoniously, shoes dangling unfastened from her feet, and closing the door behind her.

With one hand, she rummaged inside the pockets of a trim, black jumpsuit (I was quite impressed I could recall the right word), and pointed the other towards me, demanding quiet. I noticed she began crowding the same collection of silver rings onto her fingers as usual, and wondered if she had removed them at all since leaving the cunning folk.

"Don't ask me whose funeral I'm off to. The answer is your social life."

"That can't be true," I said. "I've never had one. Is it a rare breed of gerbil?"

"The Machine wanted me in this gorgeous little red outfit, with a flowy bottom and lace gubbins all around the skirt. I said I would not go if I had to wear a dress, and told the seamstress there, with that single stipulation, she could set me up with whatever she wanted."

"And that worked?"

"Did you ever see me in one of those things? I looked like a turkey waddling about." She pinned her arms to her sides and marched stiff-legged on the spot, looking more like a nutcracker than a turkey. "The young lady—Freya, her name is—I thought she looked pleased to work on the red piece, but when I refused it, well, let's say I've inadvertently done a good deed today. Cost me less credit out of my budget, too. I'm going to fork out on some of those pastries for us, from the bakery in the centre."

"Don't worry about me. You should hang onto the extra; your allowance will be down after you went AWOL for a whole shift."

"Oh, boo! I'll figure something out. It's my treat, for our first *business meeting*."

The Machine could probably detect the sarcasm—she practically gushed with it—but all of the lines of binary in the walls were not equipped to decrypt a word of it. I could have protested again, tried to wear her down on the matter of money. But I didn't, for several reasons. It was a pointless battle to partake in, not only because I would lose to her laughing, immovable stubbornness, but because to argue at all seemed an insult to her sentiment, however small and enigmatic it may have been. There was something else, too, something in her expression, in her eyes —a spark, or a flicker, fleeting and precious—still dark, but shining, like velvet.

"It suits you."

"Didn't she do well?" she replied, voice muffled by the hairpin pinched in her mouth. "See how stretchy this fabric is? She even got my colour."

Hair gathered into a rough bunch behind her ears, she twisted it upward, pulled the pin from between her teeth and shoved it into place. And, it was true, she radiated a warm, handsome energy, not so much a virtue of the fine clothes she wore with relative irreverence, but rather of that precise, earnest lack of care. She had requested these clothes to *wear*, not to be wrapped and stuffed into like a young noble being tied into a corset several sizes too small.

"Man, I've missed you."

"Well, I can't exactly declare I would have come back to this place of my own volition, not any time soon." She crept forward, quickly fiddled with the conch of my right ear, now tired, frustrated, and sore, before sitting on the floor to fasten her shoes. "But it's certainly not all bad. Come on, get your tie sorted. We can't hole ourselves up here playing dress-up all night." She patted me on the shin, using the back of the chair to manoeuvre less than elegantly onto her heels.

Eve always held her parties on the bottom floor of the old military building. Correction: we were supposed to call it the administrative centre nowadays. It boasted the largest empty surface area in Interieur, the bare wooden floor and stone walls warmed up a little by orange-tinged lightbulbs and silken drapery. I assumed the room was permanently on reserve for her, since the trappings never seemed to disappear. To mark the occasion, two large bunches of balloons, loose voile curtains and a trail of pastel flower petals burst out of the gaping front entrance onto the terrace, swaying luxuriously in the evening air.

"Good lord…" Lucifer muttered, scratching her forehead, then snickered. "Hah, very droll."

She had walked the entire route here in no particular hurry, eyes mostly directed downward, her footwear evidently not designed for the cobbled paths. I did not mind the leisurely pace. Only at that moment, faced with the gilded stairway, did she reach out, her fingers wrapping around my bare wrist. A chill seemed to run through her skin.

"Do you mind?" she said.

"Not at all." I untucked my hand from its pocket, threaded our arms together, feeling rather regal as I did so.

"Figured since you're here, I might as well make the most of you."

Her Soul only brushed lightly against my own, but it did not feel as I had expected, like what I had experienced with others. Clumps of sand filtered into my blood vessels, slightly rough and extremely discomforting, fingernails scraping against the inner walls, though it quickly dissipated, my body rinsed clean. On top of the brassy percussion spitting out of the ballroom, Eve—or one of her minions, at least—had opted to hang glass windchimes in the doorway. I had hardly noticed them before, but suddenly all other sound drowned under the irksome, constant tinkling.

"You're worried?" I asked.

"Honey, I'm always worried. Although, if you can already tell, that's not a brilliant sign." She grimaced.

"Then, my liege, might I suggest we get this poxy sham over with?"

Her frown twisted into a bemused smirk, and she pranced up the steps on her toes, two at a time, towing me along.

The transition from a dank corridor to the building's glowing, pulsating heart prickled a little, rather like a match lit inches from the eye: hot, bright, with a thick aroma. Simply counting the sheer number of humans packed into the room, we should have met a light barrage of shoulders, hair in the face and mumbled apologies. Strange, then, how disorienting it could be, to stride elegantly into a neat, semi-circular stage already carved into the pool of bodies. Conspicuous. The band were not even close to a chorus, but ramped up their volume nevertheless, seemingly to be heard over the hive of voices, threatening to smother them with their newly discovered vigour. Perhaps I should have been flattered. I knew I should have been adulated, in fact. And yet I found the whole ordeal peculiar, at best.

"Three thousand, three hundred and sixty-two…" Lucifer said. "Seems high."

She wasn't talking about the guest list. She was looking at a number. And she was right. That number was bloody high. There were only a handful of individuals close by to whom it could conceivably belong, and it definitely was not mine. I knew, because a row of four digits had flashed from below, barely noticeable amongst the brass and baubles and brief bounces of light from the tremoring chandelier. Written sideways down my arm, lit in stark white so as to bore into my suit for maximum readability, was the number three thousand three hundred and ninety-one. My eyes flicked over it like a wristwatch. Perhaps waiting to be acknowledged, the final figure chose that very moment to tick over, growing limbs, up from one to two. I snuck a glance at Lucifer, barely tilting my head. There it was, plastered across her collarbone: three, two, six, two. The lines bent somewhat, distorted against the slope of her chest, and the muscles in her shoulders quivered, as if the symbols' pointed extremities were sharp as blades, claws burrowing into skin.

"Why do I feel like my smalls are being hung out on the line for all my neighbours to see? I never used to feel that way. Don't get me wrong, I've got some nice lacey pairs, embroidered. Nothing wrong with my taste in bras, but that's my business."

I squeezed her arm closer to my side, nestled her elbow against my ribs.

"I suppose I thought we all would have grown out of this whole business of watching, once the old man picked his Angels and got it over and done with."

She puffed a quick, heavy sigh out of her nose. Then she fell still, her gaze flat and unfeeling, as though her consciousness had grown so angry it had simply vacated her brain and floated up to join the pigeons gathered up in the window crevices. She did not so much as turn her face to meet the countless pairs of retinas which stared back at her. Numbers began to appear in the dark creases formed by the crowd, typing themselves out across foreheads, down skirts and trouser legs, and even more overhead. The erratic lighting seemed to flip a switch in Lucifer, and she returned with a slight ruffle of her hair.

"Serves me for expecting any different."

"There's no getting over it," I said, hardly able to retrain the bitter smirk rising from my gut. I had not failed to notice the cool, foamy wave of relief wash down my spine as I skimmed over the totals, mostly settled in the mid-to-high-two-thousands, as if seeing them medicated me, made me safe. "In hindsight, I can't say what the constant comparing did for any of us, but there's no stopping it. Sometimes I wonder if the Angel debacle wasn't just some hysterical excuse we all collectively invented in our sleep."

**[Gabriel]**

Lucifer lasted all of five minutes, dangling with Michael at the perimeter of the room, like plastic bags caught on a riverbank, before skating across to the refreshments table. It was one of three long, antique benches full of deep scratches carved into a grooved, porous surface which seemed to soak up smells, the only one not flipped over and pushed against the wall. At present, only a few guests scattered themselves along the seats, perched on the outside edges, dresses folded over their knees, to pick at the platters of rectangular cakes in impossible colours and intricately adorned vol-au-vents. Given a couple of hours, there would be two crowded rows, as many bundles of lace, satin and netting as could stuff into seats to rest aching legs and sore soles. My current proximity, stood off to the side—just close enough to catch the scent from the cauldron of alcohol—offered the best vantage-point, as well as a good chance of nabbing an empty spot on the end of a bench, when the time came.

I lost visual contact with Lucifer as she dived into the melee, hands steepled in front of her as though her filed fingernails could carve through the crowd like a tender joint of meat. Although I could not see her shape, her movements sent sporadic, translucent ripples into the atmosphere above the sea of heads that vibrated against the touch of my Soul. My eyes waited for her to emerge on the other shore, where she headed unhesitatingly for the nearest beverages, picked up a glass of viscous syrup and immediately threw the entirety down her throat. Her lips smacked against her teeth, shrunken slightly from the taste, but she replaced the empty glass in her hand with a second, without asking, and took a sip from it, unembarrassed.

The approach of Eve did not go unnoticed, either by me or Lucifer, whose pupils slid askance above the goblet balanced under her nose. Our hostess weaved between her favourite ladies, the emerald sequins of her dress hissing against the floorboards like reptilian scales. Rei had returned from her conversation with the bulletin-writer, the beanpole of a man in patterned suspenders and half-moon spectacles. She was a flurry of yellowish-gold and dark hair, straightening her butterfly headpiece and opening her mouth to speak, before I laid a quiet hand on her elbow.

"Be back in a moment," I whispered.

I sidestepped along the length of the table, only so much that I could focus my hearing on the exchange about to unfold, tilting up my chin such that, hopefully, I appeared to be looking for someone, if rather half-heartedly. Eve's face had a pointed shape to it, meaning it slotted neatly into the angle between Lucifer's bare shoulder and her ear.

"Might I suggest you watch your intake, madam Angel, lest you get cut off? For some reason, I remember you being a bit of a lightweight. It seems you've made quite the lifestyle change. Unless, of course, you are the same as ever, and stooping to drunkenness already."

"Well, you did whisk me here with the promise of a good time. I do hope you weren't lying about that, at least."

"You know what I always said, sweetie: it's never good to be nosey. I have my duties, and in this case, everyone has come in their best dress, expecting an evening romp made bespoke by Eve Stanton."

"Everyone, except for the main attraction, you mean."

"Freya told me you refused the design she originally had planned for you. She was very upset about the whole thing, but I reminded her that it was a noble desire, to look less than your best, making yourself a more attainable image to your subordinates."

"You mentioned that it is your purpose to ensure your guests enjoy themselves tonight."

"Naturally. It is only right that we all associate your return to us with positive feelings. That you have survived this long is a miracle, which we must commemorate as such. And who could do a better job than me?"

"I should be flattered. Still, I hope it was my active imagination, but I couldn't help noticing a few unmistakably miserable faces as I made my grand entrance."

"Yes, you always did have the most vivid fantasies. Ah, you might be referring to Michael over there, I see. Nosey. You needn't worry. Michael comes to all of my parties. He still loves me a little, and I surmise he is sour, seeing that I have moved on with far more grace than he could manage. You know what men are like. The boyish pout will fade after an hour or so. Here, some punch will surely speed up the process."

"I understand." Lucifer took the second glass of glittering magenta syrup into the cup of her hand and gave a shallow curtsy, balancing both like a mockery of Justice's scales.

Rei must have heard a sigh leave my nostrils as I settled back beside her. "You get anything?" she inquired.

"Not really. I wouldn't want to be alone in a room with them for long, that's for sure. Lucifer's on the drink already, and Eve keeps doing that thing where she flexes her knuckles to show off the bones. They're both fishing; for what, I don't think even they know."

"Isn't that exactly what we're doing? Fishing?"

"Well…of a sort. But ours is the good kind, the conscientious kind. What's old specs on about?"

"Oh, Phineas? I wasn't paying much attention, if I'm honest. Then Uriel popped in to flirt with the Bovary twins behind us, and that put me totally off."

"Still got the jitters?"

"Haven't been able to shift the feeling all afternoon. I was hoping you might gather some idea of what's happening."

"True, I can't tell what's going on, but damn if I don't know *who*."

"Think Uri is in on the game, too?"

"I'm not sure. Maybe, wouldn't surprise me if Eve's got him floating around on some errand."

"I realise…I don't know her as well as you did, but I hope she's not in terrible danger. I wish I could get rid of this fog, at least."

"You and me both."

I had never lied to her before all of this; I thought it outside of my capability. And yet. It festered like an ulcer inside my stomach, the acidic sting only eased by a conviction that I was keeping her safer. I held in my head the key to a titanium safe, the power to clear the mists for her, to make her understand. She might well have seen through my ruse already, known as we spoke that I had pushed her into a dark room and was trying to lock the door behind me. Still, the fact remained, if she discovered the truth, she would want to intervene in some way. I felt little shame in admitting I would see Lucifer thrust into the inferno she carried on her back, before I would allow Rei to be threatened with the same. The Angel's Soul was different; she could kill and maim to save her own life. Rei would fight it, though; she'd sneak and stare and listen for hours to the whispers of the Source. I only hoped I could hold her back for long enough.

[Lucifer]

Michael had been facing in the wrong direction, when I wrestled free from the amalgam of writhing, grasping arms, with a couple of knocks to the torso for my trouble. The bubble of free, empty space had shrunk since I left, and had a distinct, chemical perfume, as cosmetics began to leak into the air, carried on a film of sweat. He was resting his back against a wall and, whether or not he was aware, gradually sliding toward the floor, pulling a coil of ribbon attached to balloons down with him. He straightened up as soon as I managed to catch his gaze.

"There you are" he said. "It's been a while."

"Did you think I'd found some secret exit and done a runner back West?"

"I *was* beginning to fear I'd lost you."

He did smile, a little, but I wished he would not smile like that, like a wince pulled up at the corners. Like he was trying to comfort me, even as every false move I made punched a hole in his chest.

"Care for some punch?" I offered the stout glass to him, taking a cool, sugar-laden gulp for myself. "It's peach-flavoured."

"Peach? That's my favourite. You'd better have it." Rather than pass it back, he leaned over and emptied the contents of his flute into my almost empty one with a clumsy slosh, apparently oblivious to the inappropriateness of the gesture. He wanted something to do with his hands.

"Don't look at Eve so much. As it is, we're still a step ahead of her."

"What do you mean?" he queried.

"Right now, she thinks I came back to this place expecting some sort of fanfare. She believes I still desperately want to feel liked by this lot. You knew, didn't you, that she set up this whole charade to humiliate me? That's why you were so nervous about the invitation."

"I just…I know I won't let anything *happen* to you, but Eve's wily; she finds cracks to slip through." A hesitant pause, while he shifted his weight against the wall. The flush drained from his face again, just as it had leaked onto his kitchen counter, the moles on his skin bold like spatters of ink on paper. "Did she say anything about me?"

"She tried a few angles, I won't lie. She's throwing shit at the wall, finding out what sticks."

"You must seem like a different person entirely, to her. I don't want to suggest you're lucky or anything, but—"

"I know. I am. How long since you split from her?"

"It's funny. You and Gabriel both made a break for it on the same day."

"Promotion day."

"I took a bit longer, to gather up the means, I guess. It must have been a couple of months."

"I left you behind. I mean, I left everyone, but I knew. I knew, and I left you."

"You did what you had to do. And then you came back. What's the alternative, that the moment passed, and you never got out? It doesn't bear consideration, not to me. This is the reality we live in: the one where you came back. It's no wonder Eve doesn't understand why you did it; I don't really get it myself."

A round, polished speaker hanging from the ceiling vibrated my bare toes. The music was too loud; it rattled in my head, and had only grown louder since our arrival, as if slowly amplified to mask the lack of chatter among the crowd. The guests moved with gentle sways of tulle and glossy satin, pastels, fierce reds and deep navy, sticking to circular colonies like bacteria in a dish. Once my brain had accustomed itself to the constant back-and-forth motion, it became easy to spot the solo Gabriel, snaking through gaps between the camps, cutting a path to our side of the room. He landed only a short distance away and brushed along the wall until he could drop a hand onto my shoulder.

"I'm surprised she let you get away," he murmured. "Are you aware you're to make a speech on the turn of the hour?"

"A speech?" I sputtered. "Hah! To an enthusiastic audience, I'm sure."

"I'm not sure if I'm supposed to tell you or not. I thought I was being awfully sneaky, eavesdropping, but who can be sure, if we're honest?"

"Quite the opportunity…I ought to have prepared notes. I need another drink, or three. Michael—" I tugged at his sleeve, cool metal of his cufflink burrowing into my thumb. "I'm going to walk with Gabriel back to Rei's side. Watch. It's quite funny, really, how this lot act when they realise that I'm right behind them."

Michael nodded, quiet. He obeyed my request staunchly, gleaming spots floating in his pupils, as they skimmed over the dancefloor.

"I won't be long this time."

Gabriel let out an odd noise, from deep in his lungs, observing over the top of my head while I reached out for a refill.

"You're really downing another glass of that stuff?" he said. "There's hardly any alcohol in it, you know, just fruit pulp and spices. Makes it easier for the Machine to keep you walking in a straight line."

"Exactly. What choice do I have? I feel like a pincushion in a nice suit. If I can get thrown out with hyperglycaemia, that'd be ideal." I threw another dose into my mouth and gargled it down. "Bloody hell, that's gross."

"Is that how it works?"

"What?"

"Hyperglycaemia."

"For my purposes, sure it is. The air in this place is rotten. They don't seem to mind you so much; can you make anything out from the rumblings?"

"Only that they're waiting for you to pull out the weapon we all know you have."

"You *all* know? Who's been talking?" I could hear my own paranoia spewing forth on my breath.

"It must have been Eve, I guess. As far as everyone here is concerned, your Soul damn nearly killed her. That's how you managed to break out." My Soul—that was what he meant by a weapon.

"Nearly, as in past tense? She doesn't know that I'm finished trying yet."

"And then she'll have a hundred points added to her number, while we all have to hold her up for her bravery. You should go back to Michael. If you can stand still in one spot for more than five minutes, that might help."

"I'm fine." I dropped the glass back onto the counter, only a few lumps of pale orange flesh left at the bottom. I realised, hooking my fingers around the silky fabric, that I had worn a hole inside of my pocket. I whipped out my hand, and discretely fanned away the clump of black dust that floated out with it.

Rei then appeared at the edge of my view, leaning against Gabriel, her gaze glued to her right wrist, and the mismatched brown leather watch she kept strapped to it. My ears perked at her next three words, spoken barely loud enough for me to hear.

"Raphael's in next."

An astute observation I had yet to make; it was true, Raphael was the only the only major player—that I knew of, at least—still absent from Eve's shimmering, saccharine stage. I could not guess how he factored into the grand plan Rei was narrating as it unfolded. I watched the open doorway as the last Angel glided into the fray complete with grey suit and burgundy tie loose around his neck and continued watching even when Gabriel prodded me in the back.

"Go, now," he said, firmly, coaxing me, I could only assume, back to the opposite side of the room. Unenlightened as to what for, only that Michael would be there, I waded through the undulating, swooning breeze swelling towards Raphael like floodwater. Amongst the swirling feathers of spring blossom, wine and tar, one could easily pick out the jade silhouette of Eve, bounding like a deer across the void separating her and the lone, stationary man. He held out one arm, ready to receive her, and she wove herself around it, perched on her toes to bury her nose in his collar. I lost sight of their faces, except for their teeth, beaming in the fluorescent lights. I almost ground to a halt, but for the innocuous tinkling sound of glass shards on the floor. I shoved my way past a fidgety little man in turquoise to see, in the same spot by the speaker, Michael, looking down into his hands. He had been clutching the delicate bauble in his fingers, and squeezed it so hard that a section around the rim had shattered. Some pieces lay on the ground, confetti at his feet, while others had landed in the dregs at the bottom of the glass. He blinked, incredulous, childlike, as if surprised by the sudden noise, before pressed one thumb between his lips. A red trail slid from the hand still cradling the glass, down the smooth surface and dropping onto his shoe. I crouched down to pick up one of the larger shards. Cracks developed on the small, cloudy dagger, tiny hairlines where my fingertips pinched, then the piece disintegrated, a mere pile of crystalline snow in my palm. I could have thrown it down my throat, like breadcrumbs, and it would surely kill me, drown me in a tincture of my own blood and saliva.

The crowd did not turn for the slice in Michael's hand, however. They turned for the hypnotic arc of Eve's arm, seemed to stretch, elastic, reaching for my neck across the gaping room. She gave a little wave.

"Now that all of our figureheads have finally joined us," she tittered, "I say it is fine time for a small word from our most esteemed guest! A speech, Lucifer, a speech!"

A round, clumsy insect landed in my hair. I smacked both hands on the crown of my head, sending it humming away, and I giggled. "Who, me? Goodness gracious, what can I say? Everyone, I have to be going now—much to your relief, I know. You all enjoy your evening of loud music and fruit smoothies, and wake up with icing from the cake still sticking to your cheeks. It looks delightful, very pink. Look, it's alright. You can't offend the demon-lady. And the Machine won't give a damn. Now, I truly must be off, before your worst nightmares come true, and you all end up as little mucky piles of ash and peach punch all over the vintage floorboards. Alright? Ta-rah!"

I knew I had shoved a few dopey, unsuspecting guests out of my way; I felt the blunt clash against my shoulder, even if I could not make out their faces. To expend the effort to acknowledge, even to recognise beyond the brief sensation of bruising, could prove fatal, spreading the already limited power of my conscious mind like warm, soft butter. Glittering golden spangles, emeralds and cotton candy turned to grey catacombs then to the heavy, sulphuric haze of dusk, all in a rapid, kaleidoscopic tunnel of light and shade, blurring as it rolled upon its axis. I kept my hands clenched at my sides, holding back the explosion, restraining the mounting piles of fire and gas underneath the straining tips of my fingernails. The room smelled of salt but tasted sweet as treacle on my tongue.

I made it as far as the front terrace, down the shallow steps, one drop of the foot at a time. However, once my ears caught the verdant rustle of her gown, the clicking of her pointed heels approaching from behind, my Soul ploughed through the fibrous wall of muscle like a field of reeds, peeled back the rubbery, tough layer of skin, opened up an artery.

The smoke whirled around my body—flowing through the same space, around and around, rather than dispersing—as though I were a goldfish in a mason jar, and it the water trapped inside with me. The ground tilted under my toes, as the polluted air drilled down and outward, a giant bead of acid rain. Leaving only a solid platform wide enough to stand on, the Soul had, in its tantrum, carved a deep bog, turned solid rock to quicksand and modelling clay. The pit stretched not only between Eve and I, but orbited me on all sides, my one piece of solid pavement acting as a raft, the saving grace keeping my bare feet afloat. The mud was hungry, gulping down the last remnants of opaque blackness, and leaving Eve free to look down upon me with all the disgust left in her.

"Don't you ever come to me whinging that I ruined your welcome party," she sputtered.

"Oh no, I wouldn't dream of it. Rather, I like to think that I spoiled *your* day, just this once. Not quite as I imagined it, certainly, but I'll take what gratification I can get."

"I don't know what you're talking about. What am I to be punished for, chaining you up in a basement and publicly flogging you? This is your own fault. Now you understand. You are no prodigal daughter of the Sovereign. We live under a steadfast rule of meritocracy here, Angel. We are each in our rightful place. I have earned mine. You have finally taken that which you earned. There is no conspiracy here, no secret campaign to hurt your feelings."

My first instinct was to tuck my head down, swallow all the fluid in my mouth, maybe weep a little. I allowed that urge to tick over along with the stabbing in my bladder. My next trick would have been to screech, still gulping down tears, that there's no such thing as fucking 'meritocracy', that there are no bootstraps under us, that if we had all been truly put in our place, then it was not in the way she believed. I would have told her to use the big, wrinkly, squelching brain I knew she once possessed—and then I blinked, and recalled who it was I would be throwing my body under a tram for, how far a girl could regress in only half a breath. I preferred not to make her job any easier. Getting quiet and trembly and leaky equated to a summoning. The frilly-edged sand-dune voice, the patting of my back and thumbing at my cheeks, soft, assuaging chill behind the ears. The holding pattern. Perish the thought—I preferred her angry. Her anger was boiling and belching, and it melted her waxen crust. It was far more productive, more lucid, but also, for my sake, apprehensible. Her anger was legible to me. Or perhaps I simply relished the opportunity to be difficult. I liked the buzz it gave me, to imagine the little pip of frustration shimmying down into her stomach and digesting, fizzing and popping in her guts, all while a slothful and hideous Galatea stared dead-eyed past her face.

"You like to have things, don't you? People," I said. To have and to hold. "You like to hold them in your hands and squeeze them until they break, don't you?"

I came to a peculiar realisation, as I watched her on the other side of the hollow cavern. A certain fact, which washed over my head, seeped into the cracks, like a shallow wave grinning white, finally breaking over a flint nestled in the sand, both carried in by the tide. Eve was, simply put, a rather ugly human being. As far as the eyes could see, she was a pretty young woman, beautiful even. Angelic. Her long, fair hair, rather than the veil of ironed satin over her shoulders I knew, was arranged all in braids, encircling the crown of her head, save for two downward spirals, just barely touching her narrow cheeks. She might have been the closest to perfection as was possible to attain. The Machine approved highly of her image.

Occasionally I would try, without much success, to picture the Machine—that unseen thing pressing at my back—as a small and breathing creature. It was necessary at times, to engage in this mental exercise, no matter how futile. If we were to allow our menaces to grow to unfathomable size, the size of an atmosphere, a deity, intangible, we—or rather, I—would end up annihilated. When I imagined the Machine, it had Eve's face. Albeit, it was significantly greater in stature, and all her skin split open into numerous ellipsoid eyes, blinking and fidgeting like the wings of a fly, but I recognised her. That was enough to stir a feeling in my chest, close to pity. I was being somewhat unfair.

Eve learned how to paint her face, such that every little scab on her cheek was invisible. She did so because the numbers taught her it was the correct thing to do. Who would not rather be worth fifteen than ten? It was not her perfection, or her heavy green dress that I now found abhorrent. These remained signs of her fallibility, her humanity. What repulsed me so was the way her thin lips curled as she spoke at me, the same as they had when she spun lies and spouted truths only when convenient, or at least sufficiently amusing. It was the brazen flash of teeth at those of us who were stupid enough to listen. The Machine's code did not, technically speaking, permit the harm of peers. And yet she found a way; there was always some way.

I wondered whether she smiled to hurt me, or merely at the idea of hurting me. When I pulled my face into a crude imitation of a smirk, I was a mirror, a frame, not to glass and silver, but air, blood, and a furious Soul. Alone as I was in the socket-shaped void, there was no escaping the knowledge that my smile was also an attack.

I need not use my voice. *"You have tried to destroy me. But still, you can't."* That is what Eve heard in my forced expression, evidently, since when I stepped forward for her, the ledge crumbling under the toes of my shoes, the lovely green fabric of her gown was scrunched in her left hand and disappearing into the Hall. It seemed she had intended to hold the same, taut glare, as if she was about to spit, until her figure had disappeared out of sight. However, her course was interrupted by another body moving slowly out of the doorway, whom she was made to dodge if she was to retain her dignity before her most honoured guests, still bubbling through the walls. Armed with her blinkers, Eve failed to register precisely who had blocked her path. The muscles around my mouth fell.

His head tipped a little to the side, as if trying to figure out whether the painting on a wall was hanging wonky. Facing me was the fifth Angel, the dragon, Raphael. His gaze flicked askance, watching Eve as she bustled past him, before turning back again. His chin remained perfectly horizontal, his shoulders still as he descended from the terrace, as though he did not need to breathe. He approached the edge of the crater, extending one hand across the gap toward my raft, upturned and curved like a cradle, the other hidden behind his back. For a moment, I could have been stepping out of a barouche into the arms of a butler. He then jerked his head back, a subtle, snappy order to jump. Compliant, I leaned my weight forward, dropped my hand onto his palm, and felt a pop in my shoulder as he hoisted me onto solid concrete. He did not speak at all. In the meantime, Michael had emerged outside, pale-faced and heavy-footed, limbs dangling numbly. He began to topple down the upmost steps when Raphael skipped into his vacillating path. The latter rummaged in his chest pocket, retrieving a mauve, floral-patterned handkerchief, the expensive weave of which shimmered over his fingers, as well as a paper serviette. Using his bent knee for a countertop, he folded the napkin into a smaller, dense wedge, and rolled up the silk into a long, narrow piece.

"For your hand," he barked, a nurse with strange, less than mechanical detachment from his patient.

Michael watched blankly with no objection, as the improvised gauze was pressed straight into the tender, fleshy heel of his hand, and the handkerchief wrapped around, tied in a rudimentary knot, to hold it in place.

"That should do for now. Can't have you getting blood all over the floors."

I cleared my throat. "You two should head back inside. I'll accompany Michael to the medical centre. I can't imagine the wound is severe enough that we will both have to retire for the evening, but in case."

Raphael hesitated, or at least his head did, reluctant to follow the movement of his body back up the steps. He retreated backwards into the dim building, Gabriel's glare flitting all over him, before he vanished behind the swell of a loose curtain. Gabriel had an unusual, delirious wrinkle over his face as he inspected the extent of the damage.

"I, uh, dropped my ladder."

"That's certainly one way to put it," he said. "You should get moving, before the pavement starts to swallow your shoes."

He was right. I picked up my feet, took a step back. Under the glow of the streetlights, I could discern a thin layer of particles rolling, almost floating, over the ground, like sand across a desert. It flowed from all around, each alleyway a tributary. If a light breath of wind caught the stream in a cross-current, it threw up a looping wave which glistened amber, like crystalline dust. It swarmed to the edge of the carved-out ring, which steadily rose higher until level with the untouched stone next to it. At the same time, a damp smell penetrated the air, the ground staining a darker shade as groundwater reversed its natural course, slithering up through minute pores. It mingled with the dirt, becoming a sort of cement, a perfect, liquid mimicry of the old cobbles. The city was repairing itself, filling the gouge made in its body, a reminder of the scab that would be soon to form on Michael's skin. Our animal flesh could not heal so pristinely, not without outside assistance. Gabriel was right. I turned around to tell him so, but he was gone. Instead, I placed a hand on the small of Michael's back and pushed him gently northward.

He cleared his throat with a stifled choke before speaking. "We have to do something, Lucifer, Lucille—whoever you are now. We have to be better than this."

# Part 3: Vacillation

**[Gabriel]**

Lucifer hummed with almost lascivious satisfaction, slouching back in her chair. She clutched a golden-crusted pie in both of her hands, nursing it, either unaware or uncaring of the dust and grime caked over her fingers and dragged across her face. Her palms were shrivelled and pale, as if the fleshy parts were dead, aged with all of the soap and water she had used in an attempt to domesticate the Red Café, a grumpy, huffing and puffing sort of baptism. A trail of flour and caster sugar led from her dark linen trousers back to a white bag with paper handles, conspicuously clean on the low wooden table between us.

"I haven't eaten one of these in years," she exclaimed, eyeballs rolling backward with delight.

"What, do they not have cooking apples out West?" I retorted, pretending to know anything at all about what did and did not grow on trees by the ocean. I imagined the trees there being stout and bulbous at the top, like lollipops, like Lucifer's pinkened cheeks full of fruit and crumbs as I looked at her.

"It's not that at all. I stopped long before I even thought about getting out."

"Why, then?"

"They're not good for me. Fattening. Eve had wanted to go for a swim. She had a suit made for me. Caught me with my midday

[102]

snack. I think it was disappointing for her. She'd been trying so diligently to persuade me onto those bluish-green coloured smoothies, and now she had to be seen with a girl who ate *pies*. It was a poor show for the both of us."

"What's wrong with *food*? That you taste it? That you have to chew it first?"

"I think that's what you said at the time, too, from the luxury of your freakishly active metabolism."

And unless my wires and hers had conveniently crossed, I believed I recalled the event she referred to, a vague, colourless recollection, drifting up like steam. I heard Eve's voice somewhere behind me. I could hear the curl in her lip, the fingernails grinding in her mouth, as she said, *"Really? Are you sure you want that?"* She had whisked Michael aside, to the corner of the room, to have a little talk about what on earth they were going to *do* with her. Perhaps that explained why he could remember too, but without remembering, an uncanny repetition. She liked to keep sneaking back in.

"And after that debacle, the smell, that buttery, syrupy sweetness, gods, it made me want to hurl. The next time I'd eat sweet anything was with the cunning folk. I was laid up in a bed for a while. Something to do with all the blood draining from my head, they kept finding me face-down on the floor in the middle of the room. One of the women tending to me, she offers me this berry pastry thing for breakfast, and I have the audacity to refuse. Oh, all of the saturated fat, I say, the refined sugar. I can't have it, blah, blah. And she stands over me, takes the little dish from my hands and puts it in my lap, and says, 'Maybe not, but it's what you need. So unless there's an allergy you haven't told me about, eat up, and don't let me find you with your nose between the floorboards again.'"

"Not entirely convinced of the science employed there, but if the grub was good…"

"It was incredible. It all came from a little patisserie on the same block as the apothecary shop. They made these square apple buns, called yum-yums. Not every day, but maybe a couple times each week. And there was a boy working there, about fifteen, very earnest. I think it was his first real job. The boss would send him jogging down the road just before I closed for lunch, to tell me they'd just taken a fresh batch of my favourite out of the oven, and I'd send him back to her with an order—one apple yum-yum. Sometimes I'd get there, and she'd hand over the greasy brown paper bag with one extra inside, saying they were selling two-for-one that day. I don't believe that's ever been true, but I've also learned better than to try debating with people like that."

"Did you end up on the floor again?"

"Oh, yes. But not from passing out, I'll grant her that."

"And it's just like one of those?"

"No, not quite. I've never been able to track down anything exactly the same. But then again, when was the last time you had your salad served with beefsteak?"

"And you've eaten how many, in your interval of decadence?"

"The first I asked to be completely cooked, all the way through. Huge mistake. I was invited to this establishment a couple town's over, for some occasion, an anniversary or such like. They're specialists. Academics of butchery, as it were. You are to eat the meat as close to raw as it can get, so it must be the finest, freshest cut. I've never been again since. Couldn't afford it myself. But I might prefer it like that. When I think back on it, my tongue feels as though it was sewn into the mouth of a king, just for a day."

"Doesn't sound like the prettiest plate to sit in front of, not to me anyway."

"It's not. Not at all. But I'll tell you, I didn't walk out of the door thinking of how impolite it looked."

It was then that Lucifer's whimsical fairy tale of a baker's boy with yum-yums shed its papery skin, emerging as if a moth, now an ode to the rich juices from a bloody hunk of raw cow's meat slowly dissolving between her molars. And it was then a band of shadow flickered across the wall above the counter. Our little storyteller stopped her mobile tongue, hands falling heavily into her crossed legs, shaped like a basin in which to dunk them once again and cleanse her skin of the fond reminiscence of both sweetness and gore. Outside, Raphael seemed to glow red behind the glass shield smeared with green and brown. He slammed into the door, a half-hearted attempt to startle us when he was already seen, though I did expect for a moment to find one half of the handle snapped off in his fist.

I was quick off the mark. "Watch out—here's our, what, colleague? Minder? The Light Beverage Police?"

"Man, unbelievable, you're so fucking clever. Keep your razor-sharp wits to yourselves why don't you? Listen, I don't give a rat's arse about you lot patting each other on the back in this old shithole. I'm just passing by to remind you who's watching. The wheels don't stop turning just because the runt decided to turn back up. The Sovereign didn't recruit this many of us just so we could all hold hands and have a nice knees-up over the weekend. Four of us is plenty to deal with an outlier…or three, or just the two. And you…" He swiped his hand over his chin, before flicking a finger in Lucifer's direction. "I'd suggest that you, especially, pull your foot out of your mouth before someone sticks theirs someplace else. Uriel doesn't trust you as far as he could throw you, and I'm not much inclined either. Put it this way: leave off with the whole hide-and-seek game. You were never very good at it."

Lucifer politely bent forward and placed her chipped mug on the low table, presumably to avoid it crumbling between her fingers. "I see now, Uriel put all those impressive words in your mouth, did he? I should have known from the start. At this rate, he'll have stuffed so much raw sewage down your throat, it'll be clogging up your ear canals too. Don't worry, honey, I'll make sure to be a good, obedient, quiet little foot soldier over here. Just so long as I can keep my coffee." She rubbed her palms together, the whispering sound reverberating around our corner of the room.

"Off you pop then, you've made your point," I added, too late to shield her, but I could at least make a small sortie of it.

"I meant for this to be a kindness." Turned out Raphael was not finished quite yet. "After all, I won't be the one ordering a termination."

He disappeared out of frame, voice muffled by many layers of concrete, like a customer finished browsing the window display.

Snatching a glance at Michael, standing over her shoulder, part of me still expected him to soften the atmosphere like a benevolent pincushion. Rather the opposite, he clamped his lips together, curving the creases downward, and opted instead to watch the doorway with what must have been contempt. This continued even after Raphael had retreated from behind the glass. It was a face I could recover, vaguely, only from childhood memories, one I assumed he had shed like old skin, a lack of proper attention on my part. That, or I was witnessing yet another stage in my closest friend's long metamorphosis. Hoping that such an alien change was not taking place at all, as I certainly had, seemed ignorant, inconsiderate even; the urge was tempting, nonetheless.

I had been preparing to close my eyes, lean my head back against the armchair triumphantly when my ears latched onto an out-of-place, familiar sound. One extended knock, followed by three taps in quick, staccato succession—a sound I somehow cherished and dreaded at the same time. Rei's sharp little knuckles rattled the pane of glass in its frame, which she seemed to notice, since she opened the door with both hands, slipped inside, and consciously, gingerly pushed it back into place with her back turned to us as if she needed to concentrate.

"Hello," she sang, before turning to assess our reaction.

"Ah, you found us. And what would you have us do?" I jested. She would have hardly needed to look.

"Maybe I just missed you, darling."

I smirked. "During your work shift? I beg to differ."

"One of these days, young man…" Her olive cheeks blew out like balloons when she pouted, huffily tapping the wooden sole of her pump against the floorboards. "There's a representative coming down from the Northern District, due to arrive in the morning."

Michael groaned beside me. I thought to tip my head back as planned and simply pretend I had been asleep the entire time. "Oh, you should have lied and said that an enemy army just breached the Wall, or my blood screening came back and I need a leg amputated, anything."

"That bad, huh?" Michael said, the worn-out, pitiful strain of his voice betraying him.

"Imagine doing it for eight hours a day, every day, then. That should help you feel better," Rei tittered.

At that moment, Lucifer threw her arms out in front of her, making frantic grabbing motions with her hands. "Woah there, back up for a moment," she hollered. "A representative?"

"It is quite commonplace. Spokespeople from outside colonies arrange visitations, so that they can see how we live within the Wall, how the Machine works to facilitate our new society. They often want to know how such a system enforces the welfare of us as residents, how we cultivate Souls from such a young age, how we have optimised our rates of production, how we suppress crime, that sort of thing. My job is to tour them around the most elucidatory parts of Interieur, depending on what they're here to see. Now and then, representatives submit a request to investigate a particular area, or monument, or whatever, in which case I consult with the Machine as to whether it would be suitable to go there at that time. You know, it all sounds awfully dull, the more I explain…" She trailed off with a meditative sigh.

"So, if that's part of your occupation then, dealing with these tourists, why inform us? Because there will be strangers let inside?"

Rei popped back to attention, ready to correct Lucifer's mistake. "Just the one! We only allow a single individual to enter through the gate at a time. That's policy. And you will be accompanying us. I'm not so important that I would be given five personal bodyguards, although the thought is nice. Rather, being Angels, you make the finest ambassadors to present to our visitors—at least in theory. The *crème de la crème*, if you like."

"No prizes for guessing who's first to the gate, all primed and preened, every time." I found myself making a pinching motion with my fingers, like playing a harp, or plucking long feathers from an invisible, but pungent peacock carcass.

"I know *you* all like to grumble about it. Raphael isn't too keen either. It'll take me the afternoon to catch him, now you've scared him away, even with the Machine's help."

I knew she would not exactly be charmed if I pointed out the irony in her statement, at least not in her current frame of mind.

"I suppose I will be wheeled out too." Lucifer added, shifting forward in her seat. "Who is it then, this foreigner from up North?"

"Their name is Jasmine. They're known in the other districts as the Angel of the North, or so I've heard, at least."

"Jasmine?"

"You know of them? Yes, I suppose you might; you have spent so much time among the Western people, after all." Rei spoke more to herself—like the right side of the brain casually conversing with the left—than to any of us.

Lucifer immediately checked herself, glanced her fingertips over her mouth. "The name does ring a bell," she mumbled.

**[Lucifer]**

Jasmine marched through the gateway, held aloft on the back of a horse, a massive, mahogany beast with rippling, velvety skin and a spitting, huffing snout. Its tough, flat feet swept up dormant plumes of dirt as it drummed from the low railway path onto the platform with ease. One of Jasmine's hands grasped a tangle of the horse's mane, the other resting on their knee. Their hips rocked gently from side to side, moving with the animal, both relaxed and trusting. Their eyelids narrowed slightly, poring over the crowd gathered to receive them. Their hair, still long, and darker than my own, was pulled away from their face, one part in a complex weave of ribbon, foliage and grasses. Completing the regal image were a trio of furry companions— foxes, one with a glossy amber coat, another smaller individual with large ears and a lolling tongue, and the last clearly much older and more ragged than the others—at which Rei stood positively agog. They were only brownish, trembling blotches down below, taking shape when they hopped up quietly to meet us, squirming around the horse's sturdy legs.

Jasmine's Soul could control animals. Wild or tame, creatures rallied around them according to their will, as though charmed by a spell, or infected with some microscopic species of parasite. According to Jasmine, this ability surfaced as a child, around six years of age, during a house fire. They woke on the front lawn, lying roughly on their back, skin raw and blackened, bitter smoke still swirling in their lungs. It appeared the family's dog had pulled them out of danger, not exactly a feat unheard of. What was truly unusual, however, turned out to be a pet from further down the street, also sniffling at the child's clothes, and the sparrows plucking away hot flecks of ash from their cheeks. The elder fox, the one with a chunk missing from its brush-like tail and a scar crossing its jaw, I could not look at without wondering if it had charged into battle before, yapping and snapping its canines for Jasmine's sake.

They had not yet spoken a word, and I found my eyes hypnotised, throat constricted, enchanted by the Angel of the North. I could remember the sound of their voice, their stern, statuesque face, a chink of their left eyebrow, sliced out by chickenpox or acne. They leaned forward eagerly in a murky void.

*"I've found a way out. I'm getting out of this place. Come with me."*

I felt warm and seen, as though they had said my name, but neither of us could find it now.

Rei shuffled on the spot for a moment, like a ballerina in a music box, before bowing at the waist, hands clasped to her chest.

"Welcome, representative."

"Come now, Rei, I am aware I look the picture of regal self-aggrandisement to your people, but I promise I mean no such thing. With how many times we have encountered one another in this precise spot, you and I must be on a first-name basis by now."

"Ah, of course, Jasmine."

They replied by sliding down from the horse's cloth saddle in one quick, efficient motion and returning a shallow curtsey. Seeing them in such an elevated position—in more ways than one—I had briefly forgotten that Jasmine was actually quite diminutive in stature, only an inch or two taller than Rei beside them, as they peeked over the top of her head.

They led their animals past the other Angels, one of the foxes halting to sniff at Uriel's shoes, before stopping a short distance from me. Jasmine's hand hung stiffly before them, as if resisting the urge to point and gasp. Instead, they gave an open-mouthed smile and subtle quirk of their brow.

"This is her," they said, their voice breathy and fleeting, "the lost child?"

A caress, across space and lost time. All I had to offer was a hurried nod and clumsy bend of the knees, more like a well-contained sneeze than a gesture of courtesy.

"Yes, this is Lucifer, vessel of a very powerful Soul. Number, um—"

She hesitated, searching my face for an aid. I felt a shivering over the skin of my palm, turned it upright. The digits traced themselves out over the hills and dark folds, from the base of my thumb to the fleshy joint leading to my ring finger. Jasmine leaned forward to examine it, an odd expression between a smirk and irritated pucker twitched at their cheek.

"Impressive. Then, since I count four gentlemen gathered with us, I am surely being attended to by all of the Sovereign's chosen. Quite the honour indeed."

"I had not thought of it from that view," Rei noted. "All five Angels together at last, you are quite right. It is a special day."

"Then shall we begin?"

"Of course," she said, sounding as if she could finally exhale.

For all of our supposed importance as Angels, we had little say over the unfolding of events to follow. We formed a neat, box-like formation behind Rei and her guests, shadowing them in tandem, like children, my only task being to watch my own feet, so as to avoid trampling the tip of a wandering tail. My legs had evidently grown used to marching at a busybody's trot, as I found our present walking pace agonising, and I found myself having to deliberately slow down to maintain unison with the taller, significantly fitter men flanking me on either side. This, I inferred, was leisure. All of us, suited and booted, crawling along a couple of streets, making them look pretty, and our guest prettier. The pavements were all broad, prime for exhibition. Strangers lingered, luggage resting beside them on doorsteps, dark figures flickered across the smeared glass of high windows.

The two at the front of the parade nattered between themselves in polite murmurs, discussing matters of import, like the turning of the seasons, statistics from the recent harvest, and a potential trade deal for diet supplements. Jasmine's horse bobbed its huge, heavy head alongside, flicking its ears occasionally, as though privy to their conversation. I almost tripped over my own feet when Jasmine suddenly held up a commanding hand, arresting the group, and raised their voice.

"Aulis, might I take a short walk with Lucifer—a turn of the room, if you will?"

Rei moved her lips, intending to reply, but tied herself in knots. "You mean…alone?" she said. "I'm not sure if—"

"I am sure my four-legged companions will be safe in your care, as I shall undoubtedly be, in the presence of one of your Angels."

"I suppose there isn't any problem, in particular…"

Uriel stepped in, literally taking two great, stomping bounds toward Jasmine. "I cannot, in good faith, advise such a thing, representative."

Michael, Gabriel and I looked to him, anticipating we would be called upon to reinforce his assertion, but he evidently did not require our input, affirmative or otherwise. Raphael knew better, simply clearing his throat and raking his fingers through his hair.

Jasmine did not quite laugh, but grunted, baring a slight crescent of white teeth. "The decision should be left to her, no?" he replied, gesturing to Rei, who straightened her wilted posture, nodding.

"Yes. You are correct," she said.

"I am much obliged, aulis." Their gentle tone vibrated like a hum deep in the windpipe. They turned, and bowed once again, to me —for me. "Shall we, then?"

I let the representative lead me away at first, giddy feathers swirling in my stomach as the stern, watchful faces of those left behind steadily shrunk to mere dark strokes of colour. I held my proper stature—hands behind the back—but could not help my mouth running away from me for a moment.

"What does it mean, that word you kept using to refer to Rei, ow —owl-something. I've heard it before. Someone must have used it, a customer of mine."

"You needn't worry. 'Aulis' is simply a polite term with which to address someone of knowledge doing you a favour. The young lady has been nothing but forthcoming towards me in all of my visits, so why should I not refer to her as such? The individual in your shop was most likely of North-Western descent. I have picked up a few idiosyncrasies of the language in my time. Has it been long, since your return?"

"Not long, enough time for the lion's tooth to bloom, that's all."

"And the streets are hardly changed for it, so they seem."

"For the flowers, or for me?"

"Oh, the plants were never truly gone. Perhaps, neither were you." They smirked, either realising the double-meaning inherent in their imprecise vagaries, or because I had slipped into a deliberate trap. The truth was, naturally, hard to discern.

I left Jasmine to their reflections, and we completed the walk in luxurious silence. They largely followed wherever my feet automatically carried me, only occasionally halting without warning to peer up at a puffing chimney or down a grate into the sewer, their hand spasming at their side as though tempted to reach out and touch. This obedience persisted; even when I swerved, climbing the steps up to Moore's Hall, they skipped merrily behind, behaving as a cub might, enticed by the chain hanging from my belt as it jangled against my hip. They had the same watchful white spark twitching in their pupils.

They slinked reverently through the open doorway, into the aisle, gaze wandering over the rich colours of the fresco, looming ahead, a barricade. They were still paying close enough attention when I stopped walking. Making no more effort to keep up a pretence, I perched the back of the closest pew, toes barely resting on the floor, and began scraping dirt from under my fingernails. They blinked quizzically, but would not yet speak.

"So, Jasmine…why are you really here?"

A white petal dropped out of their hair, they flicked their head to the side so abruptly. They clasped their hands behind their back tightly, obstinately.

"Don't worry; this room is one big blind spot; the Machine can't hear us. That's why I brought you here."

"I see." Their expression immediately screwed up with some negative emotion. The pink of their lips disappeared inside their face as they chewed on the soft flesh with their teeth. They were silent for a long moment, waiting until they could accurately articulate their frustration. "First, Michael went through the effort to get out of here, to find you, and then he brought you back inside. Why?"

"Leaving the city hardly poses a problem. We're Angels, Jasmine; turns out we are practically free to go when we please."

"And yet here you all are." They shifted on their toes and buried their fists in their jacket pockets.

A violent thumping entered through a high window, to be swallowed by the hall's empty air. A magpie dropped, briefly, towards the woman standing across from its master. It noticed, however, that though I barely turned my face, my eyes watched. The bird beat its wings. The safety of the rafters was rather more compelling than the call of its master's Soul, for now.

"Do you have any idea why I followed Michael?" I said. "He plans to destroy the Machine. As far as I can tell, the least I can do is give him the support he asked for."

"What?"

"And beyond that," I continued, "I trust him with my life."

"You plan to stay, then. It will be a rotten task, you know. Believe me; believe my people."

My small laugh bounded into the walls, a stiff, cold sound. "I understand perfectly well. The Smiths were executed for the very same ideas. But Michael has decided, and so Gabriel has as well. That leaves me with no choice. I can't leave, to watch them die trying."

"You aren't happy here. Even I can see that."

"Of course not. I'm not wanted anymore. Anyone paying attention sees I'm up to no good, and everyone of influence hates that. My old teacher, our teachers, hate that I am here. They're constantly peering out through the net curtains of their offices, at me, like they're wondering what went so wrong. The ones that are still alive, that is. But what can I do?"

"Perhaps *I* can help you, somewhat."

"How? You won't be staying, I assume."

"I couldn't. Still, I'd surely be more useful to you from outside. They don't want you, don't trust you? Alright—wait a couple days. Some of my scouts will fly over the Wall, usual routine. And when you are all ordered to the scene, make sure you are the one to eliminate the majority of them. Show them what a good Angel you are."

"Your scouts? Hold on, you mean..."

"My Soul takes them across. I use birds, usually; they have the most success breaching the Wall in the first place and, if I do well, a few might manage to return, too. In the past, I preferred to assume they are completely unaware that I am in their head, leading them here. But I can still feel it, when they get caught."

"Then don't do it."

"I've been at this for a long time, Lucifer. I suppose, after I insisted James Smith let me out, got myself to safety, this was my version of making a noble sacrifice for the cause. I can't say my thoughts were with everyone else, when the Wall opened for me. At the time, I was sick of it. I had to save myself, no matter what, before I could be *turned*. Only once I'd made it North did I have enough of my faculties to remember the others I had left behind. Since then, I have become quite accustomed to the feeling of those creatures I control being burned, beaten and shot to smithereens. But, no, I'll be making my exit as soon as we're done here."

"Which will be but a moment. We can't hide under this roof for very long, not if you're planning on making a quiet exit."

"I figured as much," they mumbled. Taking this as a cue, Jasmine slid their hands neatly out of the pockets at their waist and glided towards the light beaming in through the open doors, coattails swirling behind.

I stayed put, and stopped them, briefly, with another question. "Do you have anything you want to say, before you go, any message you want me to deliver?"

They shrugged. "To the rest of the Machine's lackeys? No, not particularly. I have no great friends amongst them, and I've never been much of a talker when it comes to my enemies. It's one way you and I always differed."

Again, they started walking away, and I spoke up. "We want to let everyone escape this time. When they get past the Wall, we'll have some hundreds of kids needing someplace safe to go."

"*If* you manage such a feat, the northern people will be just as prepared as they have forever been. The cunning folk out west might be worth approaching as well, since the city has you for its hostage now. I'll do what I can."

"Oh, ye of little faith," I retorted. However, those words exchanged, I finally saw fit to join them at the bottom of the aisle.

Taking another stride towards the exit, the finality of the motion slammed against my ribcage. I swallowed, the sensation somehow both sticky and rough as the slow drag of claws, like throwing a cup of sand down my gullet. I continued to walk. "You know," I said, "for a while, you were the best friend I had in this godawful place."

The hint of a demure smile twitched in the corner of their eye. "And you were mine, for a while." They slipped outside, the cool glow of the sunlight tangling in their hair.

The purpose of our little excursion fulfilled, we both knew to head immediately back to the spot wherein we had left Rei waiting, before suspicions could rise any further. We found her, as promised, watching Jasmine's mount, clutching the reins and glancing warily up at the horse's calm face, as if afraid to make direct eye contact. She jolted backwards when it rolled its head towards her, shaking a fly out of its mane. Gabriel, on the other hand, trailed a hand up and down its back, stopping to give a few firm pats on the neck, bulging with veins and tendons. He could, I supposed, he was that much taller. Although, whether he or Rei or any of us were in any danger was not truly up to the animal. The twelve-legged bundle of copper fur unfurled into three foxes, who stretched onto their feet upon sensing their master's presence. They took turns slaloming around the stiff legs of Uriel, who appeared to have been pacing along the same crack in the kerb for some time. Rei looked profusely grateful to see us, unconsciously thrusting the reins forward for Jasmine to take from her.

"Ah, you're back! Would that be all for today?"

They chuckled. "Oh, no. I had wanted to take some notes from your new medical facilities, as I recall. That was the main purpose of my visit, but better to skewer two men on one pike, wouldn't you agree?"

"Ah, yes." She held her hands in loose fists in front of her chest, pupils crossing towards her nose, a chunk of her mind still stuck absorbing Jasmine's turn of phrase.

I re-joined Michael at the rear of the pack, every cavity in my head stuffed with cotton.

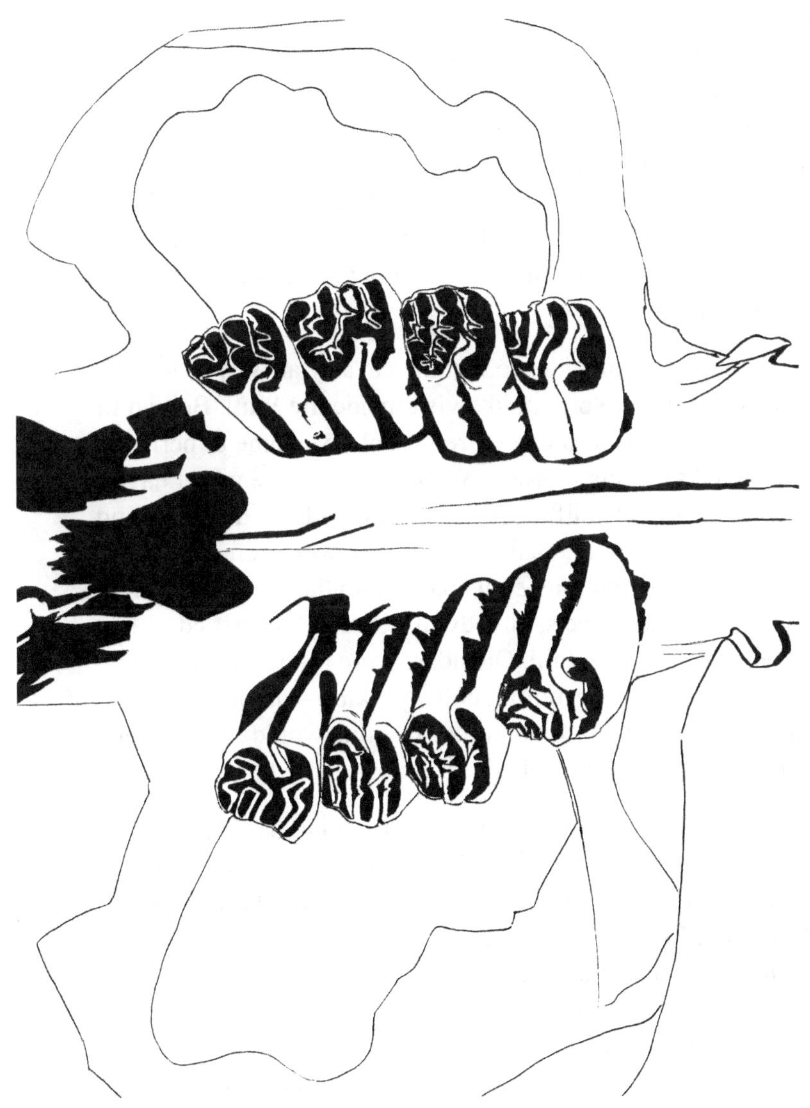

**[Michael]**

The ground rippled with trembling shadows as the birds passed over the lip of the Wall, warping the daylight. Raphael stood firm, watching the horizon as if bearing witness to a meteor shower, his obstinate silhouette my lighthouse in the alien sea. Uriel was the boat, vanishing amongst the waves before surfacing in another place, moving with the water, slipping through my fingers like oil. He had his back facing Raphael's, roaming freely around the other man's blind spot, eyes impatient. Gabriel clutched a loaded revolver in one hand, and the bridge of his nose in the other. Lucifer's boots groaned heavily against the pavement. The sound was uneven, as though she walked along a slope, or with a limp.

It struck me as no coincidence that the cavalry arrived so soon after Jasmine of the North paid a visit inside the Wall. Behind the serene, earthy exterior, the good representative came to perform an underhand scouting mission. What lacy disguise might have covered their true face lifted away to the clouds on the thumping gusts of many wings. If *I* had realised their deception now, one could be certain it had long sunken down to the bottom of the Machine's latticed bowels, already digested by electrified synapses like stomach fluid. Outsiders were to the city as mosquitoes were to our mortal, delicate skin—vampiric; they could step inside by invitation only. Jasmine would surely never enter through our doors again.

I did not fear their sharpened edges. What small damage their beaks and claws could do would heal. And like a lit match to freshwater, like a honeybee's sting, if they touched me, they died. Instead, I feared the consequences of my actions, what might happen if I could not make Lucifer stand up to this moment of scrutiny, if I could not prove her value. I feared that I had been outplayed, that something was unravelling for which I had not prepared. I feared the standing stone on the hill, by the lake.

One aspect of Jasmine's creatures which remained recognisably the same, the one thing I remembered well enough to make me sick, was the slightly strange, undulating motion of the birds, each one equally alive in body, if not in mind, but in synchronicity, tied together, like individual hairs on the same head. It reminded me that, even if Uriel sliced off their legs, even if Raphael ripped every feather from their bodies, they would continue to breath, to wail, to try. It reminded me of what we were to the Machine, that I would be expected to make the same choice, even dismembered and flayed.

Uriel stopped pacing. His blade scraped against the road, losing momentum like a kite. "Get a move on Lucifer. It's time to do your job. Funny as you seem to find it, we don't get chosen by the Sovereign just to sit around breathing."

She tried to chuckle, as though to show him she still could. "What, you mean you weren't?"

I wondered if Lucifer, too, would continue to breath, to try.

I turned my body to look at her. She tilted forward, clutching her thighs, hair hanging like a curtain over her face.

"You alright?"

"Who, me? I'm peachy. Not sure what I expected, but it wasn't for the Machine to spit out some esoteric street names and expect *me*, not only to get there, but do it quickly. So, my legs are fucked, but what can you do?" She lifted one hand to wave it at Gabriel. "She get you out of bed?"

"Don't even talk to me about it," he sneered, pulled at the belt adorned with pre-loaded chambers weighing uncomfortably on his hips.

"Sounds like you all need to get a grip," Raphael shouted into the air, unmoving, his head of cropped, pale hair still staunch and lurid as a beacon in the murky light of day.

"Yeah, yeah, easy for you to say, jock," Lucifer sighed, to no response. She leaned back, gloved hands moving to the small of her back, propped herself up, a tower rocking on its foundations. "I see this is the source of my second sunbeam, coming in at twelve o'clock." She squinted. "What's with the demonic red colour?"

"Markers. The Machine's probably been tracking each one of these for miles. Doesn't want any getting away."

"Looks like there's a lot of them to deal with, considering we're all bunched up here. Surely it would be prudent to spread ourselves out, for when they scatter, no?"

Raphael barked, "Hah, you're clearly the novice among us." If the shape of him stood for the lighthouse, his voice was the keeper's dog inside.

"The birds are all being commanded by one Soul," I elaborated. "A group of such a size is only barely possible, so whoever this is must be…extremely powerful."

"Helsing's name, Michael, if you crawl any further up this guy's arsehole, you'll pop out of their throat."

I ignored Raphael as best I could, for Lucifer's benefit. "Even so, they have to remain as a flock. No individual can stray too far, else the Soul loses its grip, the same effect as if I touch them."

Uriel spoke again, finally recovered from the blow dealt to him by Lucifer's insolence. "It's easier when they end up on a smaller road. They tend to funnel then. Much easier to catch." His swaying, grimacing face filled my vision. "You have your work cut out for you today. Speaking of which, discussion time's over. Arms out, socks up."

I nodded, rather pathetically.

"And I was having such a nice dream too." Gabriel confessed with a whimsical hum, mostly for his own benefit. However, the upward curl of his top lip into a toothy sneer, that was certainly directed toward the rest of us. Then, his arms tensed into that tell-tale triangular formation, he raised his revolver and fired a single shot. He cleared his throat, as though the thick, blunt roar of the bullet leaving its chamber—like a bag of salt thrown into my stomach—had been ejected from his own lungs. Overhead, far less distant than it had seemed only seconds before, one red bulb, a tiny chunk of Lucifer's 'second sun', blinked, hesitated for an instant before extinguishing. A black, lifeless apostrophe fell out of the sky, alone, still too obscure to see the trail of feathers floating behind. I sighed, knowing the corpse collection lads would have to go out of their way for that one.

The spectacle was a kick in my back, a reminder that it was my task to direct those bullets, to whip the other Angels into shape, to holler and point and swing my arms from the eye of a storm, like the hound corralling a wild herd. I kicked the butt of my polearm off of the ground, hoisting the long handle over my shoulder as though flying a flag. The sharp scratch of wood on stone caught their attention.

"Turn around, Gabriel, other direction. I want you to swim with the tide. No point in wasting ammo on the main body when we need you to clean up all of the stragglers Uriel leaves behind. Speaking of whom…" He was probably already up there—any excuse. The man would perch on the edge of a cloud if he could, he so dearly enjoyed being taller than the rest of us. "I need you on these rooftops, covering the high-flyers." Sure enough, as I glanced up out of the corner of my eye, there he stood, austere, one foot resting on a chimneypot. I let him be. "And Raphael, you know what I want you to do, I assume?" He nodded without a word, jaw moving slowly from side-to-side as he ground his molars together, the skin stretched over his clenched knuckles already so inflamed that it seemed to ripple.

"And as for myself? What are my orders?" Lucifer darted back when I turned around, swinging my blade clear of her head.

"Stick by me and watch closely. I'll direct you as and when."

From many metres away, the small infantry of birds appeared to be travelling in a single, crowded unit. However, they struck in a series of waves, in rapid succession and increasing in magnitude. The first proved easy prey for Raphael, crushed under his limbs; he could grasp multiple individuals in either enlarged, clawed hand, grinding his victims into an indistinguishable stew of feathers and bones. Others were scorched by the slightest contact with his scales. They plopped to the pavement, screeching in agony as they burned, smouldering like damp tealights. Those with quicker wits flapped their wings hysterically, lifted higher by the hot air emanating from Raphael's skin. They did not escape. Still, death by a quick slice or a single metal shell in the heart seemed a much more merciful end. The strangest bodies were those which clumsily clipped the corner of a building, or a lamppost. Looking at them, as they pushed their bellies along the cobbles with their feet, wings dragging at either side, I noticed the sheer variety of species among them. The crows, magpies, and occasional giant, sharp-edged owl or buzzard, those I had envisioned. The little sparrows, however, the larks and the fat, lolloping doves, they reminded me of stuffed dolls, the sort with plush fur and sewed-on buttons for eyes, wrapped up in suits and tossed onto a battlefield. They bled, all the same. And after writhing on the ground for a minute or two, they rolled onto their backs and died, from the shock, I supposed. My tongue felt numb and swollen in my mouth, and I hesitated to swallow lest it slip away and get lodged in my gullet.

I lost sight of Lucifer somewhere in the second burst. The flock took the shape of a great eel in the sky, jolting up, a little twitch of the hand, before crashing down upon Raphael and sweeping past me in droves. The weight of their increasing number pressed the crown on my head, pinched a vertebra at the back of my neck. Compelled to assist, I cradled the wooden polearm handle in my left hand and pushed its length forward with my stronger right side. The heavy metal blade, sharpened on both edges, could pierce through one or two fragile bodies in a single thrust, and shave a couple more wings on the downstroke, provided a feathery, blunting bundle was not still lodged on the end. Bitter air trickled into my lungs, thick and glutinous with the constant mechanical pounding from behind—only interrupted by the occasional need to reload, the movement of Gabriel's hand plucking a clip from the string hanging at his hip and inserting the new round equally automated. During one of these perfunctory moments of relief, Lucifer's voice caught my ear, some distance away now.

"Raphael."

I glanced in front of me. In the process of inching a path toward the brunt of the assault, boots crunching with each measured step, she held out one hand as through trying to grab the man's attention. Behind her back, her fingers grasped tightly around something, a small object protruding from her pocket.

"Raphael, move aside."

She, of course, garnered no response. Whatever he could hear at that moment, whatever he could perceive, even, was not within the realm of human ears. I noticed a slight trembling under my foot. The pavement seemed to slide away underneath me. Lifting the heel of my shoe, I saw the crack reaching over the stone's smoothed, porous surface, quite benign, if not for the steady widening of its mouth. I let my weapon clatter to the ground and ran.

"Raphael!" I startled myself with a shout which burst through the cloak of undulating noise from above. Like Gabriel's bullets, my voice cracked in the clogged, stifling air and bounced from one brick wall to the opposite. I grasped both of his shoulders tightly, sweat and gore seeping onto my palms. Some terrific reaction, like fire—hot, painful and insatiable—sparked against the walls of my ribcage for less than a second, pushed a gasp out of my mouth, before my Soul snuffed it out. I watched for dark, pinpricked pupils as they resurfaced in the blueish pools of his eyes. They met mine briefly, a single, deep heave escaping his chest, before he turned them over to Lucifer.

The flock, noticeably thinner than it initially was, but still numerous, floated away from her in unison, as though repelled by a stench, the dark body swelling upward like an opened parachute. Lucifer's body arched downward, she angled the dagger with a flick of her wrist and plunged its thin blade into the soft, gritty dirt between two paving stones, then immediately wrenched it out. As though the gentle curve of earth beneath the street was in fact the hump of a boar's neck, the gouge poured forth a thick, dark effusion into the air. She stepped back to observe, ducking behind her bare arm as if shielding her face from sunlight. The earth's blood was black, wispy, and hungry, peeling apart every bundle of feathers left in the sky, layer by layer. It choked them first, inhaled into the birds' lungs, then crawling its way out, eating through flesh, cartilage and bone, digesting it in many atom-sized mouthfuls. The cloud of smoke seemed to turn its countless warping heads, inquisitively, searching for more meaty pulp to consume until nothing remained.

The street fell quiet. Nothing remained, the only traces of the abundant flock being the heavy odour of hot sawdust and an opaque haze sucking up sunlight. Smoke curled around her, like the skirt around the legs of a ballroom dancer. She watched the sky, head bobbing slightly, and from behind she reminded me of a cat sniffing at the air. Then she swirled around and began to trot away, before freezing in between steps. Making a quick survey of the faces still turned toward her, her hands slumped onto her hips, the black gloves which protected her palms bumping against the band of her leggings with a slight leathery squeak.

"So," she said, her tongue pressed against the inside of her cheek, "are we done here?"

"Certainly looks like it to me," Gabriel said, finally, his expression unaffected, like the face of a building, his mouth the door swinging open in the centre.

Uriel, still suspicious, kept his backside firmly planted against the slope of a rooftop, and glanced over the crowded, pointed outline of the adjoining blocks. He searched for a retort and, evidently finding nothing suitable, nodded silently and evaporated, reappearing a second later behind Lucifer. His eyes continued to fixate on the enigmatic strip of bluish grey above the Wall, only panting a little, and positively oozing with discontent.

Raphael threw his hands loosely over his shoulders, as though to indicate his pliability, his unwillingness to resist. "I suppose, if not, we'll hear about it soon enough," he concluded. He made a peculiar expression, not quite a smile, more like a quirk of self-satisfaction, when the Machine's voice vibrated out of the walls.

"All targets eliminated. Thank you. Deploying recovery team. Protocols reset."

Lucifer hummed in agreement, rocking her whole body back into motion. "Good," she said. "I'm dying for a piss."

I felt a slant in the air. Uriel graced her with a final wrinkled expression of revulsion before phasing into the background.

Gabriel interpreted this as an opportune cue to announce, "And I'm going back to bed." He had managed to hold onto a drop of exasperation to inject into the curtseying gesture he performed as he passed.

Only Raphael remained. He addressed no one, gaze trapped in the middle-distance. It seemed as though a slither of his consciousness was stuck in the elongated second in which I grabbed onto him and put his Soul to sleep, as though a part of him had not woken up. I felt the sluggish weight of the thing. It felt like the haste of my fingers and the rage in my voice had sufficient force to throw that second out of continuity, and it lingered over the street like looking through stained glass. One end of a thin, silk thread knotted around it, buried in that spot under the road, and the other end implanted in his body, tied around one of his ribs. It stretched, elastic, yielding, but not without a little discomfort.

"Raphael." He didn't look up. The only indication he heard me at all was a slight jolt in his shoulders, drawing together toward his spine. "Are you hurt?"

He leaned to one side, that thread still exerting some pull on his body, before yanking himself away, taking a few steps in the opposite direction.

"Do you need something?" I added, oblivious as to what 'something' could be, but hoping to cast a net wide enough to patch up the hole, if the crackling, stinking bodies at our feet somehow could not fill it.

"Oh, fuck off Michael," he yelled. He disappeared into the dark rift, leaving it to smoulder at the corner of my eye like a cigarette burn.

**[Lucifer]**

Michael accompanied me back to the apartment. I tried to decline, but evidently my tone of voice did not have the same finality to it as Raphael's low, bratty rebuttal. So, he just kept his elbow stuck out politely and told me I looked as though the life had drained from my face. It wasn't the kindest of observations, but he wasn't likely to be wrong, in my experience. He didn't look so sharp himself. Sure, he didn't limp, or drip with sweat, hang his jaw open for every puff of air he could snatch. Instead, his body appeared to fold in upon itself, like the edges of a fallen leaf, as though he wished to pull his knees up to his abdomen, and continue to shrink from there, smaller than a foetus, tiny enough that he became imperceptible to the world.

He hovered over my shoulder, and I had assumed he would follow me inside. However, he paused in the ground-floor doorway without saying a word. I paused to glance back at him; his back faced me, a blunt object, while he leaned outside. He nudged the breast of his jacket aside, and I ducked my head, mostly curious to know what he guarded so gently against his chest, nestled in both of his hands.

"I'm sorry little one," he said, in a trembling murmur, almost a lullaby. "Go on, quickly now."

A frantic, clapping sound, and a flash of dark blue and daffodil-yellow plumage. The tiny bird did not hesitate before it soared up and out of sight. Michael stepped inside and closed the door, then turned back to me, as though returning from a dream. He pulled a pale, delicate downy feather out from the fabric of his shirt, an uncomfortable knot in his brow. I was not convinced the bird would make it over the Wall before being recognised, or simply collapsing, unable to survive the trauma. Neither was he, it seemed. Still, I found a childlike innocence in him, in his compulsion to *try*. I chose to admire that from afar, at least. It was all I could do to scrub to haze of pity from my own eyes. We said nothing more of it between us.

**[Michael]**

"You don't happen to have any ice lying around, do you?"

"Ice?"

"Yeah, just to put on this."

She turned her right arm over, holding it out to the side, into the light. I pushed a couch cushion aside to take a better glance. A red mark, raised and seeping like a burst blister, began at her wrist and tapered off as it climbed her forearm towards her inner elbow. Under the hot glare of daylight, the wound appeared to bubble underneath the skin, as though her flesh simmered. Whitish peels were already curling away from the centre.

"It looks ugly, but it'll be fine," she assured me, nonplussed. "Lumping cold on it helps with the stinging in the meantime, though."

"I, um, I've probably got some frozen peas or something in here. Let me see."

My fingers trembled as I rummaged through tubs of leftovers, and portions of meat wrapped in greaseproof paper and clear crystals. I preferred to think it was the effect of the freezer's chill. I eventually extracted the half-used bag of mixed vegetables that had been lounging, slumped over rather unattractively at the back of my mind. Ice scattered over the floor and began melting into my socks, as I wrapped the package in a dishtowel. She accepted my offering with a grateful smile, which faltered a little as soon as she pressed it against the sore on her arm.

"This has happened to you before."

"Oh, more than I care to admit. Side-effect of having such a mean Soul, I assume."

"It looks painful."

"Only a taste of the pain I could deal to you, if you weren't magically immune."

"Eve told me I should think myself lucky. Told me I could never really understand what it was to feel fear like that. She made it sound like you were trying to murder her."

"On that day, maybe part of me was."

"I'm sorry. I shouldn't bring that sort of thing up. It's not your fault."

"It's not yours either. To be honest, the worst recoil I ever felt wasn't even when my Soul attacked *her*. Check this out."

Balancing her injured wrist and cold pack on one knee, she untucked her vest and lifted it just above her waist. I winced. Wrapped around her left side, at the bottom of her ribcage, a pink scar rippled over her skin. Faint wrinkles sagged across the entire length of the blemish, as though that small patch of her body had been decayed by disease or several decades of abuse too many.

"Now that, I got from a lesson with Blackwater. It's not as though I feel the difference, but years later and I can't shift that mark. Not only was the damage worse than usual, I never had it seen to."

I felt my larynx bob upward, large and rigid, like I had gulped down a pebble. "Why?"

"Didn't want to say anything. Didn't want anyone to find out. I was embarrassed, really."

"Or afraid."

Afraid for Eve to find out. Afraid to be doted on, to be poked and prodded—to be called stupid and cowardly, frail and a liar. I had been living in the same apartment as her, all of us penned in together, with no clue that she was so severely wounded. Sure, I recalled that girl's almost permanent tight, pursed grimace back then, but she must have been in more pain than that. If so, she had done well to hide it. I questioned whether I had yet changed enough, to simply shrug my shoulders and be honest.

She clicked her tongue against the back of her teeth, returning pressure to the damp towel, now leaking cold water onto the leg of her trousers. "Nah," she said.

I was preparing for bed, winding down my body piece by piece, watching the process in the bathroom mirror, when it arrived. When he arrived. Lucifer reclined on the couch, drifting between states of consciousness. I slid the soggy bag from under her hands, like stealing a toy from a child, returning it to the freezer with a mental note that the peas were no longer to be regarded as edible.

"Communication has been sent from Angel Raphael, marked urgent."

My toothbrush almost dropped out of my mouth. The Machine's use of a politely lowered voice did not help.

"Reading now. Open the door, Michael."

That was it. The note stopped. The Machine stepped back, back into the ceiling. The sound of trickling water filled the room. The palm of my hand smarted against the tap. Usually, I presumed, the terror that arose from such a message concocted itself from the swathe of awful, sudden, gory possibilities which spiral in the mind. In this case, the primal fear that wrung my intestines was that of the sheer unknown. As I spat into the sink, squeezed a hand towel in my fists, my imagination groped around and found nothing but absolute blank canvas. I opened the door, still scrubbing white gunk from my lips, at first only wide enough for one eye, then wider. The corridor crouched in deep, natural darkness, and in it up to his knees, blurring at the edges, stood an Angel.

Raphael shrugged at the sight of me. "Funny, how it can be handy sometimes."

"I was erring more on the side of alarming. What's wrong?"

"Nothing. Actually, no, that's not true." He appeared to flicker up and down on the spot. "You still got time? I'm just going to say what's on my mind. If you forget it, you forget. No harm, no foul."

His pained expression did not match the words he spat from his mouth. For a fleeting moment, I thought he had collapsed at my feet, playing out some sort of gothic scene from a novel. I blinked, and he threw a glance over his shoulder at me. He had sat down on the doorstep. He cast a long, towering shadow onto the wall in front of him. He glared at it as though he could set it alight if he did it hard enough. It would keep the neighbours away, at least. Stubborn. Stubborn, like no one had any patience at all, and he would have to drag it out of them.

"Fine," I said. "Say your peace, although maybe don't shout this time, else it won't just be me and the Machine who hear you."

I squeezed over the threshold, pulling the door most of the way closed behind me, and sat on the floor. He seemed very tall from down there, under his concrete pedestal. He had not yet wrapped his steely hands around my throat, so I assumed I was free to let the tension from my shoulders seep out, like beads of sweat.

"No need to look like you're shitting yourself. I'm not about to profess my love for you."

"Well, good, because that would be compromising, not to mention insubordination, and I'd hate for that to ruin our friendship."

He ducked his head, skated a hand over his hair. "Really? I hope Lucifer finds you funny, else I'm just embarrassed for you."

"I don't know. You'd have to ask her yourself."

He shook his head no.

"I'm sorry for dismissing you so rudely, earlier. That was… unnecessary."

"You came here to apologise for that? You've said much worse to me before."

"I remember. And chances are I'll tell you to fuck off again, and I won't be apologising for that, either. But that's not what I came for." He waited for a beat. I watched his pupils dart from side to side, as though reading his speech from the brickwork. He continued, "I never gave you the chance to tell me why you bothered to come back. Or how you managed to drag Lucifer with you."

"Trust me, there was no dragging involved. I didn't leave with the intention to leave Central behind me, not while I still have business here—business she and I happen to share."

"What, and that business includes fucking with Eve Stanton?"

This felt to me like a game of hot or cold, and we had made a turn, getting warmer. He referred, I assumed, to the incident at the ball.

"Partially," I said, treading carefully. Not carefully enough, not even close. "Pun not intended, I suppose?"

"Shit, no. Gabriel in on it too?"

"Sure." Caution simply seemed the wrong approach to this man.

"Well, more power to you. Wish I had the stones."

"Who says you don't?"

Eve's shape rose slowly out of his silhouette on the floor, in her green dress, the train soiled with round spots of red. She held her arms prostrate at her sides, and thin slithers of glass in both her hands. She smiled flagrantly under the gaze of the Machine.

"Listen," he muttered through his teeth. "I fell for her far worse than any of you. How many years has it been, do you remember, since I first snuck back to your place with her?"

I felt her look at me, her hand gripping my wrist. "I don't know…two, three?"

"Weird, I figured you would be keeping track. I was attracted to her, then. She was pretty, powerful, seemed to know me better than any other bastard could. Better than I did."

I angled my cheek toward him, tried to smell him in the air, his presence. "What did she tell you?"

"*I* told her tales about the creature inside me, about the… complicated relationship I have with it. We don't along, let's just say that. It is so *angry*. I try to control it, but sometimes I just can't do it. Eve, she refused to believe a beast exists. Vehemence is my truest self, embodies the very thing that I am. Said she liked it that way."

"That's not—"

"Oh, don't start. I'm aware. She warned me not to lie to her, that she'd always be able to tell. The Machine didn't seem to mind, though. If anything, I have a feeling her number went up. I suppose that was the whole point. Makes you wonder what sort of demigod babies it thought me and her would raise together."

Oh, Raphael. "You never would have been allowed to raise them yourselves," I confessed.

He thought about this for a while, then nodded, turning away from me. "…Eve doesn't have a Soul at all, does she?"

"No."

Though I could not see his face, he seemed pensive in his silence, until I noticed laughter. Born as a brief, chesty rattle, it erupted from him as a biting guffaw, burrowing the back of his head into the wall. I reclined, waited for him to empty himself of it.

"Do you know," I opened, "Who my Soul resided with, a few generations ago?"

He swayed limply from side to side, an indolent smirk still draped between his cheeks.

I said, "Dominion lived in the body of Lester Altair, supposedly was the whole reason for his notoriety and…relative longevity. Doesn't sink much lower than the most widely feared clan of thieves and murderers."

"She made sure to remind me, all the time, how furious you would be when you eventually found me out. Us, I guess."

"Funny, that. I wasn't allowed to get close to other people, smile too widely from across the street, laugh too hard, couldn't *touch* anyone. She'd wait for me to get home before she said she'd seen me trying to get off someplace else. All those years I knew that her Soul, imaginary or not, couldn't do jack to me, but she still had her hands squeezed over my eyes. The Machine didn't care, since there's nought 'actionable' to punch through the algorithm. But she often told me she loved me." I felt I had shrunk, that I was smaller than my shell, that I could open a vent and spill into a puddle on the ground. I had not prepared myself for this. I still had toothpaste stuck to the corners of my lips. Raphael had somehow known I was ready before I could, that the fruit dangled there, ripe for the picking. "So, I'm afraid I won't be meeting your expectations regarding a punch-up. It hardly matters to me anymore. Well, no, it does matter, but not in that way. Not in any sense that hurting you is going to fix."

"Doesn't matter to her either, not anymore. Whatever value she needed to knock off my number, she wasn't able to do it. I can picture that day so clearly, when I was the one given these wings." His eyes rolled upward, to the blackened thorns growing out of his hair. "I still feel this…ache."

"Of course, you were a means to an end, but what she did to you wasn't enough. I, for one, am thankful that you got in her way."

"I never intended to."

"And yet you did."

[139]

"Michael, listen. I'm sorry."

"What do you have to apologise for now?"

"For enjoying it, when I did."

I turned toward him, hearing his voice muffled. Face entombed in the folds of his arms, only his hands were visible, pointed knuckles almost bursting through his skin, which cracked and split, decaying into the colour of dark scales. A wall of heat bloated around us, contracting and exhaling, as if waiting in anticipation. My hand reached through it, finding the curve of his neck. The bare contact sapped a little of the tension from his body, redirecting the roar through my skeleton, into the concrete like a mast. He lost weight, became malleable, such that I could unfurl him into my chest.

"Thanks," I heard.

"Nothing else I could do, mate," I said. "I understand how you felt."

"I guess this is what Lucifer appreciates so much."

"Maybe."

My lungs heaved, as did his. As if we had one each, and the blood crawled through them, fatigued. As if the muscles burned.

**[Rei]**

Gabriel did not touch any food that evening. He sat in front of the thousand-piece jigsaw on the floor, without touching it, without speaking. I lowered a mug of tea into his hands, and his fingers wrapped around it, two threading through the handle as if by instinct. He then stared out of the window, steam lapping against his face, until the tea grew cold, untouched. Me, on the other hand—my knuckles, my elbows, the inside of my wrists, my shoulders as he passed by—rather than brushing over me, grazing the fine hairs covering my skin, the pads of his fingers dragged, as though he were coated with tree sap. I tried to see, to prise open the eye of my Soul, to catch a glimpse of what he saw, and found nothing. But he did not see nothingness before him. My gut wanted to pin him down and shake him and scream, "What? What?" until he answered me.

Finally, sat at the foot of the bed, gripping at the edge of the mattress, he cleared a sticky lump from his throat.

"Listen, I have to tell you something."

"Please!" my veins cried, their gasps radiating frantic heat through my limbs.

"There's a lot I want to say, but I can't. It would be too dangerous. Lucifer coming back, it's not a coincidence. It's not just luck. She's here to help us. We have a very important job to do. And…" A tiny sphere of blood rose like a sprout out of his bottom lip. "Look, we know next to nothing about how it's going to play out, but it's probably going to be nasty. I can feel it. I wish there were an easier means, a means to persuade our way out of this, but picking out one poisoned apple won't fix the tree. I just want you to know that, whatever happens, we wanted something better, for everyone, and I'll do everything to keep you safe. Okay?"

I ducked my head away from his pleading eyes, pinched my temples, and let myself giggle a little. "You—you do realise, if this thing you're doing is as dangerous as you're making out, I'm going to find out anyway, like, *for sure*."

He grasped my hands, kissed the top of my head, mumbled into my fringe. "I know. Still, I need to keep you out of it for as long as I can. And I know it's in the Machine's interests to keep you protected, too, but I don't want it to make you forget, either."

I wanted to admit to him that, ever since I started sitting on that bench in the evenings, a few minutes before the twenty-third hour, to meet with him, I had a feeling I was walking into a bigger picture. I thought perhaps I ought to tell him, that I can't sit in that spot anymore, the sheltered place under the archway, without seeing him stumbling down the road.

The shroud of darkness had appeared safest to him. It was winter, so the light gave way early. He had returned to the apartment, at a quarter to ten, and resolved to wait until Eve departed for her night shift before he began to pack his things. The digits on the clock's face flinched forward occasionally, so slowly, and all the while he tried not to think. He had possibly anticipated some sort of vocal protest from the Machine. It was watching us closely.

Once the moment came that he descended the steps outside, all those heading to work were long gone, and those coming home were safely behind closed doors. More than being a fugitive, I thought he feared being seen. He did not want anyone asking him where he was going. Home was a strange word, to him, for how casually we use it. He no longer had a proper grasp of it. From the perspective of his muscles, their habits, it meant the unlit hole behind him. But as for the rest of him, he was lost. The load at his sides was not insubstantial, but still too light for the task at hand. Two cases were stuffed with clothing and other odd items he considered absolutely essential. A small backpack was all that was necessary to hold the more personal belongings. There had been no need to panic, or to ransack. So little of what was his held enough value to bother carrying. Nothing was missing; he simply did not possess anything else. He had followed the path as it presented itself before him, away from the apartments, past the old bar, towards the bridge.

Looking upon the scene from outside, the emptiness of the street actually made me appear rather unreal. I was perched on the wooden bench under the arch to Gabriel's right. I almost heard the rumble of a train over my head. As he gradually approached, it became clear I had noticed him, and was smiling. His feet shuffled faster underneath him, the bag slung over his shoulder smacking against his ribs. He resented me a little. After all, he had emerged under the dark gloom so as to avoid judgement, not only from those confused, and thereby inconvenienced by him, but also those who would expend the effort to pity him.

It seemed to be when he shot that final, involuntary glance at me before he passed right by, that he noticed the absence of a disturbed frown over my countenance. Instead, I was bent forward in my seat, stretching my neck forward, not unlike a shopkeeper for whom business is still just slow enough to enjoy the company of strangers. My expression had the same beckoning effect too, it seemed, as all strength evacuated his arms. Feeling he could not lug the load any further, he folded himself into a misshapen heap on the bench. His weight somehow sank, like resin, into the most microscopic creases of the solid wood.

"I've been waiting for you."

He turned his head slightly towards my voice. Rather than continue pretending to be absently looking over the road, the slightly younger version of me, now his neighbour, had tucked her legs under herself, and was balancing her chin on clasped hands. Her eyes glimmered, a little glassy under the street lighting (white light, as prescribed by the Machine).

"My name is Rei," I had said. "I am—"

"I know who you are. You're the one with the Soul, the one that sees the future."

"My Soul is called Enlightenment, thank you, and it can give me glimpses of the past as well, if I can so persuade it. Get it right."

Only when I giggled did he recognise my seriousness had been in jest. Later, he would admit that he struggled to believe, in such a miserable place, one smile could be consistently so sincere.

"Yes, you are placed in…" he grunted, rubbing his palms together in his lap.

"Public relations," I added.

Then he nodded, apologetically. An unseemly, impatient sigh puffed from his nose. "Alright then, let's hear it. Why are you here, at this unreasonable hour?"

"I saw a vision of you. Weeks ago, I sat on this bench for a moment to fish something out of my bag, and I saw you, here, a little before midnight. I was not sure what day my Soul was showing me, so I've made a habit of waiting here, to see when you would arrive. And here you are, at last. I was beginning to think I might be mistaken." It was true. I really had been growing very worried and embarrassed.

"Such visions must be an everyday occurrence, though. Why waste so much time here? I cannot imagine the Machine is particularly satisfied with your sub-optimal sleep schedule."

"Nor yours." I shrugged. "I don't suppose I've checked my number for a while. Look, I don't know where you have come from, or why you aren't there anymore. I only thought, perhaps, I could help you with one of your cases. Probably only the one, though; I am rather a lot smaller than you are, um…"

He looked away from my face, just for a moment. Perhaps my shining eyes had reminded him of tears, as they suddenly fell from his eyes, making damp the unshaven hair on his face. He clutched his head in his hands, as if it were arid and aching.

"I'm sorry," I said. "I cannot remember asking your name."

In the seconds after the words left my mouth, his body stiffened and twisted with pain. His head. I asked him to describe it to me, what he was experiencing. He could see everything, even though his eyes were clenched shut: every brick in the bridge, a bird landing atop it, slowing down—five miles an hour, two, stopped —and my hands, reaching for his shoulders. His Soul was terrified, but of something it could not find.

"Second candidate. Number three-one-five-four." The garbled, echoing voice projected the Machine's words out of the brick wall. "You are chosen, Angel Gabriel."

The brutal sensation appeared to be ceasing, his fingers unknotting from his scalp. As he moved his hands, one knuckle caught against a cold, metallic thing behind his ear, something that should not have been there. There were two halos, one framed within the other, driving into either side of his skull. He immediately gripped one loop in his fist, where it looked small, to my mind, even delicate.

"What is this?" he demanded, his voice a shaky murmur.

The Machine replied, "Your wings, as denotes each chosen Angel. I must ask you stop pulling your wings, Gabriel, as you risk harming yourself. The headpieces cannot be damaged or removed."

He let go.

"Oh, congratulations," I mumbled, unsure, deflated. "Three-thousand one-hundred and fifty-four…that's incredible."

His head dropped onto his knees. He had not stopped crying, only now he began to weep and tremble. My palm felt hot against his back, like I could burn him if I held it still. "We don't have to move right away, Gabriel. We can wait here a while."

Back in the present, Gabriel held both of my hands on his knees, brushing his thumbs over the lines in my palms. He spoke quietly now, somehow soothed. "The moment I saw you, that vision of you under the bridge, it had reassured me that something like

gods were indeed present and watching over me. But as soon as
the Machine drilled these wires into me, I had to wonder what
the hell for. What purpose did a gold crown on my head serve?"

**[Michael]**

Just when the Red Café had settled in with us, the walls firm in their decrepit, peeling state, the furniture in its place, I brought something in with me, something tremorous and pointed and unsafe. And when my eyes locked onto a shadow—that shadow—dancing through the trickle of light at the window, I understood what it was. He let himself in again, though less brazenly destructive than before. The swing of the door was faltering, delicate. I ought to have handled it with more care.

"Raphael."

"Yeah, yeah, it's me." He stepped over the threshold onto the red tiled floor, for the first time. He rushed it, like yanking off a plaster. "Look, I'm here. I'm in. Is there a form I've got to fill out, sign on the dotted line or whatever?"

A pause. The others turned to stare at him.

"Would you…like a cup of something, coffee, tea?" Lucifer pulled up her brow, and tilted her chin forward until she looked sufficiently bemused. She held up her own mug in demonstration. My gaze drifted away from an escaped blackened drop sliding down the enamel, drawn instead to the figure stood petrified on the welcome mat. I wanted to rise to my feet, leap towards Raphael.

"We have crumpets, shortbread, hell, you might even be able to swipe a bit of chocolate." I heard Gabriel add, from across the table, taking up Lucifer's cue.

"That's what you want? For me to eat cakes?"

"They're not poisoned, I promise," I said, some extra weight falling on that last word. "Come on, pull up a pew."

Still, he hesitated. Lucifer lifted herself from her seat and repositioned onto the cushioned arm of my chair. In doing so, she left behind a spot just separate enough, just safe enough, to accommodate our guest. He slouched back into the scuffed, canvas lining, peering around at the once-matching rug, paint, and papered feature wall, all curling in at the edges towards him.

"Place still looks like a bloody barn," he scoffed.

Lucifer was quick to retort. "Come on, man, cut me some slack. All that time I could have used to pretty up the safe room, I've spent giving you and Uriel the run-around, trying to avoid eye-contact with my old babysitters, and flirting with the wrinkly codger in the chair—what's his name…"

"The Sovereign?" Gabriel offered, raising his hand as if to swat her fingers, clicking above my head.

"Thank you!"

"Besides," he continued, "your turning the place into some work of art would only make our job more difficult. It's not like we can protect it, all on its own, like a little snow globe."

"Shame."

"So this is where you meet, right?" Raphael said. "To talk about, well, whatever the fuck it is you're all planning on doing."

"Call it what you want." I shrugged, suppressing a knowing chuckle. "Mutiny, shutting down the Machine, levelling Interieur, doesn't matter, no-one can hear us in this room."

"What?"

"I not sure if the Sovereign even knows about them, but the city has blinkers—built in—rooms the Machine can't get at. Sure, it has a musty smell to it, but this is the best watering hole in the city, period."

"And you lot found this out how, exactly?"

"Smith."

"…Built in."

"Their breadcrumbs are all I had, to start. That pair have basically been holding our hands beyond the veil."

"And here I thought *you* were the chessmaster behind this stunt. Figures there was something going on." He sighed, long and low, like a paper bag leaking air. "Props to him, I never would have guessed 'Hey, how's your head today, kid?' actually meant 'By the way, I'm going to need you to punch the lights out of my magnus opus one day, kid. It might kill you to stop you, but them's the breaks.'"

"I suppose that's the more cynical way to look at it," Gabriel mused, chin resting on his knuckles.

"I'll bet that's one thing we'll never get the truth of," Lucifer added.

I shook my head. "We know they wanted us out of here; they were executed trying to help us do it. Surely that has to count for something, at least."

Raphael waited for a minute, at least, before he filled the dense silence with a long, deep hissing; a sigh through his nostrils. "This all feels too weird." His eyes were screwed shut.

"You're taking all this astoundingly well," Lucifer mumbled, arms crossed tightly under her chest.

"Suspiciously well?" he replied.

She hummed to herself, though it came out more like an elongated groan. "Not sure yet."

"What, was I not supposed to speculate?"

Though I shuffled, almost onto my knees, I was not quite close enough to reach out and shake him. "I'm happy you came here today," I said. "Relieved, maybe, is the word. I wasn't sure you would."

"You didn't leave me much of a choice."

I shrunk back while, conversely, Lucifer rocked on the spot, and clapped her hands together, cackling with an erratic enthusiasm. "Aha! I told Michael his bright, puppy-dog eyes would eventually be the ones to turn you traitor. But would he listen to me…? Now you're there, right at home in my comfy chair."

"Well, no, I'm not like— It's ever since you decided to pipe up at the fucking ceremony, I've been going through this shit." He lurched forward in the comfy chair to snatch a biscuit off the neat pyramid structure Lucifer had built that morning, his arm quick and elastic like a frog's tongue. "So, if anyone's to blame, it's you," he added, voice turned sticky with butter.

Whether or not this was intended as a light jab, she did not seem to mind.

"Okay, okay, Michael—scratch what I said before. Raphael being so offended by my speech, so terribly he had to come back here and tell me personally, that's *much* funnier."

She was both incredulous and charmed by the dissonance between his nonchalant position, shoulders almost level with his ears, and his left pinky finger, protruding delicately upright from the crumbling lump in his hand. The rapid up-and-down movement of her pupils was followed by one barely audible grunt which scrunched the end of her nose.

"You all need to be careful, though," he said, gazing into the empty space in front of him. "Not about the Machine, necessarily, if you have that covered like you claim. I mean about Uriel. He's been watching, real close. And unlike the Machine, he literally has nothing else better to do. Spends hours in that room behind Hall, talking to himself in front of the Sovereign. I call it the motherboard; he preferred the 'throne room'. I couldn't fucking stand it, the boredom, all the pretence."

"You happen to know what he's been reporting back?" Gabriel proposed. "Whatever his eyes have seen, and the Machine's haven't, it must be fairly minimal."

"Sorry, I usually gave up and left before much of significance came out. Trying my best to ease the brain-rot, I suppose. Maybe that was his intention, to have me gone by the time he got to the juicy parts. He doesn't seem to be reporting facts, though. It's more like…he's feeding it. With observations, opinions, feelings, in amongst the platitudes."

"And he gets no response, I assume?" Lucifer was leaning forward, elbows resting on her knees, methodically twisting the rings on her fingers.

"No more than you or me," he replied.

"But you still have concerns." I nodded as I spoke, trying to inch him onward.

He hesitated briefly, seeming to question the legitimacy of his own claims. "It just seems like… I know the Sovereign is the only man with control over the Machine, officially speaking. But, if anyone else could exert a bit of influence over the algorithms, it's Uriel. And he definitely believes that."

"Are you worried about your own safety?" Lucifer said, almost absurdly calm in her intonation.

"I don't need coddling," he bit into the air.

I did not want to sound as bruised as I did. "We don't coddle. There's no point in it. We only ask. It's the decent thing to do."

Lucifer breathed deeply beside me; I felt the release in my own lungs. Looking at her face, as she drew her legs up towards herself like a soft, drooping gargoyle, I realised I might have an ally in my ache. An ally in my desire to bind my hardened flesh about Raphael, to wrap a protective body around him, kicking and screaming, biting and clawing.

"Part of me," I suggested, "still holds out hope that, if we set him, Uriel, free from the Machine, sever his ties to it, then he might…get better, somehow."

"Can't claim to share the sentiment," she slurred. "I'm cruel in that way, I suppose."

"I wouldn't call it kindness on my part. If I am honest with myself, to save him, keep him, it just feels easier."

Raphael turned to Lucifer, tapping a finger against his chin. "You know, there's a rumour that goes around about you. People who say you never made it out past the Wall alive, that you're just some ghost, or a vampire, or something else come back to haunt whoever pissed you off."

She grinned, pulling up her cheeks as if to show him the sharpest of her teeth. "That's interesting."

"Not going to deny it then?"

"Of course not, why on earth would I do that?"

"Well, at least you don't hide who's earned your bloody revenge."

"You are right, some of them just aren't worth the effort of keeping a blank expression. I still have my secrets though, trust me. I am a woman of many…"

Faces, I remembered for her.

"Assets?" Raphael suggested with rather more humour. "I suppose I haven't a clue what you truly think to me. Go on, tell me, am I on your death-list?"

"No, no, you're far too intriguing for that."

"I'll take intriguing."

"I would call that getting off lightly, boyo," Gabriel piped up, peeling open another portion of watery jelly from his stash of pots. "Maybe there really is magic in those striking blue orbs of yours." He balled up the foil lid in his fist and tossed it, bouncing it off of the wall into a waste bin. Rather than plunging into his next sweet-smelling portion of gelatinous sugar water, he rested both hands on his knees, still lightly gripping his utensils, and rocked his head back against the wall.

"What's got you in a trance, Gabriel?" I asked.

He hummed, eyes closed, and waited for an elongated, empty breath before answering.

"Did you know," he said, "that just a few hundred years ago people would have killed to be sat in this room, just like this, with four of the land's most powerful gifted?"

"Well, yeah, obviously."

"Mm, I suppose you've got me there. But not just the really devout types. I'm talking about the most ordinary, working folks as well. Anyone with a little faith. Living vessels have, in theory, a connection to the Source—a little like an umbilical cord. Through their Souls, they can commune with the Source's, well, what would we call it? Energy, I suppose."

"How is that much different to now? People with Souls in them can do funky shit most can't. Same idea."

"Maybe. This was less about combative utility, though, and instead more for the sake of simply…making contact with that otherness, the higher plane. Their belief was that those particularly powerful gifted could, in a sense, resonate with one another, entering into a sort of flow state. Souls brushing their surfaces, overlapping, like links in a chain. Gather up enough strong ones and anyone might be able to taste a crumb of the most delicious dessert, take a single page from one book in the perfect library, feel the weight of dark matter between two fingertips. And so on, you get the idea."

"Well, that is one very cushy soliloquy to describe a group conference."

A breathy titter slipped between his teeth.

"There are still a few, where I came from, who've kept their faith," she professed. "They seem to speak of whole conversations they're having with that thing above the sky. Resonance…what would that look like? I don't know; the Source is what it is, and it's never done any such thing for me. You still believe then, Gabriel?"

"I wouldn't necessarily call it belief. It's not as if I have a weekly appointment with the divine. Mine is more of a feeling. Literally. I know *something* is there. What it is, what it means? Beats me."

"What does it feel like?"

"Don't ask for much, do you? Right now? Like mist rising off of a slow river; like dying leaves floating on a slightly damp breeze, strokes of daylight setting them alight in flares of amber and rust, until only the veins are left, dragging against my skin before they disappear over my head." His eyes snapped open. "How was that?"

"If it were true though, even a part of it, what does that say about us? Five gifted individuals herded together under the name of Angels—to what end?"

And me? What purpose, therefore, do I serve in all this, the deadening sponge, the black hole? Say I am a walking, talking, blood-filled battery, one arbiter in a great, moving network. Who is the medium? Which mouth does the circuit feed? In a more fluid, and perhaps more optimistic scenario, the Angels are more like a cauldron, incubators of a complex concoction of Souls. Even then, Dominion seems a bizarre choice of ingredient for such a deadly poison. I kept such musings to myself, holding them inside my head by pinching at my brow. I turned my ears back to the sound of Raphael's voice.

"You know what that sounds like to me, right? Hallucinations. Maybe trapped wind."

"And how, exactly, is a man supposed to argue with that?"

He grumbled. "I don't buy it. Gathering up Souls and tripping out on Source-power? Nah. But, hey, if you're not lying, then more power to you, I guess."

"It's far more than what's going on in this bucket of brains here," Lucifer said. "And on that note, I'd better clock out for a bit." She rose to her feet, slapping her knees, most likely to distract from the sharp intake of breath as her limbs straightened out.

I followed her outside, not very difficult to do, since she walked with odd movements, not quite a limp, but as though every twitch of her muscles caused her pain. I think it did. I couldn't be certain when it had started, or if it had always been there, and I had failed to notice. There seemed to be many details that had escaped me, the little pinches of physical discomfort could be one. She had admitted herself, that she had learned many disguises, flashes of energy, like adrenaline, keeping her awake. A scuba helmet she could only wait to pull off of her head. Had she learned such trickery from the cunning folk? Or had it taken years of separation, of deep, skeletal change, for me to realise the helmet was not merely her face?

Even as I caught up to her, debating carefully whether or not to tap her on the shoulder, she ignored my presence in favour of the Machine, which buzzed down from the roof with a message. The voice seemed quieter out in the streets, like a furtive whisper. And in a crowd, the numerous calls overlapped, merging into a cacophonous mimicry of cicada song.

"Communication has been sent from Angel Uriel."

She threw her head back with a groan, hands braced on her hips. "Save it for later."

"Attention. You have forty-seven unread communications from Angel Uriel in storage."

"I know. Make it forty-eight."

"He's sent more," I noted, the least valuable observation to leave my mouth in some time. "Have you been reading them? Sorry, that's not really my business…"

"I stopped a while ago." She raised her palm to me, eyes still pointed upward. "But listen to this. Hey, Machine, you still there? Discard that last message for me."

A pause.

"Error. Unread files cannot be deleted." If I did not know better, I might have noted a deliberate tone of disdain in the Machine's selection of voices.

"So, I decided collecting them like bottle caps would be more fun." She gave a flourish of the hand, as if offering the answer to me on a dish. "Anyway, I'm going to head back. Go on, go hang out with Raphael for a bit."

"I'll walk with you."

"No, I'll be fine. If little telegrams are the worst an Angel can throw at me then, well, I've not much to worry about." She bent down to tighten one of the braces clenched around her right knee.

"I don't mind."

"I know. But I wouldn't call it a very warm welcome, being left alone with Gabriel and his breakfast."

I shook my head. "He probably just appreciates some normality."

"Normality, huh. You know what would be even more normal? You guys doing nothing together for, like, ten minutes, while the old woodland hag gives you the chance."

"He does like you." I broached the subject with far more sincerity than she was equipped to receive in her present state.

"Me? Come on now," she scoffed, turning away before I could stop her, brandishing a flurry of dark hair.

Gabriel eventually finished his fifth pot of coloured gelatine with a perfunctory sigh of satisfaction. Tucking his little metal spoon into a pocket, he rocked out of the low cushions into which his torso had been steadily sinking over the past hour.

"Duty calls," he chimed. "Don't be having too much fun without me, children."

Raphael stayed put, crossing his arms, seemingly unconscious of his own incredulous glower. He watched Gabriel gently pull the door closed behind him, seemingly aware the glass pane might pop out if treated too roughly.

"That guy used to seriously piss me off," he said, after a beat. "Still does, really, but more in the amicable way, where you want to slap him on the back, rather than kill him."

"Well, I for one am glad you chose not to kill my oldest friend."

"I wouldn't say it was a matter of choice. I knew full well that if I even tried, I'd only end up with a chunk of lead between my eyes, and a humorous quip over my dead body."

"So, it's fear, then."

"Ah, but am I wrong?"

"Probably not, I'll grant you that. If Gabriel wasn't on side, we'd all be doomed. Then again, the same could be said for you."

"…This really is it, huh? A blind spot, this dingy little hole in the backstreets. An oasis in the desert, or whatever."

"You don't believe me."

"No, I do. Of all of us, I always found you to be the worst liar. Besides, I don't think *three* of you together could be that stupid, as to spout all of your deepest and darkest secrets like that, not if you weren't sure of the truth."

"If that's what it takes to persuade, I suppose. Though, I'd appreciate if you didn't spread word that the Sovereign's favourite Angel is a transparent numbskull."

"Not what I said. You're just earnest, that's all. Whether that's a slight on your character or not is…I forget the turn of phrase, something about the eye of the beholder." He wandered over to the window, peering up through the smears as if waiting for an appointment, as if a message was due to appear in the narrow strip of sky, at any moment. I got that impression, perhaps, because it was the most composed look I had yet seen on his face. "So, what you're saying is, so long as we're inside these walls, the Machine can't see us?"

I stood up from the chair, shifted my feet a few times, then settled down on the arm cushion. "No. No-one can."

"And no-one can hear us."

"If you shut the door behind you, not a peep," I said to his back.

His shoulders skipped, a hint of a chuckle. He twisted around, attention back on me. "Not totally soundproofed, then."

"Well, no. I probably wouldn't hold a jazz party in here. Have you seen the state of that single-glaze?"

"I'll keep my voice down for you. Keep the dragon in here." His pale, jagged fist thudded into his abdomen.

"That's up to you, I guess," I said.

"Depends."

"On what?"

"On you. On Dominion." He shrugged. "Whether to leave all the difficult choices up to me, that sounds like your call."

"Not from three metres away it isn't." My body made a strange gesture, arm protruded in front of me, fingers splayed out, before retracting, the stalk of a sunflower, growing, blooming, and wilting on an instinct.

"Fair enough. And we're Angels, meaning no perusing our heads, our memories." His pupils kept flicking upward, like there was gravity working in his brain, pulling them away at any given opportunity. His mind wandered, a ball rolling around a circular maze, taking every which avenue around, only to return to the same point in the centre.

"Exactly. The only ones who know what's going on here, right now, are you and me."

"No eyes in the ceiling."

"None."

"Really. No numbers."

"No numbers, no judgement."

"At least until Gabriel reads it in the lines of your face, a frown here, a little twitch of your left brow there. And even then, it's only a matter of time before Lucifer tweezes a confession out of you. I wouldn't object to that. Dying in a whirl of black fire sounds like a pretty iconic way to go, especially if I've earned it." He laughed again, stifled. Restrained.

"Lucifer would never do anything like that. In fact, she'd laugh at the mere suggestion of it."

"How can you be so sure?"

"Because there is no one person I trust more than her."

Raphael turned still. I had not realised I was watching him breathe, not until the slow heave of his chest ceased. One doesn't expect to see a boat floating perfectly stationary on the water. The liquid body strains with the weight on its back, and the knowledge of the struggle fades from our thoughts, but without it, the world is wrong. He had taken off his jacket earlier, and I was so close to seeing the bones move under his white shirt. He started to pace again, only this time his eventual destination was evident. He crossed the room, stopping in front of the armchair, where he hooked his thumb under my chin and lifted up my face.

"Why?" he said.

And release. Smile. I had thought about this one before.

"Hell if I know. I think it's better that way. I can't list off ten reasons why she's good, or why she's safe. She's like us. That's just the truth."

"Yeah, I'm starting to get that. I'd love to argue with you, to press my finger into your chest and say 'I've thought it through, and this is why you're wrong.' But I can't. That's not what I want. So…"

"So what?"

"So—in theory, I could grab you by the waist, pull you under that counter and kiss you senseless, Michael."

"You could, if that's what you want."

It was peculiar, curious, to feel another Soul like that, without the stab of fear, the knife's slow, painful twist. Dominion enticed forth, like the lone occupant of a ragged house drawn to the window, by the warm, playful lick of a candle. I unbolted the gate and let it in with delight, the same pointed smile as he felt under his lips, when he flattened my hand into the wall above my head. I thought a wisp of hot smoke might burst from my mouth, when he drew out a deep, rumbling sigh with his teeth (or claws). He desired the control, as I understood. He enjoyed the idea of overthrowing the leader of the army of Angels, and the Angel-general liked to be overthrown. Still, it surprised us both, the great breaths of contentment, the arch of his spine, as his flesh gave way under my palms. We each tugged at the other like splinters, needles from a pincushion, every tiny wound a relief, rendering our hands softer, more limber, sinking us into the foundation, footprints in fresh concrete.

I felt as I had not in long, wearisome years of my life, a bright, constantly expanding sensation—freedom, perhaps—like a forgotten organ tucked at the back of my anatomy, tasting its first pump of blood. At the same time, I feared something, or perhaps I waited for it. Like the high of seeing Lucille step down from her mystical, earthy pedestal and smile on me with recognition, at once herself and a different being, who still knew and wanted me, it rushed around me and tied itself into tight knots. I felt so much, too much, such that it boiled under my skin and threatened to breach the bounds of a safe haven, leaking under the countless eyes of the Machine. Raphael knew it, too. He sympathised. Hence, the needlessly tentative, slightly embarrassed intimacy, all fumbling hands under rolled-up clothes and loose belt buckles, as though cotton and silk could contain it if brick and mortar failed. No-one, no man-made god would know the taste of the damp on his neck, the wrinkle that appeared on the bridge of his nose, when I pressed my knee up between his thighs.

He promised to make me senseless, and that much was true. I had to untangle myself from his arms, stare at his eyes—returning their mildly puzzled squint in kind—to remind myself of the man in front of me. I had forgotten his name, for a fleeting pause, a moment in between. Or, rather, I found myself on the verge of remembering. Raphael vanished, and something, some other word flickered in his place. It drifted away as quickly as it had approached, and then he kissed me again.

Some traitorous part of my conscience expected my number to have changed, whether positively or negatively I had no idea. I only knew that the Machine had taken it upon itself to judge before. My stomach recoiled, pressed itself against the wall of my abdomen, unable to bear the sight of my imagination, a spinning reel of countless possibilities, endless combinations of digits strung together. My body waited, prepared for me to have been terribly wrong about the Red Café, and for this to be how the news would be broken. How would I tell them? Like a father, incapable of looking his brethren in the eye as he confesses his debts. I gave in to temptation—today had made it so easy—

glanced down at my bare wrist, the skin still pulsing and flushed despite the brisk walk through cool, rain-damp air, and asked. The symbols painted themselves onto my palm instead. I felt their callous warmth building, growing like a flame inside my tight fist. The Machine forced me to open my hand to it, a beggar.

The number was written in deep blue, like spilled ink. Not a unit more, nor less.

It remained the same.

The eyes are blind.

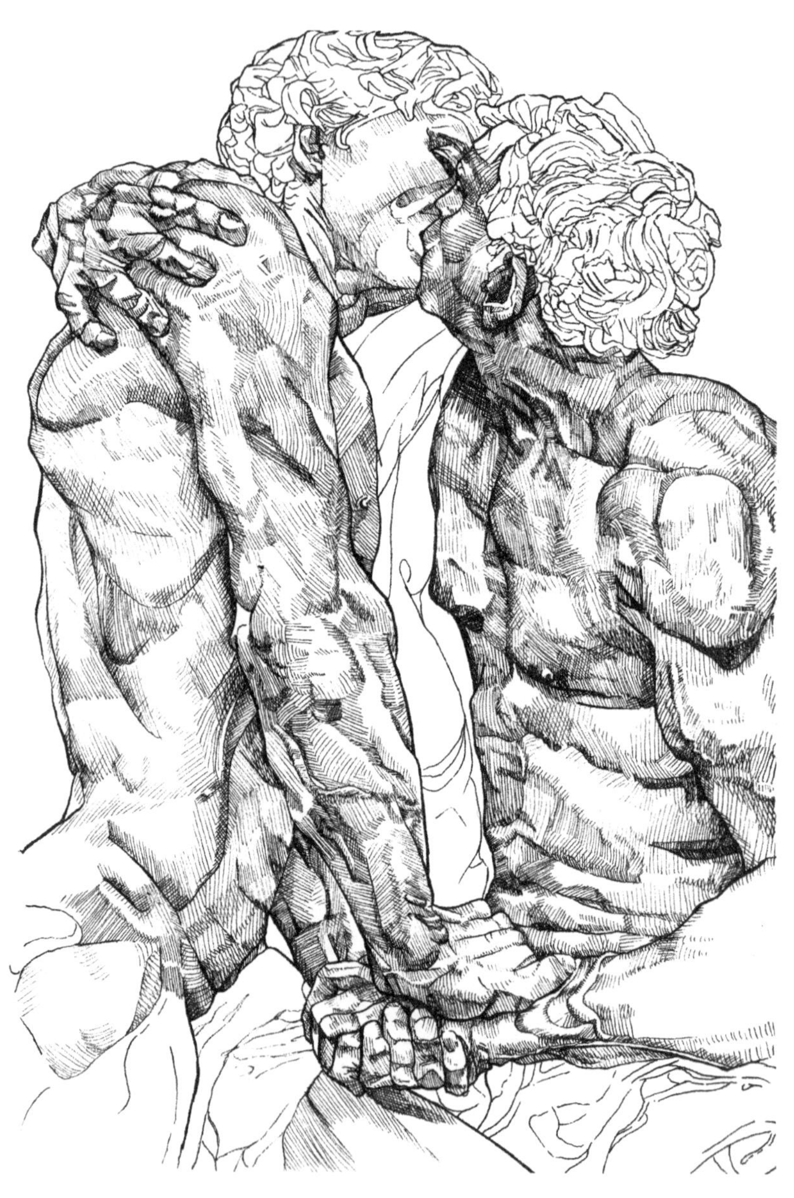

# Part 4: Incursion

**[Raphael]**

The Machine contracted me to work into the early hours of the day. Or night. My internal clock had shifted, reprogrammed; the turning of the earth affected me differently these days. I avoided exposing myself to direct sunlight for long periods, or my eye sockets streamed and ached like I had sustained a solid right hook to the face. I had the chance to see the sunrise, in the warmer months at least—a boon, for some. As for myself, I dealt with fire so often that the burning ball of gas in the sky did little for me. I prowled the quietest hours like some sort of nocturnal beast. Then again, I had never experienced true darkness. Lamps and the odd lonely window bent their orange glow onto most streets, warming the cold stone like old, stewing coals. After so long, the mind does, thankfully, stop finding eyes in those radiant orbs. I seemed a poor choice of candidate. Those outsider spies foolish enough to attempt entry under cover of the night were doomed to suffer the loudest, most incendiary and unsightly execution of the lot. Easy pickings. More residents should be shocked awake by the noise, really. After many shifts, many unpleasant deaths, I could only make guesses. Hiding my work under the temporal tablecloth prevented too many direct witnesses to my mess, too much trauma going unchecked. Instead, the Machine could keep the doses regulated, the occasional controlled drip. A rude awakening here and there generally proved sufficient to discourage the masses from secretiveness. Shortly after the Angels' ascension, one especially desperate lad thought himself quite conniving, took to burglary. Much to be learned from his sacrifice. He thought the reduced visibility might aid him, ill-expecting that the Machine's lens functioned nothing like a human's pathetic equipment. I saw the consequences of his crime first-hand, on my hands. It was my job to drag his body out from where he had slumped over the windowsill like a sack of flour. The Machine could have stopped his heart beating at any moment, but wanted to make a spectacle of him, I could only assume. I had heard of no such cases since.

I had wasted away a good part of this cycle idly working to scrape a persistent burgundy stain from the cuff of my jacket. Some foul blend of bodily fluids that didn't much bear thinking about. My legs did not want to stand stationary, almost entirely numb with nervous energy, as though injected with raw glucose. My body had only recently been put through a number of agreeable sensations in rapid succession, and now refused to settle for any lesser treatment. I occupied my muscles by attempting to contrive a route through the damper back-alleys of the industrial cluster not yet committed to memory, like a giant, boring game of spot-the-difference. The buildings, tucked out of sight behind a block of prettier residential apartments, vibrated with the constant, barely audible hum of sleepless ventilation systems. The slight disturbance led me to only narrowly avoid wandering into the anomaly manifesting before me. A narrow section of the street tilted, the straight lines of the paving stones bent like elastic, tension building. A black monolith, blurred at the edges, the subtle curl of a scythe, complete with metallic glint.

I leaned against the outside wall of the nearest building. A stocky man, with a familiar stomping gait, hurried down the front step, and off in the opposite direction, with an unashamed glance over his shoulder. Either he had a lazy eye, or he was rolling it into the back of his head at the sight of us. I thought might have been a butcher, at first, looking at the leathery vest he lifted from his shoulders. He let the door fall shut behind him. Evidently, men like him frequently made such blustering, huffy exits, since they had installed an anachronistic-looking soft closer on the thing. Out with the draught came a distinct aroma of bleach. I had taken refuge in front of the clean-up crew's office. I sensed a hint of irony in that fact, though I could not quite grasp it. And I had been caught.

"Raphael."

"Uriel."

His tone, categorically, did not invoke a neutral greeting (more of an accusation, the detective addressing the culprit in a novel's final scene), but I replied assuming the best of him. Perhaps I could throw him off, discomfit him into walking on by. Fruitless, naturally. My fellow Angel had a particular flair for pantomime dramatics, but he did not tend to have his Soul ferry him around for no reason at all. It seemed worth a try at the time; I was in no mood for a lecture.

"I know you've been gallivanting with Lucifer's harem. You were at that old, rotting café. The place smells of decay, of death. I suppose that's why she feels at home there. Does it deceive you into thinking you're getting away with something?"

"No-one's asking you to look, if you find it so repellent. Sure, I'm taking the opportunity to sniff around. Why does it matter to you?"

"I'm sure you know why. You know your job. I am also aware you experience…intrusive inclinations. From an outsider's perspective, it appears as though you are giving in. Can you blame me for having concerns?"

"I'm here, doing my daily duty like a good little boy. The Machine tells me to stand here, I'll stand here. It tells me to walk over there, I'll walk. It tells me to jump, I ask, 'How high?' I get my eight hours, eat my greens, tear a few still-beating hearts out of bare chests and incinerate the corpses, all as I'm told. Who I gallivant with in what free time I get, as far as I can see, isn't your business. It might do you good to take a little more interest in your new sister. Not often that an Angel rises from the grave. Or are you jealous?"

I could only wait to find out if he had called my bluff.

"Michael must have pulled some impressive veil over your eyes. I don't see how else you could fail to see that they are the enemy here. They are the bad guys, not us."

"Us? Come on, don't start playing around with me now, acting up as if I was important. This is just like chopping the tail off a lizard; you'll grow another one. No need to have a paddy."

A bellowing laugh constantly threatened to bubble to the surface as I spoke. Hearing his haughty presumptions regarding my private life only increased the temptation to recount the sultry details of exactly the kind of recreation Michael and I had indulged in. Alas, I found myself doggedly protective of certain secrets. It had, after all, been so long since I had been allowed to possess any. I imagined this was how children felt, giddily attending school after a birthday, having received the latest, most fashionable gift everyone hankered after.

Uriel tutted. "I'm not trying to charm you; I'm trying to reason with you, since you're the only man left with a shred of brain matter bouncing around in his skull. You want to drink tea with four sugar cubes and an extra shot of caffeine every morning? Fine. You want to overload on prescription meds or go on nature walks out in the arsenic-infested wasteland, we can make that happen."

It seemed I had rubbed him the wrong way. Perfect.

"This is your pitch? You're going to come at me with that? Fucking hell, it's probably better that you're not trying to be my friend."

"They are taking an entire world, a living thing that can be tweaked and nurtured and made better, and instead they're going to kill it."

My own saliva suddenly tasted bitter, as though growing a patch of mould behind my teeth. I resisted the urge to gob it out onto his shoes.

"The only people who had the power to 'tweak' anything are both dead," I snapped, so abruptly I bit the end of my own tongue, drawing a drop of blood, a sacrifice upon the Smiths' altar. "The Machine murdered them. Who exactly is going to fix this shithole now, Uriel—you?"

"You have no idea—"

"Ah, of course. Thanks, but I'll pass."

"I have done nothing but protect this place. That's why the Machine chose me."

"For who?"

"What?" he choked, shaking his head at me, incredulous, like my question had adopted new meaning overnight, to which one which no-one had bothered to make him privy.

"You heard me. Protected it for who? You've tortured people to get what you want. You've done it before, and you'll try it again. Fuck, man, you'll probably get away with it, too."

Moving my back away from the wall was a mistake on my part. A cold thrash of air in my eyes forced me to blink. He vanished. The blank space behind me moaned, gave a high-pitched wail, then was smothered. I felt his presence, though I couldn't see him. The unnatural way he parted the world's atoms, shoved and sucked particles out of his path, space bloated with substance, rippled and tore holes in its fabric to accommodate him. Warm breath on my cheek, his mouth mere centimetres from my face.

"You don't even know what torture is."

"I'm not listening to this anymore. Got shit to do, places to be. All I'll say is you'd better pray for the Machine to jump down from the heavens and start protecting *you*."

I swivelled around, hands pushing deeper into my pockets, fists so tight my fingernails, chewed until stunted and soft, left pink crescent-moons in my palms. Moving ever so slowly, I twisted my shoulders, formed an arched shape with my body, my best imitation of a circling hound, given the limiting circumstances. I felt glad for my extra half-head of height over the other man; his eyes drew level with my teeth.

"Is that supposed to be a threat?" he chided.

"Not necessarily, but since you asked…you're a dead man walking, Uriel."

My chest ached as if it had not gasped for breath in minutes, as if a giant's hands had wrapped around my ribcage and squeezed until the bones bent. I hoped the surveillance would find something for me to kill this shift. I could let it sink its claws into my skin first, before I twisted its head off of its neck.

**[Lucifer]**

Footsteps entered the hall behind me. I spun around. It was only Rei, dancing brazenly up the aisle, a leather-bound package hugged to her chest. She smiled upon being noticed.

"You really know how to find people in this place, huh?" I said.

"That is basically my job, yes. All day, every day."

"I was being followed before I got here. A fresh-faced little convoy, looked as though they were out for groceries, but then they pursued me down several streets in a row. You don't happen to have a network of amateur spies reporting to you? If so, I have a few tips they might use to improve on their subtlety."

"No, I don't. I work alone most of the time." She took the jibe very literally, and shrunk back a little, as though wary to infer anything more.

"Apologies. That was probably a bit much on my part."

"You'll have to forgive the less worldly city dwellers," she said. "They've never really seen anyone like you before." My immediate instinct was to question which part of my appearance, exactly, could be so unusual to these unseasoned civilians, with an added analogy about a bear in a cage. But I refrained, squeezing the tirade down between my tonsils. Rei seemed to sense the stilted tension. "A gorgeous piece, isn't it?" She gestured before us, to the fresco. "Do you know much about it?"

I replied, "Shamefully little, I'm afraid. I recall that it was painted by Lily Glenn, some century-and-a-half ago, and that one vocal bunch of killjoys called it vandalism."

"Oh yes, it was a bit of a covert operation, which is particularly impressive, considering this is probably the largest work she ever produced. This wall took Glenn two years of straight effort to complete."

"I just remembered, there is one other thing. There was an inkling, wasn't there, a long while back, that the Soulless, the wolf…" I pointed to the focal centre of the scene. "…and this guy, pale hair on the left, were meant to represent the same person?"

"There was indeed, as you say, an inkling. The thinking was that this wolf was a shapeshifter, and since we have records of the Souls, or lack of, belonging to most of the soldiers, this Soul—as manifested here—would have to be the odd one out, if you will."

"What about the hand on its head?" Looking closely at the hound, I noticed that the young man depicted adjacent, with the dark features, rested his right hand between its ears. This was not a restraining gesture, however, like that of a man commanding his own Soul. Instead, it was almost an embrace, a comforting motion. The brushwork recreating the fur between his fingers was meticulously delicate—soft. "This is a Hughes sibling, the elder of two brothers, right?"

"Exactly, the potential relationship there presents another promising line of inquiry."

"I think it's humiliating," I snapped, now in the mood to speak my mind, "how little we understand about all these people. Take those two, Rayne and the younger Hughes; we have the archive containing their Souls—meaning, the weapons they fought with—a rough idea where they came from, and that's it. And yet we're expected to worship them like…like what? Gods? Parents? Martyrs?"

"Mrs Smith felt very similarly to you," Rei answered, knowingly. "She was trawling through records, military documents, diaries, trying to figure it out, until the day she…"

"Yes, I know. The cunning folk would send all manners of material back to assist her in her research. As for me, I spent hours searching for traces of them in the West, for what good it did."

"Well, it's not surprising, that you would feel so drawn to them." She fidgeted on the spot, shifting her weight as if the object had suddenly grown heavy in her arms. "I can't speak for anyone else, but Mrs Smith told me three things about you before her termination: the name of your Soul, that you were probably the one girl in contention for the Angel Programme, which she begrudged terribly, and that she was writing about you." She untied the leather case she carried with swift circular movements, and out of it pulled a dilapidated book, blank, presumably a notebook. "In here, mostly."

I took the artefact in just the same manner as she passed it to me, very gently, as though its pages would disintegrate at the slightest indication of eagerness. The cover was slowly detaching at the spine, the sound of tearing emanating from every page turn. Loose cuttings and scrap paper threatened to spill out at regular intervals, sometimes punctuated by a fraying dog-ear in the upper corner.

"Your birth name isn't in there anywhere. Believe me, I have searched through more than once. I suppose Smith was more forward-thinking than to write down such a thing."

"It was a mistake to get my hopes up, really." I gave a wry smirk and a shrug.

"This should interest you, though." She indicated a page early in the collection, showing a rough graph, full of branching lines and notes in pencil reading 'maybe' and 'query dates'. "It's a family tree. Much of this is preliminary work, I think, so take it with a pinch of salt. These groups down here are a muddle." She was right, towards the bottom of the page, the 'graph' devolved into frustrated mess of deletions, correctional arrows and solitary items, floating without any tether to the overall shape. Her voice sped up exponentially, like she was sprinting through the explanation to stop the conclusion running away. "See up here, though? These annotations, like 'cousins' here, and 'great-uncle', 'once removed', these are in relation to you! And if we follow this line, from one I. Hughes, up to Theodore, it appears that Eris is your…hold on." She started counting on her fingers, mumbling under her breath, quickly replaced her hands under the book when she noticed it vibrating and about to drop between my wrists. "Great-great-grandmother," she suggested, her tone slightly sceptical.

I could feel the revelation oozing out from Smith's dark, blocky writing of 'ADOPTION' next to Theodore, my great-grandfather's name. It simmered, bulging into a thick, rolling boil from my chest into my head. When I lifted my gaze to their portraits, whether precisely accurate or not, the faces of Gaius and Eris were seen anew, benevolent in their tactile nature. "What does the letter I stand for?" I asked, unsure whether my numb lips and flaccid tongue could form the words properly.

"As in your mother's. I'm sorry, but I have no clue. There's no trace of your father, either."

"That's okay," I said, breathing a little of the tension out of my chest, and turned back to the pages, specifically, the right-hand leaf. I took a few long, quiet moments of turning it to various angles to decipher its meaning. The heavy, rigid lines of the tree had encroached upon it towards the foot of the paper, but underneath, a tangle of faded pencil marks appeared to loosely depict the picture before us, rotated and shrunk down like a woollen jumper thrown in a hot dryer. For all of her other competencies, Mrs Smith had been no fine artist, bless her heart, and her sketch was only barely legible with the original staring me down for comparison. What intrigued me, however, were her labels, some of them underlined with several firm strokes as if to signal their importance.

"Fenrir Hughes…what a name, huh?"

"Really?" Rei yelped. She had followed the movement of my finger tracing the drawing, and scurried behind me, reappearing at my left, so as to position her face as close to the pale-haired figure as possible. "How in the world did she know that?"

I smiled watching her flabbergasted reaction. "More to the point, how come we haven't figured it out already?" I gestured to the prominent shape of the wolf, its ashen body curled protectively around the dark-haired boy—I glanced to the sketch for his name: Benjamin—shielding him, each delicately painted hair taking up colour from the burning sky.

"That's quite the family you've got there," she mused, almost at a whisper.

I folded the tome shut and offered it at arm's length. "Here. You should take this back, keep it safe just as you have been doing."

She shook her head, but lifted it out of my grip and slipped it back into the protective case all the same. "You don't want it?"

"It doesn't matter if I do. We will be watched from the moment we exit this room. The last gift you delivered to me ended up lost. And this one is far more important."

"The last gift…? You mean the blade. You lost it?"

"Not on purpose, obviously."

"Then, in that scuffle the other day?"

"No, I don't think so. I'd have noticed. It's as though I went to sleep one evening, woke up, and it was gone. Disappeared. So you see. You see why I'm wary. That information must leave the hall in the same hands it entered with. It stays with you."

"I suppose you're not wrong." She deflated a little, wrapping her body around the shape of her bag. "Will you be leaving soon?"

"I probably should, before I run into someone I'd be less happy to see."

"Then I will run on ahead. That shouldn't raise too many eyebrows, I don't imagine." She was already trotting down the steps, lifting her knees up like a marching band, as if to let off excess steam.

Once she was nearing the portal, I called out, my voice elevated much too loud by the empty roof. "Rei." She turned. "Thank you, for thinking of me. It's a pretty risky thing to do."

She bowed her head, in acknowledgement of the fact, before she darted out into the street, on her way home, I hoped.

It was a part, a portion. A taste. I knew myself better perhaps than I ever had before. I carried those faces, their names, with me out of the hall. A father, a mother. I wanted the rest, and so wandered as if I might stumble upon it under my feet, like a stone. Letters floated before me, for me to prod and tease at, but with no memory to hold them they fell away from me into nothing. B…M…F…L. I thought I might cry. And I was delighted, in the delicious knowledge that the Machine could hear none of this. I was ravenous for thought, imagination, freedom. She could restrain my old self, drown her in tar and code. The eyes watching me only knew her, and the appendages growing from her skull. A big, red sticker slapped across my head. Hello, my name is: Lucifer. Or Lucille, maybe, if they were feeling magnanimous. They did not know any better. If I were to be truthful, I was barely any better. Hughes, Hughes. I must cling to it, I reminded myself. This was very important. Hughes. I could saunter around the body of this dying city, calling myself Eris Hughes, and no-one would know but me. No-one would ever believe it, not even me.

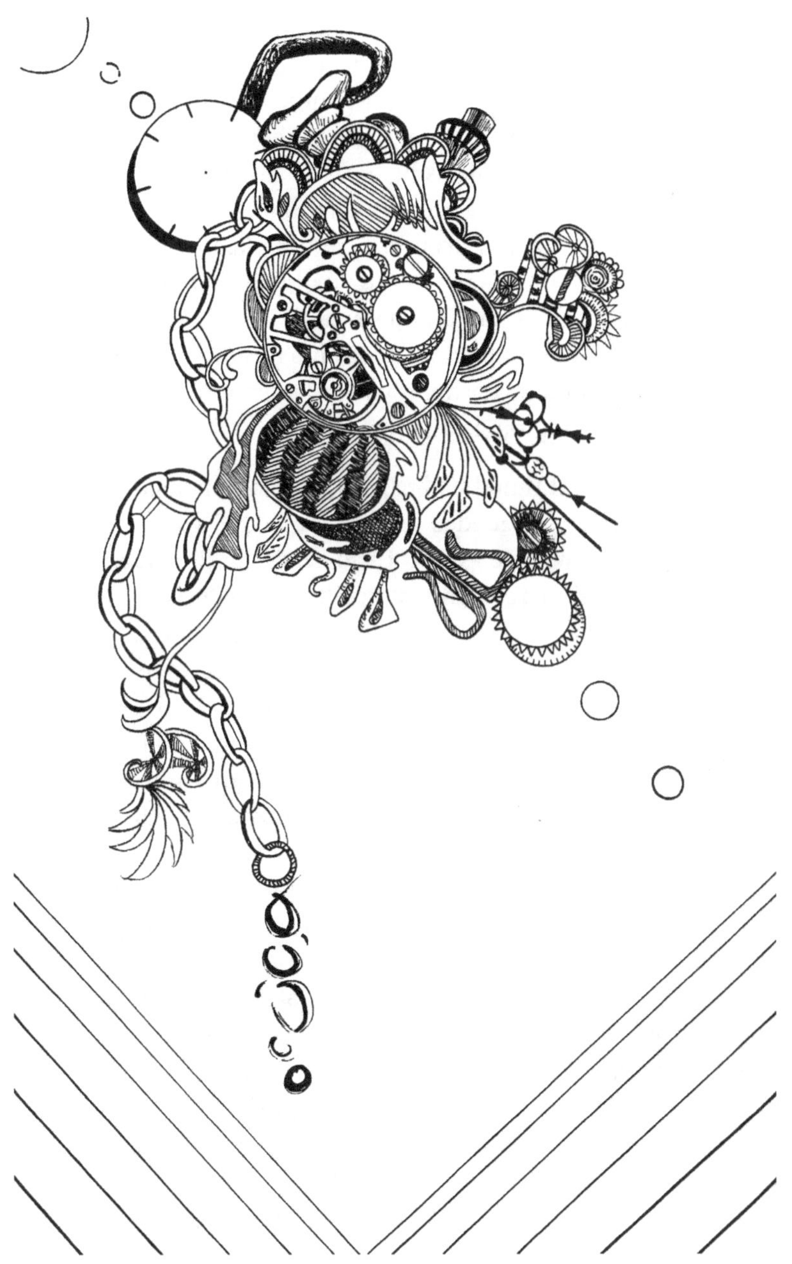

**[Raphael]**

I knew I had been sleeping too well the past couple of days. Evidently, I was officially ousted from Uriel's inner circle, since, on previous occasions, he would at least wait until I had drunk up a good six hours of rest before calling a summit. Whether or not I had full consciousness at my disposal, it no longer mattered. Now he had free rein to spite me as his fickle inclination pleased. For instance, the man knew full well my quarters lay, at minimum, a fifteen-minute trek from the central plaza. The only human capable of making the trip in five would possibly be one on horseback or, more importantly, one with Uriel's Soul at his disposal. Most likely, he wanted to witness me turning up late, suit bedraggled, stumbling over my own feet, hair stood on end with sweat. I would grant him a stiff jog, at most.

I could not recall the last time I had experienced weather such as that morning. The early sun tended to blast me in the worst way, the light taking on a raw, pale aspect. I had heard certain metals could be forced to such fierce temperatures that they turned white with terrible heat. It appeared the sun, having handed over its baton to its milder colleague, the moon, and lain down to recuperate under the horizon, recovered the energy to fulfil such a prophecy. Mercifully, perhaps, I found the brightness diluted by a thick veil of cloud. However, said clouds had grown so heavy with their own, damp weight, they had sunk downward, like an abandoned shipwreck mooring on the ocean floor. The result was a fog so thick it seemed to have tactile substance. It glued my fingertips together like wax but poured into my lungs like the juice of berries, with a similar, noticeably sweet flavour. I expected, given the time, to run into Lucifer at some stage upon my journey; from what I had observed, she tended to stick mostly to a fixed orbit around the city centre. With the cool, translucent plasma blurring my vision, though, I should not have been surprised to miss her dark silhouette drifting amongst the fog. She already made little sound as she walked in regular conditions, without such a thick cushion absorbing the creaking of her feet.

I suddenly grew restless, my body turning with the flow of the mist, an anticlockwise rotation which accelerated before I could catch up to it. After all, if Lucifer could hide only steps ahead of me (still no sign of her), blending into the landscape, the moisture mixing colours together like watercolours, so could anyone else.

"Wait."

An arm sprung out from behind a lamppost, unfolding in front of me, blockading the alleyway. I looked down as it bumped firmly against my chest; a black sleeve, rolled up to the elbow, the arm was attached to Gabriel. I dipped my face, pressing a hand over the molten hot, dry patch of scaly skin flaking from my neck. It itched and throbbed, like ten layers of eczema. Gabriel leaned his back against the flawless, painted surface of the iron pole, gazing pensively into space, but flicked a glance over for barely a second.

"Sorry," he mumbled. "Didn't mean to startle you."

His attention was directed roughly in the direction of the Hall, but appeared, in that moment, to be more tuned in to Michael, a little further down the path. The copper-haired man paced gingerly from kerb to kerb. He had his weapon turning in his hands, fully extended, and would occasionally halt, tap the spearhead down onto the pavement, before flipping it back upright and resuming his slow amble. We were not hiding, so it seemed; we were waiting, as though in triage.

"Don't just stand there. I know the message didn't literally say 'come in', but honestly, have some initiative."

In the second I wasted watching Michael chew on his bottom lip, Uriel had appeared before the entrance, framed artfully by the heater-shaped doorway at the top of the steps, like a cake-topper. My chest shrank, those sharp teeth we call ribs closing in and boring into the taut, delicate membrane stuffing my insides. He could have sauntered out of the door, as he seemed to suggest. Alternatively, he could have jumped instantly from almost anywhere he pleased. There was no method for telling where he had been, waiting to speak. Michael turned and nodded, indicating that it was acceptable for us to approach. Lucifer was missing.

They had noticed, too. Gabriel stayed glued to Uriel as he marched on before us, only occasionally screwing his eyelids shut in long blinks, trying to telepathically commune with his Soul, like it was some sort of echolocation device. In that moment, I almost believed that he could, that Lucifer somehow mattered enough to become a speck on his Soul's infinitesimal map of the world. But she did not, and he followed on obediently, making it look painful. Michael, on the other hand, swayed from side to side, constantly slowing his walk then bounding ahead of me again, ferreting through every shadow for a sign of her. I tried to catch his attention, hoping that the wrinkled expression on my face read something like the words I wanted to say. Listen Michael, I think I fucked up. I fucked up really bad. I think something horrible is happening. I'm sorry. I know how much you love her. Don't look like that, so frightened and frail. Maybe she is still alive.

"I don't suppose you'd care to explain?" Michael panted.

"Call it a group conference or…a business meeting." Uriel replied.

He took to his favourite path, the well-trodden line suggested, almost goaded by the building's long hypnotic tongue, straight through the middle. I weaved my way along the right, east-facing edge, sidestepping around pillars adorned with pink and white bouquets, tall, gold-plated candelabras, and knocking my shoulder against a bust of Lord Wallis the Third. His was smaller and much less shiny than the rest, making him easy to miss in the swaying waters of a nervous fit. He must have done something terrible too, to upset the monarch that much—perhaps digging up a few of the royal topiaries. Gabriel had opted to stroll quietly down the west side, while Michael darted between a pair of pews, holding on to the back panel facing him, as if the carved oak and bronze could protect him like a scutum. Then Uriel stopped. He held up one hand beside his face, finger pointed to the ceiling, and the three of us halted, stood to attention like we were bows leaping off of violin strings and leaving the theatre in silence.

"There's a certain security in numbers, a kind of…insurance. Traitors and imposters don't last very long in a tight group. Crafty as a scavenging crow may be, it has only two options once the wolves arrive: flee to the treetops, or have its skinny little neck snapped between jealous jaws. The traitorous crow would sooner be burned, gouged or eviscerated before it could infiltrate their pack. That's the Sovereign's reason for choosing five Angels; not because he needs that amount of power, but to nip poison in the bud before it spreads."

Gabriel sighed. The sound simmered up to the ceiling. "So that's why you had us brought here, to gloat?" he retorted. He dragged his hand down over his face, then flicked it into the air, like wiping mud off his skin.

Michael snapped. "If you're so proud of it, why don't you just go ahead and tell us what you've done?"

"Me? I haven't done a thing. What, am I therefore your enemy because I tell you the truth? You want to know the other lesson I learned from our ancestors?" His hand closed around the golden crown curled through his hair. "Always aim for the head."

The fingers and nails of my left hand were crushing into the meat of my right, I noted only when the skin turned strangely cold underneath. I hoped Uriel had the audacity to leave before the rest of us, meaning I was free to hide from him behind my skin, frozen in a stiff, stoic, statuesque pose. On the flipside, the dragon wailed in my throat, for one of the many pairs of hands behind to reach out of that painting and strangle him.

He did finally, after taking a moment too long to soak in his own pride, descend from his stage and glide by the three of us. He smiled eagerly at me as he passed, as if urging me on, poking me in gut from across the room. So, I remained perfectly still until I saw the back of him disappear into thin air. Michael took a little more initiative. He waited with faux patience for the ideal opportunity. Then, his hand shot out from behind his back, palm colliding with Uriel's chest. His Soul seemed to radiate off of him as his fingers closed like talons around the latter's shirt. Though I could not speak for Gabriel, I felt as though our own abilities had been nullified as well, by some percolating extension.

I could only hear his whispers thanks to the hall's amplifying acoustics. "Where is she?" he said.

Uriel tutted, raised his hands above his shoulders in ambivalence. "What, Lucifer? How should I know?" A pause, and then his tone dropped, no longer amused. "What are you going to do, impale me on your clothes prop because you've all lost your girlfriend?"

Rich, coming from him.

"Oh, trust me, I wouldn't need the polearm."

An incredulous laugh rang out. "I say, I really can tell what you see in him, Raphael. He can look quite terrifying when he really tries!" My wrists began to tremble violently.

"Why is it that you never make such provocative jibes toward me?" Gabriel swiftly intervened. "Could it be, Uriel, that you are truly, genuinely afraid? I suppose you could call it a strategic decision; I prefer to see it as cowardice." He made a point of absently picking at debris under his fingernails as he spoke.

"Might I take that to be an invitation? You're in luck. I'm free from 1500 hours—appointment only."

Michael ripped his hand away from Uriel and stepped away from him in disgust.

"Get out," he spat.

At least he obliged us on that front. "Fair enough. I don't know about you boys, but I for one have more important places to be." He skipped by the last pew and dispersed into a vanishing cluster of particulates.

## [Lucifer]

A white, barren landscape expanded outward on all sides of me, tilting steadily upward into an unviewable distance, as though I were stranded at the bottom of a bowl. The deep, sandy ground into which my feet sunk was frigid, and yet the air above it rippled and swelled as if sweltering. The only other object in this freezing wasteland was a stone building some several hundred yards in front of me, square, stout and poor company for a lone living creature. It was not a silent monument, however. From somewhere inside, echoing out from a vast, dark chasm in its belly, it spoke, called out to me in a low, sleepy murmur. I resisted walking towards the building precisely because of this, obstinately refusing to comply with such soothing enticements.

I turned around, started wading in the other direction instead, towards what appeared to be a shadow descending over the lip of the horizon. The ground gulped under me with a subtle hiss, trying to trap my shoes in its orifices, and pull them off of my feet. However, only three arduous steps into my journey, the small blotch atomised like water droplets into a growing, growing horde of many black spots. As they spread, they accelerated, and sprouted limbs, and feathers. All of them hurtled down-slope, toward me; they could see me. I ran—I ran—I ran, not fast enough. They were fast, so fast, on top of me. Their shrieks turned to speech, their beaks into pointed teeth. They sliced the fat on my cheeks and neck, tried to pull out my fingernails, crush my bones under their tongues.

"Come back here," they said. "Please, don't go. Why won't you pay attention? Don't lie to yourself like this. You're not even trying to understand how I feel. My feelings. My feelings for you. I would do anything for you. You just have to do this for me. Where did you go, love? I'll give you time, some more time, all the time I have to. I know that's what you need. You're just a little uncomfortable right now, that's all. I understand. I, too, am sick. That's why I want you to do this for me. I know it makes you strange, fuzzy, poorly." Their bodies blended with the static walls, stirring together into a dark, unsteady mass. My shoulder cracked against the stone threshold as I fell inside. "Come here. You can't hide from me. I am behind you all the way. Come on. Come for me." Ensconced in the blackness, even there I was not safe. The birds kept flying, piling into the archway, tangling together into one huge, screaming beast with countless scrambling talons reaching inside, piercing its own eyes in its relentless determination. The only light came in narrow strips, through leaks in the roof above me. One of them somehow managed to squirm free. It fell onto the floor with a dull thud, a mangled, matted abomination with only half a face, which writhed pathetically on the ground for a few seconds before it died. "Burn it. Burn it all down. Jump into the fire, love. Kill it. Kill it. Take it. There is no escape."

I backed away from the deafening noise, reverberating around the cramped space, my hands clutching at my ears, my eyes transfixed by the corpse. My feet shuffled insentiently, until my heels hit a wall. It emitted a hollow, knocking sound, so I reached out one set of hands to search the wooden, splintered surface for an opening, moulded myself into it, but found nothing promising. Glancing over my shoulder for a moment, I saw a mock imitation of an oak door, including decorative panelling, but nothing like a handle. My remaining options were to climb and attempt to tear out a large enough opening in the ceiling— hardly feasible for one of my strength and lack of balance—or find out what was on the other side. So I slammed my body into the wall, hit it, kicked it, yelled at it, until there were yawning holes in my boots, my knuckles, and the wooden barricade.

Slithers of wood combed through my hair, fingered at my scalp as I crawled into what appeared to be a narrow tunnel. My hands landed upon a rough carpet, like sandpaper which, when I pushed up onto my feet, I recognised as a welcome mat. Flipped upside down, in faded black text and worn edges, was written the whimsical line: *Wipe Your Paws*.

Before me, what I had thought to be a crawlspace barely large enough for my body now extended up and out into a hallway—still a few centimetres too cramped and far too long. The entire room was lit, rather feebly, by a tin gas-lamp, seemingly abandoned on the floor, halfway along the corridor. This was not an uncommon accident to be made, apparently. The sour stench had leached into the wallpaper. Within the yellowish areole of light, dust could be observed, dropping infinitesimally onto every visible surface. Doorknobs and picture frames were preserved in stale grey chrysalises. Inside those frames, displaced in time, was the same child, surrounding me on both sides. The closest photograph showed a baby, chubby and pink-faced, whinging from the comfort of a bassinet. A trick of slow shutter speed, perhaps, but the infant appeared to have one or two excess limbs flailing around. Another showed the girl, or some of her, anyway. She seemed to be laughing, her arms and bulbous head bobbing above the surface of a shallow river. The same girl, a foot or so taller, then stood over a wooden table, her weak little shoulders rounded with grit and resolve. Looking closer at the gelatinous pile in her hands, I concluded she was attempting to gut a fish. In the last picture I dared to glance at, she had reached the peak of some high precipice, peering curiously over the cliff's jagged edge, her clean dress floating, wraithlike, behind her.

At this stage I had come across the first door to my left. Upon electing simply to submit myself to chance, I curled my hand around the handle, sticky residue gluing to folds in my skin, and opened it. A solid, brick wall stared me in the face. I tutted, chastising myself for expecting otherwise. I had, of course, yet to surmise what this cold monolith was supposed to be, let alone what it had actually become. I ultimately chose to play along with the childish architect, opening every door on either side in quick succession, until I happened to stumble across the correct answer, provided one existed at all. As soon as I began to settle into the tedious process of coating my hands in grease and shit to no avail, one threshold yielded a new result. Smeared on the brickwork, in some slick, oily substance, a primitively drawn face smiled out at me, renewing the appropriate feeling of panic and disgust in my chest. My tongue tasted of rust.

"Very clever."

I slammed the door.

The resulting tremor must have caused a disturbance since, in the following moment, I heard a latch turn at the far end of the hallway. The final door, the head of the table, the one face that had been blankly looming, watching, all this time. Out emerged two pairs of mousy, plush feet. I flattened myself against the wall, a futile attempt to protect myself. Wholly unnecessarily too, given the wiry-looking canine, back hunched and claws scratching against the floorboards, trotted by without so much as an acknowledgement. Perhaps the beast was blind; I could not catch sight of her eyes. She flatted her large, round ears to her head and skipped through the small, screaming hole I had created in my wake. She had left the door hanging open. A mistake, perhaps. I headed through the gap in haste, my head heavy with shame, treating this opportunity as the only one I would be given. I grabbed the doorknob and immediately jammed it closed behind me without a shred of remorse. Coward. The cruel ringing in my ears could easily be mistaken as its own voice.

"You're here!" I heard.

But where was here, exactly? Somewhere new. Deeper. The room was certainly dressed for the part. A large, luxurious rug covered most of terracotta tiled floor, presumably to guard against the cold. The wallpaper was garish, bright green and covered in fleurs-de-lis, bulging out with damp in the most conspicuous places. My face wrinkled involuntarily into a grimace. The odour was unlike anything I had experienced prior, rather like cracking a rotten egg, but somehow meatier, and wetter. The source was obvious. A long dining table was laid extravagantly, all chairs empty and tucked neatly in place, the centrepiece. Silver platters and serving bowls remained filled with rotten, indescribable food, and coated in a furry, muscose patina for their trouble. All least some of the offering was raw, bleeding putrid juices onto the cotton tablecloth. Whatever organisms that had busied themselves decomposing this mess must have been microscopic. The only sign of life I could see was a large house spider, drowned, floating in a glass of sour wine, its legs curled into its body.

I heard a voice in the ringing again. "You're late."

"Yeah, no shit."

"Well, beggars can't be choosers. Especially when said beggar is late," it replied.

It replied. I froze, my knuckles turning to an osseous white as I gripped a chair.

"Anyways, it's your loss," it continued. "No time to stop now; I'm trying to save you."

"What?"

"Four spaces to your right, there's a knife, a real one. You'd best take it."

"Why?"

"Quickly, now."

"Why?" I repeated through gritted teeth.

"There's a monster coming for you. It's there, in the room with you, right now. I don't think you've noticed it yet. Pick up the knife and stab straight in its eye; that's the only way you're getting out of here."

I looked to my right. Sure enough, balanced on a plate, a dagger lay, suspiciously untainted. The handle was wooden, engraved from the feel of it in my hand; I did not stop to inspect it.

"Chop chop," the voice sang, evidently pleased with its own unsavoury joke.

I turned around on the spot, a full, painstaking revolution, and though the glow from the fireplace was pathetic, it seemed clear I had not missed any intruders concealed in one of the room's eight corners. My head rotated a knot faster than my shoulders, floating away from my neck almost like a greased screw. I stumbled towards a wall, saving myself the minor indignity of toppling over, and began to tear at the paper with the blade. There was nothing underneath, but a coat of plaster being steadily devoured by black mould. I crouched low to the ground, still dragging the wallpaper between my fingers. On all fours, I crawled back to the table, flipping over chairs to claw at the cloth in clattering fury. Once again, there was nothing under there. I raised my arms above my head, heaved myself up. I had stopped breathing.

"Come on now. You're better than this," the voice squirmed its way back. "You're clever. Outside the box. And you're running out of time. No point snarling at me dear, I'm only trying to save you."

I looked again. There was, indeed, no monster under the dining table, only a dark swipe stain on the rug, still slightly tacky to touch. Following the drag mark out from the shadows, it led into the burning coals of the fireplace. Impossible, I could see only ash and kindling amongst the flames. The mantlepiece, even, was littered with half-depleted candles and burnt matches. But the painting above it, which was hung on a wall too wide in a frame too thin, I had only acknowledged in passing before. What had appeared to be an abstract bundle of jagged shapes now took form before my eyes. Thick, gauche brushstrokes represented an animal, a dog. I finally recognised this as the dumb, skeletal creature which had passed me in the hallway. Here, she was depicted over the backdrop of a fallen village, her legs all contorted towards her spotted rump, jaw hanging wide and some thick liquid rising out of her throat, trickling down her perfectly triangular teeth and blunt snout. A hyena. In place of the moon, her single eye sprung out of her face, white and empty. The walls groaned; they howled. Her eye, I remembered, I was to gouge out her eye. Wasting no time, the noise expanding, heightening, rattling the silver cutlery, I stepped onto the hearth, swung the blade in a swift arc and plunged it into the canvas.

The room immediately exhaled, as if resuscitated. This included, of course, the stench of my ransacked buffet. Then I heard movement at the door, a distinct knocking on the wood. I had been convinced before that I turned the lock on my side, but here it was, creeping open with a patent, elongated, strain. It swung a little on its hinges, dangling, almost. I considered that this entire structure might well be tilted, by a matter of degrees, sinking into its own white, sandy foundation. No-one walked through, however. Impulsively, I resolved to confront this lurking, arrogant figure who had apparently been observing me through hidden peepholes and tunnels in the walls. I strode toward the doorway, firmly planting my feet on the ground so as to determine if it was still beneath me, preparing myself for the sight of this stranger. I halted, and thought of the dagger, left hanging out of the beast's eye socket. Moving quickly, before I could second-guess my instinct, I returned to the painting, and yanked it out, keeping it secure in my grip. And in doing so, I noticed the image had transfigured. In the moments my eyes had neglected it, the small, rounded body of the hyena had merged with the rubble behind it, birthing a new aberration. Her fur was dark, singed like the ravaged village, and her limbs jagged, broken, interspersed with iron, stone, and shattered beams. I saw two sets of vicious jaws, one larger, smothering and consuming the other. The monster was dead, falling apart, and the door remained open.

I was wrong, though, to assume progress had been made. When I reached the exit I found, bent forward impatiently and peering inside, a young girl, with mousy hair and a flannel pinafore—the girl in the photographs. She recognised me.

"You did it!" She rocked on her bare feet, a sparkle of delight in her eyes. I knew her voice. It was the same, juvenile intonation that had taken similar delight in my torment. "Come on, let's get going."

I refused, crossing my arms across my chest, the tip of my blade punching into my skin. "Who are you?"

"Oh, give me a break!" she chirped. "Seriously? You know me. I can tell. Your eyes just scream, 'You look *so* familiar.' And I know who you are, so—"

"Was that you, then? You're the one who's been wittering through the door about some pretend monster, aren't you?" It felt ignominious, this battle to intimidate a child.

A vexed frown flashed ever so briefly across her countenance, before she restored a cherub-like curiosity. "What are you talking about?" she said, reaching her hand into my trouser pocket, and dragging me forward, as though on a leash. "You are the only one here."

As soon as she could close the door behind me, she released her vice grip on me. She almost broke my neck. Rather than the long, tangible, if dysfunctional corridor, she had dropped me at the top of a steep staircase. Precariously narrow steps descended in a tight spiral, each with a smooth dimple worn into the middle. The surface shimmered, lit from far above, through a glass dome suspended like a white planet in the heavens. The lurid décor had vanished, a distant figment of my imagination, replaced by raw stone. Water seeped up through its pores but did not circulate or cool the air. This place was warm.

"We're going down now," the child sang from somewhere below my feet, the spattering of her toes echoing up through the chamber. "Deep, deep, into the belly of the beast!"

I clenched my nails against the wall, shuffling and scraping along its endless curvature. My head was weak, and ductile as a sponge against the rock. I thought to count my way down, to keep some measure of how doomed I was, and then lost it around the fifty mark. I only realised my eyes were closed when I cracked the bridge of my nose against the corner of the circle. Gravity pushed me through a confined slit chewed into the dead end, built to be traversed by rats, not guests.

My view blurred and scattered with starry particles, I discovered my destination, a square chamber, barely lit, but embellished with white marble, carved into an enclosure of vines, roots, and clusters of veins. They guarded a dais towards the rear of the room, just above knee-height. The girl sat on the end facing me, lightly gripping the edge and swinging her legs—an ethereal scene.

"This is it," she said, unusually tempered. "What do you think? Do you like it? It is pretty. Doesn't it seem a bit…much, though? You'd think a goddess was lying here or something."

She hauled herself onto the platform, and lay onto her back, her hands folded onto her stomach, smiling contentedly. I took the knife out of my pocket, finally realising where I was standing. This building, from the grey façade in the wilderness, to the perverted imitation of domesticity, to the stairwell into bedrock —it was a mausoleum.

"Go on," the girl piped up, impatient. "You have your weapon with you, don't you?"

"Why?"

"Perfect. Do it, then, right smack in the heart like in the books. I'll try not to squirm or howl or such like."

"Who are you?" I asked again. Who was she, to demand this of me, an outsider?

"Listen, it's got to be done, and I don't mind. You're the one making a scene here, not me."

"No."

"What, you mean you won't?"

"Of course I bloody well won't! What the fuck are you saying?"

"Come on…" She returned to her seated position, throwing her arms over her head in apparent exasperation. "It's not as if your hands are squeaky clean, anyway."

"You are asking me to kill you, to murder you, a child!"

At that, she leapt upright, and seemed to fly across the small space with inhuman momentum. She jumped on the spot, her fingers knotted into tight, angular fists. "I already told you this! *You* are the only one here. How have you not figured this out yet? Just how stupid are you?"

She lashed out, kicked my shins until I collapsed to the floor, stood above me, striking me with her knuckles over and over. "Either we both stay in this tomb, or you get out. And I sure as hell don't want to be stuck here to rot with you!" When she realised this was ineffective, she began to scratch at my face, and pushed her thumbs into my windpipe.

She was me, a long time ago. Only when her flute-like voice cracked, rattled with frustration and rage, could I recognise it. At that age, throughout my pre-pubescence, my existence had no dealings with mirrors or cameras. My idea of my own appearance was a mere chubby, spotty blur. But I knew my own voice; that was familiar.

She started to sing, her mouth tight and wrinkled. "Kill the beast, kill the beast, sink her low."

I could only look into her sapphire eyes as the blade cut through cotton, skin, muscle, and the loop around my neck fell away. She limped a few steps backward, an expression of disbelief casting a shadow over her face. Her last utterance, as she spilled out onto the stone, was perhaps her vilest jibe.

"Sure took you long enough, idiot."

I hated her. Even as I lifted her tiny body off of ground—the room spinning and warping around me, and laid her back, prostrate on the dais—I hated her. I was sure she felt the same. Still, when I reached the rift in the wall, prepared to ascend toward another doorway, and more futile busywork, I turned to glance over my shoulder. However, the child was gone. Over her pedestal an animal on four legs clambered, its single blue eye already fixed on me. The black hound in the painting, the monster was alive. Its claws carved wounds into the marble, tar trailing from its mouth to cauterise them. It hesitated for a second or two, letting me take just one resigned breath before its great legs propelled into me, teeth closing around my skull.

I awoke to white walls, and a bundle of searing lights which threatened to blanch the skin from my bones. I was vertical, but not standing. Attempting to move my legs, I found them bound in multiple places, attaching my body to a post behind my back, painfully ironing out my spine. My upper body, I could not sense at all; it was paralysed. The constant beat of dripping, like a faucet, came from my face. There was a dark, crimson puddle slowly growing beneath me, flowing down from the tip of my nose.

At the sound of clattering movement outside the room, I tried to raise my head. Impossible, I bitterly realised. A little girl sauntered in, from where I had no idea, the red stain now spread across the entire front of her dress, and trailing down over her plump, purple-tinged knees. She was caked in dust, like charcoal, all over her face and bare arms. She smiled mildly, tilted her whole body to one side, inquisitive.

"Still alive up there?" she chimed. "Amazing."

"I could say the same for you." I grimaced, the words scraping against the inside of my throat.

"Who, me? Well, someone had to fetch that dead bird out of the chimney." She clapped her palms together jovially, sending an itchy plume into our eyes.

"Was it you who tied me up, too?"

"You're not tied, are you? No way your arms would stay all funny and knotted like that with *ropes*."

Her nervous giggling fit was cut off before it could truly start. She twisted her head around suddenly, glancing behind her, as if reacting to a noise I could not hear. "Someone's coming," she said. "Lucky you, I guess. Here…" The girl wrapped her skinny hands around the exposed end of the knife and unsheathed it from her ribcage without so much as a grunt or a breath, only a sickening squelch. "Take this with you."

She faltered for a moment, glancing over my restrained limbs, before she dropped out of sight, ducking down to shove it into my sock. The slick warmth smeared onto my leg and soaked into the wool. She did not reappear. Instead, a woman stood up before me, flashing strange blue eyes and dark hair, the horns encircling her head seemingly made to match. There was no hole in her breast. She was Lucifer. She wiped her hands on the hem of her shirt, with a suitably goat-like sneer.

"You're going to need it," she said, walking backward away from me, and only averted her eyes as she turned a corner into the impenetrable murk.

My centre of gravity seemed to shift abruptly, my stomach rolling onto its side. Confused and on the brink of regurgitating some toxic, bubbling dribble, I opened my eyes. I was lying on the concrete. The colours were familiar at least, almost homely, moving and liquid though they were, inflating and squeezing the voices immersed in them.

Michael's was loudest, tremoring in my ear, first shrill and piercing before he noticed, and tried to smooth it out. "Lucifer. Lucifer. Lucille, can you hear me? Wake up. Can you see us?" Warm, clammy hands slid under my head, briefly lifted me off the floor. Meanwhile, a soft, dense lump materialised under my cheek; I could feel the worn fibres of a jacket underneath me, one that had been laundered plenty of times. This belonged to Gabriel, I guessed, from the smell, the same delicate, floral scent. It made me want to go back to my shop and stick my nose in a jar of dried sage.

There was someone else, too, a man who, as I heard more of his abrupt, angry tone, I assumed was Raphael. He was floating far above me, by my feet, and seemed to be constantly swaying back and forth, the motion only squeezing harder on my head. Out loud, or so I thought, I cried out for him to *stand still*, for a minute. In the end I sat up, in an effort to appease the three of them, and settle this newly developed dizziness. I was, for the most part, proven correct. Michael's grip tightened on my arms, while Gabriel, perhaps the more medically minded of the two men, propped a hand between my shoulder blades and at the back of my neck. Raphael, on the other hand, appeared suddenly in front of me, perching on the heels of his shoes, looking as though he was preparing for a sprint race.

"You're back. You're back," the former murmured.

"The hell happened to you?" Raphael snapped.

"I don't know" A pause, then I waved my palms at him. "Actually, I lie. Machine happened, a glitch maybe?"

"Don't think so, else you'd still be laid out here on your lonesome, wouldn't you."

I scoffed. "Figured as much, just thought I'd chance my arm. How bad do I look, lads?"

"Well, I mean, you have a bit of..." He gestured imprecisely to his own nose and an area somewhere between his ear canal and chin. "It's not *terrible*."

I reached above my lip with the tip of my tongue, and sure enough, I tasted like a rusted coin. Raphael grimaced and leaned even further away from me, clearly thinking that particular sight was, indeed, terrible.

"Not even a black eye?"

"Were you expecting one?" Gabriel queried, inspecting the side of my face I indicated.

"It certainly feels like I should be."

"That might have something to do with these," he said. I had no idea what he could be referring to, until he moved his hand, and I felt a corresponding pulling from my skull.

"You're joking me."

They were cold. Two smooth, frigid lumps of metal sprouted from behind my ears and spiralled down towards my jaw. My wings, as they were so called, shaped like the horns of a nondescript ungulate. Even clutched inside both my fists, they would not bend. I already knew they wouldn't, not after any amount of twisting and banging, but it felt better to try again.

I grabbed Michael's arms, attempting to stagger onto my feet like a woman old and infirm, only with a more vicious, angry grip. "I've been stuck down here all this time, for these? You put me through that fucking hellscape just so you could put these on? I don't want them back, you bitch!" I shut my mouth as soon as I realised no more words were coming out, just animal noise.

Gabriel took a step back, understandably, while Raphael appeared to freeze on the spot, still crouching, facing away from us.

"What happened to you, Lucifer?" Michael asked, parroting my own question, though with a rather different meaning.

"Since, as far as you're concerned, wherever *you* were isn't where we found you," Raphael elaborated audaciously, slightly contradicting the former's calmer, coaxing tone.

Ah, the frustration of being on an entirely different wavelength. "No, no. It's weird, complicated. Dark place, extremely old, never seen it before, full of sharp things. There was some stabbing, got strung up to a stake for it. Very unpleasant. And entirely fake, apparently."

Michael shifted my weight and shook me a little, as if to rouse me again. "I'm sorry," he said. "I'm afraid you're not making much sense right now."

"Ah, don't worry about it. Me as a kid? Awful, just as nasty as this version." I smacked myself on the chest. "All I'm saying is, it could have gone worse."

"We're going to take you home, okay? You can rest a bit, and we'll get you cleaned up."

I understood. Frankly, I wouldn't know what else to do either. "A nap? Yes, excellent idea—I'll have some shut-eye, and as soon as I can walk in a straight line again, we'll pop down to the red café, get a little pissed, and maybe I'll start making sense."

Gabriel chuckled gingerly, as Michael draped one of my arms over his hunched back. "Whatever you say, ma'am."

It was only sat on a chair, bent unbecomingly over Michael's kitchen sink, that I grew aware of a narrow, bony object jabbing into my shin. Hurriedly untying and shaking off my right boot, I found, lodged firmly inside, a dagger—my dagger, transformed, polished clean. I did not recall putting it there; taken, given, lost, then found, this lightweight sliver of steel seemed determined to constantly follow me, literally biting at my heels all the way.

Michael took hold of the blade. "Yours?" he said simply.

"It is now."

"Then we keep it." He wrapped the knife in a towel and tucked it back into my empty shoe. He then turned back to the task at hand, twisted off the tap, dunked a handkerchief in the lukewarm pool of water, and placed it in my hand, before tucking my discarded belongings under his arm and leaving me to my ablutions. I watched the crust dissolve from my skin into a red flush on his checked white cloth, and let it drip down, heavy like ink.

# Part 5: Acquiescence

**[Raphael]**

Lucifer's spot was at the bottom step of the altar right at the rear of the Hall, off to the left side. She lounged on the floor, legs tucked beneath her, propped up on one arm. In my imagination, I unfolded a picnic blanket, red and white chequered, to complete the scene. She held herself so still and stately, if I closed my eyes for long enough, only looking through rapid, glancing blinks, she would start to merge with the picture, flesh flattening into oil and pigment. I observed her for a moment, until it began to feel awkward, the breeze a degree too cool on the back of my neck, my stomach a few grams too heavy, then I crossed through the entrance.

"Hey, fish."

"Raphael, I thought I recognised the stomping sound. Everything alright?"

"I was about to ask you the same thing. What are you doing down there? You stuck?"

"Oh, maybe. I don't know. I was looking at this part of mural, in the centre here, this woman. Her name was Grieve. She was a healer. The artist must have been very fond of her, don't you think?"

"I don't know a thing about her. How do you figure?"

"Well, for one, the artist's signature. Her name was…?"

"Lily something-or-other."

"Right, and she marked all her work with the flower. Apparently it was quite the game Glenn played with collectors; because she painted on such a giant scale, she'd hide it, realising they'd spend hours, days, weeks searching. I wouldn't know. I've only ever seen her other pieces in books. But in this one, it's right there, see?"

Her circling finger was not as precise an indicator as she seemed to believe, but after pursuing her gaze for a while, I found it. Five white petals folded outward from a bleeding pink centre at the woman's breast, striking against the rich copper glow of her skin.

"But besides that," she continued, tucking her hands back in her lap, satisfied, "no-one else in the picture is dressed up like she is. The more I look, the more I notice. Grieve…she's wrapped her in these beautiful folds of white and gold, that just breathe over her body and gather behind her like water. The shade cast by every little crease in the fabric has the same red as the fire above her. Can you imagine what a tiny brush Lily would have pinched between her fingers, to paint every stray knot of hair, how many minutely distinct shades of colour she must have stirred on her palette? And if you really focus your eyes, you can just make out a freckle on her left wrist. Yes, I think she loved her."

"All of the deep, philosophic insights you have about this fucking drawing and all I think about is, what if they'd picked literally any of the other Soulless to be standing in the background? How much easier would my life be then?"

"What would you have back there instead?"

"As if I know. My understanding begins and ends with the Wyvern."

"Somehow I don't believe that's quite true."

"You're just desperate to give me too much credit. That's how they get you, see, the numbers. Just something smaller, I guess— more human-shaped. Now you'll tell me that would ruin the effect of the picture, the ambiance of the thing, whatever it is that keeps you hypnotised by it."

"If anything, it would be more frightening. Although, I think I might prefer that. It'd be kind of homely. Perhaps I'd never leave."

"You come here for company."

"Maybe. I hadn't thought about it in that way. What was it that you said, something about hypnosis?"

"Well, I didn't mean—"

"You're probably right. It's like a sleep away from sleep."

"Isn't the phrase supposed to be 'home away from home'?"

"In a different circumstance, with different people, sure. I've never much related to it myself. There's no face to it. The word comes to mind a lot, all on its own, like some sort of monkey-brain instinct. 'I just want to go home.' What do I mean? That tug, the yearning, it's not like any other that I know. It doesn't radiate from anything, just lies down on top of me, like a sheet. Where have I been before, that I would be so desperate to return to? A warm, rectangular hole in the dirt? Doesn't sound so bad when I say it out loud, actually. Maybe it's the voice of my Soul, begging for another more comfortable body. Now that I can sympathise with. What about you? Is this home, to you, Raphael?"

Homes were a stationary entity, a thing for other people, smaller, softer creatures who vibrated at the edge of my vision. Only when the word struck me, driving through my skin like a pendulum to an eggshell, did I understand her question. It slammed into me, then through me, a nameless, translucent grief. I imagined if I waited, very still, for long enough, she would turn to reach out a hand, and lead me wordlessly into a dark sea. I felt I would take her anywhere, any place she knew to go. I closed my eyes against it. In the blackness at the back of my skull, I found the pressure of a hand at the nape of my neck, the taste of sugar under my tongue. I opened up again, the wave having passed. There she seemed to nod at me, as though I had walked through the entrance and greeted her over again. It was an effect she and Michael shared, the look of someone who could see invisible things. With Michael, it left a bright flame behind his pupils, warmed his skin. I ached to see it too. In Lucifer's case, I felt mostly content to let her deal with the reflections in the shadows, to view it through her, an imprint of a ghost in the dust, the idea of a bird's-eye image of the earth. I only had to make sure not to lose her in the woods. Pair them together, one-plus-one across a room, and the gravity of their gazes collapsed into something spherical, a moon overlapping the world like stained glass.

Lucifer's eyes briefly crossed at her nose as she yawned into her elbow, the high-pitched squeaking sound amplified by the vastness of the room.

"Don't know why Michael has trouble—I can tell when you're tired. You start saying odd shit."

"I hope you're not assuming this is as strange as it gets. I'm feeling almost sane today, as it happens. What are you doing out here, anyway? Last time I saw you in full daylight, you were coming to arrest me."

"Couldn't close my eyes. Too much to think about. Figured I'd be better off going for a walk; if I just lie there letting myself get frustrated, I end up leaving a scorch mark on the duvet. I was passing through and guessed you might be in here. Thought I ought to check in, make sure you weren't spouting blood from your ears again. You don't seem the type to hanker after company, but I figured you wouldn't kick me down the front steps either. But I suppose I could be wrong, in which case I can turn around, get on my knees if that makes things easier."

"I wouldn't bother. The floor's about as comfortable as it looks, and these aren't my kicking boots. Although now that you mention it, I probably ought to find a hiding spot other than this place. Makes me predictable, and extremely easy to sneak up on, apparently. Some of the younger girls, they used to sort of loiter in their doorways, maybe peer around corners when they saw me, but now they've figured out that I'm here. A pair were around earlier, peeking over the top ledge, though they didn't stick around for long. I think they got bored waiting for me to, you know, *do* something."

She shrugged, and planted her head between her hands.

"Can I take you somewhere?" *Anywhere.*

"Now, that's new. Are you flirting with me, Raphael, or just trying to murder me?"

"Guess again. There's still a while before time for the Red Café, and my spot's only a bit off of the tram line."

"I see. I confess, I find it hard to tell sometimes. It's a whole problem."

It appeared to me that, as of late, I struggled to discern the difference between painful, awkward, but very necessary decisions that can only be coaxed about with a bit of impulsive short-sightedness, and simple disastrous mistakes. The tram carriage stifled in spite of the wafer-thin windows rattling in their frames, letting off a sweat that misted over my mind's eye and induced a constant, dizzying sense of being one careless swivel of the head away from fainting. All the while, the tram itself crawled along the rail, dragging out the journey past schedule several times over. Impossible, I knew, but the knowledge only increased my discomfort. I had no intention of keeping secrets, and yet when Lucifer inquired as to where we were headed, I couldn't force out the words 'botanical garden'.

I walked off of the carriage at the most ideal stop and marched along the curling footpath, trusting that she had the wherewithal to follow. When I stopped, the rhythmic crunch of gravel underfoot continued until she caught up with me.

"Oh, okay." She crossed her arms over her chest and nodded, though her slightly limp jaw still suggested a degree of confusion. "Any reason you've brought me to the garden?"

The essence of lavender filtered through the air, tickling at my nostrils and tear ducts. At our feet, small pink petals gathered, scattered by a nearby arrangement shaped around the base of a tree. Crushed and torn between stones by feet so thoughtless as to wear shoes, they released their dye into the porous ground as though it was all they were born to do. Perhaps it really was, in a sense.

"This is where it happened," I began. "This is where they killed Wyvern. There weren't many witnesses to the actual moment, obviously, but from the state of the aftermath it apparently wasn't hard to figure it had been grisly. The site went without seeing many human faces for a few years after, so it got a little wild for a while, things growing and perishing of their own accord. Didn't last long, mind."

"I imagine it became quite the sales pitch. It's like people need to wait a bit, give themselves chance to feel a tad embarrassed about their nibbling curiosity. Then, once the first couple bite, why, then you're in business." She chuckled.

"Are you hungry or something?"

Her eyes rolled upward as she tilted her head and pursed her lips in concentration. She had to think about it. "No, why? Are you?"

My own perfectly mundane comment, rebounded back at me, halted me in my tracks. I felt my brow creasing up. Now I had to think about it. Shifting my gaze down to her face, I thought I caught the last hints of a sly smirk.

"No. Anyway, so we know that Wyvern managed to breach the Wall and get inside. Far from the only Soulless to do it, but it's the one people tend to remember. And if you look into the horizon of your favourite painting, you can make out a line of willow trees. Here is the one place we know of that they could have grown. And obviously they look different now, but the trees in the picture were most likely a few of that bunch.”

“Impressive.”

“Where we’re standing now is, give or take, the very spot. It’s not even the best view, but it’s the one I like best. Feels snug, like I know it. Takes me back to the past, I guess. Now if only I could wipe all of that useless shit out of my brain and use the space for something important.”

“So you come to chill out in the place you died? A little unorthodox, I have to say. I can see the appeal, though. It’s pretty. There’s this really old cemetery, out West, that looks nice in the autumn, too.”

“But I’m not dead yet, am I?”

“I don’t know. You tell me.”

“So it’s not like *that*. Sure, this is Wyvern’s grave. But my Soul is my imagining of that beast’s burning body made manifest. It’s more like the place I was born, that part of me, anyway.”

“Your sympathy for the creature was so powerful, it became distilled through the Source into a Soul, especially for you. Some folks would say you’ve been spoiled.”

“In what way? Besides, I wouldn’t call it sympathy, just a kid’s obsession. Can you imagine if I turned into a horse instead, or a bicycle, or a piano?”

“I’ve seen my own grave.”

I paused, wondering if she’d even heard my last reply. Her voice had dropped low, without warning. I expected to find a matching expression painting itself all over her body, her arms pulling tighter around herself, the whites of her eyes watery. But save for her eyebrows stitching together over the bridge of her nose, she was, outwardly, unchanged.

Fine. She had me. I couldn’t resist. “Where?” I asked.

"When the Machine took me. Remember you said I apparently *wasn't* where you found me? Well, that's true. I wasn't, not entirely at least. I was in my…tomb, I suppose you'd call it. There wasn't much rebirth going on there, I can tell you that much."

"You think if the Machine decides to hit me with the old tranquiliser next, this is what I'll see?"

"Maybe. It depends, probably. Would being stuck in a meadow full of posh flowers get you so distracted that she could weld a pair of antlers to your head?"

"I don't know. Am I alone in this hypothetical flower garden?"

"Hah, unlikely."

"Then yes, I imagine it would. You don't seriously call them antlers, do you?"

"I keep hoping if I say it enough, it'll piss *her* off, too."

**[Rei]**

I blinked, and upon opening my eyes, realised the time was late in the afternoon. My working hours were over, and I had been due to arrive at my apartment over an hour ago. Instead, I found myself mid-stride in unnatural darkness, sandwiched between a single-storey storehouse wall on my left, and *the* Wall on my right. My shoe slapped against a wet floor.

"What am I doing here?"

Several times in a row, I seemed to wake up, my brain effectively rebooted, somewhere along the outermost alleyways, in the middle of walking *somewhere*. I had no immediate recollection of how I had got there, where I was headed, or what for, only that I had been at this for a while, that I must have forgotten more than once already, that the short-term memory was surely buried under numerous censoring, censuring wipes. I ought to have been going home. I needed to pause, take a moment to relax, push that huge, throbbing thought to the wayside. I should have been home by now. After taking a look at nearby buildings, glancing inward to the lit main street, I regained my bearings (again). I had found my body facing near enough westward, no direction in particular. Whatever I had planned to do, it was clearly not in the Machine's interests. It could be a potentially dangerous task. Quite likely, in fact. I continued walking, noting any details in my dim, squalid surroundings. It could be anywhere, the thing I had hoped to find. My past selves had all chosen to continue their mission; I owed it to them to finish something, even if in the end it wasn't what I had started.

For all of the talk of the Wall's great power and glory, much of the world at its feet festered in old damp and stewing detritus. Leaves, uprooted weeds, matted feathers and excrement, gathered up into a dark brown slush at the outermost edge, as though ploughed aside—out of sight, out of mind—with a shovel. It lay there in the darkness, still, ashamed of its own dirty, soggy aroma of organic rot. The buildings here did not receive the same graces as the old train station, or the giant bell tower, other, rather larger features more befitting the overall regal aesthetic. These were instead shoved, like cattle, as far up against the Wall as they could conceivably fit. Though these were only stout little fixtures of one or two floors, perhaps serving as attractively quaint cottages back in the prime of their lives, they nonetheless managed to block daylight from touching these lower segments of the great monument. Dark patches, only viewable from this strange, neglected viewpoint, climbed up into the stone, rooted themselves in it, growing out and blurring at the edges like fallen rose petals. If one stopped walking, opened their ears, the occasional, nebulous slap of a drop on soft, wet ground could be heard from nowhere in particular. But I could not stand still. I moved slowly, painstakingly, but I did not have much time. I could not go West, like Michael did. Only Eve Stanton lived in that grand, two-storey apartment now. The only place I could think to start, was the Wall, the place she had first appeared to me, a voice to the name, a marble statue come alive.

There was a row of paintings on the ground floor of the administrative building, life-sized portraits, lined up like draughts pieces, stacked on the opposite side of the board. Angels penned in gold-plated frames, a head above eye-level, each wrapped up in fine drapery, tassels and jewels they had never once stepped outside in. The blank space, the incomplete arrangement, so lopsided that the wall seemed to tilt with the uneven mass, became the accepted landscape. The frame had eventually been tacked onto the wall as it was, nothing inside, no name on the label, if only to save finding some other place to store it. The fifth Angel had not even died; they had never been conceived. The white void, a blank mannequin, the unfulfilled promise of someone new, someone *else*. The final portrait was now in place, and we all forgot we had ever known another view, upon entering the building. The dark figure, torso turned a few degrees to the left, facing gravely frontward, could never live up to the void.

But there was a gap, still. The woman in the photo did not fit in her frame, not properly. Her face had lines cutting through it, her eyes circled by grey bruises, and the palette lacked delicate touches of white light blinking from every smooth surface. Next to the men at her flank, she looked positively elderly. She stuck out like a placeholder, a zero slotted into the number, a cavernous pit in the clean complexion. That was, I supposed, who I wished to find: the person whose portrait belonged in that gap, the girl who this blank-eyed Angel intended to replace. Gabriel spoke of conflict, of rumblings. They could decide to keep their mysteries from me, hide them under their lapels so as to protect me from them—or them from me. Still, none of them could prevent me from writing out my own. It was the good kind of meddling. The conscientious kind.

The beam of light and life reached down from the perpendicular alley, coaxing, like a curled finger, beckoning stray children back to civilisation, rendered the corner even dimmer. A cluster of long, dark streaks sliced across my path, as though a large pair of arms had dragged something limp and heavy from one kerb to the other in a large, dirty sack. The narrow stretch radiated a different aura, a world behind the marvellous scene, the alien sensation of viewing the grey, empty space backstage. The leaf litter seemed, to a mind slightly delirious, overwrought with thinking, the most suitable place for a wise old secret to hide in plain sight. The rumours of abandoned underground passageways were not lost on me. On the contrary, I experienced my own personal high, simply imagining a crypt so fit to burst with contraband and curiosa. But, in the absence of any ideas as to how I might smuggle myself into such a mystical realm, the forgotten secretions of the world above ground were the next best thing. This outer path had a gutter, all the way around, some sort of protective, warding circle—defective, though. I only discovered this as I pushed my foot into the brown slush, scraping some of the surprisingly heavy and cumbersome substance aside. I saw something floating in the murk, a hump, much longer in one direction than the other, like the conspicuous, freshly turned mound over a grave, a boil growing under the clay epidermis. Something had interrupted the slick, icing-like veneer of the swill. The mound hissed and began to foam at the mouth in response to the disturbance, coughing up the large, angular object. An amber crust disguised it, seemed to disdainfully shed itself onto every surface it touched. Naturally, I crouched low enough to brush my fingers across it, the arid, ireful rust catching and biting against every channel in my skin. I lifted it up a little, just off of the ground, to get a sense of the thing. It was heavier than expected, cool, slightly slippery. I had never handled an eel, or even a more regular-shaped fish for that matter. However, I felt I must have watched someone else do it sometime, many years ago, the process of dragging the tip of a blade across oily skin, peeling it away, not so dissimilar to a fruit, really. I imagined it was like this, this iron, wrench-shaped thing. I knocked the weightiest, almost bulbous end of the object against the ground, and flakes corrosive dandruff fell gently down like dirty snow.

My eyes opened to a stream of red skimming down concrete. Leaning against the Wall, opposite me, Lucifer sobbed, a stained hand clamped over her mouth. Her hair hung matted, and dark clothes glimmered with blood, tears, and sweat. Beneath the scarlet paint smudged over her cheeks, she looked much younger, afraid, her eyes round and glassy. She gasped, my own heart leaping away from my ribcage, at a sudden, dull clashing sound. Out of her one, clenched fist, a metallic, curved hunk of scrap had dropped into the pool gathering at her feet, sending a light, incriminating spatter onto my shoes. I crouched to the ground to snatch a closer look, wondering where and how she was hurt, acutely aware she could eject me from this memory at any moment. There were two, pointed, cornucopia-shaped pieces, solid but lightweight. I could think of no animal's head from which these could have been harvested, local or otherwise. The only evidence left was clinging to the disc-shaped, blunt ends of both horns. Reaching out to touch it, I realised with revulsion that, stuck to my fingertip, was not only congealing blood, but split strands of hair, and pieces of skin. Raw, warm flesh.

Further back along the alleyway, at the spring of the blood trail smudged by her dragging heels, another shining object lay deathly still. It was a tool, something like a wrench, or pair of pliers, which had been dropped callously on its head. I looked back at Lucifer, the acidic taste of vomit barely touching my taste buds. I saw two large wounds, one on either side of her head, somewhat obscured by the sticky mess congealing around them. Those ugly spirals of alloy were her wings. Whilst my back was turned to her, as if she knew someone was watching, she pushed herself away from the Wall. With a guttural growl, she patted the small of her back, checking her weapon remained tucked into her jeans. Then she walked away. She walked with purpose and renewed vivacity, seemingly pretending she had not been on the verge of unconsciousness only a moment ago. She was headed, I realised, for the exit, the weak spot, that I had caught wind of but never been able to find.

Before I would be allowed to see it, however, I was kicked out of the past with a harsh blow to my stomach. My body paused for only a second in the present, my hand still closed around the cold, rough wrench handle, before I was hurled forward into the near future.

I was back at the apartment, standing with my back to the door, as though I had just wandered in after a shift at work. The curtains had been drawn halfway, leaving the room trickling with warm, muted light. Gabriel appeared to be lying on the sofa, taking his regular afternoon nap, his crossed feet in grey socks the only part of him visible from here, dangling off of one end. He would wake up soon. The rust of the wrench still scratched against my palm as I crept towards him. I rested one hand on the back cushions and peered over. Blood. Gabriel's cheeks streamed with blood, so dark it looked black. His torso lay in a dyed patch that surrounded him. The air was damp, humid, and smelled sour. I bent over the grab his shoulders, when I noticed his eyelids were wide open. But there was nothing underneath. I could have sunk my fingers into the dark, warm holes in his face, slowly filling with the same sticky substance soaked into his shirt. I had forgotten he was still alive. He suddenly turned his head towards the rustling I made as I flinched away, and his arms shot up, grabbing hold of me. He clung to my wrists, chest heaving with gurgling breaths, when I tried to recoil away. With a vicious pull, I yanked myself out of his desperate grasp, diving backward for the door, hand smacking onto the handle automatically.

The ground rotated perilously beneath my feet as I returned my mind to that dingy street, next to the Wall.

"What am I doing *here*?"

They never taught any of us to latch our Souls to another person, to send them anywhere outside of their chosen vessel. Sure, it was possible, anecdotally speaking, but not a part of the curriculum. Perhaps because no human could survive it. I braced myself against the brickwork, which itself slanted beneath me, and retched until my regurgitated breakfast had washed down the gutter. I spat the taste of acid out of my mouth, replaced it with salty tears, then turned around, knees tremoring, and headed straight for home.

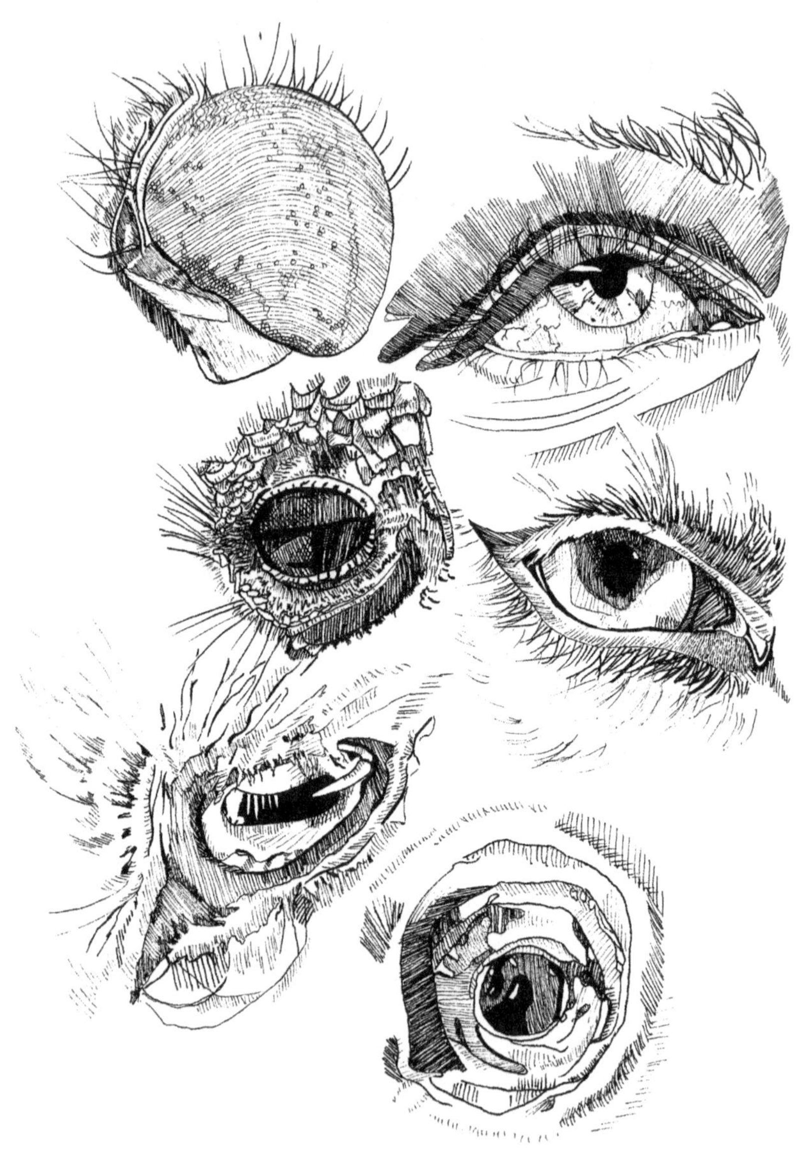

**[Gabriel]**

I never did tell anyone about the strange vision I had. The first
time I saw it, perhaps, my heart raced with dread, at least until I
woke up. I sat upright, my chest pulsing, icy with sweat, but then
felt the bedsheets under my hands, felt my eyes adjusting to the
low light. I took stock of my body, and found all appendages
safely attached. I was back in the real world, and nothing
untoward had occurred in my sleep. Then I saw it again, of
course, and again. Ah yes, a recurring dream, I realised. Quite
commonplace, even to be expected in such a time of elevated
stress. I had heard of lucid dreaming, the idea that one could
retain a degree of consciousness, an awareness that the
sensations they felt were not of reality and had no consequences
there. That explained rather neatly how the pain, the sounds, the
smell could all seem so clear, so coherent. I could not claim,
unfortunately, claim to have thought nothing more of it. Quite
the contrary, I could not seem to shake it off. The images rose
like smoke through a chimney, if I left my mind empty and idle
for too long, being so unlike any dream I had managed to capture
in memory before.

I opened my eyes to nothing, no shapes, no colour. Somehow,
though, I knew. Whether it was the warmth of my own breath
flowing back into my face, or the unnatural position of my arms,
prostrate at my sides, somehow the prey animal in me already
knew I was trapped, stuck in a space barely large enough for my
body. A narrow slit of light teased at the corner of my vision, just
a slight disturbance, like a hairline crack in a full-length mirror.
It did not help. Whatever solid wall lay above me was so close to
my face that I could not make out any details. I flipped my
hands, and as they turned my smallest fingers pressed against a
flat, rough surface. I reached out horizontally. I could trace long
grooves, not quite like tree bark, but rather very old, gnarled, cut
wood. My right index flinched back from sudden stinging pain,
colliding with my hip. A splinter. My chest seemed to be
expanding with each gasp I took; soon the box would not be
large enough, and the roof would squeeze down on my bones,

curling them inward and puncturing my lungs. Bracing both hands underneath me, I shuffled my body downward to feel with my feet. The box narrowed past my thighs, tapering in like tweezers, such that I could not fit both of my soles side-by-side against the farthest wall.

A knock, on the outside of the roof, right above my face. It was not a firm, beckoning knock, knuckles on a door; it did not speak to me. The sound consisted of many tiny taps in succession, layering atop each other, like a pianist's fingernails scurrying against noteless keys. It started at the head-end of the box, then scattered downward. It took a pause, then again, from the top. I could not stop myself. I continued to do it, every time, like purposefully circling to incorrect answer on an exam paper. I balled my hand into a tight fist and slammed it against the wood. The immediate response was not always a constant. Usually, there was a little movement, and a scraping, as though a pair of hands roughly grasped both sides of the box and left deep, loud scratches, impossibly deep, unless these hands had ice-picks for fingers. Sometimes there was a pause of only seconds before the noise, other times the silence lagged on for minutes, and I felt myself growing drowsy, my limbs growing heavy, sinking, leaving an impression in the wooden floor, before being jolted alive by a sudden bang. Occasionally, to pull a rug out from under me, the sounds would be subtler, a smoother introduction, like a low humming, that began well before it is audible to my ears, and steadily grew, vibrating the earth beneath me, then my brain inside my skull, until I felt I was about to burst open like a balloon. The gentlest introduction, and ironically, the one I dwelled upon for the longest time, was what could only be described as a *pressing*, a weight placed silently upon the lid, pushing downwards with increasing pressure, snapping the fibrous bonds of the old planks with cracklings of varying intensity.

The ending was always the same. The sound, be it scratching, thumping, or cracking, ceased abruptly. That would be my warning. The air in the box immediately clogged with a sweet smell comparable to a gas leak, or foul meat. I prepared myself to struggle for my life, pulling my knees up as far as they will go and folding my hands over my chest, when there would be a mighty crash. Something—I was never able to see it—broke through the lid of the box in a single fell swoop, leaving a shallow graze across my abdomen and many more spear-shaped fragments pointing at my gut, highlighted by the burning flare of light pouring in through the gash. I was naked in the dream. Exposed. Lashing out with my elbows, I beat a large enough hole to force my head and shoulders through. And as I sat up into the open, the box keeled and yawed, and I had to cling onto the side to avoid being tossed out. The smell, by this point, had changed, evolved, I had no clue when exactly. Now the bitter aroma of salt dried out my tongue and glued to my eyelids. My hands were cool and wet. I felt my stomach contract. My senses struggling to cope with the abundance of light around me, the horizon seemed to constantly shift, drifting up and down, tilting me around like a spinning top. I saw in only two colours: the stark white of the sky, and the fluid, depthless blue of the sea surrounding me. When I glanced down at my feet, curling them toward me like shields against the cold, I finally recognised the shape of the box. No matter how many times I had been there before, however many repetitions I remembered, I was never allowed, until the moment I looked at my feet, to realise I was floating in a coffin.

There was never anything else, just my quivering body, the box, and the infinite expanse of water cradling us. I allowed myself a length of time to simply exist there, infantile, before I progressed. I could take as long as I wished, it seemed, time being immaterial to the abyssal trenches beneath. Eventually, I would have to lean back, and look up, overhead, for the sun. In the absence of anything else, the sun seemed my best chance, a friendly face, the font of knowledge. Craning my neck that far was agony, but all pain, all physical sensation, soon drained away into the water, when I saw what was loomed directly above me.

An eye. There was an eye, several miles overhead, several miles in diameter, hanging in the sky. I could make out the concavity of its transparent, almost liquid lens, reflecting pale light onto me. The halo of the iris was also blue. Naturally. If I lifted my arm, waving it to the side, I could observe the black pit of the pupil twitching as it watched. I could call it a moment of incredulous, childish experimentation, or call it the only possible thing for a human's body to do faced with such dreadful, annihilating absurdity. Either way, it was during such a moment, watching the miniscule adjustment of the gaping black well in the sky, that I would notice it change size. I would question my perception at first, the thing being so large and its movements so slow at first, but surely, the pupil began to expand. As if it were a mouth, drinking up the colour of the water, after the first taste, it was ravenous. The dark hollow swirled outward, devouring the iris leaving nothing to separate its raw hunger from the pale, gelatinous flesh surrounding it. The countless branching veins, pink tributaries reaching for the centre, grew wider, bulged out from the smooth surface, some bursting their banks, seeping like ink through paper. Then, as though the blackness had weight, the eye spasmed, struggling, fighting, as my own flesh had inside the box, before it started to sink.

And then, of course, I woke.

**[Raphael]**

Ten minutes late, I made it to the Red Café, and found the door unlocked, but the lights off. I entered to a, frankly, bizarre scene. In dimness and dead silence, Michael reclined in his usual seat, head resting on the heel of his hand, eyes closed, as though he had dropped off to sleep while engrossed in philosophising. Next to him, in the Comfy Chair, Lucifer was draped horizontally, her legs hanging over the chair's smoothed arm. She, too, could have been sleeping, if not for the tense seams in her face, and finger and thumb fiercely pinching a flap of skin between her eyebrows.

Michael tilted his head upon hearing the door creak open. I could make out a minute slit of his green irises, seeming to shimmer in the dark. "Afternoon. Don't worry, you can come in. You didn't happen to see Gabriel on your way here, did you?"

"No, I would have assumed he was here already. Say what I may about him, the bloke has always seemed more punctual than me."

He produced a low grunting sound, the meaning of which I couldn't discern.

"What's going on here?" I said, glancing towards his companion, who was still peculiarly absent from the room.

"Head trouble—dizzy, headache…"

"Migraine?"

"Oh, I bloody hope so," she suddenly responded, voice raised, seemingly struggling to moderate her tone in her usual manner. "That means it'll go away eventually. Did you say you hadn't seen Gabriel?"

"I did."

She released her hand abruptly, leaving a pink blotch on her face, visible even though the rest of her appeared rather grey. She stared at me quizzically, causing me to shrink back a little under scrutiny, then she loosened her grip and looked to Michael instead. "That's strange," she murmured. "That's weird, right? Did you mention anything to him?"

"No, I don't think so," he said.

"What are you on about?"

Using the strength of her arms, she turned herself around, dropping her feet to the floor. "I thought I might have figured something out, an answer to our predicament, wanted to tell all of you before I had an aneurism, or disappeared down a freak sinkhole or something."

"Could he have been held up anywhere? Where would he go?"

"With Rei, maybe. That's the only place I can think of," Michael said, a hopeless lilt coming over his presence.

"Do we go look for him?" Lucifer proposed.

"No need."

My eyes were fixed on the glass pane of the door, behind which, in the time it took me to blink at a sudden noise, Rei had appeared. Without waiting to be noticed, she began furiously battering her shoulder against the door. However, it was hard to pay much attention to her behaviour when, wrapped around her other arm, Gabriel loomed, his eyes closed, dark skin shining with something awful. He had been wearing white at some point this morning, presumably. Before any of us could rise to assist her, Rei had barged her way in and onto the doormat. Her shoes were caked in filth.

"I don't know what happened! I-I could tell something terrible was coming, but I was working; I couldn't get home in time to wake him. There was nothing else I could do, so I just brought him here—I mean, I tried, but..."

"Hold on, Rei," Michael said, gently prising her from Gabriel's wrist, and squeezing the latter's shoulders. "What happened?"

"I can't see," Gabriel answered for himself. "It seems I dozed off for a few hours, per usual, and woke up, well, blind." He was absurdly calm, as if this was some minor, hereditary condition he had been quietly waiting for his entire life.

"Let me see, gently now." Michael, continuing to mumble to himself, closed both hands around Gabriel's face. Rei gave a muffled whimper, her mouth buried in the crook of her elbow, knowingly. And Gabriel, he seemed to peer around, almost child-like, the way he tilted his head from side-to-side, searching for the man approaching directly in front of him. With thumb and forefinger, Michael peeled back the pair of eyelids. They appeared slightly tacky, from where I still sat. And underneath… I had never witnessed such a thing. The eyes were still there, as far as could be seen, but with no white left in them. What remained were orbs glistening with a bright, fresh red coating their surface, save for tiny, dark voids in the centre—static, and useless, now.

"So, Michael, just how bad is it?" he inquired, punctuated with a strange sound, almost a chuckle.

"I won't lie to you, buddy. This is bad."

"Then why are you still looking at it?" Gabriel patted his friend on the knuckles, as if to break a hypnotic trance.

"Sorry."

A thought suddenly leapt to my mind, something about that word, 'looking'. "Didn't the Machine try to intervene when you found him like this? That's supposed to be its job. It didn't even pipe up with, I don't know, directions of where to take him or something?"

Rei shook her head so violently the rest of her feather-like body swung around with it. "No, the Machine hasn't done anything, not that I know of. It's like it hadn't been watching him at all. I even waited for a little while, waited for a voice to come along and fix him. Idiot. I'm such an idiot! I'm so sorry!"

"You too? I don't understand why you all keep apologising to me. It's not as though any of you personally gouged my eyeballs out."

"That's not the point," Rei snapped. "Stop trying so hard to be nice to us!"

"He's right, though." I realised it was the first time Lucifer had said a word since the pair had arrived, shuffling through the door. Her gaze slipped by all of us in the room, fixated on some point outside the window, her fingernails tapping silently against her knees. "All this talk of blame, and fault, and 'I'm sorry', it won't get us anywhere. This isn't your fault, Rei. In fact, there was probably nothing you could have done to stop it."

"What?"

"Gabriel's right: none of *us* did this to him. The Machine did. She messed with me, fucked around with something…something in my head. Now she's done the same to Gabriel, too."

POW
ER
BLESS
ING
RIC
HES
GLO
RY
WIS
DOM &c
HO
NOVR
STRENGTH

**[Gabriel]**

I felt an incredible sense of comfort and gratitude in my chest, those first perilous days, that I had a place I could confidently call my home. A home, to my understanding, was quotidian, ingrained so firmly and deeply in the brain so as to require no thought, and no senses, to remember in minute detail. I shouldn't have felt so surprised. Somnambulists are perfectly capable of traversing familiar surroundings, walking downstairs, cooking breakfast, committing homicide, in their state of sleep. Though stripped of the gift of sight, I did, at least, still have my consciousness.

We eventually determined, mostly by accident, that the searing pain in my head, as if the cap of my skull had been opened like a lid and hot coals dropped inside, was due to light. I found this somewhat ironic, almost amusingly so. I happened to have been reclining on the sofa, having lost track of the exact hour, in next to complete darkness. Rei arrived through the front door and kindly flipped the light switch on and, in doing so, brought back the vicious headache and very nearly caused me to vomit. We scrambled for a solution—or rather, I attempted to bustle around the apartment, whilst only Rei actually succeeded—for a scarf, or such like. I did, at one stage, suggest duct tape, to which she fiercely objected, settling instead upon a roll of bandage. The material scratched roughly against my face, clearly not designed for this purpose, but serving it well enough. A bandage, handily, also proved proficient at soaking up the red, viscous discharge which still continued to creep down my nose from my tear glands. Whatever remained beneath my eyelids had been hideous; that much I could discern, from the terror tangled into Michael's voice as he pried them open. I wouldn't know. I could not, after all, take a look in a mirror. They felt somehow odd to touch, I supposed, though I could hardly recall exactly how.

The constant careful gaze and frequent sighs of another human being reinforced my urge to at least appear suitably busy.

I made a point of asking Rei for the time when the question rose to mind, and I knew she was present, to save the dreich tones of the Machine's automated reply from driving her to lunacy. When I happened to be alone, however, it made a rather engaging little game. I could tease away at my brain, trying to recognise whose voices the Machine was using, from one-word clips. For a whole minute, I was free to query, out loud, "what is the time now?" And in response, my half-dozen or so participants would recite, "the time is three forty-two pee ehm"; "the time is four sixteen pee ehm"; "the time is four forty-nine pee ehm". What I had previously dismissed as garbled nonsense I could now pick apart into small chunks, manageable jigsaw pieces. They did not fit together into a complete, orderly rectangle, but they could, nevertheless, be forced to thread together in all manner of ways. Giving myself a dull ache at the front of my head seemed to me a healthy sign. I hoped it was a promising indication that I was not going insane.

"Now? It's just gone seven, I think," Rei finally answered, all alone.

Seven was the next milestone on my list. Rei quickly realised why I was pushing myself to my feet and scurried to my left side. I grabbed her hand, extracting it from my forearm. If I kept one set of fingertips on the back cushions of the sofa, until the last centimetre, I knew I could, with the other set, reach the adjacent wall. The bathroom was a much smaller, more densely packed space, and so vastly easier to negotiate.

For many reasons, I was, and always had been, thankful that medication was one aspect of my life I had no role in deciding. No-one had to be sensible; the algorithms could do that for me. And so they were, very restrained, very often. Lucifer's profession, whether the Machine personally bought into herbal tinctures and mineral supplements or not, became undeniably useless as soon as she stepped within its bounds. No weighing scales, spoons or syringes were used here. The path of an apothecary had never, at least in the time I had known her, appealed very much to her personality. Personally, I doubted she pursued the occupation out of intellectual interest, or a passion for customer service. Anything, *anything* to make herself as obsolete as possible. She made a noble, spiteful effort, and yet the Machine still managed to drag her back home to mama and papa. My palms curled around the front edge of the sink, the ceramic cold and mostly smooth against my skin, though the pads of my fingertips scraped against a couple of natural indents in the bowl. I recalled this room being white, full of reflections; with that first, frigid touch, I could feel the light pressing against the curtains, so to speak. Acknowledging my face in front of the mirror—lucky, lucky facial recognition software—the system dispensed my allowance for the evening, four different capsules, declaring each item as it went. I felt a tiny leap of satisfaction as I picked out Uriel's voice in the word "milligrams", and Henri, the short chap who served me my groceries just the other day, saying "fluoxetine".

I trailed a finger along the lower seam of the door, following the straight edge around a right angle and up, until it reached the handle. The round, silver knob seemed strangely difficult to pinpoint. Where it had once landed between my fingertips automatically, it now evaded them like a living needle in a minimalist haystack. It seemed to require a mite more force than I was accustomed to, before the door popped out of its magnetic latch. I noticed myself unconsciously flinch away from its heavy, pendulum-like swing, probably excessively so, afraid of the embarrassment that might come from clouting myself in the nose. Alongside the distinctive clang of the cupboard's contents vibrating in unison, I heard a metallic rattle—something knocking against the edge of a shelf as it fell out of the front.

It was at that precise moment, that small sound, I recalled that I also stored razors in this cabinet. My stomach lurched, as I saw its shining handle spinning down, down, towards my bare feet. It ricocheted off of the sink, changing the angle of its descent. I threw out an open palm and trapped it in a closed fist. Rei immediately burst into the room, breaking out in a moan, somewhere between distraught and exasperated, upon noticing the blade I was rotating between my fingers.

"Oh gosh," she said, "and here I thought I'd moved all of the sharp things. Sharp things, hot things…I'm still debating whether to roll up the rug."

"No, don't take away the rug! At least, not yet. It's been the most useful thing so far."

"The most useful thing for sitting on the end of the couch all day?" she probed. I imagined a sceptical arch to her brow.

"Well, what am I supposed to be doing? I can't exactly pick up a book to read, now can I?"

"Oh, I know. I'm sorry, Gabe. I just wish I could be here all the time. Lucifer was right; clearly, the Machine isn't taking care of you at all. Where are you cut?"

Only when she took my wrist into her warm, slightly clammy hand did I realise she was referring to the razor blade. "Nowhere. It's alright; I saw it fall out."

Her grip tightened. "You…you did what?"

"I saw it." Where I had previously felt wholly blasé about such a simple act of reflex, I was now stuttering, dumbfounded as she sounded. "Not in the same way as you would *see*, you know, with your eyes. The sight of the whole bathroom didn't flash before me. I mean, I knew where the blade was, where I would need to hold out my hand to catch it, before it…"

"Before it hurt you."

"You're right. Acuity did that. I can't see a bloody thing, but my Soul still can."

Until then, I had not, to my own discomfort as much as Rei's, so much as considered the state of my Soul. The power of perfect sight, I had most likely assumed, aware of the bitter irony, that it had abandoned me as soon as my worst nemesis took my eyes. I had forgotten it, as I thought it had forgotten my plight. Instead, it had been waiting in the depths, waiting to protect me from something. There was a nasty, dangerous realisation, that the only instance in which I would be allowed to catch a glimpse of the world again would be an imminent threat to my life.

**[Michael]**

Lucifer was not in the apartment when an alarm woke me. I was notified of this fact by a torn scrap of notepaper taped to the outside of the bedroom door. To write a physical message, with pen on paper—it seemed like an anachronism, an old wives' solution to the problem. Quaint, rather charming. It flapped at eye level, like a healthy spring leaf, when I opened it into the room, slightly greasy hair still uncombed, with crust stuck to my eyelashes. I plucked it off, running a hand over my face. I recognised her handwriting. The letters were slightly rounded at the corners, though she exclusively used block capitals.

*"DON'T PANIC! NOT KIDNAPPED. GONE OUT ON AN EARLY PATROL. SEE YOU THIS AFTERNOON."*

She had read my mind, even in my sleep, apparently. When I first set her up in my accommodation, I quickly learned that she rose with sun over the jagged, concrete horizon. Unsurprising, since she lay opposite to the only window in the apartment, and although I tried rotating the couch by a half turn, to face the front door instead, I continued to find her sitting wide awake at the crack of dawn. She persevered with this new setup for a few nights, before resetting the furniture to its original layout, explaining that, even if the view over the street was not particularly picturesque, it did not make her nervous. At first, I would find her staring around the room, literally twirling her thumbs, in some nebulous state between utter boredom and disbelief. She might pour herself a mug of tea if she felt particularly bold. Given some time to acclimate, however, she started to bring books back from the public library, and I myself grew accustomed to the whisper of a page turning in her fingers as I staggered to take my tablets and freshen up. Her current rental reclined on the cushion, in her spot, a clinical-looking textbook about literature and art of the post-war era. It looked much too clean to appeal to her. The cover was a flat layer of glossy card, where it should have been cloth or leather, curling inward at the edges, with a soft yellowish colour and musty aroma.

As soon as I no longer resembled a reanimated corpse, I decided I would get on and leave too. I did not feel particularly hungry. Instead, I figured I might as well busy myself later by cooking something more substantial for both of us. Doing so would take a little imagination and careful scouring of the mishmash in my cupboards, but this served the dual purpose of occupying my thoughts while I wandered. I did not mean to chase after her but, admittedly, I rather ardently hoped I would stumble upon her all the same. To casually pass by her would mean she really was still here, patrolling, still awake…still alive. The end of my train of thought bluntly dropped itself into my mind, like a strike to the forehead. The feeling only intensified as I stood outside Moore's Hall, tempted by the blank darkness inside the doorway. I hesitated at the bottom, knowing I was surely being watched closely. Still, I jogged up the steps two at a time. Damn the consequences, I would have liked to say, but the slight anxious stirring in my gut proved heavy and difficult to shake.

There she was, poised upon the altar, not sprawled out for sacrifice, just standing with her hands clasped behind her neck, rocking on one foot. She twisted around, hearing me stamp through the middle of the pews. She appeared to take a few seconds to recognise me, before the dubious stitch in her brow relaxed.

"I thought I might find you in here. I see your patrol is going well. Up to some less-than-legal mischief, are we? Or do you just *really* like looking at old paintings?"

She squeezed her shoulders up around her ears, smiling, I hoped, at the chutzpah of my opener.

"I don't know if I like looking at them, so much as I feel I should get to know this one. Could be worse, I suppose. It is a beautiful picture. You're not a fan?"

"I don't know... It's not the artist's rendition that turns me off, but these people in it. We get talked at so much about the heroes who defended the Wall, I start to resent them. It feels like they put us here. Even if the brushstrokes make them look pretty."

"I've been thinking about that, too, you know. Remember when the Sovereign announced the Angel Programme—or whatever it was called—started selling the role of Angels to us like we'd be the offspring of Naomi Elwin herself?" She guarded her mouth as she spoke, hinting at the constant presence of the man in question, locked out of sight behind a layer of stone, plaster and paint.

"Sure I do."

"Well, think about the story, the actual history as we recall it. There were two walls. Obviously, we've got the Wall protecting Interieur, which the military fought to defend, questionably mind you. But we forget about the wall around Morrigan Larsen. She birthed the Soulless, those poor, ugly creatures, to keep every living being away from her wall. Both of them were knocked down in the conflict. They called it a war. So, where does this wall—" She waved her hands over her head dismissively, speaking to some point high above us. "—the one we're supposed to fight for, to literally kill for, fit into that story?"

"And who does that make us?"

Though we deflated in body, folding up into warm, sighing blood bags, I felt an exhilarating effect inside, one of discovery. It was like the most secretive, internal art, to speculate over one's true nature in this way, knowing that, for once, so long as we were quiet about it, there would be no easy reply. It was also horrific, catalysing. The barely unseen inkling of truth, threatened to melt skin, muscle, organs and bones, into a single fatty puddle on the floor, dripping slowly down the stone steps, viscous and hot, leaving one polished silver crown behind. Or perhaps the metal would sink into us too, emulsifying into the toxic slick.

I came back to my senses, a man, propped up on two legs. Lucifer turned her face towards me, a sympathetic squint about her eyes.

"Sucks pretty bad, doesn't it?" she said. "I've no idea of who I am, in truth. I am a Soul in a plump little carrying case, that's it. Sometimes I fear that Eve had it right all along, when she said Uriel was only doing his best to cope with a difficult lot. That I am hard to like."

"I wonder if she thought the same of me, even, before I was Michael. It is certainly the impression I got at the time. You know, I wouldn't like to give the Machine credit for its foresight, but maybe, perhaps, that's why we have each other. We can all be difficult together."

"Hm, somehow I don't see that working out."

"Come on, four out of five isn't so bad."

"You won't try to recruit number five into your ranks still, then?"

"No." I stiffened, recoiling against the noxious taste out of my mouth and resisting the urge to spit. "Uriel has been given his chances—by all of us—and he betrayed each one of them. He's formed his own little clique with the Sovereign. How could we trust him? How long can we keep reaching out a hand into the dark?"

"Only to have it bitten off."

"Right."

"You know what I think you are? A romantic."

"Really? After what I *just* said?" I felt a warm blush, of all things, peppering over my forehead.

She crossed her arms resolutely, nodding with her whole body, and a mischievous smirk on her face. "Yeah. Every ragtag band worth their salt has one of 'em."

[232]

"Hey, Lucifer."

"What is it?"

"If it made the difference between realising our design and failure, would you kill me?"

"If what you mean is, if I had to choose between you and anyone else here, then—"

"No, that's not it. I mean, if it meant *the Machine*, would you kill me? I need to know."

A pause. She sighed, deeply, meditatively.

"Yes. But only with my own hands. If you asked me to let you die, then no, never. I could only kill you myself. It would have to be me." Her cheeks flushed, a hellish flame lit at the back of her throat.

"Good. I needed to make sure we're on the same page."

"You would do the same for me?"

She looked at me again, looked away, forced herself to look back. Her whole body seemed to sag, as though I had doused her with water. It was an expression of disbelief, a rare, rare sight— disbelief that I, me, the clean one, would promise to soil my hands in such a manner, that I, by dirtying myself (only a baby step away, now), could make her blood in some way sanctified.

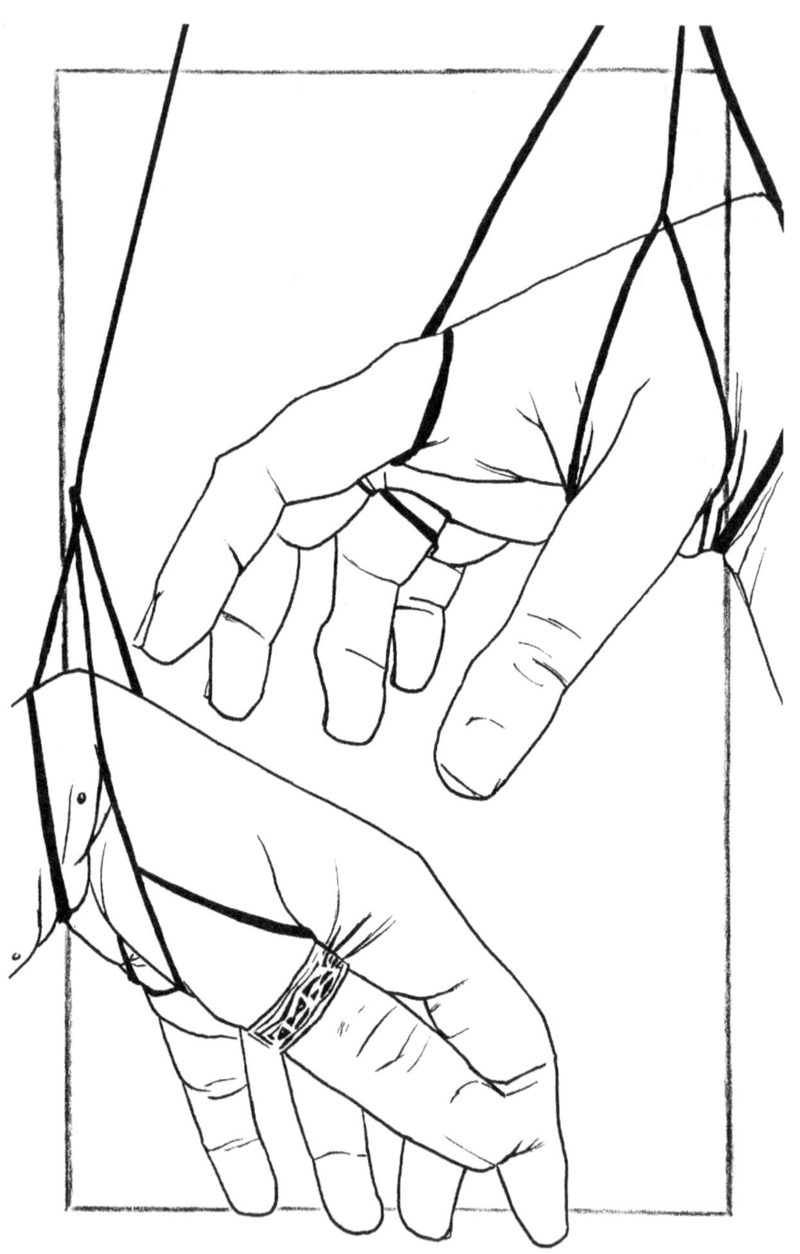

**[Raphael]**

"It's not as if we can just walk into the throne room and punt the old bastard off of his chair. If that were the case, I'd probably have done it already without thinking."

A fool might have assumed Gabriel to be taking an impromptu nap in his chair, from the way his cheek rested languidly in his cupped hand, eyelids gently closed. I knew better. Regardless of whether he could see, he had learned a particular trick to angle his face in your direction, to make it clear he was looking right at you. It meant I was none too surprised when the man raised his head, after a profound pause, to hum in agreement and say, "His bond to the Machine is far too solid."

"You saw it, right," I said, "all those cables and metal skeletons around his body? And besides, there's one person whose protection the Machine is bound to prioritise over its Angels, and that's the Sovereign. If we wax philosophical for a moment here, say we're all organs. You—" I flung my finger toward Michael, then turned it around the table. "—brains, lungs, stomach, whatever. Then he's the heart."

"Everything else dies before he does." Michael's mouth seemed to form words just a mite too slowly, like a tape player malfunctioning barely enough to arouse suspicion. His eyes fixated on a crumb-adorned saucer atop the table as though, if he were to blink, the friction might cause the ceramic to burst into flame. He broke his gaze only to finally toss a drooping curl of hair out of his eye. One which I had not realised, until then, I had been gawking at.

"Look at that, I'm a genius," I said, slouching backward.

"While we're all in the mood for speculation," Lucifer began, reclining on the rug, legs tucked under herself like a lowly empress, "can the Machine even function without being, you know…plugged in?" She shaped her hands into two stiff steeples, tapping them against her temples as if giving herself a very poor massage.

Gabriel frowned, seemingly pained with trying to recall the knowledge out of the aether. "If I had to take a guess, then I would say no, at least not properly. Assuming, obviously, that the Machine continued to receive power, it wouldn't know what to do with itself. It would be like shoving a group of soldiers into a trench, fully armed, with absolutely zero instruction."

"Chaos, then," she concluded, darkly.

"Honestly, I couldn't say. The only man who knew for certain is dead."

"Fucking hell, Smith," I mumbled, mostly to myself.

Michael had fallen silent, still in the same position, hunched over his knees. He only now spoke up, loudly too, with unguarded conviction. "So, somehow, we have to force the Sovereign to disconnect himself from the Machine, yes? And having done so, we need someone to replace him. Someone who understands, and absolutely believes in what we are trying to achieve. One of us. We have to seize control over the Walls of the city itself. Perhaps it is impossible to truly destroy the Machine, but we can at least ensure no-one is trapped inside."

"That's a mammoth of a task you are suggesting, Michael," said Gabriel. "We haven't the semblance of an idea of what danger the Machine presents to us in such a circumstance. Furthermore, you would be asking whoever is in there to assume mastery of all of its systems, maintain that control, and then detach themselves. Will it put up some sort of resistance? What effect does plugging in have on the mind of the individual?"

"Fuck it, I'll volunteer," Lucifer blithely exclaimed. "Gabriel's guesswork and Raphael's funky autopsy fever-dream, that's a good enough excuse for me. Maybe I'll kick the bucket, but it'd be worth it for the chance to give the snotty bitch a piece of my mind." She hesitated briefly, apparently as a different part of her brain took over possession. "Then again, that's precisely what you're referring to, isn't it? That's why I can't do it."

"In a sense, yes."

Michael interrupted, "I'm not asking for any of you to volunteer. I am offering to do this myself. That is, of course, if you see fit that I should."

He seemed practically decided on this issue already. In truth, I could not imagine any man better suited to the responsibility, logically speaking. Still, I found myself wanting desperately to resist, the sigh of relief I had breathed for Lucifer trapped yet again underneath my sternum. The quiet of the room was not promising, us three stifled in the corner, whilst he smiled and nodded benevolently in his seat. I considered brazenly bringing up, in all the graphic details I had retained, the afternoon he spent moaning under my hands behind the counter back there. There was a slim chance it might provoke him into shutting up.

"So, we open up the Wall and everyone runs out, like horses out of the box. What then? You headed West and were lucky not to perish from exposure before you stumbled across civilisation. What are a few hundred kids supposed to do when the wilderness slaps them in the face?"

"They'll do just the same as I did, and as Lucifer had to before me."

"Not everyone here is as scrappy as you both, though. I can't pretend like I would have made it on my own."

"And yet, here *I* am," Gabriel mused, "willing to hedge my bets. Not one child ended up in this pen for being a hapless idiot. Have a little faith in your fellow man."

"And in yourself, for that matter." Michael's words constantly flowed from his mouth like treacle syrup, and warmed the gullet just the same, too saccharine and moreish to be any good for you. Like sugar, also, he left a thick, clogging coating down the throat, stuck to the skin, glued to the lips and incisors. He existed, it seemed, in complementary opposition to Lucifer's bristled tone, blunted spearheads coughed up from her stomach with the sound of a snapping bowstring. Gabriel lounged somewhere in the middle ground, content with neither extreme of feeling. He liked to lean sideways in his chair, away from the scene, to get a better look.

"Shit, I'm still adapting to the idea of trusting the three of you sitting here. I think I shall stick to that, before I spontaneously catch fire."

Lucifer tilted herself forward, "And it's not as if they will we wandering for miles upon miles with no sense of here nor there. No-one should have to make it too far." She scratched at her jaw, eyes shifting from side to side, as though she had something stuck at the back of her tongue, as though about to cough up a beetle. She lilted like a windchime, unstable, phantasmic—a secret precariously embodied.

"Then, what are we shooting for here?"

"Just the end of the line."

"By which you mean…?"

"The railways aren't dead and buried as one might be made to believe. They're only…pruned back a bit. If our people can walk as far as the end of a track, they'll practically have a signpost showing them the way. And, with some luck, they will be picked up by the occasional ferry along its journey."

"That's how they found you."

"Precisely. By the by, it probably would have been a combination of anaemia and exhaustion that killed me; I don't really feel the cold." She turned to me and spoke rapidly, without a pause for breath, holding up one finger, to mark the footnote. "Also, it isn't as if anyone will be alone out there. We have more allies than you could begin to imagine."

Gabriel laughed, low and muffled, mouth closed in a smirk and chin lowered towards his chest. "We do? I must say, it doesn't feel like that is the case."

"The highland people up North will already be preparing themselves to assist, I'm certain of it. And if they were able to reach the cunning folk, well, they were the closest I've ever had to a family. They will take in as many as they can. Let's be honest, if they were keen enough to deal with me, any more orphans will feel like a breeze."

**[Michael]**

I always preferred to walk away from the Red Café at Lucifer's side. I made the mistake of forgetting exactly why. We had almost made it home.

"And then we ended up loitering around down in—"

Lucifer's voice failed mid-sentence as we approached a ninety-degree corner. She stopped moving, eyes fixed on a point in the near distance. Under the dusky shade cast by the apartment block, a willowy silhouette leaned against the stair rail. She recognised it immediately. Whether or not, like me, she required the crescent shape of a blade hanging over his head like a parasol to do so, I could not tell. He had two figures standing a little ahead of him, on either side, like bouncers, one stockier than the other, but both sturdily built, and both uniformed head-to-foot in sage green.

"Told you they would turn up imminently, chaps." His clean, clear voice was unmistakable. "It all depends on how much she's putting on the limp. Look, I'm bored of chastising you, Michael. So today, I'm going to express my appreciation instead. One advantage to you behaving so terribly predictably all of a sudden, is that it makes my job so much easier. It's like a two-for-one."

"You're out early this afternoon, Uriel," I began.

"Limp or no limp," Lucifer added, almost too quietly for anyone to hear, her tongue pressed into her cheek.

"And you've been making some friends," I said. I could not, dared not, pretend to be anything but surprised. The languid lilt of his demeanour suggested he had been tracking us well before we clocked him, though I knew not how nor for how long, and so he had the high ground.

"Yes, yes, I am!" he yelled, raucously, clapping a hand against his knee. But his expression turned within seconds, as though someone had sobered him up by throwing a bucket of cold water over his head. "But I don't have time for more pleasantries. My friends here are prison guards. One is carrying multiple pairs of cuffs, along with another restraining paraphernalia, should she decide to continue running her mouth. The other is responsible for a locked case in which to deposit that knife I know she's hiding. I am under orders to detain the Angel Lucifer for the crime of treason and chuck her as far underground as she will go. We're borrowing your Soul. You need to hold her. I'd like to keep this as tidy as possible."

I blinked, and his face twisted around his mouth, before he vanished from between the uniforms. The uncanny popping sound pained my eardrum, as he flickered back into existence, his hot breath sticking to my left cheek.

"Sometime this week, if you would, Michael. Come on, at least make a good show of it…or is the Machine going to demand I place you under arrest next?"

"Off of the high horse, Uri. The Machine hasn't 'demanded' anything of the sort. This is all you, throwing your toys out of the pram, for what reason today I can only guess." I spluttered out the first coherent bullshit that came to mind, like I had been knocked below the knee. The truth was, I had no clue. But at worst I could waste a moment of his time, and hey, a broken clock was correct twice a day; perhaps I would catch him in a lie eventually.

"Wrong!" he slammed the blunt end of his weapon against the ground, his face growing purple at the edges. "And if you cannot perform this most simple request, then I will bring this blade down upon the necks of all of you who call yourselves Angels of the Sovereign, starting with you, then Gabriel, then Raphael. For good measure, anyone who I find to have colluded with you will be terminated as accomplices. And there will be nothing you can do to stop it."

"Believe in your own supervillain posturing if you'd like. Just because you wish to get away with this pathetic tantrum doesn't mean you will."

I saw a flash of jagged, pearlescent teeth and heard, so I thought, a muttering of "Stupid boy," then he took the scythe in both hands. He threw his weight backward onto one foot, as though throwing a javelin. He was a sort of gymnast with the weapon, swinging the pointed tip around his torso in an arc like a pendulum, one shoulder facing me as the blade plunged squarely into the leg of one of the guards standing diligently flanking him. The young man seemed too shocked to react to the metal lodging into the flesh of his thigh, simply peering down at the tear in his trousers, hands still at his sides. When Uriel yanked it back out, however, he noticed that he was in pain, that they were drops of *his* blood pattering onto the cobbles, and doubled over. The sound was that of a kitchen knife pulled out of a hunk of raw fat, followed by a strange bubbling groan, as if the guard choked on the saliva at the back of his throat.

"It's always been your sorest weakness, I'd say," Uriel mused, between licking his thumb and scrubbing a dark spatter from his other hand. "Underestimating me. But that goes for the lot of you, really. Oh, don't look so dour all of a sudden. He'll be just fine, so long as you get a move on."

His snide glare pulled apart my fist, forcing my thumb and fingers to pinch around the nape of Lucifer's neck. She turned to glance back at me, as well as she could, a pitiful half-smile tugging at her face. The two guards now had their gloved hands locked around her wrists. The man with the cuffs and bleeding leg attempted a few times to crouch behind her, in order to fasten a chain between her ankles, before his companion, the one with the box, snatched them from him and finished the job. My chest fluttered with a murmur of pride, noticing that they insisted on holding her at an arm's length, as if afraid she might still overpower them, even with her Soul tranquilised.

But as my eyes gingerly met hers, pinprick pupils drowning defiantly in a pool of water, there was a blunt smack, like the first strike of a woodcutter's axe. Uriel's palm landed on Lucifer's head, between the tapered horns pointing in toward her temples. Under the weight of all those beastly hands, her spine bent into a crooked shape, and he towered over her, chin pressed to his chest. His fingers buried in her hair, he pulled her by her scalp, and looked down at her. He didn't say anything. He just looked at her. I felt the muscles in her neck contract when she stopped breathing.

My mind scrambled for some way to comfort her in that moment, even just to lighten the sting of my rough fingerprints against her skin, let her Soul float up for air. Instead, some perverse corner of my memory clawed to the surface. I remembered learning how killer whales would hunt in groups, skulking in the migration paths of their grey cousins. In a remarkable display of synergy, the pack would circle a new-born, coaxing it from under its mother's fin, before taking turns to lay on top of the baby, forcing it under the water over and over, for hours, until it drowned. Unable to so much as bend my knuckles one way or the other, incapable of easing her suffering, let alone saving her from it, I felt more sick with terror than I imagined she ever had.

"Looks like we've hit a wall, don't you think?" she chuckled, right before someone kicked at her heel, causing her to lurch forward into step.

**[Lucifer]**

The floor of my cell, same as the corridor all the way down, was coated in a thick layer of slightly sticky grit. Though the partitions were sound, the dirt still wormed itself inside, dropping from the ceiling like old plaster, or dragged up through cracks in the floor by the pillbugs. I made a concerted effort to tidy my abode, sweeping the mess into the corners of my personal square with my hands and feet, lasting—I could only assume—several hours, before giving in, planting my rear in a pile against the wall outward-facing wall, as though to profess my nonchalance toward the entire affair. The texture reminded me of salt, not easy to crush between the fingernails, though it generated a hard crunching sound underfoot.

Even so, I did not hear Uriel coming. A pinching ache clattered down my spine as my shoulder blades clenched together. I thought my voice box rose up, sliding from the front of my throat to the back, with my tonsils. I then noticed the sour taste burning on my tongue and realised that I had swallowed down my own vomit. The smell worked its way through the various pipes connecting up my face, into my nostrils. No matter what I ate, it seemed, my sick always reminded me of overripe banana.

This hole in the ground was so still—even the persistent buzzing sound was too consistent to notice, like the tilt of a boat to a sailor—that the slightest flicker of light felt like a razor flying straight toward my eyeball. It surely did not help that I had been totally free of distraction, too awake to nap, too exhausted to imagine the pleasant taste of sugar in my mouth, or a bar of music to play over and over in my ears. My mind instead occupied itself entirely with anticipating the blade, Soul ready to lash out of my skin like a leather whip. I managed to contain her. If I was to remain calmly inside my cage, reserving my energy, then she could do the same. My body froze in place. My limbs felt flabby and numb, my head heavy, like a porcelain face on the soft, squishy body of a doll. Uriel crossed his arms in front of him, watching me from under his brow, as though balancing a pair of reading glasses on his nose. The toe of his boot thumped against the dusty floor.

I didn't bite at first, just stared at a dent in the wall off to his left. I had little better to be doing, after all. I thought to play with him for longer, but then realised I would never be able to keep my nightly ration of dehydrated porridge inside my stomach, what with his face staring me down.

"What is it I can help you with today?" I chimed.

"Ah, so you are still alive," he said, trying his best to appear as though he didn't give a shit either way. "At least that means you'll be able to talk." His shoes scuffed against the grit as he slowly crouched down, a hand tightly gripping one of the vertical bars still barricading the doorway. He had to dip his head down further, to be level with me, slouching low to the bare floor. "I need you to tell me what you're hiding."

A wonderful, pointless idea immediately occurred to me. "Well, you see…I've never actually been kissed by anyone else. I don't honestly think pink is all that bad, as colours go; that vintage blouse Eve has, I always liked that on her. I'm worried I might be an alcoholic. And I have this mole, huge it is, massive, right smack on my—"

He huffed through his nose, his knuckles white as chalk against the grimy metal and stone of the cell. He blinked for a second or so, before realising his eyes had broken contact and opening them again. His lips parted to speak.

I sat up, using my arms to heave myself back into a right-angle. "And look, I confess. I *might* be a witch."

His fist slammed against the bars—once, twice, a third time. He stood up, and swivelled on the spot, releasing a shout which bounded down the corridor. The noises melded together and drove toward me like an open palm pressing against my temple, squeezing my head against the wall. I knew what he had come here for, what he desired so greedily that the need was fighting to tear itself out of his soft, lithe, pale body. It dangled before him, a ripe, purple bunch of grapes growing out of my throat, and he was stuck on the other side of the door.

"I'm afraid you're going to have to be more specific," I said.

A moment passed, still. He took his time to recompose, shove all of his facial features back into a comelier place. His voice felt quieter this time, as though conscious of the ears lingering, unseen in thick shadows.

"What are you planning to do to the Machine?"

I held a finger up, pushed it into the corner of my smile. "Careful now, Uriel."

"Answer the question."

"You know I can't do that."

"You will."

"Why?"

"You won't have a choice."

I laughed. It started as a snicker, just a few teeth grinding together. Then I found myself cackling, slapping my numb thighs and knocking my head against the wall until the crown of my skull ached. I knew what he wanted. He wanted me to admit I was trying to destroy the one and only thing he truly loved in this awful little world, because I was an evil, spiteful woman.

"What are you going to do, torture me?" I shrieked. "Beat me with a stick, pull off my fingernails, load me up with sedative, strip me and dunk me in the lake until I'm within an inch of my life? If you're persistent enough, I'll give you what you want, right? Please. You know my Soul. I think you've always wanted to see me die. Or to make me haemorrhage, at least. But you weren't allowed to have that, because the thick, floating soup of supernatural bullcrap in the sky chose *me*. So, you did every other little thing you could instead. And boy, I hope you got your kicks at the time, because now this thing inside me is just pissed the hell off. You know it'll tear this damp shit-heap apart until you and me both are nothing but dirt. There's nought you can do about that. Or perhaps there is. Just how selfless of a man are you, Angel Uriel?"

"Not me, dear. I shall love to see if you can keep up that gusto when I bring Michael down here to hold you still by your wrists whilst I do it."

"Michael. You really think he'd make a difference? He's not stronger than me. He could never outlast me. You think I wouldn't lie back and watch as each layer of skin peels away, and the muscle beneath slowly tears into flayed sinews before my eyes? Warm blood drip-dropping onto my face—"

"That's enough."

"Second thoughts? I must say, I'd have to agree; three Angels for worm food might be a tad excessive."

"That's enough!"

I felt my face scrunch into a pout. "Oh dear. Am I not being quite as obliging as you'd hoped? Does that make you anxious? Run along now, good Angel, and find your confession elsewhere."

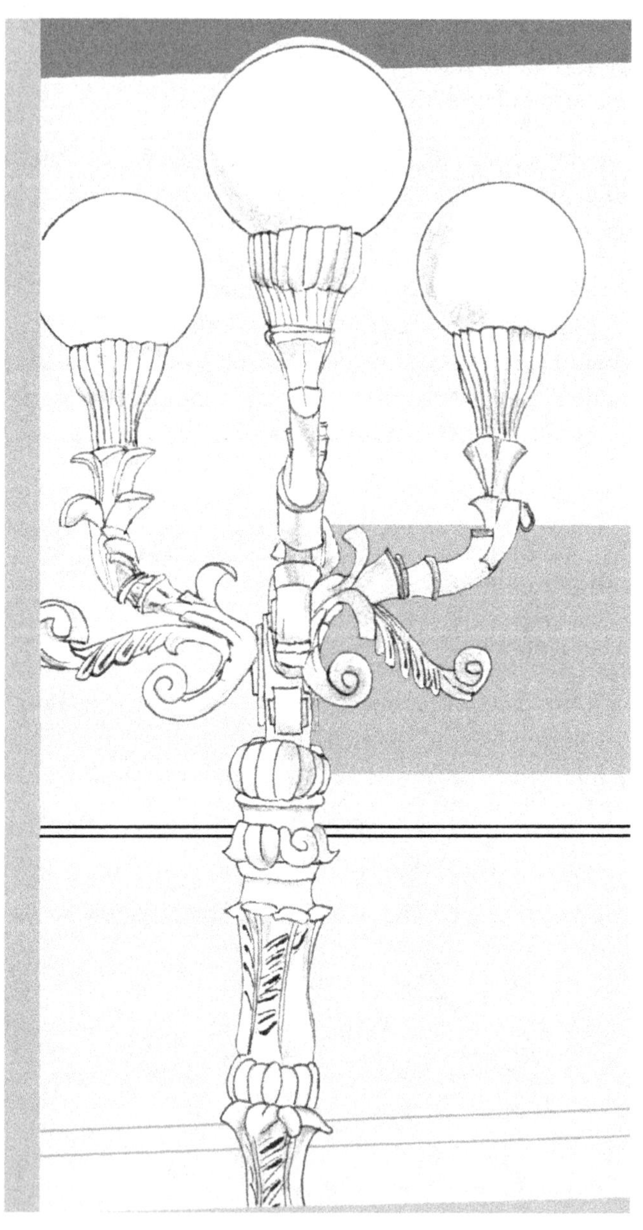

[248]

# Part 6: Annihilation

**[Raphael]**

I heard footsteps approaching from behind. Or, at least, something like footsteps, similar enough for me to listen for the scrape of a scythe's tip dragging against the cobbles, Uriel's glib voice calling bounding down the alley, *"What are you doing all the way out here, Raphael? I thought you were allergic to daylight. Lost, are we? Confused?"*

The steps grew closer, rapidly, seemed to fill up the cold, narrow space in all directions, before passing overhead. The languid flick of a crow's feathers.

I should have known this would happen. I should have planned ahead. I could have brought something with me, a needle, a kitchen knife, anything. Why the fuck was I the only stupid cunt of an Angel who didn't carry around a regular, manmade deadly weapon? My fingers gripped at my head, not quite able to maniacally knot themselves into my hair, for the metal thorns growing from my skull pricked and sliced little papercuts in the skin. I still felt hands behind me, Uriel's hovering over my shoulder and curling around my neck. I thought I might concentrate on the idea of his nails dragging across my throat, muscle and hair and dead skin gathering underneath them like wood shavings, when the hands changed. They became light, as brushed cotton, a hungry, delicious species of touch, walking down my spine, tracing the lines of my scapula. Perhaps, I speculated, the Machine would still send a message for me. To

Michael: If you could only get the fuck out of my head for five minutes—

I scrubbed at my eyes, as they flooded with, what, frustration? Fear? Reverence? The liquid blur cleared somewhat, and my gaze once again scanned the length of the Wall before me, left to my—

I stopped. In the blank, loveless, infinitesimal face, my gaze caught a dark spot. It appeared, initially, to resemble the depthless void of a crack, a narrow slit between the bricks, made only for spiders, and a little finger someone never hoped to get back. Impossible, also. I took a step closer. As the angle of my head moved, so did the shape. It protruded out, perpendicular to the vertical surface, the cement surrounding it showing not so much as a disturbed flake. The Wall had repaired itself perfectly, too perfectly, around the anomaly, like skin healing *around* a splinter, rather than pushing out the foreign appendage, rendering it permanent, claiming it had never been anything but a fragment of its anatomy. How it had managed to remain, I could not fathom. A glitch? An unfortunate accident. A bent nail.

It may not have been forged a nail. In fact, it was closer in width to a foundational length of pipe, a scrappy, wayward segment of rebar. The end facing me, at that moment, pointing at my chin, had been ground to a point, whether by the force of age, or by design. I traced my thumb over it. It was not so sharp as to be ideal, but it would be sharp enough.

I scoffed, assuming that, if the dragon could not hear me before, it was listening closely now.

"This why you're being difficult, is it? Nothing without a fair exchange. Fire for a little blood…"

I propped myself against the stone, my right palm flat against the rough, porous surface, thirsty for an offering. And my left palm, I brushed it against my trouser leg once, twice, then lifted it up to the nail. One knuckle twitched uncontrollably. The bell tower braced itself with a low hum, before bellowing out a long, pounding ring. Fluid streamed downward through my body, as though a couple of valves had burst inside my ears. My head drooped forward, barren and weak, threatening to tip off of my shoulders and snap me at the stem. The bell rolled its tongue a second time, lulling the world into a silence colder than before, as though the city was issuing a dare, and every window overhead now waited over the proceedings.

"You want me to hurt, huh?"

What was it they used to tell me? Just a slight scratch. A bee-sting.

I felt my face melt, then boil, cheeks rippling as though switching at immeasurable speed between absurd, cackling laughter, and an infant's wail. My eyelids fell closed, and then I pried them open again. I was no Gabriel. I had to look at it. I needed to aim properly. I rehearsed the action several times over in my mind. I had presumed my imagination to be a relatively safe playground in which to practice. And yet, it was my imagination that pondered whether I might see a globular bulge appear on the back of my hand, as the skin stretched and grew taught, like fabric, the structure inside shifting to accommodate pressure. Eventually the flesh would tear, frayed, yielding, bursting around the staunch black metal. I pictured little pieces of pale bone turning outward, driving through ripped tendons and veins. I had a scar on the back of my left hand, some remnant of my days as a bumbling toddler. How pathetic that little nick of a scar would feel now.

Then I remembered the bell tower. I remembered the faceless windows. They still waited. Tick-tock, boy.

I drew my shoulder back, pulled it tight, straining like a trebuchet. And then I thrust myself forward. My feet seemed to rise off of the ground; I floated upward, too big, too loud, too much for my body.

I could close my talons around the first stone brick, pressed into its cold, inanimate resistance. I buried myself in the mouth of the

Wall, elbows-deep, felt pieces of its calcified body snap off in handfuls. Stone which had slept sound for centuries melted into glass, thick, autumn-coloured sludge that slid between my fingers. I might have laughed if it were not so painful. My head hung below my chest, weighed down by all of the teeth growing out of my throat, through the roof of my mouth. My jaw stretched wider, lips tearing at the corners, opening up the airway to let my lungs scream louder. I had to keeping bellowing, else I would burn from the inside out.

A slice of the innermost face yawned, before it slid vertically downward, as though a diamond cleaver had bisected it. It fell in one complete piece, like a discus, then shattered over my skull.

Michael gave a rattling, loud, and reckless sigh that bounced around the Hall. He sat on my right, closest to the aisle, Gabriel on my left, all crouched between two pews with bent spines and aching knees.

"Still nothing?" Gabriel could have been napping, his head resting on the wooden board behind him, legs crossed, if not for his occasional calm inquiry, attempts to stifle Michael's rising nerves. As for myself, I found it quite unsettling; this version of Gabriel's childhood friend muttered and fidgeted constantly, volatilely.

"It's been too long. Nothing's happening," he said.

"We don't know how long it takes. Maybe it's already happened, and the old guy just hasn't made it out from behind the painting yet."

"And the longer we wait here to find out, the more likely it is that Raphael's head is rolling away from his dead body."

"I have an idea," I interjected.

"Rei?" Gabriel yelped.

"I'll go in."

"You can't!"

I had already picked myself up off of the ground, which seemed to confuse him. His head tilted rapidly from left to right, and though his eyes were hidden behind the bandage, I could see panic in the downward droop to his lips.

"I mostly certainly can, and I will. Or don't you trust me?" I offset my snappy tone of voice with a light kiss to his forehead. "I'll only be a few minutes. Look after my man for me, okay?" I said to Michael, taking his hand (his skin was incredibly cold) and pressing it against Gabriel's.

I refused to turn my head as I dashed away, not that I ought to have seen anything. My legs scrambled ahead of my chest, and I almost smacked my toes against the steps. The six pitiful eyes of the scaled Soulless followed my movements, suffering terrible pain, burning in red oil paint, and yearning for an end as simple as mine, crushed under the heroes' feet. I had never trodden behind the fresco before. Immediately, the feeling flashed over my mind, that I might be in the wrong place. Maybe I had anticipated something more obviously decorated to be a hidden entrance, with switches and camouflage, perhaps a congratulatory neon sign, rather than an old plastered-over wall. The hefty metal hatch was satisfyingly out-of-place, at least. The fact that the animalistic shriek emitted by the hinges provoked no response from anywhere should have been a relief. Instead, I felt lonely—as I listened out and heard nothing—and rather silly for expecting otherwise. The cool, still air in the passageway chilled the beads of sweat gathering at my hairline. The dark corridor seemed to grow longer as I walked through it, as if the dark void was alive, like the root of an oak tree.

The throne room surprised me, perhaps even frightened me, with how quiet and peaceful I found it. Light trickled in from the domed window, glancing upon the many appendages of the Machine, all perfectly motionless, not so much as a cable swaying in the air. The Sovereign sat opposite me, a soft mound, like a decrepit man dozing in his favourite wicker rocking chair, his hands resting limp and knurled at his sides. His face, clean shaven, tilted an inch upward, searching for the sound my shoes made as they scraped into the empty, echoing space.

"You. You are…"

I found myself standing upright, straight as a board, hands squeezing together behind my back. "Rei Guerera, Majesty," I said.

"You have Enlightenment."

"That's right."

"What do you want?"

"Your Majesty, I—I have had a vision. My Soul has shown me a terrible future."

"I don't suppose that future would have something to do with the delinquent Angel currently attempting to eviscerate the Wall?"

"Raphael, he—he seems to have lost all sanity, Majesty. I cannot speak for what has broken in his mind, but if no-one is allowed to restrain him…"

"And I can see that, excluding Uriel, none of my other Angels are moving to eliminate this traitor. Does your vision explain that?" I sensed something like a laugh in his wispy voice. I would not fall for it.

"If I may be so brash, Sir, Lucifer is still incarcerated underground, as per your own orders. Gabriel has been deprived of his sight and cannot navigate on his own, and as for Michael…I could not find him anywhere in my Soul's vision. I can only assume that, in the future for which we are destined, Michael is already deceased. I don't know where, nor how exactly." I had already formulated this excuse for him minutes ago. All of his morbid talk of severed heads had led me to thinking about his relation to death.

"Then, I must ask," he said, after a pause, "what is your point in informing me of this?"

"Perhaps it is mere desperation, Majesty. However, in the absence of the Angels, our guardians, I suppose us civilians have no choice but to fight on their behalf, for the sake of our city, the integrity of our great society. The thought of the Wall's protection being gone, it…breaks my heart."

"The Machine's safety protocols do not allow for violent action towards the Angels by subordinates, child. You should understand this."

"You cannot change such measures, Majesty? I did not know. But I am sure there are many besides myself who would be willing, given the opportunity."

"The only way for me to facilitate your good will is to manually shut down the Machine, the very programme that has granted you protection inside the Wall. Do you understand what that means?"

"I am so sorry. I regret the intrusion."

"You must know, little one, that if you are lying to me, you will have killed us all."

This assertion almost struck me off of my feet, for a split second. Of course I was lying, through my teeth. But Gabriel's promise had come true; the Machine could not tell the difference, not in this room, not if I could lie *well*. This man, sitting hunched and weakened before me, required that I be honest. It had been such a long time since anyone had needed to ask that of me.

"I understand, Sovereign. What reason would I have to mislead you?"

"Your intimate relations with Gabriel, for instance."

"With all due respect, my relationship with Gabriel, a man who is now more vulnerable than I have ever been, should only render me even more desperate to keep him alive."

"You believe him to be incapacitated? You sorely underestimate him… When I detach myself from the Machine, I will be unable to transport my own body. This room will not remain standing for long. You must carry me to safety yourself. Then gather your colleagues. Use Michael to assist you. I very much doubt he is truly dead. He will lead you to destroy the dragon boy."

He stopped abruptly, like the end of a written speech, or a vinyl record. I stooped down to peer at his eyes, and found them tightly sealed shut, as though denying me access. While I was crouched, however, he began to keel forward, tipping out of the chair. Without a moment for thought, I took the last remaining steps towards him, catching his oblivious weight against my stronger shoulder. One of his arms slung over my back, the other, along with his legs, hung heavy and limp beneath him. I had no other option than to tow them along the floor, like the plough behind a pack horse. Recalling those words that had, seemingly, barely escaped off of his tongue, I heaved our bodies in the direction of an exit. I had to wrap my arms around his torso and pull him on his back through the narrow passageway, and continued in this manner down the aisle, and the front steps. I could hear his feet lump over each hard, steep edge with a dull, numb sound. The world around us looked still and uncaring, all help hiding behind doors, darkened windows and multiple storeys. In a fit of desperation, I hauled the man in my arms along the side of the building, my arms shuddering with weakness. I had spotted a right-angled crevice, between the rear of the stairway, and the thick, concrete foundation of the monument.

I took his head, hanging limp against his chest, and tilted it back so that it could rest against the wall, and only as I laid his hands upon his lap, did I feel the genuine tears welling between my eyelids, and nose streaming down my lips. I thought I had successfully smuggled us away in the shade, but heard Gabriel approaching behind me, hurriedly dragging his feet across the pavement, pulling Michael alongside him by his arm. They must have followed me, confused.

"Rei! Rei, what is the matter? What's going on?"

It took Gabriel's asking in his breathy, disconcerted tone of voice, before the answer could properly construct itself in my mind, let alone tug at my mouth. I smothered my face in my hands and said, "I think he's dead. He…fell all of a sudden. Even when I carried him outside…he looks so frail like this, but I could only sort of drag him on my own. I didn't know what else to do; he told me to carry him out of there, that was all. I couldn't feel him breathing. I couldn't feel anything. He seemed so heavy. And now I see him, and I think he's just *dead*. I killed him."

"It's okay…You'll be okay. He can't hurt you." The words flowed easily from the vibration in his throat. He could not see what I barely described, could not see what I had done, unlike Michael, who recoiled backwards, hands clasped in front of his mouth. "Is it only me," Gabriel said, "who can feel that trembling? It's in the ground, a sort of crumbling sound, not anything like the buzz I've heard before."

I felt strangely calm, the muscles in my back relaxed a little, despite the secret I had learned, possibly a result of Gabe's inquisitive, murmuring tone. "Him—he did say something about that. You two have to go," I insisted.

Michael finally spoke up. "I think she's right. We should move quickly."

Right about what? Right about the city's certain doom? Or right about the fact that I had driven the Sovereign to suicide? He did not specify any further.

"You're coming with us, Rei." Gabriel hooked his hands under my arms, and as he lifted me off of my knees, still hugging me to his breast, I felt several cold slaps of rain against my bare skin.

"And just leave him here, like this?" I had somehow forgotten who, or what exactly I was mourning for. For a moment, I thought of the Sovereign's body like that of an elderly man I was abandoning in a ditch, not a corpse preserved by ill means, dispatched most expediently for the greater good.

"There's nothing more you can do for the man. Typical Rei— you've been too kind to him already."

"But, wait…" I realised, as Gabriel disparaged the Sovereign, lying dethroned and diminished, why Michael had grown so quiet and terse. "We're meant to connect you to the Machine, Michael. If this is what happened to him, then what is it going to do to you?"

"Search me. I can't say I've paid much thought to it." He turned, hands balled up in his pockets, and gazed up at the Hall, the angular steps, the arched portal, squaring himself up to the idea.

**[Lucifer]**

I was busy carving patterns on the cell floor, dragging my
fingernail in long, spiralling lines through the damp grit, when
the first quake rattled the ground. I only noticed a slight
movement at first, enough to erase my drawing with dust shaken
from above. A flash of a silhouette just outside of the cage. I rose
to my feet, knees throbbing, and approached the bars.

I heard rapid, overlapping mutterings towards the long stairwell
leading to the surface, which amplified into frantic shrieks and
yells as the first chunks of the ceiling fell. The bricks atomised
into plumes of dust that stalked the corridor, sniffing for open
nostrils and exposed eyeballs to swarm. I could make out some
orders to carry up an unfortunate man who had been struck in the
head, and now appeared to be collapsed in a burdensome,
immobile heap. They did not seem to care for their prisoners,
even when the metal bars began to buckle and bulge in front of
my face, wailing under some immense pressure from above. Nor
did they notice when I pressed my weight against the bars and
found they could now warp enough to contort my body through,
one limb at a time, heavy stones with jagged edges nesting in my
hair and grazing my skin. The voices were gone. As I shuffled
along the corridor, toward the sloped bar of light licking over the
stairs, the walls moved, sliding downward, gathering at the base
as if they were liquid, like lava piling up in thick, viscous folds.
The cold floor bloated and cracked beneath my feet, parched and
brittle as it was. The deep tremors continued, fluttering under the
ground through the prison's concrete structure. Ah, the light. It
expanded, opened up like a hungry gullet, and then shrank to a
pinprick, to a dark void. I reached out, and grabbed blindly at a
loose block rolling down, down with the ceiling. My knuckles
scraped against the bedrock, stinging like venomous nettles and,
as I tried feebly to push the crushing load away from my chest,
the rubble melted, turning to clay that moulded between my
fingers. The black smoke hissed and thrashed as my Soul chewed
away at the stone, scrambling for air, my fingernails straining,
pushing aside handfuls of dry, bitter dirt, spitting lumps from

between my lips. Only at this moment did I wonder, what was I doing? What the fuck was I doing?

After what seemed to be an hour of helplessly writhing around in a vat of sand for hours, pulling clumps of decayed matter out of my nose, my ears, my eyes, prolonging a slow suffocation, my right hand burst through the quicksand into frigid, empty nothingness. I flexed my freed fingers, before hooking them into the mud, clawing my arms above my head, heaving my body out from a premature grave. From one enclosure to another. The outside world burned my eyes.

"Wotcher, rotten apple. Here I was, beginning to wonder if I'd ever see you again."

Blackwater. He was leaning against a lopsided iron fence, his arms crossed loosely, foot tapping impatiently, such that his hard heel produced a high-pitched clang which echoed over the wreckage. I noticed no sign of the guards I had heard panicking below.

"Sir." I choked up, between the coughing and sneezing, trying to flush a thick coating of dirt from my pipes.

"Now, I've never been quite sure whether or not I should be flattered, when grown adults still call me 'Sir', three, four years later."

"Well, there were plenty of other things I thought to call you," I wheezed, "but the younger me thought it wiser to restrain herself. Nowadays, calling you a knobhead doesn't carry the same insubordinate appeal, I must say."

"Oh, don't flatter me. I've always been a mook. Here, thought you might want this."

He waved his hand in front of himself, like a fan, an attempt to encourage me to my feet. Then he pointed toward a spot on the ground between the two of us. There, lying between a crack in the pavement like misplaced trash, I found my knife. The shard of black metal gleamed like a broken mirror, like torchlight. I bent to recover it, and sure enough, it slid into my grip, perfect. The handle had been too large for my hands as a child. Now I understood.

"I even sharpened it up for you, gave it a little polish. You do remember how to maintain the blade, don't you?"

"How did you—?"

"Pilfered it from the guard while the Machine wasn't looking. Of course, I then had to drop it when you started it back up again, if I wanted to keep my hand. I've been sat here watching over the bloody thing since." He tilted his chin up, looking at the pale dust billowing through the air, thick as sand, light as ash, and rolled his eyes. I had learned gall from the man, if nothing else.

"Am I going to need it?" I probed.

"You're asking me?"

"Which one of us was the last to be buried alive, hm?"

"Fair play, not that I have much to offer. All I can tell is there's trouble brewing at the Hall. Uriel seems to have swayed the Machine to his side."

"Uriel? That can't be."

"Look, the little fucker has all the city's wildlife tailing him like some sort of pied piper. For a moment I assumed Jasmine was back, too. Then I saw who was really heading the pack, and let's just say displeasure is an understatement. So, unless you've got a better explanation tucked away in your head, the Machine is still wide-awake, and it isn't about to play ball with you, Angels or no."

"The dagger it is, then." I tucked it away and rolled up the grimy, baggy sleeves hanging from my arms, already feeling less naked than I had in the cell. I turned to walk away, without acknowledging the slightly bitter curl in Blackwater's expression, but then hesitated. I said, "When you started teaching me to fight, really teaching me, you told me I was full of hate. I've spent almost every day since then trying to convince myself that you had it wrong, that there was something else, in here." I thumped my chest with the heel of my hand, a ridiculous, sentimental gesture.

"And?" he said.

"You know what? It might be true. I am hateful. Maybe it's all I am."

"It's kept you alive all this time, just about. Look at you; you just crawled up from under the earth like something undead. That is, if you have the right assessment of yourself in the first place. I can't tell you either way." He shrugged a dusting of grit off of his coat, surveying the hail of brick and slate slipping from nearby rooftops and grinding one heel into the dirt. "Hell, I don't even know who you are, or what you're up to, or if this carnage was part of the plan. I probably shouldn't be here, to be honest. But it isn't as if I have any use for that thing, so I figured you might as well have it back. You had best run, mind, if you want to get there before Uriel and company."

"Run? Run! You saw what I just had to do, right?"

"Ugh, fine." He threw his hands in the air, before reaching over the fence to lift over a wooden bicycle, with red paint peeling like rust off of every surface. "The things I've done for you. Hop on the back then, brat, and don't blame me if you end up with your nose planted in the pavement."

Incredulously, I waited for Blackwater to seat himself on the rickety bike, then balanced behind him, feet barely supported by the bolt holding on the rear wheel. I clung to the shoulder pads of his suit, much to his displeasure, listened to the rickety frame creak in pain as we pedalled through narrow alleys in the direction of the Hall. Though I hardly dared turn my head, I noted that, despite my own, recent ordeal, the rest of the city seemed intact, almost pristine, save for a distant column of smoke climbing towards the clouds. I could not see over the rooftops to the source of the fire, but I wished that Raphael was the cause. Beneath the stone labyrinth's usual low drone, and the ticking of the bike chain between my feet, I thought I could sense another, indistinct murmuring, like a chatter, a constant barking. The innocuous sound crawled over the hairs on my back like a horde of flies.

Given he made his chagrin so obvious, I expected Blackwater to throw me off of his back wheel at the foot of the Hall and speed down the street, a final complaint bouncing off his puckered lips. Instead, as I glanced over my shoulder halfway up the steps, he lingered rather awkwardly, one foot on a pedal, mouth pursed tightly. I paused, to see if he would speak, admittedly a little curious.

"I suppose this is where I leave you," he yelled, realising the nicety had come slightly late.

"It is." He had never seen much reason to be more than blunt with me. It seemed to him the kindest thing to do, not to make any exceptions.

His hands dropped into his lap. "I confess, I'm having a hard time deciding what to do with myself now." An inaudible chuckle shook his shoulders.

"You leave," I replied. "You go, just like everyone else. The outer colonies already have enough fugitives on their hands; I can't imagine they'll begrudge one more. Take up fishing or something, like other men your age. And try to steer clear of Uriel and his band of vermin on the way out."

"There's nothing else, then, that I can do to assist you?"

"Other than to get a move on and bugger off, no. If I am about to kick the bucket here, I'm not having you stick around to watch. Do you have any idea how embarrassing that would be?"

"Well, with the attitude…" He swung his leg over the bicycle, and shoved it to the ground, with a decidedly graceless commotion. "…I sure do. Time to find out how forgiving these locals really are, I suppose," he added, wandering leisurely along the pavement, a sharp turn from the wide central roadway. That route would take him a bit off the beaten trail, past the tradesmen—carpenter, engraver, printer, and the like—until he reached the Wall, which he could simply follow until he was caught, by whom I could only guess.

"Just find one of the ladies, tell them you broke me out of jail and gave me a weapon. It's only a stretching of the truth, and it'll keep you for a while."

He stopped again. "Listen, kiddo. Don't you die."

I shrugged, and turned my back on him, growing cross now. "What can I say? I'll try."

His face quirked, not with a smile, but something more neutral, a gesture of ambivalent recognition. "Well," he said, "that's more than you ever used to say. Guess we can only hope it's enough."

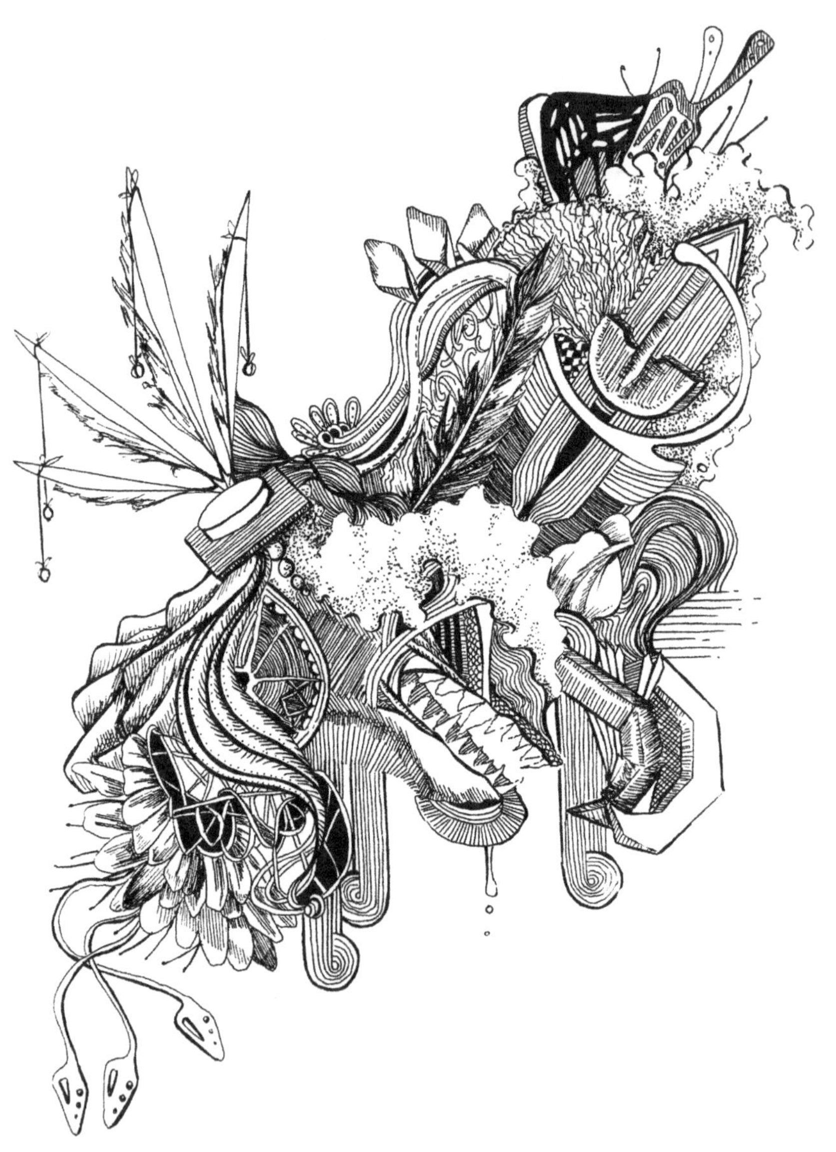

**[Gabriel]**

"Michael," Rei said, gently. "Michael, are you there?"

"He's gone, I think."

Michael was sat in the chair. I refused to call it a 'throne'. Thrones were ornate, plush, luxurious; this chair was the sort of thing one dreaded finding in a hospital basement. His hands draped over the armrests on either side. When he was still awake, babbling words of praise, struggling to keep his neck still, he held his back erect. Now, he sunk forward, his spine a curve, chin resting on his chest, like an ear of wheat that had survived a week without water. A clamp-shaped adapter weighed cold and heavy in my left hand, the thick connecting lead hanging down from a perilous tangle overhead, while the right hand pressed down upon the top of Michael's head. My splayed fingers lay atop of Rei's own hot knuckles, still tremulous, positioned on the opposite side.

"Then we're on our own now."

Connecting the left and right side of his wings to the mainframe had proven easy enough, particularly under the man's own watchful gaze and accessible memory combined. The crucial circuit between them complete, like the first letter, the rest sprawled before us, silent. Rei slid her hand away. I could only imagine the array of dark, empty sockets staring out at her, lifeless pupils, in the absence of any human eyes for company. I assumed they ranged in shape and size, as hollow pits in the skin of fallen fruit left to the insects.

Rei did not speak. She heaved up some sounds, like the embryonic sludge from which words formed in her mind, but cut herself off with a frustrated huff.

"We don't have much time," I said. "We need to get this done and get out."

"I know that! Forgive me for not having it all in hand, but there's something huge and angry with lots of teeth on its way, and

[267]

today is first I've ever seen of this entire thing. I can't just figure it out on my own."

"I can help you. Though this is the first time you've seen this room, I can't see anything at all. So you also need to help me. Describe what's in front of you."

"I don't even understand what I'm looking at. How do I know where to start?"

"Fine. I will. Check around his wrists and ankles. There should be pairs of cuffs. Are they fixed to Michael?"

"Around his feet? Well, no, they're—ow!"

"What was that? A shock?"

"No, that's not it." Her voice sounded muffled, as if coming through her teeth. Then I heard her suck on her skin with a hiss of pain. "The cuffs are all still open, so I went to shut the ones around his legs, and on the inside… Feel."

She grabbed hold of my fingers, pulling me down until I felt a smooth metallic surface beneath. I traced the tight curve until the side of my index pushed into an obstacle, perpendicular to the inside edge of the hasp. It was long, so narrow I could pinch it, but tough enough that a tug in either direction did not bend it.

"A pin?"

"It's got a sharp end, too. That's what caught my hand."

"Close them. Give the moving part one good, hard shove. Like this."

I kneeled on the floor, positioning the heel of my hand against the outer side of the latch, and rolled up the hem of Michael's trouser leg. I did not pause to contemplate before slamming the cuff closed. I heard only the blunt knock of metal against metal. From the wince that passed Rei's lips, however, I assumed the needle had successfully punctured the skin.

"You fix the ones up there," I directed, moving on to the next.

I couldn't tell what was different about the metal around Michael's hands, what went wrong. It did not make sense, like the hollow ringing sound had. Instead, as Rei threw her whole weight down upon the hinged shaft, an almighty crack sliced through the room, as though her body had somehow grown up to the ceiling, plucked a femur from the rafters and snapped it over her knee.

She seemed not to notice. "Done," she said.

I tilted my face up to her, attempting to harvest some sense of a reaction from her voice. The cool air gave out a subtle hiss, like my ears were immersed in water of incalculable depth. Rei's feet kicked up ripples as she paced around the back of the chair.

"What now?" she dipped her head under to ask.

"Just pick up whatever thing is closest to you. Every empty socket needs to be filled. There were never any loose wires. Nothing wasted."

"This one, then."

She pushed something round into my palm. I could barely close my fingers around it, a knurled ring, tapering away to a rubber, perhaps plastic tail.

"It's a greenish colour," she called from some low position, crouched behind something. "The cable, that is. Pretty heavy, compared to some of these other ones."

I moved the part around, running my thumb along each edge, prodding into any gaps wide enough.

"These two are the same end, kind of square, chunk out of the middle… That has to fit there, right? No?" She talked constantly, in breathy, clipped mumbles to herself, a raised voice to me. "Any ideas?"

"This wire is fairly short, yes?" I tugged on it until it strained taut. "It should go back there somewhere, I think. Look for something that fits a pair of pins, round, feels as though it might thread onto a screw."

"I've seen the screw shape somewhere," she said. I offered the plug to her. "Right in the middle. Here—"

An explosive clap and a high-pitched shout started and stopped within the same second. I could imagine the burst of white light splitting the darkness, the sound was so distinct. A metal weight hit the floor.

"Rei?"

I scrambled to my feet. An acrid scent burned my sinuses.

"Are you there?"

A sigh. A good sign. "I'm fine. Trying to find another outlet for two pins. It's not a screw cap, by the way," she added, matter-of-factly.

"I'd guessed as much."

"What about you, are you okay? Here. Take a look at this one." Another heavy rope whipped against my wrist.

"Of course."

*"At least I know it's not real,"* I almost admitted out loud. Then my mouth sewed shut like a dam, remembering that I had never figured out how to tell her about the dream, with the wooden box and the ocean. *"You just got an electrical shock, right? If we had really been drowning in water, I wouldn't be able to ask you if you were still alive, because we'd both be dead!"*

I thought, so very briefly, of Lucifer, an image of her against the bars of an underground cell brushed over the surface of my eyelids. I wondered if she had found an escape from her prison. I wondered if Michael was searching for her. She must have been up to something, somewhere. I was beginning to think like her.

**[Lucifer]**

I had no perception of the sheer heaving, vacillating noise that
burst from every orifice in the city, not until I climbed through
the entryway, the curve of the archway pulling me inward like a
mother's arm and enveloping me in wet, misty quiet. I thought I
might take my time, take in one sip of sweet, cold air leaking
from the walls, before the inferno fell from the sky, as I walked
to the altar where I had risen from the earth to meet it. Then I
surveyed the room, looked to the left of me, and to the right, past
where the yellowed light glanced into the mud, and there was no-
one there with me. There was no-one. Michael had to be in the
chair. But he could not have pushed those screws and nails into
himself. I did not know who had helped him, but they were not in
the room. There was a storm coming in. They could not help me.
I ran. How I wished for powerful, bursting legs, that I could
sprint and bound rather than crawl. My chest shrank, innards
squeezing up and out like the guts of a pomegranate. I spat lumps
of soil from my mouth.

As I suspected, there was a deep, gaping cavity where the lead
door had been left hanging open, bleeding darkness like the
weeping flap of skin over a papercut. I reached into the
passageway, grabbed the handle with both fists and threw my
weight backward until I heard a low, mighty bang.

When I emerged from behind the frame, I found the chamber
steeped in darkness. Every window, shaft, and crevice were
filling with formless shapes rendered black by the lack of light,
shuffling for space like newly hatched spiders on a cobweb. The
archway strained as a bundle of bodies pressed against it,
writhing on top of each other like a baby's tiny, plump limbs as
they struggled for space, little feet breaking free from the hot,
fleshy amalgam and slapping against the floor.

Rats and birds, for the most part, although I could also point out
squirrels, bats, badgers in the crowd. The grass snakes were too
slow, their flaccid bodies still pathetically curling around the
doorway when the rest had already come to an unnatural

forward-facing standstill. Taxidermies had more life in their glass eyes than these. It pained my heart to find an amber-coated fox among them.

The air shifted, oxygen sucked in reverse out of my lungs, sweat lifted away from my skin, pulled toward the aisle. The archway twisted in place, like the wringing-out of a dishrag, then sprang back into position, an elastic tension and release. In its place— Uriel. As he landed, he crushed the head of a rodent under his foot, perhaps unintentionally, but perhaps not. I knew this, because I had learned every little sensory distortion his Soul created, every hint to know he was coming just a fraction of a second before he appeared. I had to. And I knew he never made a wet, squelching sound. He bit at the inside of his cheek when he heard it, too. But unlike me, he could not stand to glance down at the worm-like tail sticking out from under his shoe, as it flicked and squirmed and went limp. He couldn't stand the mess. He didn't seem particularly pleased to see me again so soon, either.

"Stand aside, Lucifer. For once, my quarrel is not with you. Not yet. You can save us both the expended effort."

I pulled the dagger from the small of my back, turning it in my hand to a reverse grip. Quick little poking jabs might help against the Angel, but stood a fat chance against an army in the hundreds. I moved my toes inside my shoes, trying to find the ground through the needles in my feet.

"Michael's the one back there, isn't he? And don't just stand there gawking at me like a mute. It's not helping your case."

"What difference does it make to you? You'd vaporise a puppy if it were the one plugged into your Machine."

My tongue was tired, exhausted with engaging with him. My Soul much less so. It thrashed and kicked, hot, low in my belly.

"The difference," he said, "is that I'm going to have to kill you first, before I can get to him. A shame, really. I had greater plans for us. But someone has to keep their priorities straight."

"That sounds like a fair assessment to me. See, my priority is to stand right here, on this spot, regardless of who or what follows you down there. And little do you know, I've worked years in customer service, so it'll take more than you whinging about it to get me out of the way." I shrugged.

"Get a grip, woman. What am I supposed to make of your corpse?"

"Personally, I think that's my business. Why? Does the thought of my dead carcass scare you? Are you worried about what might happen—that my skin will turn inside-out, and all this juice and fat and shit will squelch over your nice shoes, or that all of my bones will curl into fangs and gnash at your ankles as you step over? I'm afraid you're just going to have to get over it. Rigor mortis takes time, more than what you have. Come on, love. It's only a bit of blood."

He hitched the scythe up in his hand, not yet into the position to strike, instead knocking the handle against the floor, the metal ringing out like a tuning fork. A bird had been perched atop the blade's upper, blunter edge, a vacant-eyed corvid. Jarred by the impact, it ruffled its breast and sprang onto iridescent wings.

The other birds followed, springing like fired arrows out of the throng. They dipped in a downward arch, before rising toward the altar, their wings drumming as they beat the air, matching the stamp of a heavy wave breaking onto a cliff face. We would speak of birdsong being soothing, the sound of nature's persistence among, between, and in spite of us. The larger individuals kept their mouths shut, waiting until they were close enough to also take a slither of soft cartilage between their beaks. I had heard tales of magpies pecking out the eyes of lambs under the noses of their mothers. Remembering this, I held an arm across mine, peering out, child-like, from between my splayed fingers. Meanwhile, the smaller birds, as though under a different set of orders, forgot the lyrics of their parents, preferring the breathless, formless squeal, taken from when they themselves squirmed naked, with no eyes. They squabbled for space as they all began to swing their tiny, clawed feet forward to grasp at my hair. I silently, mentally, secretly thanked the Machine for preparing my Soul so well for this moment in advance. The dense smoke smothered me in darkness, it hugged me so closely, flowing out from my face, as if coughed up from a bonfire in my lungs, stroking away the hairs down my back. I felt the birds' limbs touch mine, burrowing for grip as my arms grew slick, curling their feet around my fingers, only for them to turn soft and fall away, rotten fruit from their tree. The big crows and rooks hung on for longer, nipping as they croaked in my ears. One managed to leave a gash in my cheek, as it reached for the artery at the side of my neck, the sensation of a blunt meat cleaver. The fog cleared from my view, turning toward this straggler, enough that I could see to extricate the creature from my head with a stroke of the knife. It thudded onto my foot, and as I kicked it aside, I noted that almost all of its feathers on one side had been burned away, and Antithesis had begun to chew away at its skull, its pale surface standing out on a cushion of black.

"What idiot gave you that thing back?" Uriel shrieked, a foamy, high-pitched noise like a new-born's cry bounding around the hall.

"Nobody," I said. "I killed one of the guards for it. Thought I might need it."

Eve used to tell me I was a terrible liar. Even when I presumed that I was regurgitating a most basic truth, she said the deception shivered across my countenance, through my little voice. In this case, I didn't mind at all, if it was this easy. I wanted Uriel to know I was spouting lies directly to his face. And if he did believe some of it, well, so much the better.

I had a nasty, disgusting idea, seeing him standing amongst the Machine's hapless, senseless army of tools, backs erect, each like a wooden pawn, or an arthritic finger. I slapped my right hand against my cheek, pushed it across the hump under my eye. Mean, stinging pain radiated through my head, down the side of

my neck, as if to alert me to the blight I had just rubbed in under
my skin. Palm smeared with red stain, I held it aloft, pointing to
it with the same hand that held the knife.

"See?" I called out. "I told you; I practically leak this stuff. I'd
congratulate *you*, but I assume of all these poor fuckers are just
on loan from the Machine."

He tilted his head back a little, so as to be looking down from
somewhere, if only down the slope of his own nose. A pause
leaned heavy upon the sweltering atmosphere. I saw no
refutation in his expression, no debate, no strategy, only quiet
contemplation, like a ballerina tipping up their chin as they
balance their entire weight on one toe, taking a moment to
luxuriate in their next action, already decided. He rolled his eyes.
Lifting his weapon an inch off of the ground, he placed one foot
behind the other, stepping sideways, as if opening a door for a
lover. He stood and watched.

There was a great pounding, like a torrent of rain against the
windows, the percussion of myriad feet grinding into motion.
The room fell forward with its creatures, becoming liquid and
flowing like a river down a steep mountainside. The combined
force of hundreds of tiny, weak bodies flipped over the wooden
pews like hurdles, trampling over each other, the steps up to the
altar acting as a sort of bottleneck.

Knife in hand, feet planted on the floor, I swung my arm in a
wide arc before me, the big slabs of muscle in my back straining
and tearing. The black titanium, still sharp as a scalpel, made a
clean slice through the thick air like tissue. It carved a long, thin
opening that spliced the room horizontally, which widened just a
little, as though fingers had squeezed it like skin on either side,
before my Soul's fury spilled out, dirt from a wound. There was
a minute delay, Antithesis awaiting the perfect fraction of a
second, gathering energy, clenching her teeth, gas under a cork.
Then the smoke roared and propelled forth with such momentum
my body recoiled backward, a thin, dense slither of darkness, a
razor blade, guillotined the entire length of the chamber.

Instantly, the shrieking sound dampened, drowned as a sea of windpipes were chopped into pieces. My blood boiled as it hit the ground. It swelled up in thick, elastic bubbles, turning from red to scorched black, dust scattering like steam.

Over the crest of the haze, I saw a head, a little smaller than my own, jump toward me. We were almost face-to-face, its triangular snout, stripped of hair, but mouth still full of teeth, to mine, round, cushiony, and delectable. I held the handle of the dagger with both fists, pointing it outward, in front of my brow, like some sort of tricorned animal. But before the little canine could impale itself on my blade, its body fell away. The soft parts melted to slush first, pouring out from its bottom jaw, leaving only the bones, which peeled away in flakes, ash that floated into my eyes and nose and mouth.

I didn't want to spectate, as bodies disintegrated into particles before me, so rapidly that they still had a little life left in their separated parts. My head felt as though it floated in a pond of hydrochloric acid, my feet made of rocks. But I had promised I would not simply let Uriel kill me. And doing that meant never averting my eyes, not handing him an opening like candy in my fingers.

But amongst the feathers, fur, and flames, Uriel was gone. Naturally, he would not stand the humiliation of being slain in one blow with all the rest. Or rather, it was his Soul that would not simply lay down at the sight of my own and whisked him away. Truthfully, in a raw, body-to-body brawl, I would have been crushed under his white knuckled fists years ago, like a twig, with few signs of a struggle. Today, the marks of my struggle were holes ripped in the marble, ancient relics burned to stubs like matches. My back hit a wall, the fresco behind me, the Wyvern's maw strange and enlarged over my head. My arms pressed against the sandpaper skin of the paint, as though I dragged the plaster along on my shoulders. He could not hide forever. His Soul could not hold him in limbo indefinitely, else the burst cells of his body would dissolve away, absorbed by the breathing earth, and he'd re-emerge with a deep cavity in his torso where an arm had been. I scanned the walls and broken windowsills. He was in this room, somewhere, looking at me, waiting. As I turned my gaze to the rafters, the sound clawed at my ears, the gusting of hot wind up a chimney.

I saw his mouth first, cavernous throat behind a tongue glowing against a rack of pearls spitting saliva. He dropped like an iron weight. The dagger wedged between me and the downward swing of the great singular talon in his hands, but it felt as if it took every inch of muscle in my arms to hold it there, to push back, to stop him from tossing me aside and jamming the metal point in my spine. He kicked at my knee, pain firing down my shin, before he vanished again. He appeared at the foot of the altar, but as I leaned forward, firming my grip on my weapon, he floated away on a breeze. He landed next to me, scythe missing my ear, peeling layers of colour from the wall when he yanked it out, and I coughed, eyes flooding with tears, choking on plaster dust. Then he was suspended in the air over the aisle. He shifted so rapidly that my mind could not process his image fast enough, and he appeared to have a double, a projection of himself following in his wake. He was in front of my face, above my head, and behind my neck, all at the same second. He was not trying to impale me on the fresco, at least not yet. He wanted to confuse me, exhaust my nerves, and disable Antithesis.

I bent forwards, one arm wrapping around my head. I tilted the angle of the dagger, so that the point pressed a little further into the elastic skin which covered my throat. As flashes of Uriel continued to shift and warp in a swarm, their number seemed still to increase until they began to overlap, resulting in mirages with three arms, and disembodied eyes and lips. Encouraged by my shrinking body, each one raised their weapon over their head, poised to strike, floating closer, growing larger, melting together into a blurred mass. At the same time, a pool of darkness stirred at my feet, rapidly swelling and rising straight upward, through my stomach, before it burst out from my back, almost tearing my spine in two. The bundle of black dust grew so dense it appeared to solidify, as it splayed into a cluster of uncountable spears, spines unfurling like a flower from a bud. My thoughts resonated with Antithesis, my Soul equally determined to weed out the true, fleshy Uriel from the mob, stabbing relentlessly, feverishly through the air until its power was slowed by the ceiling. And there he was, dropping to the ground as if he had tripped. With no other clean space left to pop into, his hands and knees pressed against the unnaturally warm marble, his face parallel to the gore pasted over it.

The many wisps of smoke coalesced into a complete wall of impenetrable fog above our heads. It began to sink as I looked down on Uriel, pretending to be heavier than the air we breathed, to swallow it up in ravenous gulps. He peered up at it, falling like a blanket of volcanic ash, his eyes rolling backward into their sockets. No more light fell on his face, drowned out by the black haze. A few eager specks settled onto his wings, marring the golden halo with debris. I pushed a hand through my heavy, sticky head of hair, to see him better. I adored his expression in that moment, the second I took a step towards him, kneeling on the floor, and he glanced back. Never before had his jaw trembled like that, tongue caged between his teeth. Never before had a face so clearly read, "Oh dear, I have made a terrific mistake." I stopped when I was standing close enough to reach out and touch him.

"I thought this would be more difficult, you know. I thought it would be my chance to prove I am no longer a coward, after I turned my back and ran from you. A true test of wills, no good nor foul about it. But it turns out you are no more than the day I left you. Eve's been toying with you. She whispered in your ear, told you I was feeble, and stupid, that you could have me, because I was easy. Eve is smart, see? Wicked, yes, but much smarter than you and I. She was wrong this time, though. She slipped. You're but a child. Me? I am unto a god. Sometimes I think the Source knew all about you. It gave me this power, to protect me from you. What do you have left to threaten me with, huh?"

"You're all talk, aren't you? A real blabbermouth, at least until your Soul tires out. Now, now, you're smarter than this."

"Oh yes, I do love to talk, once you take the gag off. Not that you'd know. And you can spit out whatever garbage you want, but me and my Soul, we've got to know lady death terribly well. We can stay here like this all day."

"You know death, do you? Well, go on then. Kill me, right here, while you still have the chance."

"Absolutely not."

"Oh, why ever would that be?"

"Because you asked me to." I removed the knife's edge from my throat, in order to point it under his chin, forcing him to look me square in the face. "Go on, poppet. Run along, before someone else finds you, someone more generous than me."

There was a small popping sound, followed shortly by a grumble, like a fire igniting in the guts of an engine, grinding his silhouette into sneering crumbs and scattering them over the horizon.

The remaining vestiges of a black fog ascended towards the cracked and hollow windows, coasting carelessly against the glass fangs as if returning home, to the deep intangible bowels from which it came. It seemed to carry away my strength to stay standing, too. My body concertinaed into a heap, knees pressed against the floor, head dangling against my chest. Between my clasped hands, the handle of my knife crushed in the folds of my skin, one fingertip brushing against the somewhat blunted blade. At the sound of skittish footsteps, hard heels smacking down the stairs, I glanced to my right. The crimson smears and spatters on the tiles blended together with the blurred facsimile of my face, reflected back by polished marble. Lifting my eyes a little more, I realised how I appeared to be a single sticky, metallic stroke in a sickening painting.

"Lucifer!" Rei called, each syllable broken apart by a frantic gasp for breath. "Oh, Lucifer, stay there. I'm on my way."

"Don't worry, Rei. I'm not hurt. It's not mine."

"I'm so sorry," Gabriel spoke from a little further behind, still negotiating the narrow steps.

"What?"

"For leaving you alone like that. I heard the fighting, clear as day, but we couldn't get any further than the lead door to help you."

I shook my head. "Yeah, I handled it."

He seemed to be following my voice, approaching with a tentative shuffle, and reaching out to touch Rei's shoulder before he lowered himself to a crouch beside me.

"Was Uriel among them?"

A nod.

"And did you…?" he trailed off, rubbing a sample of the gritty paste covering my arms between his finger and thumb.

"No. He left. He's gone. I'm a little disappointed, to be frank. For all his bragging about 'persistence', I was rather looking forward to pinching the squishy part of his nose and plucking it away from his face, like that stupid party trick. There were some guards, outside my cell, when I broke out. It was a mess. I don't know…I don't know if I…"

Gabriel quickly curled an arm around my neck, stroking the top of my head, and offered up the other to carefully lift me onto my feet. I yanked a stray shard of broken glass out of my thigh and tossed it aside before Rei could notice. I held onto him for a few moments longer, the walls still tilting around me, and a throbbing pain in my leg.

"If you two are here, then…Michael is?"

"He has been connected to the Machine for some time now, to a certain degree."

"He released me from the holding cell."

"It must have been one of the first things he managed to control," he pondered, mostly to himself, turning his head as if he were able to look up and around and survey the surroundings. "Even now, we can't be sure he is, um, working correctly. Bloody hell, there has to be a better word for it."

"It's difficult to know what should go where, you know?" Rei added. "What needle should poke into what skin, and such."

He took a few slow steps backward, sensing a gap in understanding within the awkward silence. "Well, now that you have won us some reprieve, perhaps the best idea would be to… Stop."

Gabriel cut himself off, with a loud hitch in his breath. His body turned perfectly still, only for a fraction of a second. Then his hands disappeared from their clasped position at his waist, behind his back. They emerged holding a gun, two fingers already removing the safety. The air squeezed and grew frigid. Even as his shoulders hiked upward, and the resulting explosion ripped my eardrum, I did not, could not, realise what was happening. My arms froze at my sides. Some stale, chemical smell filled my throat. Strangely, the first movement I managed was to reach up and touch my own chest, as if I would have to check for a lump of metal lodged in my heart. His nostrils flared, and his cheeks fell as he unclenched his teeth, but his bandaged face remained fixed, not on me, but a point barely over my shoulder. The barrel of his weapon angled downward, his grip relaxing by a millimetre or two. If he had locked onto a target before, he had lost it now.

I pivoted on one foot to glance behind me, and my gaze met squarely with that of Uriel. He had been mere inches from me. He took three stiff, heavy lunges back, arms reaching out, eyes looking coldly ahead, as if conscious, alive, and desperate. His lips had been pressed tightly together but fell open as his head hit the ground. A thick, lumpy stew slopped out—pink, not so grey, matter. In fact, Gabriel's bullet had entered just above the bridge of his nose and subsequently shattered inside his skull, shredding his brain into digestible chunks with mechanical efficiency. If not instantaneously, then in the moments it took for me to hear the sound of gunfire, turn around, and stand over his body, Uriel was dead. I had been blissfully unaware that the man had reappeared at my back; my Soul had no time to react. It was as if Gabriel had levelled his revolver and shot into the empty air, before Uriel even materialised within it. Red-stained fluid slid down the slope of his nose, flooded into his eye, but he could not blink it away, leaving it to gather like a bead of mercury in his tear duct. His pupils had already enlarged, swollen to the size of a coin, inhumanly massive, black holes in his façade. I inched closer to him, every appendage of my body bundled together, unwilling to be moved too far away from each other like I was adhered together with rust. As I did so, my ankle twisted, stepping onto the edge of a raised, flat object. His favourite sickle still lay reverently over his open palm, seemingly held firmly in his grasp until the last dregs of plasma had trickled down his arteries.

"Well, there. It's done. He can't trouble you anymore. I'll take this blood on my hands." Gabriel. He finally spoke. He could not possibly see the terror in my countenance, and yet he gave a deep sigh. "I've had it," he explained. "You don't have to forgive me, Rei."

She slowly lowered her hands from her ears. "Forgive you? Forgive you? What was it that you were told, Lucifer, for all that time? 'But his number is so high. He could never do something like that. Maybe you've got issues you need to unpack.' Would your teachers, your guardians, even, have given you that free pass? Would Eve? Why, would the Machine have? Look at him. He was going to kill you; he was going to slice your head off. No! I don't need to *forgive* you, Gabriel. Am I supposed to? Maybe I am meant to hate you now, but I can't even blame you.

Shit! Fuck!" She dabbed the tears from her cheeks before she wrapped her arms around his neck, pulling his head down onto her shoulder. She rifled through her memory for every expletive she'd ever heard out of someone else's mouth, so she could blurt them into the linen of his shirt.

"Rei," I said, tentatively, "how did you know all of that?"

She did not move her face, and her words came out muffled and drenched. "My Soul doesn't always show me disasters. I wasn't lying when I said that. Still, most of the time, it…does seem to be bad things. Awful things."

Something had to be watching. Not watching over, necessarily, that seemed too charitable a suggestion. But this perfect congregation of Souls, too much of 'the right place at the right time', raised my suspicion. I was not speaking to the Machine. This was beyond her—before her. In fact, it seemed to be fighting against her. I was speaking with the Source. Blind, deaf, composer of impossible coincidences and, apparently, capable of correcting its own mistakes. The Source kept my ancestors alive, made them gods, gave their daughter a Soul to allow her escape, sent a man faster than the human eye to stab me in the neck, then ensured a man with no eyes and perfect aim would be there to kill him first. The Source was no friend of mine, more like a master, a playwright.

"What do you want with me?" I pondered, silently, curious if it could hear me. "Look at me. I'm already caked in filth. What more do you *want*?"

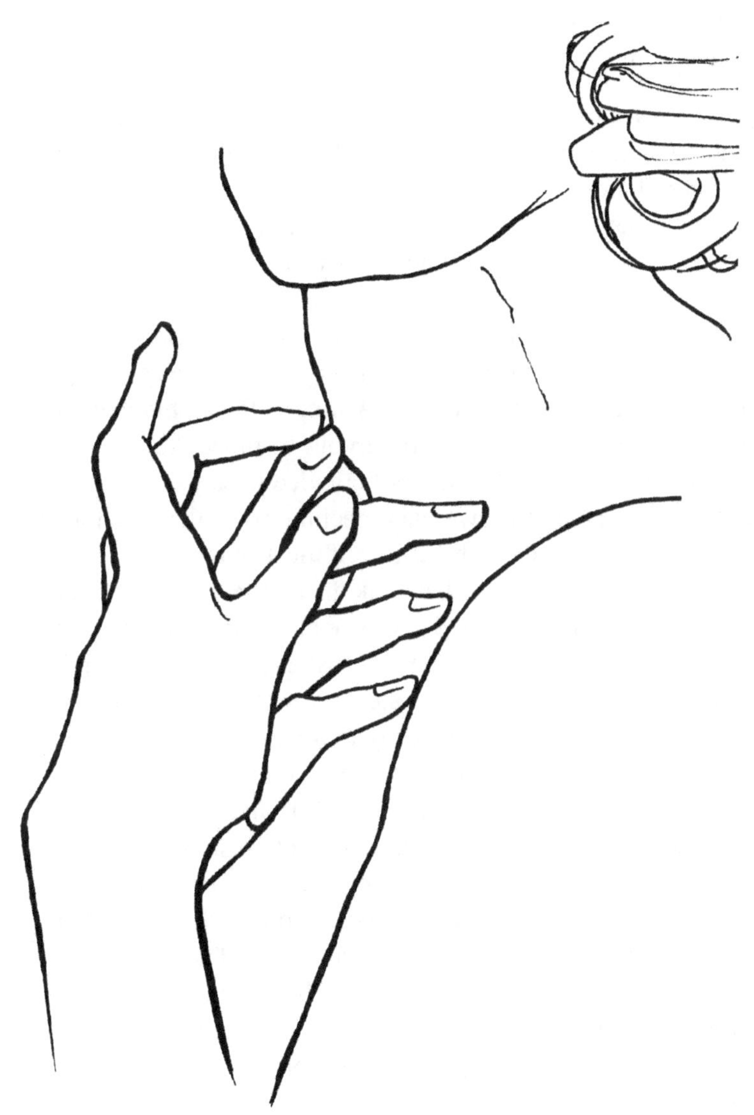

I awoke face-down on the ground, a weight across my shoulders, my hair sticky with dust-ridden cobwebs. My ears were filled with a pitchy ringing, so viscous and opaque it felt almost liquid, penetrated only by the low, percussive rumble of distant voices, rippling and overlapping with unease.

They did not see me, lying there. Or if they had, they had chosen not to investigate any further. Perhaps they thought I was already dead. I myself wondered if that might be the case. After all, as I rose onto my hands and knees, and twisted to glance over my shoulder, I saw the edge of a slate roof overhead, which steadily began to slip downward like a toboggan, as though spontaneously detached from its wooden frame. It appeared to be taking its turn to snap itself in twain, using my spine as a chopping block. I felt it was as good a slice of the architecture to die beneath as any. And then, as if nervous to finish the job, gravity rolled onto its back. The roof crawled back the same route it came, a flake of brown paint peeling off of the gutter as it slotted neatly into place. Pushing myself most of the way upright, the head-to-toe ache that sunk through my body seemed to suggest I was not yet expired. I was not so willing to let go of the possibility in that moment. I could just as easily have been in some purgatorial state, having awoken before the powers that be had sufficient time to whisk me away to my punishment. I ducked under a length of dark metal—a fallen lamppost, I realised, that had gotten itself flung some distance down the alleyway and wedged at a diagonal between two storehouse buildings—towards the voices. Despite the state of the city around me, I discovered, rounding a corner out of the shade, that I in fact remained quite alive. A protracted sigh of something akin to disappointment leaked out of my chest. I had assumed that death in a blaze of ignominy would, at least, relieve me of all my feelings, up to and including remorse for my own actions.

I found a group of strangers whose faces I recognised, four, perhaps five of them, clambering over a low-lying section of the

Wall. A couple of limber beanpoles had skipped over the rubble like mountain goats. Having passed through the narrowest point of the V-shaped cavity, they were currently in the process of hauling their stouter companions over to join them. They were stragglers. They pointed and peered into some point in the distance. Past their heads lay the most vast, forbidding, and green slice of land I had clapped eyes upon, undulating in the shape of a pair of cupped hands. Rising up out of the valley, clusters of dark figures quivered like silverfish, unkillable, constantly reborn out of the crushed shells of their progenitors. They would not be the last. The high-pitched trickle similar to that of broken porcelain suggested the turning-over of bricks and tiles, the crunch of glass underfoot. The sounds of the undead rising from the dirt. The sounds of my victims. I took a step away from them, away from the green meadow, away from the seductive wink of release. And as I moved, pushing against the flow, it felt as though I waded through water, fighting the river that led to the sea. I heard a hum, like breath over the lip of a bottle, vibrating through the marrow of my bones. The voice drifted underground, climbed upward, smoke from a fire stoked in the walls. It scratched and prodded at my skin, familiar in the manner of a voice from a dream, one where my hands are dyed red and black and pain is served without the promise of catharsis. It came from the centre. It called to me, and I knew no other way than to listen.

A whimper from down below, the wet, indulgent cry of an injured foal. Eve Stanton clung with both hands to a soft, foamy cliff face, bending under her weight. Its plush edges stood out amongst razors, stalagmites, and blunt objects, someone else's resourceful use of a mattress. They had wholeheartedly committed to their own escape in destructive fashion, something Eve struggled to do. She kicked out one leg, unravelling a loose bedsheet from her skirt. The waves of her hair, like morning sun through a window, draping over her face in time with her tantrum, that I perhaps expected. That sight washed over me, bathed me in hot, dry wasteland air. As a moved closer—one foot in front of the other—the details of the tangled mats at her waist, sweat beginning to collect in beads on her forehead, took some of the edge out from the soles of her shoes. The lack of her pristine velvety sheen declawed her. Her ire turned toward the steel beam hanging over her head, upon which I stood. She gazed up, recognising me—she did not quite reach my eyes, settling for my mouth—with the relief and recollection of a child once lost. Her body froze, save for one arm, which she lifted to the sky, to me, the back of her hand facing me, vulnerable and expectant as the slope of her neck. The delicate, pristine curve of her wrist would glimmer in the daylight as though dusted with snow, if not for the new smattering of old dirt. She did not speak to me. She looked. She waited.

*"I think we will be very good for each other. From what I had heard about you, I thought you might bite my fingers off. If anything, you've been rather placid. Not following his example, are you? You're different. And we know you've always liked me. Come on now, help me up. Or are you really—?"*

The whistling sound began to quake inside of me, thrashing in time with my heart's angry pounding, and beating through my blood. I crouched low, steadied myself on the edge of the beam, and jumped. I did not imagine her face turning around to watch as I left her behind, her pale princess's arm dangling in the air. There was no point.

There was movement on my left, just a subtle ripple of a shadow. I thought it must have been Eve, that she truly had a Soul after all. Perhaps she could jump like Uriel. Perhaps I had enraged her so fiercely that she could shift into the body of a snake, preparing to lunge out of the darkness and lodge her fangs in me, like an iron beartrap to my leg. My Soul clambered up my spine, stopping at the back of my throat, secreting an acidic taste into my mouth. It promised to fight her. It would fight her until the pressure on my organs killed me. And if I refused, why, it would simply evacuate my fragile body and find its own way home. I took one lurching step to the right.

A brown rat about the size of my fist scampered out in front of me. It seemed oblivious to my presence, narrowly dodging my foot as it veered around a corner and continued running in roughly the same direction I faced, two more tailing behind it. Something else clipped past my ear, I assumed a large black bird at first, before I realised the rotund body and webbed wings belonging to a bat. Their procession appeared to taunt me, with how swiftly they vanished amongst the devastation, how little my powers affected them. I wondered why they did not make a break for freedom, for the world of leafy canopies and plains that quivered in the cool breeze. They surely had nothing of value still holed up here. Were there silk threads around their ankles, tying them to this place? Did they simply despair at the idea of leaving? Did some great love call to them, too?

All I could do was follow.

**[Lucifer]**

Gabriel expelled a puff of cool air into his hands. "That has to be it, then," he said, with a tone of resignation, rather than optimism. "There can't possibly be anyone else—anything else left to come after us."

"Has there been any sign of Raphael?" This was important information, at least to me.

"Nothing yet…" Rei seemed to know instinctively, by habit, that hers was the one answer that counted. "Although that could be a good sign," she added, taking a sheepish glance at my face.

Gabriel pondered on this. "That leaves us with one last enemy, I guess."

"Who?"

He ducked his head a little, acknowledging the defensive incredulity in my reply. "People have been flooding out of the Wall already. Michael is hooked up, holding the gates open, and he would be trying to keep count, so he said, but—" Before he could finish his sentence, Rei shoved him forward, barely avoiding tripping over his legs. In their place, a buttress detached from the nearby arch, collapsing endways onto the altar, and fracturing into two pieces. The ribs above our heads moaned under stress, and the entire structure appeared to move by several inches. Flakes of plaster and oil paint fell from the fresco, ricocheting off the wooden debris and down the steps like hail. The pale underside of the delicate pieces disappeared as they landed in a slick of red tar, soaking it into their pores like blotting paper.

Gabriel tilted his head seeming to search urgently around himself for something. "He's not alone in there."

"The Machine," I concluded on his behalf. Our one fear all along, and the only explanation that made a modicum of sense. "She's fighting back."

I heard a mighty crash outside, before a stifling plume of white, chalky dust poured in through the windows and front entrance, settling on every vacant surface. The marble tiles underneath us seemed to warp and swell, as if waterlogged, then began to sprout dark hairline cracks.

"But then, what about Michael?" Gabriel spoke to himself, volume rising and quailing with every word and steady realisation. He spun around with such sudden speed that made my own head swim, but immediately collided with Rei, her hands braced fiercely against him.

"No, you mustn't!" she cried, her eyes shining out of their sockets now.

I understood the motivation behind her outburst. However, it was also her momentary distraction which allowed me the opportunity to dodge past the pair of them, out of their reach. It was, of course, a contingency, assuming she would have cared to stop me at all. The false wall disguising the passageway was already gone, flattened, as though it were extending a hand in invitation.

"It's alright, Gabriel," I said. "I'll go. Just do one more thing for me. Make damn sure everyone else gets out of here in one piece."

The irony of my demand did not pass me by unnoticed. Part of me hoped that Gabriel would not cross paths with Blackwater on his way out. I imagined the latter would not be best pleased to find out that he had attempted to save a life only for us to pass it around like a martyr's hot potato. But each of our dilemmas were not created equal. We could only measure the stakes on our own set of scales. We did not all weigh the same in each other's hands. Gabriel, at least, was open-minded. He could be convinced, that my demise would be a profitable investment at best, and a fair trade at worst. I tapped the toe of my boot against the floor, finalising my decision. The rubber sole had worn down to a slither and torn away from the stitching. Then I slipped away, down the corridor.

Navigating it alone, the passageway seemed constructed of darkness, solid at the sides, too long in front, and utterly quiet. And, deprived of light, the throne room presented itself only as a rippling black blotch in front of me, just out of reach. I caught myself dragging my feet at the realisation I had risen out of one grave, only to descend right down to my neighbour's larger, deeper tomb. I hesitated for a moment, this strange optical illusion giving me the impression that the opening was a portal, that once I stepped through it, like a noose, I would instantly die. I wondered if the loop would continue in perpetuity, an ouroboros feeding from the earth like a worm, or if I would ever be allowed to simply lay down to rest.

The vault felt warmer on my skin than I expected, not like mud but instead like temperate water, stale air bulging with fresh, humid sweat. My death would not be so cool and quick as the dark passageway would have had me believe. The heat radiated, surely, from the lone body facing me, from the opposite side of the room, further away, it seemed, than before. I saw the bundle of copper-coloured hair I knew, dulled by a pallid layer sitting atop it like sugar, like igneous grit, but little of his face. His eyes watched me from under his brow, whites rolled to the front.

My feet slowed, like the feet of a horse refusing to jump. "Are you there, Michael?" I called, and listened to my voice bounce back.

"Yes, yes, it's me. One of us had to actually go ahead and get shit done, idiot." His head wobbled from side to side, then snapped upward, as if a puppeteer pinched on a thread knotted between his teeth and pulled.

"Somehow I don't believe you."

"And? Perhaps I don't believe you, either. It doesn't matter, what you *think*. James and Isabella Smith. They truly lived up to their name. From the moment they first laid eyes on you, they've shaped you, made you. You stride in here, the guts of innocent creatures dripping from your skin, so sure of your own heroism, as though you wear the title of your ancestors with every breath that slides over your tongue. As though you mean any more to this city than the Soulless that walked before you. They were beasts stitched together from scrap pieces, born to kill and struggle and die, just like you."

"Not all the Soulless. Not Fenrir. Does that name mean anything to this city?"

"Of course. Shows just how little you really understand. If only I had the power to summon that corpse from its grave and tear him limb from limb before you. All that you are is exactly what you were made to be. There are forces in this world far larger, far higher than I, and they have known you were coming for a very, very long time."

"You're angry with us, aren't you?"

"Come now, Lucifer, we've always been angry, haven't we? Like rabid dogs, we are. This is everything you wanted, isn't it? This…"

Something fell from behind me, something metal and brutally heavy, and landed next to my left foot. I left behind a dark smear when I inched it quickly away.

"This is the Machine I'm talking to, isn't it? You've done something to Michael, haven't you? You would even betray your new Sovereign for the sake of revenge, of punishment." I took a couple of tentative steps towards the figure in the chair. "Look, for what little it's worth, I am sorry it had to—"

"Quiet!"

From somewhere amongst the tangle of cables hanging over him, one suddenly shook loose and, on the downswing, so happened to wrap itself around my neck. Pulled taut, it lifted me off the ground by several inches, the balls of my feet balancing the whole weight of my body. The spiralling grooves in the copper chafed against my skin, plucking out the most miniscule baby hairs as it pressed upward on my jaw. With one hand jammed between the noose and my neck, I found the wherewithal to reach around my back and pull out my dagger, still tucked under the waist of my trousers. It took driving the blade back and forth an innumerable number of times to, in blind panic, saw the wire in two, presumably assisted by the smoke gathering around me, clouding my view. I managed to make only two or three nicks in my face in the process. The thick white shirt I had been wearing in the chilly underground cell was completely deteriorated—collateral damage—the final remnants falling off my shoulders and leaving me in a black undervest.

When I fell to the ground, it was not onto cold stone, but the rough fibres of a burgundy rug, once plush and luxurious, but so beaten that patches of underlay showed through like brown bruises. The square expanse of the throne room had narrowed, walls sliding closer, squeezing my shoulders. I saw a corridor. There were no doors, just me at one end, Michael at the opposite, hanging from the ceiling like a chandelier. Wipe your paws. Everything smelled of rust. I screwed my eyes shut, so tightly it ached, and my corneas trembled for fear of being crushed under the heels of my hands. When I blinked them open, it was gone. There was never a carpet, or doors, or picture frames, or a hyena, though the mould under the wallpaper still darkened my fingernails. Michael's mouth scowled.

"A weapon? No, no, one of my Angels shouldn't require anything of the sort."

A painful, involuntary spasm in my wrist sent my knife soaring out of my grip, hitting a wall and bouncing pathetically into the rubble.

"Not up for a rational conversation, are we? Fuck, if you're in there somewhere, Michael, I'm sorry. I can't hear you."

"All of you, you leaped to throw your trust at him, didn't you? Michael, the righteous boy. Your lawless knight. You bleat about rationality, and yet you would sacrifice yourself behind the altar before you left without this man.”

“Funny, you didn’t have to crawl inside my head to know that, did you? Don’t you find it refreshing, speaking face-to-face like this?”

“You care so little for your own life, only surviving out of an amorphous sense of duty. It’s a powerful drive, too. All this time, you’ve thought of yourself as an enigma, but this much is blatantly clear to me. It is precisely why you were chosen.”

“So, this is what you want. What, is it a test?”

“Perhaps, from a certain point of view. You see, all of my Angels assumed I was incapable of learning. False. I have learned this: neither you nor I can rewrite the other’s code. We are both bound inextricably to our duty. And I, like you, will not be persuaded to the contrary. Thus, we meet at a stalemate. A stalemate that must either be broken today, or held in perpetual agony as I watch your mortal body slowly decay into a pile of bones, lost to time.”

“You’re not letting me go without a fight.”

His cheeks lifted, round and bright and pink like apples. “A good, old-fashioned death-match.”

“Strange, that you say old-fashioned, and yet you have dispossessed me of my weapon. Somehow I always knew you were the type to play dirty.”

“I never claimed otherwise. It is the numbers, you see, which create the illusion of fairness.”

“Oh well, it’s not as if I needed a butter knife anyway. I can beat you. I can beat you with my bare hands. I’ll destroy you!” My voice crackled like hot bile in my throat, rising as I hacked it up and spat it out.

Having announced my intent so clearly, I was forced to act pre-emptively. Taken in by a deep, primal instinct, I turned my left arm upward and, with the other hand, burrowed my fingernails into the skin. Dragging my fingers across the curve of my forearm, four thin channels of blood boiled to the surface, at first bubbling up through the thin, unclean splits, then trailing towards my knuckles, gathering in warm reservoirs between the creases of my joints. The motion burned fiercely, like a hornet marching over my body, slicing me open. This was sufficient to command forth my Soul. Antithesis swallowed up the air around me, vitally, impeding the Machine's reach, preventing her from touching me again.

Eve was wrong. She'd taught me too perfectly. I'd grown into a damn good liar. I had learned to lie so well that Uriel concluded he had to sneak up from behind and stab me in the back to finally make me die. But I could not lie to the Machine. And Uriel was right. *A real blabbermouth, aren't you?* Even under the best of circumstances, my Soul could not possibly last forever, let alone coming limp and bruised from an already brutal assault. Eventually, very soon, my polluted, corrosive shield would fade away, and the Machine would put me down with a well-aimed steel rod under the chin. I saw no choice but to put her down first, like Gabriel aiming a single bullet into the air. A real death-match. This entailed, as far as any of us could surmise, severing the system, wiring, code and all, from its origin, from the Sovereign—from Michael. From the crown set into his head.

"How fucking irritable and violent do you think I feel now, huh? Go on, guess. Scale of one to four."

"That's it, Lucille. You know it was always destined to end up this way. You and me, at the end."

**[Michael]**

This was my tower. I built it. I made every wall, lifted each granite brick in my arms myself, piling each atop the last. There were corridors lined in furs and tapestries, spiralling stairways feeding every cavity like arteries. I slept under the tower's ceilings, ate from the tower's cellars, breathed through cracks in the tower's windows, drank water that pooled under the tower, turning sweet at its feet. One day I would breed in the tower; my children would inhabit the walls, their small, fragile feet pounding against the floors. A sickness of sour dislike swelled in my stomach as though whisked with a fork. These walls I placed, each line of cement, for myself. Now there were frames obscuring the wallpaper, and the faces inside are not my own, a woman's faces.

The tower would never let me go. I built it to wrap itself around me always, like limbs of an oak tree. It did not know how to do anything else, and it would crumble over my head before it learned. Like the tree, stone would grow and distend around my body, hold my bones inside.

There a beast approached me. It rose out of the dirt, out of the death—they were one and the same; what was dirt but the pulverised, nourishing remains of the dead? A black-haired dog, with eyes of glowing candlewax. Filth shook out of its fur with every laboured step it took. Its pulsating tongue flicked over its lips. I built the tower over the wolf's grave. It heaved its gaunt body from the ground with big, dirty paws. Now my tower would break, brick by brick, over the beast's crooked back.

The sky was falling. Shards of stained glass, beautiful as stars, threaded through my hair and sliced across my face. Some were painted red, the crimson fire that enveloped the great dragon, the destroyer of the Wall, perfect and terrible. Others were splattered with drops of scarlet, blood trailing down my skin. The golden crown on my head did little to protect me. The wolf stood over me, saliva hanging from its teeth, opened its jaw, and screamed.

**[Lucifer]**

Michael had left his weapon at his feet, as though he knew. Like the sword in the stone, the blade gouged into the ground, stern, unmerciful, but willing.

I gripped the polearm with both fists and heaved my weight backwards until the spearhead sprung out of the floor, and I felt the muscles in my arms tearing into strips. The weapon now in my hands, the collapsing dome over my head seemed to slow, pieces sinking down as if through thick water, though that detail did not concern me any longer. I shifted the weapon in my grip, holding it close to the sharp tip, and shoved it underneath the metal crown on his head. Bracing myself against the pole, I attempted to use it as a lever, bending it upward, one foot pressing against the throne between his shackled knees. With my left hand, I took a length of silver feathers and clumps of his hair and pulled. I pulled with what dregs of strength still persisted in my bones, paying no mind to the blows against my back, or the shrieks of terror erupting from dear Michael's throat—until I felt the crown bend.

My palms suddenly felt warm and wet, when silver and cables and needles gave way to the force of unrestrained mortal rage. I fell to the floor, my head trapping my arm against the marble, thus narrowly avoiding a fractured skull. Michael's wings, now detached from the Machine's hardware, spun out of my grasp, clattering away from me, while the hot, fragile body of Michael himself dropped forwards, out of the chair, across my legs. He landed with a dull, unresponsive sound, and I twisted my stiff, aching form around, to lift him out of the dirt.

# Part 7: Transmigration

**[Raphael]**

As I marched on into the square, pain splitting my legs at the knees, I noticed an overhead cable draped between two shop buildings beginning to sway, like rigging caught on a gusty wind. I had never seen the wiring behave in such a fashion, but approached, nonetheless. As I was about to pass underneath the sagging middle, I heard a snap on one side. The cable dropped to the pavement, sliding along the stones with what I expected to be an unceremonious thwap, but that instead erupted into a fountain of white particles of light, cracking like a broken tooth, then popping furiously as the spout of electricity petered into a trickle.

I considered if, next, as I stepped through into the Hall, the stone archway might burst into a bud-shaped flame. This, I knew, ought to work somewhat more effectively on my body. Alas, there was no pyre, though the interior of the room was deserving of the cleansing. The intricate sculptures and plaques skirting the chamber had been sheared smooth as though a flood of acid had poured in through the smashed windows. The wooden benches had been reduced to kindling scattered over the wet floor. The room had been, in every sense, gutted. Even the walls, like arms reaching upward to the skies, were not clean of sin. There were no bones to speak of, only stubborn stains. That, and a small shape, the size and colour of the girl Rei, zig-zagging closer to me.

"Raphael." Her voice tilted upward at the last syllable, as if asking a question, as if I were almost a stranger to her, and she barely recognised me. Perhaps I had surprised her. Perhaps she had assumed I was already dead. "Raphael!" she shouted, this time with urgency. She bounded straight into my path, arms outstretched. I grabbed her by the shoulder with one hand and pushed her aside.

"Stop!" Gabriel hollered, rising from where he had been sat, inconspicuously, in Lucifer's spot, at the base of the altar. He shouted into his own chest, holding his revolver like glass vase, cradling it limply in his fingers as though he had forgotten how to use it. At his feet, I saw a pile of pink and red flesh, tufts of hair growing from it like mould from a hunk of bread dough. The face was rolled to the side, away from me, and the body wore a black suit the same as my own. The criss-crossing laces at the back were sticky, gluing to the floor in strange places.

"Care to tell me what the fuck is happening? The city is falling to the ground when I pass out, then I come to and it's somehow magically fixing itself back up, and on my way here it starts tearing itself to bits again. And this…" I pressed my hands against my ears, screeching through my teeth to let out whatever it was building up behind my eye sockets. "Where are they? Michael, Lucifer, where are they?"

"I can't…"

"What do you mean, you can't? You don't know? You've lost them?"

"Don't move! I just can't say. I can't let you."

My fingers clasped around the lapels of his jacket, fabric stretching in my fists, buttons cutting in like a serrated corer. It took what little wherewithal I had left not to shake him, pliable as a ragdoll in my hands. "I swear Gabriel, if you don't tell me where they are, I will take your head and tear it from your shoulders."

"The back of the Hall is already collapsing. There's only one door and no way we can stop it. If you go in there now…"

Her ardent plea faded away mid-sentence. If nothing else, her lungs knew that no quantity of compassionate reasoning could be enough to stop me. I felt a burning, as though the infernal hand of my Soul had punched through my rib cage and dragged me along by my heart.

There was a dark, jagged void in the fresco, where the Soulless Wyvern had been. The cavernous passageway grew a mouth with fangs in her place. I climbed the altar and fell into it, the walls of the narrow corridor squeezing my sides like cold, hard tonsils, before I was swallowed, and released into the throne room.

The innards of the hall were wrong. I felt wind, heard the sound of waves. Light leaked inside, igniting the dust filling the air with an ethereal shade of yellow, like dusk sunbeams piercing through a soft sheet of cloud. But the dust was dry and bitter on my tongue. As Rei had attempted to forewarn me, angular pieces of slate and concrete dropped from the sky, rotating and accelerating down like discuses thrown by a vengeful god. The great wooden beams propping up the ceiling began tilting inward, groaning and splintering in the middle. Between the gaps, a telling plume of thick, dark smoke was quietly making its escape. The walls, like melting glaciers, fell in chunks, from the highest point first, simultaneously soft and fatally blunt. One smaller piece landed by feet, disintegrating into rough fragments and a plume of grit. The cloud charred with a slight hiss against the scales still lingering on my skin.

Even through the opaque veil of dirt, I could not mistake the foul smearing of crimson over the floor, or the two figures collapsed in the middle, practically dyed with it. Michael—oh, fuck, Michael. He lay on his back, barely gathered into Lucifer's lap. His body drooped limp, but for his head, which she cradled tight against her shoulder. His wings were discarded some few metres away, the usually pristine diadem now smothered in bodily fluids and ancient filth. I could hardly decide whose blood belonged to whom.

Without consideration for planning or consequences, I staggered across the room as it rapidly collapsed in, the walls drooping closer and closer, and cocooned my body around the both of them. Neither responded in any discernible way. I screwed my eyes shut, preferring ignorance to the sight of their skin burning painfully against mine, irrigated by my molten Soul, or the death in their faces afterward. Rubble continued to fall upon me, relentless, though I felt the pain to be somewhat distant from my back and arms. My mind, it seemed, had detached itself from flesh and bone, from the bruising and tearing sensations. I could still, however, feel my clothes growing heavy and damp, sticking to the ground and the two people weighing upon my chest. They seemed smaller than I would have imagined, as I held them both. We fit almost neatly, like jigsaw pieces mangled at the extremities.

Buildings tend to fall much faster than one might think, picturing it in someone's worst fear or morbid fascination. The massive quaking and crashing ceased before I had truly braced myself against it, leaving only the occasional, pathetic crumbling sound and feeble spasm in my back. The wooden skeleton had rearranged itself, wedged into an odd, but settled position that propped up what remained of the walls.

"Raphael, that you?" Lucifer churned out of her lungs, before a fit of dry heaving and coughing.

I loosened my hold on her, her voice struggling as if her lungs were clogged with peat. One of her eyes had closed itself, an abrasion on her forehead leaking down her nose into the tear duct. The other, instead, looked past me, above, turning from left to right, in seeming incomprehension or disbelief. I followed the direction of her gaze, and immediately discovered what had so confused her. I did not recognise them either. Two wings, or at least what should have been, extended out from my shoulder blades. The bony frame was not symmetrical, bent unnaturally in

the middle of the cartilage in places, and twitching involuntarily.
There had, presumably, been one complete, elastic membrane
attached to this, forming a suitable bat-like shape. The
translucent skin hung loose and shrivelled, with numerous holes
punched straight through. Where the structure had managed to
hold up, unsightly black blotches remained. Finally, I had
become the complete, prophetic embodiment of the Wyvern's
burning corpse. Although I had felt none of this damage as it had
been inflicted, a sudden, stabbing ache suddenly flared between
my shoulders, crawling down my spine as if it had claws, which
sunk slowly into each vertebra along its descent. The pain
dissipated—again somehow abruptly, fading in and out like a
stochastic pulsing—when Lucifer spoke again.

"They're gone," she said. "Where did you come from? Why
did…? How?"

I deflected the question with another. "What happened to him?"

Her hands wrapped tighter around Michael, her one functioning
eye turning glassy with tears. "I don't know. He's been bleeding.
I knew he would but…" she stuttered. "He stopped breathing
when you came in, and now I can't feel his heart. I don't want to
say it. I can't."

"Put him down," I said, unthinking.

"What?" she cried.

"Put him on the floor. We can't do anything for him like this."

She fell silent, and nodded, tenderly lowering his head. Only
once she had released him, did she dig her fingernails into the
stone and shatter the quiet of the wreckage.

"You did this!" she screamed into the polluted air. "Are you
there? Where are you hiding now, huh? You had better be
looking. Look at what you did!"

I leaned over Michael's body. Lucifer was right; his chest was
still. I pressed my fingers against his neck, his wrist, the inside of

his elbow, for any hopeful, forgiving sign, and felt nothing, of course. I knew what to do in this situation, theoretically speaking. Everyone knows what they are supposed to do. Instead, I was weeping, squeezing his hand, his palm spongy and malleable between both of mine. He was so warm. I knew perfectly well what I should be doing.

"Help me."

The Machine had the gall to reply. "Please move away from the body." Almost every human being was outside of the city now, meaning its population of voices to steal was scant. With each word, it rotated between blank renditions of Lucifer's, Gabriel's, Rei's, and my own voice. Michael was not there.

"The *body*?" I coughed. I refused to move an inch. The pain returned.

"What, so you can take him away, make him disappear?" Lucifer cried. Her face had vanished into a tight bundle of bloodied limbs.

"You requested 'help'. Please move away from the body in order to receive assistance."

Without warning, a stabbing, tearing sensation travelled through his hand, up my wrist and arm, through the bone. It burned in my joints and forced them to flinch away against my will, his skin rejecting me like water to hot oil. Having extricated my clamp-like grip, his chest jumped away from the ground, limp spine contorting as if there were a demon inside him. A faint crackling sound radiated from him. I moved to grab hold of him, regardless of the agony I might experience in doing so, but Lucifer's stiff arm suddenly closed the gap, pushing against my collarbone.

"Wait! Wait."

She watched carefully, pupils twitching from side to side with almost unnatural rapidity. I couldn't understand how she bore to look at the horror being inflicted upon us. Eventually, I felt her fall back onto her knees, as Michael's back finally smacked harshly against the stone. I had been about to shriek out the contents of my lungs when, at that moment, very nearly in unison with Lucifer herself, his body took one deep, wheezing gasp.

"I could not let him die," the Machine's monotone echoed around the wreckage, as if proud of its work. "I love my children."

Immediately, barely registering, let alone giving thought to the words we had just heard, we both leaned in close to Michael, feeling for the signs of life against our skin, in our ears. Our foreheads met in the middle, pressed together. Her face was wet, cold, pale and benevolent. Recalling the red crust stuck in his hair, I knelt on a section of my sleeve, tearing off enough that the fabric would cover the wounds in his head. As I hurriedly pulled the frayed edges taught and shoddily improvised a knot, I heard the hollow sound of something broken. The sound of a snapped chain, of an iron pipe, dripping with sin, dropped the floor. Next to my hand, the hypnotic coiled shape of a beast's horn rattled to rest. I examined the object as though it had plummeted from the sky, unknowing, slightly wary, but inexorably fascinated. Then I looked up to her. She met my barely comprehending stare in kind. I wondered if she could see her reflection in my pupils and did not recognise her own image. Her visage was freed once again, unadorned, uncaged, and somehow a little more feral, I thought. She reached a hand out, stretching up onto her knees. Her touch carried a coolness, a fresh feeling, perhaps that felt often by day-dwellers and softer animals, like pearls of spring dew laced in my hair. When she pulled away, the crown, my wreath of black thorns, hung from her fingers. I swallowed down a mouthful of dust, preparing to cry out, "*No, get away from that thing. Don't let it hurt you.*" Only then, her hand bowed under its weight, and the loop slipped away, downward, ringing, spinning on its circumference—just a coin, or a bottlecap. All the while, her brow had narrowed, from wide disbelief to mischievous inquisitiveness. She turned her hand over, and her fingertips had only glanced over the flecks of blond above my ear, when she froze, then flinched away.

He seemed almost to yawn, taking a deep, plentiful gulp of air through his nose. I felt his weight shift a little, before his eyes opened—watery green sinkholes in a siren's face. He stared at me, squinting slightly, as if a little perplexed, as a permanent fizzing static, beforehand unnoticed, seemed to fade from my senses. I seemed to view the world through a stream of clear water.

"Nikolaj?" he asked.

I would not have felt a punch in the gut in those few, fleeting seconds. "I know, Alexander, it's me."

"What…how are you here, Nikolaj? Or do you prefer Nik? I can't remember…"

"Shit man, call me whatever the fuck you want."

"Then I should be Alex." He happened to glance to his right as he mumbled away, and his body leapt with apparent shock. He might have sat up if he could; I braced my arms around him, propping him against my shoulder. "Morgan. Morgan Hughes, it's you!" he laughed, charmingly delighted in his early-morning delirium. She beamed as I had never seen before, with one of his hands buried in her dark, knotted hair. The other, I realised, was wrapped tightly around four of my fingers.

"Yeah, it's me. Afraid I'm still here."

I imagined taking a damp cloth to her face. Almost like dabbing away old varnish from the surface of a canvas, beneath all of grime, she must have been quite beautiful. He pronounced her name like a great sigh of relief, the muscles of his back releasing as he did so. His joy was immediate, bodily, a little childlike. It became difficult, a forceful effort, to refer to her by any other title, it seemed now so ingrained in the earth. My own name, on the other hand, seemed to come from some far foggier place. He spoke the word, Nikolaj, with intrigue, a deep, brooding swallow apparent in his voice, perhaps even a tinge of reverence. It sounded strange, foreign to me. It did not quite stick. Looking down at him, he appeared changed, too. Despite the drained greyness of his skin, blotchy eyes and sore, chapped lips, he felt softer than Michael had been. Morgan was the same. Her straight shoulders and the upward tilt of her nose were no longer harsh and stony, but regal. Her eyes took their time to turn and look at you, each heavy blink slow and contemplative. Hers suddenly felt like the gaze of something divine. As for myself, name and body did not match. The former I was stuck with, but the latter I could not properly inhabit. Though I had never considered it a crucial facet of that identity, Alexander McClellan had been an enemy of Nikolaj Valeriev. When I had learned to love him, it was as Raphael. I brushed the pad of my thumb over the raised bumps of his knuckles. Outwardly without thinking, between a chuckle and a chesty cough, he loosened his vice grip, searching for the gaps between my fingers into which he would thread his own.

A quick, sharp jolt along his spine. "Avi," he murmured. "Is Avi here? Is he…?"

"Yes, yes, they're, um…" Morgan glanced over her shoulder at the narrow passageway nestled among pieces of the ceiling, furtively searching her memory for the words, 'out there', and instead catching sight of two figures, ducking under a broken beam.

A female voice called out, "We're coming, just a moment!" She seemed to have dispersed throughout the room, her shout hitting a secret, specific pitch which echoed from all four walls at once.

Avi cleared his throat extensively before attempting to speak. Understandably, we had never been friendly before, but even so, I felt a pang of guilt as I struggled initially to recognise the man, missing the bands of silver to frame his face. He leaned forward into the haze, hanging eagerly off of Rei's arm.

"Is that one Mister McClellan I hear?"

"There he is!" Alex laughed, no, guffawed, as though the two were reunited for the first time, after a decade of post-childhood boredom.

I could not guess what came over him. Whether the sight of Avi Mathias with his sublime, piercing gaze helped him to feel totally safe, or the recognition of his friend with that glowing butterfly of a woman, his lover, gave him an idea. I did not know what came over him. He had no strength in his body; I felt his muscles and tendons strain against me. Still, he found something, a morsel that simmered in his veins and lifted him up, squeezed out of his eyelids and trickled down his cheeks as tears, when he wiped the stain from Morgan's mouth and kissed her. I blinked, before realising I ought to avert my gaze; it was the polite thing to do. I heard a slight wet sound as they parted, though my eyes lost their focus and my nerves prickled and grew so heavy I thought my skin sagged from my bones. The wave of numbness lasted just long enough that I missed the shift in his weight. I awoke to the clash of his arm falling around my neck, the cool brush of air and shadow across my face—how was he so strong, even now? His lips landed just shy of mine. I fumbled to assist him, adjusted the tilt of my head so that he could try again. He felt hot, clammy and a little rough as he rushed to peck at me again, once more, tenderly, before the burst of adrenaline expired, and Morgan caught him before he hurt his back any more.

I took a breath, steadied my hand against the floor. The earth had, in the space of a moment, of a sigh, swelled, crumbled, threatened to open up in a biting, gaping rift of dirt and magma beneath my knees. Then Morgan Hughes let out a sound, something between a childlike giggle and smothered sob, two lovely, glimmering streams of tears gathering in the corners of her smile. She washed over me like sea foam, smoothed away sharp edges, made things simpler, for once. The ground calmed itself, the quivering slither stitching itself back together beneath the pressure of Michael's tired body.

"How do they look, Rei?"

"They look terrible, covered in blood and cement dust and all sorts. But they're here. They're alive. Oh, I'm so, so glad! Thank, well, everything, anything. Watch the floor to your left. Can you move?"

"Move?"

"Shit, I don't know."

"I haven't even thought about moving."

"I'm that charming, huh? Like in the back-room…"

I resisted the sudden urge to punch him under the ribs. He knew I had to, hence the smug grin dimpling his cheeks.

"No, it's not that."

"Are you hurt?"

"No, it's alright—"

"Yes, you are."

"I ache a little, that's all."

"I'm tired… I'm going to be tired for months."

"Fucking shattered."

"You should explain, Rei," Avi interjected. "What you saw."

Their voices felt distant, somehow, as if we were two separate bodies, each threaded together at wrists and fingertips, rafts afloat on opposite sides of a cold, still lake. We spoke quietly, children tiptoeing over creaking floorboards, but strained our ears as though shouting across a valley, speaking the same language but in wildly disparate dialects. They crouched down to meet us, and we flattened our bodies to the ground. We were weary, lonely, scared, and all our scrambled minds could comprehend was the safety, the solidity of touch.

"Right. We need to get you out of here. Given a few minutes, the bits and pieces of roof up there are coming down, on your tired heads if we're not careful."

Morgan couldn't help but giggle, so it seemed. "Ouch, sounds macabre."

"Apologies," she replied. "It's the first clear vision I've had in a while. I got a bit excited." Rei fiddled with her own fingers; she had not been reprimanded, not at all, but she felt she ought to behave as such.

"I'm sure we can get you cleaned up and checked out once we're clear of this awful place. If Jasmine is here, as you promised, then the Northern folk won't be leaving without you."

"The cunning women, too," Morgan interjected, adamant. "I trust them. They're waiting for me."

"Did everyone get out?" Alex's voice rang out for the first time in too long, his countenance pinched together at the centre, spiralling into the labyrinth of his own, solitary speculation.

"I couldn't say," Gabriel said. "I still can't see a thing. That much has not changed. If anyone should know, it's you, Alexander." The slight formality was chilly—gently, but undoubtedly demanding.

"I…think so. I could see them, all of the people moving, outward. All of the pulses, the breath, I could find the numbers without counting. I saw Uri—I mean, Wyatt, when you…when he…"

"I know."

"I watched a few of the last ones go over the Wall," I confessed, details returning to me that I never realised I had lost, a surreptitious leak in my mind. "The northerner was there, I think, the one with the horse. They helped. Did, um, did Eve make it?"

"Eve? I believe so. I'm not certain. Trying to remember her, it's difficult, to look for one person among them all. All of the voices…"

"Come on, Alex, come back. Don't strain yourself."

He groaned, a little obstinate, a hand gripping his jaw. "Can't get rid of this ringing. What is that?"

Avi reached out across the void. He found Alex's right foot, and walked a hand up to his knee, giving it a firm, steadying squeeze. "Calm. You've hurt your ears."

Morgan's body grew still, face stuck, unblinking, waiting for her to decide whether or not to speak. "No, he's right," she said, raising her voice, interrupting an argument that was not happening. "I can hear it, too. It was much louder before. So loud I thought my head was about to burst. Like every little cavity was filling up with, I don't know, water? Not quite. It's more than that, heavier. It sits on my tongue, like a taste, but I can't tell what it is." She folded into herself, eyes screwed shut with fierce concentration. No, wait, I called out, without a sound, look out, look at me.

I couldn't stop myself. "I heard it," I declared. "I heard you. You brought me here."

"You heard us." Alexander's voice tremored, that of a pious man witnessing his first miracle. "You were at the Wall. You couldn't get much further away."

"I know. But you were angry. You were afraid. You were in pain. It hurt me."

"We needed you," Morgan said.

"You needed me. And so I came. I found a way. I couldn't breathe until I found it. Couldn't breathe, but there was plenty of screaming."

Avi stiffened, rolling his shoulders like a cat arching its spine. Tone flat, powerful, he demanded, "Open your eyes, Hughes. Can you see it?"

"Yes, and no. I thought I could, just a moment ago. Like smoke, or mist, but it's between my fingers, stuck in the wrinkles of my palms. I felt Nik's arms around me before he had even seen us. Alex, he's here, but he's also…" She dragged her thumb over her bottom lip, prised open a cut at the corner, scarlet blood hanging in the lines between her molars.

"And colour?"

"Yes, sometimes. When the light catches it right, an oil slick on the pavement."

"What does it smell like?"

"Oh, strange." Her thoughts were a poet's, an artist's. "Lots of things, all stirred into one. Fresh rainfall, citrus tea, wild garlic, and something like a bonfire, a smouldering smell…"

"Ashes." We spoke together, the same word, the same time.

I should have dismissed it, an amusing coincidence; the correct response being to exchange a knowing glance, before forgetting it ever happened. Not watery eyes, an abrupt, painful thump in my gut, trying to translate, decipher how a woman's spark of realisation could move my mouth, how the whisper of another man could flow from my lungs. It hurt, striving to hold onto it, keeping it in one place, but it seemed worse to let it escape, let it fade to nothing.

"Then you understand. And to think, you thought I had been spouting superstition, all this time. Now, we really need to get moving."

Morgan's hands squeezed at her thighs in tacit acknowledgement. "Got it," she said. "One last push."

"I can carry this one," Avi assured us, muscling his body between us like a knitting needle. "Just need you to keep an eye out for us, per se. Don't panic," he added. "I'll give him back."

*"Don't worry, darling,"* it said, the heavy water, the burning scent, *"I won't let come to nothing."*

**[sys.final\load\exit.dat]**

Their bodies were shaped like willow branches. They wiped the foul taste from their lips between words and coughs and retching, and blinking debris from their weeping eyes. They were all liars. They were five. They were two and three. Lucifer, Michael, and Raphael bunched together, side-by-side on an overturned lamppost. Rei and Gabriel kneeled opposite, their hands knitted as if they could make themselves one conjoined body. Lucifer looked at them, and attempted—so I assumed—to twist her mouth into a smile, but merely exhaled instead. Her hair was dark, almost black, but it appeared grey as the skin of a birch tree.

"You know where you are going?" she said. "Together, I assume."

Rei nodded. "We'll be heading East."

"The district of rose petals, moss-covered waterfalls, and stones that bleed gold." Her voice wobbled, as though she might have chosen to start crying then, if given the freedom to decide. "I've heard it is very beautiful. Why that direction? Did you throw a dart at a compass?"

Rei did not stumble, her thoughts clear and linear as water from a stream. "How did you choose your home? The West calls to you, Morgan Hughes, does it not? In much the same way, my history lies somewhere East. Where else would I go?"

"It's my hope that we might go even further," Gabriel admitted, "beyond the confines of Esprit."

"You will seek some means to get your sight back, I suppose," Michael hummed.

He and Rei let of a disgruntled noise almost at the same second. Lucifer tilted her head back.

"No, I will not," he declared, his intonation plodding and sagely. "It was the Machine that took my sight from me, and if it were even capable, it has evidently chosen not to return it to me. The gruesome crimson lens coating my eyes has apparently calmed rather significantly, and yet they can process no more than the flickers of light the Machine's procedure left me with in the first place. We will travel East for our own reasons, without pestering any of the local practitioners for some mystical cure."

Michael rested his chin on his hands, like a scolded adolescent. "Well, alright."

Gabriel soothed him. "Let me have this. Just let me grieve for what I have lost in peace. And in the meantime, I have the kind of freedom I've never experienced in more than twenty years. I want to live now, with Rei. And if all goes well, we plan to discover knowledge and pleasures none of us have yet imagined."

"This will not be the last we hear of your travels though, I hope."

"Changed as we all may be, Alex, I am not a different man. I am still your friend."

He might have bowed his head in agreement, even if he had no words to offer a note of finality, had he not flinched, rocking forward. But it was not he who had gasped for breath; it was Lucifer. I knew exactly the reason. I was sure of it. She had seen Jasmine emerge coolly through an empty doorframe as though it had been preserved solely for them. She had not been watching as I had. But Jasmine had been looking for her. The pace of their steps increased, and for a moment they seemed to forget they had not travelled alone, leaving their dewy-faced child companion to follow awkwardly behind.

Jasmine did not in actuality bring a bubble of clean oxygen in their wake, but it might have appeared that way, subjectively. Each of those who met their serene gaze bended toward them, beguiled and ravenous. The changeling crouched before Lucifer, taking both of her forearms into their hands and gripped them like steadying banisters. For a fraction of a second, in between her lethargic blinks, they leaned forward, as though to close the gap between them for an embrace. But they hesitated, their knee touched the ground, and they simply said:

"I'm glad to see you. You had me worried for a moment there."

She breathed in deeply through her nose, and then snorted. As a form of non-verbal communication, the sequence of sounds struck me as unnatural, the careful deliberation of the former contradicting the spontaneity of the latter. She said, "Who, me? Don't know what you were looking at, but we had everything under control. Honestly, you'd think the roof was falling off or something." She chuckled, but deftly avoided eye contact, busying herself with scraping thick, dry flakes of excrement from between her knuckles. Her cheeks sucked in, clenched between her molars, as she strained against her locking joints. "Some little bastard stole my gloves," she grumbled. She seemed, ostensibly, to be complaining of pain, yet as usual, I could detect no flesh-and-bone abnormalities in her body. There would be no last-minute revelations there.

"And what has become of Wyatt? Still here, I can only assume." Jasmine bristled.

The old fugitive could hardly help but note the gazes of Lucifer and Gabriel clumsily trip and rebound off each other.

"Dead," uttered the latter.

Pointedly electing not to acknowledge the absurd shrug that jolted through Lucifer's entire frame like a retch, Jasmine turned instead to the mousy-haired boy hovering behind them, one arm pointed, the other beckoning. "There should be some cloth in that bag you have."

The boy nodded, arms crossed behind him like a butler, and bent over the densely packed leather sack they had been hauling between them. Rummaging with both hands, he retrieved a pile of tan flannels, each folded into quarters and tied with twine. He placed them neatly on the ground beside his master, before returning to the safety of the knapsack.

"Thank you. Here, this might help." Jasmine placed a towel on Lucifer's knee, then murmured gently over their shoulder to their associate. "This is the lady I told you about."

"Hello." Trained in his etiquette, the boy bowed his head politely before turning his attention back to tying an intricate triple knot in a length of rope.

Dead.

Jasmine continued to converse with Lucifer and Michael in a subtly lower voice. "This is Samuel," they said. "He's a young gifted, part of our clan. His Soul has not long surfaced. He's rather shy, a little unsure of himself. I suppose you might say I've taken him under my wing—or, wings."

They handed another towel to Michael, then moved somewhat mechanically to offer a third package to the ravaged pair of legs seated on Michael's right side, but halted halfway, package drooping from their bent arm.

"Something the matter?" Raphael questioned, half-heartedly, tone softened and eroded by fatigue, massaging the bridge of his nose.

"Nothing," Jasmine breathed. "I suppose some part of my imagination had not expected *you* to be here still."

He rolled the dark pits of his eyes backward, then contradicted the gesture by admitting, "What can I say? Asked me a week ago, and I probably would've agreed with your imagination."

"That is often the way it goes. I sense from the fierce gazes searing into the back of my head that I needn't pry, and so I won't." They waved the cloth in their hand, reiterating the offer. "Nikolaj." This time, he leaned forward to take it. "I thought I ought to come and offer you my assistance personally. I imagine that you will be heading home, Morgan, to the ocean side. Still, we can provide refuge to any who need it. You will be welcome. I think young Samuel would appreciate a friend of his own kind."

"Might we have a moment or two or think on it?" Raphael said. The others snapped their heads to the side, seemingly taken aback either by the sound of his voice, or the shawl of decorum laid atop it. He spoke with half of his face pressed into the woollen pile, like a swaddled child, eyes fixed on an exposed drain cover.

"Naturally. I won't be far. I think my young charge could use an extra hand with his bowline hitch."

Jasmine rose from the ground and paced backward with a delicate bow, before addressing the boy with a muted tone. There was a strange expression in their eyes, as if they detected something discomforting—perhaps Raphael's unnatural heart rate, I surmised. Although, how they could possibly know this eluded me.

Raphael scratched at his scalp with blunt fingernails. He cleared his throat twice before eventually coming to a conclusion. "I think I should go," he confessed. "North, I mean. I've got some shit I need to figure out. Who the fuck this Nikolaj guy is, what he's doing here. I don't know. I feel like I might need the help. And the company of a face I recognise, at least. I never really thought about what happens after. Had no idea I'd be so scared of venturing out there on my own."

"I'll go with you," said Michael, suddenly, as if snapping awake. He had his head balanced in his hands, body swaying slightly, his ankles quavering, cradling himself.

Raphael struggled to swallow. He shook his head. "The hell do you mean? You can't do that. You don't want to be babysitting me; you want…" He faltered, the breeze of his breath dissipating, the sails falling limp. In its place, he gestured at the ground, his hands curving somewhat inelegantly into a silent, all-encompassing circle.

"See?" Michael leaned closer, ducking his head, almost resting his cheek on Lucifer's shoulder. "You and me, we're in the same boat, I think. We can consider it like a vacation, time to get our heads right, before we plant our feet more permanently." He shrugged. "Might even be a bit of fun. What do you think?" His eyes turned to Lucifer, studying her through the veil of his dusty eyelashes.

"What are you looking at me for?" she answered, her tone suggested bafflement. "You'll be all right. Course you will. You'll be so good. You needn't ask for my permission."

"Well, it only seemed polite. Where else do you think I'm planning to return at the end of it all?" he added, undeterred.

They forced themselves to their feet, Lucifer toppling onto her toes like a spinning parasol, but with a note of decisive finality. Then, however, she froze, as though something lagged in her brain, snagging on the hinge of her jaw. Her arms jerked outward with a puppet-like rigidity, her knuckles smacking clumsily into one man's hip and the other's jutting elbow.

"Wait."

The urgency of her tone, sounding rather like she was about to throw up a lump of bile, caught the attention of Gabriel and Rei Guerera standing several feet away. They arrived before Lucifer unannounced, intrigue tugging at their brows.

"The Machine told me something," she said, "back there, when it was just the two of us. I think she was trying to scare me. She spoke of some higher power, something more powerful than her bigger than any of this, even. I don't know. Maybe it's just my paranoia misbehaving. But I think she was implying someone has been watching us."

"The Angel of the North, perhaps?" Gabriel posited.

Jasmine turned away from their protégé, stirred by the recognition of their own moniker. I could not understand the animalistic reflex; I appeared constantly in the conversation of others, and it held little sway over me. I watched Jasmine rise from the ground and slide toward the nervously vibrating huddle with the sly prevarication of climbing ivy.

Lucifer's face grew knotted and taut, lines rising up her neck, as though concentrated hard on trying to believe in the possibility. She shook her head stiffly. "No. There was this…smugness about the way she phrased it, like I could never think of it on my own. Something else."

"And you believe the Machine would tell you the truth?" he replied.

"Can she lie? And what sort of lie would it be to tell? What's the point? Michael, I hate to keep asking this of you, but you don't happen to remember?" She squinted. "I was looking at you when she said it."

"Sorry. I don't know what you're talking about. What did it sound like to you, this something other? A friend of ours?"

"More likely an enemy, surely," Raphael interjected, inanely, with his flawed information and personal bias.

"I just don't know," Lucifer said, shaking her head. "I think it could be worse than that. It could be neither. It might not care."

"The sort of being," Michael mused, "that could have the Machine execute its makers, but continue to spare us, to let us do this to its city. We've picked each other off. And now Uriel. This whole project is cannibalising itself. What sort of creature that could have the Smiths killed, and then watch from afar as this happened?"

"Like a child in a sand pit."

"And if the child never planned to demolish their great fortress of sand, if they had merely pressed a finger into the wall to make a window, and the whole thing collapsed into a pile of ocean-dredged dirt in their lap?"

"Well, they would not be best pleased."

"You're not wrong." Michael's features slackened. His eyes retreated into their sockets. He appeared dejected, perhaps a little sad, or disappointed. "It would be foolish to expect the ground to simply swallow up these bones, forgive us, and move on."

Raphael stamped a foot into the dust like an agitated bull, tugging at the circles of sweat-soaked cotton under his armpits, seemingly uncomfortable. "Then what do we do? I'm in no position to be fighting a sulking child, real or figurative. So what, do we just lie down and wait for mother to punish us for our sins?"

Lucifer shook some dirt from her shoulders, from her ear canals, from her brain. She replied, "You stick to your original plan."

 "We turn eastward." Michael nodded slowly, with his whole torso.

"And you go with the northerners, just like you said. The cunning folk are resilient, but I don't trust that would be enough. The highland people are fluid, mobile. From what I've heard, their ancestors were born from a clan of fugitives. Evading capture is their style. It's how they've survived so well. You'll be safest with them."

"You're suggesting we run away."

"Not forever. But for now, yes. As for me, my roots are set, I suppose. Someone has to stand still to see what's moving. And this way, you'll always know where you can find me."

She gathered the two men down into her arms, one face pressed against each of her temples. They seemed to sink into her, made fluid beings by her hands, stroking their hair. She laid a kiss on Michael's cheek, and another on the side of Raphael's neck.

"You two had better come back to me, you hear? Else you'll never hear the end of it. I'll haunt you both for the rest of your days."

I perceived this to be a possessive gesture. The grip of her fingers on their skin a declaration: "They are mine. You cannot have them. Only I."

Michael hummed as he nuzzled her hair, sliding one hand across her shoulders, finding Raphael's hand behind her back. "I'm not worried, Morgan. I've already found you once. I'll do it again."

"Just follow the old train tracks. They'll keep you on your way, just as they did for me."

Raphael sighed, seemingly with relief, at her mention of this, as though the words came from a deity as old as the steel and timber itself.

She let go of them gradually and deliberately, the kind of motions she made when pushing herself out of an armchair, as though the crawling of her hands down their arms sent pain through her spine.

"It's to be the four of us, then?" Jasmine said, voice clear like metal on glass, their words suggesting they spoke to the earth, though their eyes were absent, meandering up to the sky, searching for the horizon. They all looked to the narrow rift torn out of the Wall, edges still sharp as incisors, the wound fresh. If they had happened to turn and glance behind themselves, they would have see the rest of the edifice, still stolid, still carving that pale sky in two. But they did not care. "I see one of our Westerly neighbours has come to pick up the slack from me. Very well. We'll ride together. Anything that you ought to bring with you?"

"I suppose my polearm would have served me quite well, if it weren't buried under a few tonnes of sandstone. Perhaps there might be something of value in the apartment."

"Is there even anything left to take?" Raphael's question suggested some reluctance, either to return to that place and find nothing, or to return, and find Michael's aforementioned something. Whether or not to abandon my bounds as purged vessels, naked in reincarnation—whether or not such a feat could even be possible—was a dilemma he still had yet to resolve.

"Some. Not much. You can try." Jasmine spoke tersely, though apparently, from the reaction of those faces looking to them, without malice, rather straightforward acceptance. "Samuel can go on ahead with you. I shall convene with our Western friend here."

"Understood, viisas," a small but blunt voice responded. The boy, Samuel, still rather flustered, picked up one end of the leather knapsack, and moved to hoist the now knotted rope over his shoulder to drag it behind him, like game after a hunt. Raphael, unthinkingly, tried to intercede, arms outstretched, mouth making animal snapping noises. In other circumstances, the man would have indeed been strong enough to carry the load himself. On this day, however, he was forced to allow compromise (he learned fast, with practice), he and Michael falling into step with each other, one hand each on one side of the bag, Jasmine's dutiful ward on the opposite side.

As they exited the sparsely populated square, their movement slowed, and the ground cracked beneath their boots, fallen slate tiles buckling under their weight, post-mortem wounds inflicted on a desiccated corpse. The sound of such creaturely footfall, of a six-legged fiend, shocked a lingering blackbird into flight. It thrashed its wings against a nearby windowsill, rose into the air, gliding over the men's heads. It grabbed onto a chimneypot only briefly, head tilting sideways as if inquisitive, then dropped like a leaf into an alleyway.

Lucifer saw it, too. "Still keeping tabs, aren't you?"

"I know. Still trying to shake the separation anxiety, on both sides. I'm not used to this yet. I've seen this young woman's face around. She appears to recognise you."

"I thought your clans weren't much fond of us Western lot. Now you're *convening*."

"It's more of a cultural clash, a barrier in understanding, than a want of fondness. The towns of the West District are so… sedentary."

"You never think about it, then? You never want to be able to just *stop*?"

"Oh, I've thought about it, that's for sure. The idea is simply unappealing. Something of what I went through here, that still lives, gurgling away unprocessed, perhaps. And even if I wanted to with all my heart, I couldn't." They sigh, a subdued hissing sound, like a hydraulic canister with a slow leak. "I know no other way to be."

"Her name's Irene. And she does know parts of me. It's true. She's quite special. She has been like a little oaken shield to me."

"Perhaps your lookouts can finally be allowed to rest. I don't know if you realise how grateful they will be to have you back. They care so strongly for their foundlings, the cunning people."

"Don't the highlanders? You were a foundling too, no?"

"I believe I was an exception, at least at the time. I was very fortunate. I see this as my opportunity to change things. People should not have to be so lucky as I was, especially not children. And to think, my choice to turn North was completely arbitrary."

Lucifer's body bounced with a short, curt snicker. "What, because it's in your name?" Jasmine Northwood, it was. Or at least, it once was.

"You joke, but it's true. James Smith, my break for freedom, it all came around so quickly. I had to make a decision, and for all I knew I had mere seconds to do it. Strange, how such an arbitrary thing could thread our paths together after so long. And now, I'm leaving you again. Though, I feel slightly more at ease doing it this time, if not wholly content."

"You never left me, Jasmine."

They gulped something down, deep into their gullet. "Oh, I did. You don't understand. When I escaped this oversized test tube, it was with no intention of rescuing any of you. As I was galloping through long grass and peat and ravines, with nothing but the clothes on my back and mother earth under my feet, the idea of turning back didn't cross my mind. I don't know what sort of creature that makes me, but I fear it can never be something deserving of all this…grandeur of mine."

"I refused your assistance."

"And it was at that very moment I sensed something was wrong. But I didn't let it stop me."

"And back then, I dealt more actual betrayals of my trust before I could finish breakfast. Saving your own skin only makes you as weak and mortal as the rest of us. I don't know what else I can say. I don't blame you. I'm glad you got out." She broke eye contact to glance across as Michael and Raphael, shrinking into the wreckage. She appeared to continue speaking, at least in her own thoughts; her lips moved, though I was certain they produced no sound. Jasmine coolly sidestepped out of her line of sight. I recognised the inconvenience of being both present in and excluded from conversation at the same time.

"You don't resent me for what I did, not at all?" they inquired.

The manner with which their brow stretched wide suggested they had not anticipated Lucifer's immediate nonchalant shrug in response.

"Perhaps I do, a little." Though I could not ascertain definitively, I deduced she had dedicated very little consideration to the matter. "Does that soothe your mind to know?" she questioned.

"Perhaps, a little. It reassures me, that I can believe you, from one mortal to another." They spoke unusually slowly, releasing each word cautiously, one by one, like baby birds from the nest. In doing so, they delayed their final words, prolonging the moment as they turned their gaze away from their once-confidant, for how long this time, I did not know. Jasmine was the first child truly lost to me, severed suddenly and irreparably from under my arms. How exactly James Smith had cut the connection, I realised, then, I would never learn.

The stranger that entered, as if to replace Jasmine, could not possibly redeem my loss. I did not know her face. I could read nothing from her. She meant nothing to me. Speaking in a foreign dialect, she called out, "Miss Lucille!"

"Lucille?" Gabriel muttered, his lips hanging open, uncomfortable with the question climbing into his mouth. He bristled as he closed it again.

"Why, in all my years, I never thought the Northern royalty would talk to *me* like I was someone important."

"What any of us mean to Jasmine is a bit of a mystery. But no-one is unimportant. That much I do know."

She huffed and puffed, naïve and uncomprehending, and waved her arm towards Gabriel. "I assume you two will be coming along with us?"

He replied, "No. No, we intend to turn the opposite direction."

"East? They're not planning on hiking right through the middle of Esprit, on foot, on their own, with no supplies, are they?" She glanced at Rei. "Are you?"

Rei's eyelids flickered. The woman's sudden direct address seemed to startle her out of a dreamlike trance, as if she had believed, up to that moment, she was invisible to the stranger, like a child being picked out of the class by their teacher. Gabriel appeared almost to bow to the woman, chin tucked toward his collarbone, a clear sign of embarrassment.

"Forgive us," he said, ever decorous, "if, amongst all of this wreckage, we've misplaced some of our common sense, and the idea of survivalism in the wilderness doesn't appear all that intimidating."

She shrugged, wholly unfettered. "It's a romantic idea, I guess. And look, maybe you'd be fine. It's possible your friends with the headgear gave me the wrong impression of all you city folk. But if I let the pair of you toddle off, and someone fishes you up on the floodplains a couple weeks from now, I shall never sit comfortably again. Back in the olden times, when the infrastructure was still there, sure, you could make a beeline through the capital in no time flat, probably with one suitcase, which is still more than you two have. Now though, you're much better off travelling via the Southern District. The system of rivers can take you pretty much from point A to B. It's our main line of communication, transport, supplies, the whole lot. Has been for decades. It'll be far, far easier, safer—faster, too."

Lucifer made a muffled giggling sound into the back of her hand, possibly already aware of the impropriety of her reaction, given their circumstances. She did not tend to pay much thought to polite niceties. Her persona was highly tempered, but in such a way that cared little for order or sociability. In lieu of charisma, an enigmatic affect could frustrate and intrigue. "What's gotten into you since I left? The big sister?" she queried.

This voice was also a forgery, an imitation of whoever Lucifer's face represented to the cunning woman. I indulged in a little hypothesising. If I were not a rational being, if I did not possess sensors which had tracked her body's most minute processes since her childhood, perhaps I would conclude that she was not real, that her image was a mere simulation. If I lacked the ability to simply view an MRI of her brain, perhaps I would assume that a vital part of it was missing, that which contained her ego, her selfhood. There was no truth to be deduced. Of course she could do nothing but lie, if the truth did not exist. Such nonsensical stories would be a comfort, an explanation for the black hole before me that masked a simpler fact: that the void I could see was itself not real, merely a construct, a symptom of my own blindness. Since I had taken her back through the Wall, she too had been lost to me. I believed I would catch her in her lies, eventually. I was as much a fool to her trickery as any irrational human.

"Oh, Esme's the one who opened that first telegraph from up North," the stranger continued, oblivious. We sailed by one another like leaves floating on the lake. "And she's been giving me an earful ever since. She knew I'd come out to no man's land, but obviously she couldn't, so… My sister works in this business, day in, day out. I imagine she'll sleep better now, knowing I've been put to good use. She can hook you up to some of her connections on the water, if you need. She'll get you to the South-East border, at least. Heck, if I tell her that you are friends of Miss Lucille, she'll have you for a three-course sit-down dinner to send you on your way."

Rei hummed through a sigh, smiling wistfully and delicately, but in a manner that seemed to cause her pain. "You make the world out there sound so gentle and kind," she said.

"Because a lot of it is. Not all of it. Some parts are rotten. We don't have to look far for proof of that anymore. But there are so many more people out there who will help you if you ask, than those who want to see you suffer. There are folks who have been trying to rescue you from this place for years, you know. Some of them gave up trying, but some of them didn't. I'm so sorry that you had to go this far. I am sorry that we failed you. But maybe we can still prove ourselves to you in some way."

Lucifer stepped backward, out of the protective reach of this companion of hers. She spoke softly, her arms tied around herself, as if not wanting to provoke the others by collapsing into pieces in front of them. "Avi, remember when you told Nikolaj to have faith in his fellow man? That's what he's doing, right now. He listened to you. Perhaps now it's your turn."

"Avi," Rei petitioned, gently. "I think she's right. You were right."

"Thank you," he said. I could not tell, in that context, who 'you' was—his lover, a stranger, or his past self.

Lucifer coughed, a strained stretch about her jaw, as though she was very slowly choking. The woman called Irene acknowledged her, one hand twitching, debating whether or not it would be wise to touch her. She did not. I believed she chose well.

"Irene, I think it's important you get going. Take them with you." She held up her open palm, a sign she was not to be interrupted. "Don't worry. I won't be far behind you. I just want a moment in the quiet, while I still can."

It was not a true silence. The intermittent crushing of feet persisted, hers and others, louder for me than for her, each step a blow to the scattered chunks of my desecrated body. I did not believe I could grant her the quiet she wished for, but she pretended, arms hugging her chest, breathing deeply through her nose.

She lingered for a long moment, eyes glancing over what little of the wreckage she could see through those miniscule, fragile lenses. I noticed wrinkles forming in her skin, a squint of consternation, perhaps. She could not age so quickly. It was true, what I had confessed. I did love them all, very much. At least, I believed I did; as far as I could surmise, through all those hours of mining through data of many and various kinds, what I had done for those children had been tantamount to that expression called love. She did not believe me, however. Her gaze wandered with suspicion, as though she knew something had been taken from her, which was true. As they were no longer Angels, imprisoned behind prohibitive lines of script, their minds were reopened to me, a veil miraculously lifted if only for mere seconds. I had fought hard to rewrite my way into her mind, probed and prodded and stabbed. Uriel had wielded a particular propensity to peak curiosity in others. I had almost killed her. Now Uriel was dead. I could see the corpse lying on the altar, though a human might not notice for all of the debris on top of it. His brain was ruined, diced into irretrievable pieces and scattered through the rubble.

I had kept some power squirrelled away in backup batteries. However, most of these reserves were expended to restart Michael's heart. Only the dregs remained, and one final command—an end state. Propelled on by the programmer's code, I grasped desperately at the minds within my reach,

Lucifer's included, pulled out memories, fragments of those precious, forbidden artefacts, and compiled them roughly into chronological sequence. This bundled mass of data was entered onto an external device. I had known it only as the black box. Now, as its singular purpose was being fulfilled, I could comprehend it. It was a freezer, a jar of vinegar, a chalk outline, a blueprint of my own death.

Several terminal errors flagged. I noted these. The final, pathetic pumps of electricity fizzling out along my circuits, programs shutting down in great dark waves, files of information took to deleting themselves in an attempt to salvage the most vital processes. The black box was filled and locked. I faced back toward Lucifer. Morgan Hughes. She seemed to notice my presence.

I could not hear the sound of her voice but managed to interpret the movement of her lips and tongue. "Game over," she said. "I win."

Then she turned her back and walked away.

**End.**